All The Pretty People

BARBARA FREETHY

BARBARA
FREETHY
—BOOKS—

Fog City Publishing

PRAISE FOR BARBARA FREETHY

"Barbara Freethy is a master storyteller with a gift for spinning tales about ordinary people in extraordinary situations and drawing readers into their lives." — *Romance Reviews Today*

"Freethy (Silent Fall) has a gift for creating complex, appealing characters and emotionally involving, often suspenseful, sometimes magical stories."— *Library Journal on Suddenly One Summer*

"If you love nail-biting suspense and heartbreaking emotion, Silent Run belongs on the top of your to-be-bought list. I could not turn the pages fast enough."— *NYT Bestselling Author Mariah Stewart*

"Hooked me from the start and kept me turning pages throughout all the twists and turns. Silent Run is powerful romantic intrigue at its best."— *NYT Bestselling Author JoAnn Ross*

"An absorbing story of two people determined to unravel the secrets, betrayals, and questions about their past. The story builds to an explosive conclusion that will leave readers eagerly awaiting Barbara Freethy's next book."—*NYT Bestselling Author Carla Neggars on Don't Say A Word*

"A page-turner that engages your mind while it tugs at your heartstrings ... DON'T SAY A WORD had made me a Barbara Freethy fan for life!" —*NYT Bestselling Author Diane Chamberlain*

"*On Shadow Beach* teems with action, drama and compelling situations... a fast-paced page-turner." —*BookPage*

ALSO BY BARBARA FREETHY

Standalone Novels

ALL SHE EVER WANTED

DON'T SAY A WORD

GOLDEN LIES

SUMMER SECRETS

Suspense Duos

SILENT RUN

SILENT FALL

TAKEN

PLAYED

Off the Grid: FBI Series

PERILOUS TRUST

RECKLESS WHISPER

DESPERATE PLAY

ELUSIVE PROMISE

DANGEROUS CHOICE

RUTHLESS CROSS

CRITICAL DOUBT

FEARLESS PURSUIT

DARING DECEPTION

RISKY BARGAIN

For a complete list of books, visit Barbara's Website!

ALL THE PRETTY PEOPLE

For more information on Barbara Freethy's books, visit her website:
www.barbarafreethy.com

PROLOGUE

I FELT an overwhelming wave of panic. I wanted to cry, but I couldn't. Tears would only make it more difficult to escape.

I ran through the tall trees, my heart pounding against my chest. I didn't know where I was going, and the thick foliage and dark skies confused me. If I'd been in this area before, I couldn't remember it. I hoped I'd run into someone who could help me, but there wasn't a soul around, except for the person who was after me.

The wind gusted as the rain pelted my head. My clothes were quickly drenched, the water on my face freezing with the cold wind. My foot slipped as I hit a rock. I stumbled, hitting my hand against a tree to steady myself. The wood left a deep scratch, and blood dripped down my fingers, but I couldn't stop.

My breath came hard and fast.

A crack of thunder was so loud it almost knocked me off my feet. Seconds later, there was a flash of lightning. Maybe I could use the storm to my advantage. Perhaps the rain would make it more difficult to find me.

Then I heard someone crashing through the brush.

I sped up.

Crashing through the trees, I came to a terrifying, dizzying stop as I realized I was at the edge of a bluff. I looked down at the whitecaps below, the dark, churning water ready to suck me under. I couldn't let the sea take me. I looked to the left, then to the right.

One impossible choice.

Would it be the right one?

I turned to the left and sprinted toward another thick grove of trees. I needed cover. My lungs strained from the pressure I was putting on them.

Within minutes, I was running out of gas. Exhausted and disoriented, I didn't know which path to take, which trees to cut through. Every turn led into a deeper, thicker forest, paths that seemed untraveled by anyone.

Tears pricked my eyelids. The worst thought I'd ever imagined raged around in my head. *Would I die tonight? Was this it?*

A voice rang through the trees. "There's nowhere to go. Give up."

"Never," I muttered, not daring to scream the words, because that would be stupid, and I'd done enough stupid things already. I broke through another thick patch of trees and found myself back out in the open, with only a few feet between me and the edge of a cliff. I'd run out of room.

I'd made the wrong choice.

CHAPTER ONE

THE OCEAN WAS ROUGHER than I'd imagined. I knew going back to the island would be difficult, but I hadn't thought it would start with the worst ferry ride of all time.

"Willow? Are you coming downstairs? We want to toast the bride," Rachel said impatiently.

"Later," I bit out, as I gripped the rail and tried to ward off another wave of nausea. "I'm a little seasick. I need air." I couldn't tear my eyes away from the horizon, needing something solid to focus on.

"Brooklyn really wants you downstairs."

"Just go ahead without me." I drew in another breath of salty air as Rachel left, hoping to quell the queasy feeling in my stomach.

I was torn between wanting to get to dry land and wanting to stay far away from Hawk Island. I hadn't been to the island in ten years, and I would have preferred to never return. But some things are more important than bad memories, and my younger sister's wedding was one of those things.

Ever since Kelsey changed her venue from Seattle to Hawk Island, one of the smaller islands in the San Juan chain off the coast of Washington State, I had felt anxious and unsettled. Now that the island was only minutes away, my stomach was churning, and it wasn't just because the ocean waves were tossing the ferry like it was a toy boat in a bathtub, it was because everything about this trip was wrong.

I wasn't just going back to the place I had summered every year of my life since I was twelve years old, I was going back to that last summer, when I'd been seventeen and filled with optimistic dreams about my future. Many of those dreams had been fueled by my best friend on the island, a local girl named Melanie Maddox. We'd been innocent, idealistic, believing in a world and a future that had ceased to exist after August nineteenth—the last day I'd seen Melanie. *The last day anyone had seen Melanie.*

In the days that followed that night, the search for sixteen-year-old Melanie Maddox had taken over the island. Endless questions from law enforcement had hammered home the terrifying reality that my best friend was gone, and I didn't know how or why or whether I could have prevented the worst from happening if only I'd made other choices that night.

My breath came faster as the guilt ate me up. I'd thought I'd made peace with the tragedy, but that had just been a lie I told myself. My stomach heaved, and I had to swallow back the nausea.

The thickly forested hills of the island loomed larger in front of me. I could see the waterfalls near the south bluff, the beach at Pirate's Bay, the caves along the western edge of the island that could only be accessed at low tide.

My hands suddenly itched to take a photo. It was a strange feeling, one that felt both foreign and familiar.

Summers on the island had been spent with a camera in my hand. Melanie and I had searched endlessly for the perfect shot. I'd taken photos everywhere, hoping to enter them into photography contests, maybe even get one published in a travel magazine. I had been so full of hopes and dreams back then. The future ahead of me—of us—had been infinite. So many possibilities.

I'd never imagined that future would be cut short for Melanie, or that I would come to hate the camera I had once loved. It was probably still on the island, still in my room where I'd left it.

I'd left my dreams of being a professional photographer behind, too. After that summer, I'd gone to college in San Francisco and majored in business. Then I'd moved from one boring job to another, finally ending up last year in a real-estate office where I turned out to be the worst salesperson they'd ever had.

It turned out that it wasn't just my dreams I'd given up on, it was everyone else's. I couldn't sell people their dream houses. I couldn't make them see their futures in overpriced old homes. When I'd asked my boss for time off for the wedding, she'd suggested I take all the time I needed to find another job, something I might actually enjoy.

I couldn't imagine what that would be. But it wasn't my future I had to worry about now; it was my past. The wind picked up, and enormous waves splashed over the rail. I forced myself to let go and move under the overhang. I didn't want to arrive on the island soaked and shivering.

As the ferry rolled with another wave, I grabbed hold of a pole to steady myself. I was surprised to see the bride, my younger sister, Kelsey, and Carter Chadwick, Kelsey's soon-to-be brother-in-law, having an intense conversation on the other side of the boat. I couldn't hear what they were saying, but Kelsey waved her hands in frustration. Then Carter grabbed her by the shoulders. He leaned in and said something to quiet her.

It was an odd moment, one that made my stomach twist for an entirely different reason. It felt like there was too much intimacy between them. I had to be imagining that. Kelsey was in love with Carter's brother, Gage. Kelsey had been crushing on Gage since she was fourteen, but it had taken eleven years for them to go on an official date and another year for them to get engaged.

Like his brother, Gage, Carter was tall, blond, and good-looking. Kelsey matched his looks and then some. At five-foot ten, with silky, straight blonde hair that drifted past her shoulders and striking blue eyes, she was stunningly pretty. She was also bone thin in a pair of white jeans and a clingy tank top under a white leather jacket. Kelsey had always been slender, but during the last few years, she'd become almost gaunt. It was a look that kept her in high demand in the modeling world.

Kelsey suddenly pushed Carter away. He whirled around, storming toward the back of the ferry. Kelsey turned, freezing when she saw me.

Was that guilt flashing through her eyes?

Kelsey's expression shifted and a deliberate, somewhat forced smile crossed her lips. She moved across the deck to join me. "Willow, I was looking for you."

"Were you? It looked like you and Carter were arguing."

"We were," she admitted.

"Why? What's wrong?"

"Carter was trying to defend Gage for missing the ferry this morning because he wanted to finish up a contract. I took out my frustration on the wrong person. It's not Carter's fault that Gage is putting work ahead of our wedding. I'm just disappointed."

"I get it. But Gage will be here tonight, right? Then you'll have his undivided attention."

"Yes. He should make the last ferry."

"So, it will be fine." I wanted to make her feel better. Kelsey was my younger sister by thirteen months, and I'd always wanted to make her happy. That was a sentiment shared by everyone in the family because Kelsey was the baby, someone we all took care of. But she wasn't a little girl anymore. She was twenty-six years old and four inches taller than me.

Kelsey crossed her arms, a distant look in her gaze. "I know it's not a big deal, but it just feels like Gage has been putting work ahead of our relationship the last few months. I've basically planned this entire wedding with Mom."

"I bet a lot of brides feel like that."

"You're right. I just need to relax."

"I'm sure everything will be perfect."

"That's what everyone keeps telling me," Kelsey said.

"But you don't believe it?"

Kelsey's display of nerves surprised me. She loved being the center of attention, the life of the party, the woman everyone was looking at.

Kelsey hesitated, then shrugged. "Ever since my original wedding venue canceled, and I had to scramble and reset everything on the island, I've felt off."

"That makes sense. I still don't understand why you didn't just get another venue in Seattle."

"Because everything was booked, Willow," Kelsey snapped. "I didn't want to postpone my wedding for another year."

"Why not? It's not like you and Gage need to rush. You're only twenty-six. This can't be about wanting kids."

"Of course it's not about that. It's about marrying the man of my dreams, and I want to do that this year, not next. I want to move on with our lives. Mom convinced the Belle Haven Lodge to make room for us, and with Jenny as the event coordinator at the lodge, I get to work with someone I know. The island was the best alternative. Plus, Mom and Gage and Gage's parents all think it's romantic. We first met on the island as kids and now we're getting married there. We're officially joining our families together."

"I guess, but still…"

Kelsey frowned as my voice drifted away. "It was a long time ago, Willow. Ten years."

"This August," I agreed, meeting her gaze. "It feels like forever, but also like it happened yesterday."

"It's tragic what happened to Melanie. Not that we know what happened to her, but it had to be bad."

"Yes. It had to be bad." I murmured, trying not to think about just how bad it could have been.

"I know you haven't been back to the island since that summer, but I have, and once you're there, Willow, once you see the house and our friends and all the fun places we used to go, you'll remember the good times. We have a lot of great memories on Hawk Island. Long summer days, sno-cones and sunburns, endless beach parties. Remember those times, not the last time."

"I'm trying."

"The Belle Haven Lodge has also been completely renovated,"

Kelsey continued. "You won't even recognize it. The island has changed, too. It's more developed now, new houses, shops and restaurants, and more people living on the island full time and working remote. You'll see how different it is."

"Are you trying to convince me or yourself?" I asked dryly.

She sent me an annoyed look. "You, of course. I want you to have fun at my wedding."

I couldn't remember a time when Kelsey had cared that much about me enjoying myself. She wasn't a bad person, but she thought mostly about herself.

Kelsey shivered as the wind lifted her hair. "It doesn't feel like summer. I hope the rain won't ruin everything."

I gasped as the boat took another big bounce. "Oh, God! Why is it so rough?"

"You look pale. The Dramamine isn't working?"

"I didn't take any. I forgot it, and then I was late for the ferry, so I couldn't stop."

"Well, we're almost there. You should come downstairs and have some champagne."

"No thanks. I need air. I'm going to stay right here until we dock." I clung to the pole like it was a lifeline.

"All right." Kelsey paused. "I'm glad you came, Willow. We haven't seen each other much in the past several years."

"You've been traveling the world."

"It has been an exciting time."

"I'll bet. Every time I go online, I see your face. The cameras follow you everywhere. You're a celebrity."

"I'm even more popular now that I'm with Gage. The former football quarterback turned sports agent and the supermodel make a great headline. A TV producer approached us about doing a reality show next year. He's going to come to the wedding and shoot some footage to use in his pitch to the network."

"Really? Wow! You and Gage would be on TV?"

"Our agents think there's a good chance. They're both excited about it."

There was an edge to Kelsey's voice that gave me pause. "Are you excited about it?"

"Why wouldn't I be?"

"I don't know, but you seem a little tense."

"There's just a lot going on. I haven't slept well for the last few days. I just need to get to the island and get married."

"Before…" I queried.

"Before nothing," she said sharply. "Everything is fine, Willow. But there is one thing I have to tell you about. I don't want you to freak out."

"That sounds ominous. Why would I freak out?"

"We're going to have a bonfire tonight."

I started shaking my head before she finished speaking. "No. No way."

"I thought it might feel weird, too, but Gage really wants it. Jenny said a lot of brides are doing it as part of their pre-wedding celebration. The lodge sets it up for all their wedding parties. It's not on the same beach. It won't feel the same as the ones we had as teenagers."

"Kelsey, you can't have a bonfire. It's going to bring back bad memories for many people, not just me."

"Jenny showed me photos from other weddings, and the bonfire looked beautiful, not like our drunken parties. This one will be classy." Kelsey played with her necklace, running the heart charm up and down the chain. It was something she often did when she was feeling stressed. "Mom wants it. Gage's mom wants it. I can't go against everyone. I'm sorry, Willow. It is what it is, and I need you to get on board. You're my sister. You're a bridesmaid. You have to be part of everything."

This wedding was getting worse by the minute. "I'll try," I said, with little enthusiasm, wondering when I had suddenly become so important that I needed to be part of everything. I'd spent most of my life being overlooked.

My older sister, Brooklyn, came up the stairs. Brooklyn was three years older than me and four years older than Kelsey, and she'd been trying to manage both our lives since we were born, although she'd given up on me a long time ago. She and Kelsey had much more in common, including the fact that they looked very much alike with their blonde hair and blue eyes, while I'd inherited my father's dark hair and brown eyes. Brooklyn gave us an irritated look.

"Kelsey, Willow, what are you doing up here?" she asked.

"Willow is seasick," Kelsey replied, making me her entire reason for being on deck, which wasn't true. But I sensed she didn't want me to say anything about Carter, which only made me more suspicious of what I'd witnessed between them.

Brooklyn's sharp gaze landed on me in an accusing fashion, as if I was conspiring to keep Kelsey away from her friends. "Didn't you take something, Willow?"

"I forgot."

She gave a long-suffering sigh. "Well, that figures. Anyway, I need you both downstairs. We want to do another toast and take photos."

"Sorry, but I'm going to stay up here until we dock," I said.

"It's not always about you, Willow."

I bit back a laugh at Brooklyn's comment. "Believe me, I know that."

"It's fine," Kelsey cut in. "There will be plenty more toasts and photos before the end of the week."

Brooklyn shot me a dark look, then went down the stairs. Kelsey gave me a tentative smile. "I know you're worried, but everything is going to be okay, Willow."

"I hope so, Kelsey. I want you to have the happiest day of your life."

"I really want that, too."

As Kelsey left, I turned back to the horizon, my gaze following a hawk as it circled over the island. I used to love watching the red-tailed hawks soar through the trees, with their wild warning screeches to the other animals to stay away from their nests, from their territory.

I'd followed the hawks all over the island. But after Melanie's disappearance, every time I saw the birds, I'd worried that they were leading me to a discovery that was both wanted and terrifying. It had been a relief to leave the island behind.

Now that worry had returned. But it had been ten years, I reminded myself. Nothing new would be discovered now. I was going back to the island for a wedding. I would replace the bad memories with good ones, and maybe it was time to do that. Maybe I needed to face the past, so I could finally let go of it.

CHAPTER TWO

WHEN THE FERRY DOCKED, I was the first one off. It felt amazing to have solid ground beneath my feet. As I waited for the others to disembark, I glanced around the harbor. Almost all the slips were full. Apparently, the rough seas had kept most of the pleasure-seekers in port. But that didn't mean they were staying inside. Tourists crowded the long pier, shopping for souvenirs, grabbing a gelato, a coffee, visiting the arcade, or the photo booth where they could pose for funny shots with their friends and family.

I'd loved the pier since the day I first set foot on it. And I'd spent a lot of time at the harbor because Melanie's parents, Sylvie and Holt Maddox, owned the two-story building at the beginning of the pier with the big colorful pink sign for the Crab Pot.

Holt was an ex-Marine turned fisherman, who spent his early mornings catching the day's specials. Sylvie cooked those specials up with her own special blend of French and Portuguese spices. The restaurant was often the first stop for ferry-goers arriving on the island and the last stop before they headed back to wherever they'd come from.

I'd spent a lot of time in that restaurant, helping Melanie bus tables when it got busy. I'd never minded the work. I'd loved the loud, warm, friendly restaurant, and I didn't care that Sylvie paid me in crab cakes. I hadn't needed the money, but I had needed the love.

I could get lost in my family, but I always felt like there was a place for me at the Crab Pot. Sylvie was a nurturing woman with a big heart and a generous spirit. She treated every kid on the island like they were her own, and I'd savored the attention she'd given me. But while Sylvie had been welcoming, Holt, Melanie's dad, had been the opposite.

Holt was a rigid, cold man, who barely cracked a smile unless he was swapping stories with one of his fishing buddies. The rest of the time, he appeared unemotional and detached. Melanie had told me he suffered from PTSD, that little things could trigger him, make him think he was under attack. That's why he always had a tight grip on himself, and on his surroundings. She'd said it had been worse when the family lived in Seattle, when there was too much noise, too many sounds to trigger him. His condition had gotten much better when they'd moved to the island when Melanie was seven.

I'd felt sorry for Holt, but I'd never really warmed up to him. And that last summer, Melanie had been fighting him about every little thing she wanted to do. It was tragically ironic that the girl, who probably had the most overprotective father of all, had been the one to disappear.

I turned my head away from the restaurant as Rachel Connelly walked down the dock. A dark redhead with fair skin and a smattering of light freckles across her cheeks, Rachel was the epitome of beautiful sophistication. She wasn't a model like Kelsey, but she worked in marketing for a fashion house in New York, and her clothes were always cutting edge. Rachel's family also summered on the island, and our parents were close friends. But while Rachel had tolerated me as Kelsey and Brooklyn's sister, we'd never been close. I'd actually been surprised when she'd taken the time to check on me while we were on the ferry. Although, in retrospect, that had only happened because Brooklyn had sent her to get me.

"Are you feeling better?" Rachel asked.

"I'm better now that I'm off the boat."

"You still look pale. Or is that just because you're still anti-makeup?" Rachel asked with dry amusement.

"I'm not anti-makeup anymore, and if I look pale, it's not only because of the boat ride. I feel weird being back here. But I seem to be the only one."

Rachel waved a dismissive hand in the air. "I've been back many times before, so it's not weird to me. I suppose it will feel a little different this time with all of us in the same place. It makes me think about the past, about our summers together."

"I really don't want to think about the past, but I can't stop myself."

"Well, try to think about the happy times. It's important to make sure that Kelsey feels nothing but love and happiness this week."

Rachel's warning reminded me of another reason we'd never been good friends. Like Brooklyn, Rachel enjoyed giving unsolicited advice, and she could be extremely judgmental.

"What is taking so long?" Rachel complained, as she impatiently tapped her foot.

Despite her recent words to show nothing but happiness, she seemed out of sorts.

"Is something wrong, Rachel?"

"No, of course not."

"You're sure?"

She shrugged, giving me an annoyed look. "Fine. I'm concerned about James and Brooklyn being together again."

"They're not together; they're just both in the wedding. They haven't been a couple for years."

"I know that, but James has been acting weird ever since he realized he was going to see Brooklyn again. He downed half a bottle of champagne on the ferry. I don't like what your sister does to him. He finally had his head together and now he sees her and falls apart again."

"I thought the breakup was mutual. And wasn't it like six years ago?" The details of Brooklyn's relationship with James were hazy in my mind now. They'd dated from the time they were in high school and through most of college, but they'd broken up in their early twenties, which didn't seem that unusual. *How many young relationships went the distance?* None that I could think of.

"I don't know if it was mutual," Rachel said. "James has never told me what happened, and Brooklyn just brushes me off with some vague reason that makes no sense. What I do know is that they're toxic together. I love them both, but they don't need to take any nostalgic trips into the past and recreate something that wasn't that good in the first place." She straightened. "They're all coming now. Don't say anything to anyone. Promise."

"Fine, I promise. But I think you're worrying about nothing. Brooklyn has dated many guys since James, and I'm assuming he's dated many women. Just because they have to walk down an aisle together doesn't mean they're going to fall back in love."

"Exactly. But don't say anything."

I didn't want to say anything, because butting into Brooklyn's business was never a good idea. My older sister could take care of herself. She certainly didn't want or need my help.

Brooklyn and Kelsey led the way down the dock, followed by Rachel's brother, James Connelly, who did look a little unsteady on his feet, and Carter Chadwick, who looked more grim than happy. Behind them was Alex Hamilton, a handsome man with short black hair and a perfect smile, Peter Jacobson, a tall, stocky man who had been one of Gage's defenders on the football field throughout his pro career, Dahlia Perry and Trina Alton, two ridiculously skinny model friends of Kelsey's.

As the group moved down the pier, I fell in behind them, steeling myself as we drew closer to the Crab Pot. The restaurant patio that edged the pier brought back a flood of memories. I could see the table where Melanie and I had sipped chocolate milkshakes and watched the tourists get off the ferry. We'd made up stories about who they were, what they were doing on the island, and their family secrets. Every imaginative tale had made us laugh. Then we'd simply kept an eye out for cute boys who might make our summer more fun.

When we reached the patio, I stiffened, shock running through me. I'd been expecting to possibly see Melanie's parents working the tables, but not her older brother—Drake Maddox. I thought he'd left the island years ago, but here he was, looking at me with his soulful blue eyes.

My heart jumped in my chest. My breath came short and fast. I felt slammed with emotion—from love to hatred and everything in between.

Drake had been my teenage fantasy—dark-brown wavy hair, broad shoulders, and powerful arms. Besides his physical gifts, he'd also been a smart and creative writer, and a guy who had always known what he wanted and went after it with stubborn determination.

At one point, I'd thought he'd wanted me. When he'd smiled at me, when he'd kissed me, I'd felt like I'd fallen off a cliff. I'd tried not to let anyone know. Not that anyone would have thought one of the hottest guys on the island would have been interested in me— the shy, often awkward teenage girl, who was three years younger than him.

Melanie might have guessed, but I'd never told her about Drake, about the times we ran into each other at the local news- paper office; the night we'd gotten caught in the rain.

My stomach churned as my steps slowed. I couldn't believe Drake was back on the island. He lived in Seattle now. He was a journalist, and according to my parents, he rarely came home, even though his parents still lived on the island. But he was here now, and that seemed like a bad sign.

I heard Kelsey squeal with delight. Then she ran straight toward Drake. She opened her arms over the low white picket fence to encourage him to get up and give her a hug.

Her friendliness shocked me. Drake also seemed taken aback. But he got up from his chair and embraced Kelsey. Up close, he looked even better than I remembered. He was the same age as Brooklyn, so he would be thirty now. I didn't see a ring on his finger, but that might mean nothing. Not that it mattered. I'd gotten over him a long time ago. And he'd gotten over me long before that.

"How are you, Drake?" Kelsey asked.

"I'm all right. I hear there's a big wedding happening this weekend."

"You heard right." Kelsey flashed her giant diamond ring in his face. "Gage and I are getting married on Saturday."

"Where is Gage?" he asked, his gaze sweeping the group.

"He'll be here soon. I had no idea you were going to be here this week, Drake. You must come to the wedding. It's on Saturday at the Belle Haven Lodge. Jenny is organizing it for me."

"She told me. I'm sure your guest list is set."

"Don't be silly. There's always room for one more. We'd love to have you there." Kelsey turned toward the group. "Wouldn't we all love to have Drake at the wedding?"

There was a vague chorus of half-hearted agreement. I couldn't bring myself to add to that chorus, and I couldn't imagine why Drake would want to come to the wedding. He'd accused all of us of knowing something about Melanie's disappearance. He'd even punched Gage in the face. We might have all been friends before that, but not after.

"I'd like to come," Drake said, shocking me with his response.

"Great," Kelsey replied. "Do you still have the same phone number?"

"I do."

"I'll text you the details."

I couldn't understand why Kelsey would want Drake at her wedding. And as I looked at Brooklyn, I saw a worried gleam in her eyes as well. At least I wasn't completely alone in thinking that Kelsey should have kept her mouth shut. But that was Kelsey. She never thought before she did anything.

"The limo is waiting," Brooklyn said sharply. "We need to go."

"We'll catch up later," Kelsey promised as Brooklyn pushed her down the dock, the rest of the group following.

As I drew even with Drake, I couldn't help saying, "Why on earth would you want to go to Kelsey's wedding?"

Drake's gaze swept across my face and down my body. I flushed a little at his scrutiny.

"Well?" I demanded.

"Hello, Willow. You look...different."

I stiffened. *Different* was never a compliment. "You didn't answer my question. Last time you saw Gage, you accused him of lying and knowing something about your sister's disappearance. Why would you want to see him marry Kelsey? Why would you want to see any of us? You hate us."

Drake stared back at me, an unreadable expression in his gaze. I'd always thought his eyes were like the sea, bright but murky, sexy but dangerous. I'd never known what he was thinking. That hadn't changed.

"Maybe I was wrong about what happened back then."

His words stunned me. "Seriously? You think you were wrong?"

"I was furious and frustrated. Your family, your friends, were stonewalling the investigation. But perhaps I overreacted."

"So you don't blame me anymore? You don't think I'm responsible?"

His gaze hardened. Before he could answer, Brooklyn shouted impatiently from the open door of the limo. "Willow. We will leave without you."

I believed her. "I have to go."

"Don't you want answers to your questions?"

"I know the answers. What I don't know is why you're here or what you're up to. Don't come to the wedding, Drake. If you like Kelsey at all, don't mess this up for her. She doesn't deserve that."

Hearing my name called again by a furiously impatient Brooklyn, I hurried down the path. As I squeezed into the limo, I was surprised at how quiet it was. Drake had put a pall over the entire group. For the first time since we'd all boarded the ferry, I wasn't the only one remembering the past.

Melanie's Diary—June 18th

Summer is here! I'm so excited to see my friends. Any minute now, Willow will get off the ferry and come staggering down the pier, probably seasick or falling asleep on Dramamine, but I don't care. I can't wait to see her. We're going to have so much fun in the next two months. Hopefully, some fun I can write about.

Mom gave me this diary for my sixteenth birthday four months ago. She thinks I need an outlet for my feelings. But it has been so dull on Hawk Island, I haven't felt inspired to write anything down. Hopefully, that will change soon.

In the meantime, I'll tell you about Willow. We were twelve when we first met, but it took us two years to become friends. Willow is shy and quiet and is always in the background. At first, I thought she was kind of boring, to be honest. But then she got a camera and became this super cool, imaginative kid who wanted to explore the island. And since that's what I love to do, we got to be best friends.

We've been all over the island together. Willow wants to be a professional photographer and travel the world. I think she'd be great. She sees amazing things through the lens of a camera. I look at flowers and just see flowers, but Willow sees patterns and designs in the petals. She sees the tiny spiderweb wrapping its way around a stem. She sees drops of water on a stone that looks like a seagull. I feel like I see the world differently when she's around.

But Willow doesn't think she's special at all. She's always fading away. Sometimes we'll be at a party, and she'll be right by my side. Then I'll turn around and she's gone. I'll find her later in the shadows somewhere. She always seems surprised that I was looking for her.

Anyway, I have one more year of high school and then I'm leaving Hawk Island. It's not that I don't like it here. It's just too small. The kids who come in the summer have such exciting lives. I've had the same friends since my family moved here when I was in the second grade. I love Gabby and Jenny. Ben and Dillon are like brothers to me. My high school class has forty kids in it. I know everyone inside and out. They're great, but I want more.

Instead of watching the ferry come in, I want to get on it and go somewhere else. I just wish I could leave now. Willow is a year *older than me, and she's going to college in San Francisco in the fall. I'm so jealous. She'll have so many adventures. It will also be good for her to get away from her family. She needs to find her light instead of being in their shadows. I don't need to find my light; I just need to be free.*

I know I should write more about myself and my feelings, except I'm kind of scared to write them down. That's probably why I've been talking so much about Willow. Maybe next time.

CHAPTER THREE

MY MOTHER, Monica Kent, stood by the lunch buffet, which had been set up on a massive deck overlooking Puget Sound. She wore a long-sleeve, body-hugging teal dress that showed off her curves and accentuated her blonde hair. In her late fifties, she could have easily passed for mid-forties, thanks to her dedication to fitness, diet, and cosmetic surgery. She loved when people were surprised that she'd had three kids. Sometimes, I was surprised as well, not because of how she looked, but because she'd never seemed to enjoy being a mother.

Oh, there were some things she cared about, like shopping with Kelsey. That had always been one of their favorite things to do together. With Brooklyn, my mom could talk business, because Brooklyn had followed in my mother's footsteps, going into the investment company that my mother's family had started fifty years ago.

My mom loved me in her own way. I didn't really doubt that. But we had never found common ground. We didn't like the same things or the same people. We just didn't connect. I exasperated her, and she frustrated me. I hadn't really noticed how distant our relationship was until I got to know Melanie and her mom, Sylvie. They would laugh and tell inside jokes. They had such an ease and affection for each other, it made me envious. I'd wished I could find that connection with my mom, but it had always eluded me. Whatever closeness we'd had when I was a child had faded as I grew up and continued to disappoint her with my life choices.

My mother had wanted me to go to college in Seattle; I'd chosen San Francisco. She'd wanted me to either work for her or for my dad's law firm. I'd done neither. I'd had seven jobs in seven years in a variety of industries, most recently real estate. She'd wanted me to live near the family and vacation on the island the way we used to. She thought I should have gotten over that tragic time in my past years ago. But then, she'd never really known how close Melanie and I were. She'd never known a lot of things.

It was weird to look at the woman who gave birth to me and not really feel that much. *Was the problem with me? Was it with her?* Maybe it was with both of us.

I accepted a glass of champagne from a passing server, who was prepping the crowd for the first of what would probably be many toasts over the next several days. I wasn't going to drink, but I would need to clink my glass with everyone around me.

My sisters had joined my mother now, standing on either side of her, a trio of beautiful blondes. I didn't see anyone waving me to join them. My dad, Larry Kent, was off to the side. He was also attractive and looked younger than his years as Mom made sure that they both kept in shape. His dark hair held no streaks of gray, contributing to his youthful look.

My father stood next to Gage's dad, Sean Chadwick, and his wife, Eileen. Sean had brown hair and eyes, while Eileen was a curvy blonde with a sweet smile. Next to them were Marie and Michael Connelly. Michael was looking at his phone, a bored expression on his face, which was not unusual, while Marie, a born cheerleader, was giving my mom all her attention, obviously wanting to show her support. Most people in our circle of friends believed that Marie and Michael were in a loveless marriage, but Marie had all the money, so Michael would never divorce her.

The younger members of the wedding party were gathered in

front of the bar, James and Rachel Connelly, Carter Chadwick and his big brother, Preston Chadwick, who had his arm around his wife, Gabby, while their five-year-old girls were coloring at a nearby table. The Hamiltons were also present, Louise and Rob and their son Alex, who had come in on the ferry with me. Trina and Dahlia were hanging with Alex and Peter. There were a few other people my parents' age I didn't recognize, but that wasn't surprising; they'd always had a lot of friends.

My mom tapped her champagne glass, getting everyone's attention.

"Thank you all for coming," she said. "I can't believe my baby girl will be married in four short days." She gave Kelsey a proud smile.

"Aw, Mom," Kelsey said, smiling back at her. "Let's not get emotional yet."

"Don't worry. I'm not going to cry, not today, anyway."

I wasn't worried that a tear would drip down my mother's cheek. I couldn't remember her crying about anything. It would mar her cool, controlled image.

My mother continued with her speech. "It means so much to Kelsey and Gage that you've all made the trip here. I can't believe it's been so long since we've been together on this beautiful island. You're all very special to us, and we're grateful for your presence. I want to especially thank Eileen." My mom waved her hand toward Mrs. Chadwick. "Eileen put together this lunch, and all the gorgeous floral centerpieces. Many of the flowers came from her greenhouse. Aren't they beautiful?"

There was a round of applause for Eileen's flowers, and she gave a shy smile. Then my mother took back the attention. "As you all know, Gage has been delayed, so we'll toast him when he arrives. In the meantime..." She lifted her glass. "To Kelsey. May today be the beginning of a beautiful celebration and an amazing future filled with love and happiness."

"To Kelsey," the crowd echoed.

I dutifully raised my glass along with everyone else. Then I set it down on a nearby table and moved through the French doors leading into the dining room.

I hadn't been to this house in a long time, and I wanted to take a few minutes for myself. My parents had done some remodeling over the years, and I hoped that would make being here feel different.

I paused by the dining room table, my gaze captured by the magnificent glass sculpture that my mother had commissioned for the wedding. It featured two lovebirds in a beautiful glass tree, standing about three feet tall. Apparently, it would be the centerpiece for the wedding buffet. It was extraordinarily beautiful, and a sign that everything about this wedding would be first class and luxurious. I wouldn't expect anything less.

I left the dining room and grabbed my suitcase, which was by the front door, then headed up the stairs to the second-floor bedrooms. When I got to my former bedroom, I barely recognized it. The bedding was new, as were the curtains and the rug. There was nothing personal, no mementos from our past summer trips. That was actually a relief.

But when I opened the closet, I saw a stack of boxes with my name written on them. I couldn't remember what I'd left behind, so on impulse, I dragged the first box off the stack and set it on the floor. It had only one strip of tape holding it closed, so it would be easy to open. But just because it was easy to open didn't mean I should open it. I was trying not to go back into the past, but I couldn't stop myself.

I opened the box, and the first item sent my pulse racing. On top of a pile of clothes was my digital camera, the one I'd taken all over the island when Melanie and I went exploring.

My breath came a little fast. I could pick it up. I could click on the screen, but anything on that camera would take me back to seventeen, to a summer of innocence that had ended in despair.

I closed the box and rushed out of the closet. I went straight to the window and threw it open, needing air. I felt as unsettled as I had on the ferry earlier. The ground kept shifting beneath my feet, and I couldn't even blame the waves this time.

As the cool air washed over me, my breaths finally slowed down, and I noticed other little details. The tree outside my room had gotten even higher, and the wide branches were still inviting to climb out on, not that I was going to do that now. Although it was tempting. Using that tree, I'd escaped my life and this house on many summer nights. Even Kelsey and Brooklyn had used the tree to get out without being noticed. It was probably the one secret we'd all been in on.

Beyond the tree was the carport in front of the three-car garage. My room looked out over the street that ran along the bluff where at least ten mansions boasted stunning décor and spectacular ocean views in the neighborhood known as Chambers' Point.

A shadowy figure at the edge of the property caught my gaze. Someone was standing near the garage and a grove of trees. I couldn't tell if it was a man or a woman, but there was a sudden flicker of light and then it was gone. Probably one of the serving staff out to have a smoke, which reminded me I needed to get downstairs. Lunch would start soon.

As I left the room, I heard a shockingly loud crash, followed a moment later by a scream. I ran down the stairs, halting at the entry into the dining room. There was a pile of shattered glass on the table and floor. The caterer, a middle-aged woman wearing a white shirt and black pants, was staring at the disaster in horror.

My mom and dad came running into the room with Kelsey and Brooklyn, the rest of the group crowding in behind them.

"What happened?" my mother demanded.

"I heard a crash," the caterer replied, shock and worry in her eyes. "When I came out of the kitchen, I saw this." She waved her hand at the mess. "I don't know what happened."

"Is that my wedding sculpture?" Kelsey asked in shock.

"All the servers were outside," the caterer added quickly. "I don't know who could have knocked this over. Everyone was on the patio. I don't know what to say."

"It was in the middle of the table, safely away from any casual contact," my mother said. "I made sure of that. It took some work to break this." Her gaze swept to the caterer once more. "You're sure you didn't see someone knock this over, Dana?"

The caterer shook her head. "I did not. I'm sorry."

"I can't believe this. It was so beautiful." My mom shook her head in despair. "It took months to make."

"Every wedding has one thing go wrong," Brooklyn interjected. "This is it."

I thought the one thing that had gone wrong was when the original wedding venue had canceled, but I wasn't going to put myself in the middle of this mess.

"We won't have a centerpiece for the table," my mother moaned.

"I'll help you find something to replace it," Eileen Chadwick offered.

"It will work out, Mom," Kelsey said, a tense expression on her face. "Let's go back outside. We don't need to worry about this now."

"I suppose," my mother conceded. "Dana—"

"I'll clean it right up," Dana said.

My mother allowed Kelsey to lead her away, and the rest of the group followed, with Brooklyn staying behind.

She gave me a sharp look. "Did you see anything, Willow?"

"I saw what you saw—the broken sculpture and the caterer standing next to the table."

"Do you think the caterer did it?"

"I heard her scream. I guess it's possible. But if she did, I don't think it was deliberate." I saw a worried glint in Brooklyn's eyes. "Do you think it was deliberate?"

"I don't know. Maybe someone wants to ruin Kelsey's wedding."

"Like who?"

"One person comes to mind." Brooklyn's lips tightened. "What were you talking to Drake Maddox about?"

"I told him he shouldn't come to the wedding."

"What did he say?"

"That everything happened a long time ago. But it doesn't make sense. I don't understand why he'd want to come. I thought he hated all of us."

"So did I. Not that he had a reason to hate us. We weren't responsible for Melanie's disappearance. Did he agree not to come?"

"No. But Kelsey should disinvite him."

"I don't know what possessed her to throw out that invite. Gage will have a fit when he hears about it."

I suddenly wondered if that's why Kelsey had done it. She was angry at Gage for missing the ferry. Perhaps she wanted to get back at him. But this wasn't the way to do it. "Maybe Gage will get Kelsey to take the invitation back."

"But it will cause trouble between them. This is not good, Willow."

"I know. Kelsey shouldn't have moved her wedding to this island."

"I agree."

"You do?" I was shocked that Brooklyn and I seemed to be on the same page for a change.

"Yes. I told her not to do it, but everyone else thought it was a great idea, and Kelsey didn't want to postpone the wedding."

"I don't know why not. It's not like they need to get married right now. Why couldn't they wait and get another venue in Seattle or in LA where they'll be living after they get married?"

"I think it had something to do with this reality show that's in the works. Anyway, it's too late now, Willow. We're here. You need to help me make sure this wedding goes off smoothly." Her gaze moved back to the glass on the floor. "I really hope this was just an accident."

"I can't imagine someone doing it on purpose."

"I can. The caterer is a local woman. She could know Drake."

"You think Drake is behind this?"

"Possibly."

The caterer returned with a broom and dustpan and a large plastic bag to collect the bigger pieces of glass.

"I didn't do this," Dana said again, her gaze completely stressed out. "I hope you both believe me."

"I do," I said, seeing the truth in her eyes.

Brooklyn said nothing, just headed for the door. I followed her onto the patio. She stopped abruptly; her gaze moving to James, who was laughing it up with Trina. The two seemed like they'd had a lot of champagne, and there was definitely a flirtatious air between them.

There was something about Brooklyn's expression that made me wonder about her relationship with James. *Had their breakup been mutual? Was it really over?*

"How is it seeing James again?" I asked.

She stiffened, turning back to me as if she hadn't realized I was still there. "It's fine. Completely fine. Why wouldn't it be?"

Her aggressive tone told me I should drop it, but I didn't. "You dated a long time. You even thought about marrying him. I just wondered how things are between you now."

"There's nothing between us. We were over a long time ago."

"You don't talk at all?"

"We have no reason to speak to each other. Why do you care? You don't still have a crush on him, do you?"

"I never had a crush on James," I protested, shocked at her suggestion. "He was your boyfriend."

She rolled her eyes. "Whatever."

"It's true. Why would you think I had a crush on him?"

"Because he told me you did."

"When did he say that?"

"It doesn't matter," Brooklyn said. "I don't want to talk about the past."

"Then I think we're in the wrong place," I said dryly.

"Let's just worry about what's happening now."

"Oh, trust me. I am worrying about what's happening now."

"I'm going to get something to eat."

As Brooklyn headed toward the buffet table, she took a wide detour around James and Trina. Despite her words, she was clearly bothered by James's presence, but she wasn't going to tell me why.

It didn't matter. Brooklyn would never let her feelings about James get in the way of sending Kelsey off to marital bliss. The real problem was going to be Drake.

My gaze moved to the farthest table where Gabby and Preston Chadwick were eating lunch with their twin girls. While Gabby might be a Chadwick now, she had grown up on the island. She'd known Drake since she was born. Maybe she could tell me how much I needed to worry about him.

CHAPTER FOUR

AFTER FILLING MY PLATE, I took a seat across from Preston and Gabby, and their adorable five-year-old girls, Lucy and Rebecca. Preston was Gage's oldest brother by three years. He was an architect who'd reconnected with Gabby, a local girl, seven years ago. They'd fallen in love and married quickly, their girls coming a year later. Now, Preston made his home on the island, while commuting to his offices in Seattle during the week.

Preston was not as blond or as handsome as his younger brothers, Gage and Carter, and at thirty-three, he was already developing a bit of a gut. But he had always been friendlier and warmer than his brothers and very nice to me. Gabby was a pretty brunette, who still hadn't gotten rid of the baby weight, and seemed to be very uncomfortable in her tight-fitting sheath dress, constantly tugging it down and covering her stomach with her napkin.

"It's nice to see you, Willow," Preston said. "Where are you living now?"

"San Francisco."

"Beautiful city. Love the architecture," he said. "Are you working in photography?"

"No. I'm in real estate."

"Really?" Gabby asked in surprise. "You never put down your

camera when you were on the island. You were always exploring with Melanie. You were always talking about being a photographer."

I drew in a quick breath. "Yes, well, I left my camera here ten years ago, and I never picked up another one. I don't even use the camera on my phone." I grabbed my glass of water and took a long sip.

Gabby gave me an apologetic look. "Sorry, I didn't mean to bring up bad memories."

"It's not you. The memories are all around me."

"It doesn't get better, but it gets easier the longer you're here."

"This is your first time back, isn't it?" Preston asked, giving me a thoughtful look.

"Yes. And to be honest, I didn't want to come, but I couldn't miss Kelsey's wedding."

"No, of course not." Gabby fiddled with her napkin once more. "I miss Melanie, too, Willow. I don't want you to think any of us have forgotten her. But Melanie loved this island. I try to remember that."

Had Melanie loved the island?

She'd talked a lot about leaving that last summer. The island was too small, too restrictive. She'd wanted to spread her wings. She'd wanted to fly, and I'd wanted to fly along with her.

"Daddy, can we play over there?" Lucy asked, pointing to the grassy area where we'd once played badminton and volleyball.

"It's fine," Gabby said with a nod. "But don't go anywhere else."

"We won't," Rebecca promised.

"I'm going to get a drink," Preston said as he rose. "Can I get either of you anything?"

Gabby shook her head, and I said, "No, thanks."

As he left, Gabby said, "Preston doesn't like to talk about Melanie, either. He can't stand how sad I get when her name comes up. I can't believe it will be ten years this August. Melanie never got to grow all the way up. She missed so much."

My heart tore at her words. For the first time, I felt like someone else was sharing my pain.

"Jenny and I probably cried every day that first year," Gabby continued. "We'd get our hopes up with every wild rumor about Melanie being spotted in Seattle, Bellevue, or even in LA. We kept thinking maybe she'd run away, and one day she would come back. Sometimes, I still want to believe that."

"Me, too. But it's not true. There's no way Melanie would stay away this long."

"You're right. But she was so restless and out of sorts that summer."

"Yes, she was," I agreed. "She wanted to be done with high school. She wanted to be leaving for college, going somewhere else."

"There was definitely a lot on her mind that she didn't want to talk about it. Instead, she'd scribble away in her diary. Do you remember that?"

"I do. She hated the diary at first and then she was always writing in it."

"Jenny and I looked for her diary after she disappeared," Gabby said. "So did the police. No one ever found it."

"She must have had it with her that night."

"I guess we'll never know what happened to Melanie."

"I don't think the diary would have given us that answer."

"It might have given us a clue. I thought she might have been seeing someone. Do you know if she was hooking up?"

"No, she wasn't involved with anyone. We were all just hanging out together."

"Not just hanging out," Gabby said dryly. "There was some messing around at many a Saturday night bonfire."

"Well, sure, but I don't remember Melanie spending a lot of time with anyone in particular."

"You would know. You two were together a lot."

I sensed some jealousy in her words, which surprised me. "I guess we were. Did you feel like we were excluding you?"

"Maybe a little, but I know it wasn't on purpose. You two were just on the same wavelength. It was like you could finish each other's sentences. Anyway, it doesn't matter." As she finished speaking, Gabby's gaze drifted to her husband, who was talking to Rachel. A frown brought her mouth downward.

"Everything okay?" I asked.

"What?" She gave me a distracted look.

"You look upset."

"Oh. I'm fine. It's just... I'd forgotten how pretty everyone is." She gave me a sheepish smile. "Sometimes, I wonder why Preston picked me. He could have had any girl he wanted. Now his brother is marrying a supermodel. Kelsey is gorgeous. Rachel is attractive, too. They both look so sophisticated, not frumpy, and squeezed into their clothes."

"They're attractive, but Preston loves you, Gabby. You two have a beautiful family together."

"I know. It's just that being a mom, being home with the girls, I feel like I've lost sight of the world outside this island. Not that I don't love it here, I do. And my mom needs me to help her run the ice cream parlor, so I need to be here. But with everyone coming back and looking so good, it reminds me of how small my world has become."

"Maybe you need to take a break. You could come visit me in San Francisco."

"That would be fun, but it's difficult to get away. I don't know if I have the energy to make it happen. But thanks."

"It's an open invitation." I sipped my water, then added, "Did you know Drake is back on the island?"

Uneasiness ran through her eyes. "I heard he was coming, but I haven't seen him."

"He was sitting at a table on the patio at the Crab Pot when we got off the ferry. Kelsey gave him a big hug and invited him to the wedding."

Surprise raised Gabby's brows. "What? Why would she do that?"

"I don't know. I haven't had a chance to ask her. But it's a horrible idea."

"What did Drake say?"

"That he'd love to come, which makes no sense. Drake was convinced that someone from our group knew something about Melanie's disappearance. He was so angry with Gage; he broke his nose."

"I remember that. But Gage knew nothing. No one did." Gabby gave me a thoughtful look. "You don't think anyone did, do you?"

"I don't know. It's strange that Melanie could disappear with no one seeing anything, but I also can't imagine anyone doing anything to hurt her. Have you and Preston ever talked about it?"

"No. Preston and I didn't start dating until almost three years after Melanie disappeared. She wasn't at the center of conversation anymore." She cleared her throat. "Anyway, I hope Drake doesn't come to the wedding."

We both turned our heads as Kelsey let out a sudden squeal. For a second, I thought something else must have broken, but then I saw Gage Chadwick storm across the patio and sweep Kelsey into his arms for what felt like a dramatic movie kiss. They were so beautiful with their golden hair, perfectly fit bodies, and incredibly attractive features. They were the golden couple.

"I thought you weren't coming until tonight," Kelsey said when Gage finally let her breathe again.

"I couldn't stand being away from you another second, so I hired a boat to bring me here," he replied.

"I'm so glad. I missed you."

"You have me now," he said, kissing Kelsey again. Then he turned to the rest of the group. "Let's get this party started."

Laughter followed his words, and it reminded me of how often Gage had been the leader of our group. Everyone followed his cue. Kelsey seemed brighter, as if Gage's arrival had taken away all her worries.

Gage had never had that effect on me. He'd had little time for me, and I'd never had much time for him. We hadn't been enemies, but we hadn't been friends.

"They're so perfect together," Gabby said. "Preston said they're going to have a TV show."

"I heard something about that, too."

As Gage and Kelsey moved around the patio to say hello to everyone, they eventually got to me and Gabby. I stood up and gave Gage a brief hug, feeling awkward, but we were going to be in-laws, so I needed to get over that.

"Hello, Gage," I said.

"Willow. You look good. It's been a while."

"It has. Congratulations."

His smile sparkled as he glanced down at Kelsey. "I'm the luckiest man in the world."

"I'm the luckiest girl in the world," Kelsey returned.

As Gage put his arm around Kelsey's thin shoulders, it occurred to me that Kelsey's smile was nowhere near as dazzling as her groom's. There was something off. I just didn't know what or how serious it was.

"Kelsey," I said impulsively. "Can I talk to you for a second?"

She hesitated as her gaze met mine, but then she shook her head. "Later, Willow. Gage and I want to say hello to everyone."

"Okay, sure." I told myself everything was fine, but I didn't believe it.

"I should check on the girls," Gabby said. "Maybe we can chat more tonight—at the bonfire."

I sighed. "The bonfire, right."

Gabby gave me a sympathetic smile. "It will be fun. You just need to stay in the present, Willow. Nothing is the same as it was. Time didn't stand still."

That was probably true for most people, but I'd spent ten years trying to move on, and I was right back where I started.

CHAPTER FIVE

GABBY WAS RIGHT. Time had moved on. The beach by the Belle Haven Lodge was nothing like where we'd had our teenage bonfires, I thought, as I walked from the lodge parking lot to the sand Tuesday evening.

I'd gotten a cab to the beach. My parents and sisters had taken the two cars we kept on the island, and they'd all seemed to have other things to do on the way to the bonfire, so I'd been left on my own. That was not unusual. I was often left behind, but I didn't really care. I wanted to make my stop at this bonfire as brief as possible.

This beach was wide and flat, which differed from Miramar Beach where we'd held our teenage bonfires. That beach had been secluded and accessed by a steep trail, which made it more difficult for adults and sheriff deputies to patrol. Not that the sheriff or his deputies had ever been that interested in stopping our fun. As long as we weren't drinking and driving or being totally stupid, they left us alone.

I wonder now if the sheriff had changed his attitude after Melanie's disappearance, if the kids who came to visit the island after that had been held more accountable.

Probably not. Our freedom had come because our parents had

money and the locals wanted to keep the summer visitors happy. Melanie had told me that bonfires weren't allowed outside the summer months, even on warm spring days. There had been different rules in the summer because the tourist money kept the locals going for the rest of the year.

That was one reason Drake had been so angry after Melanie vanished. He'd thought the sheriff was going easy on interrogating the rich summer kids. He'd thought someone was being allowed to get away with...I didn't even want to say the word. I preferred to think of Melanie as just being gone. I didn't want to consider how she might have been hurt, how she might have been killed.

The word hit my head before I could stop it, and my steps faltered. I drew in a breath and let it out, wanting to drag my mind back to the present. But the present wasn't any more relaxing than the past. Despite the change in bonfire location, I still felt a sense of dread.

It wasn't just that Melanie had disappeared after one of our bonfires; it was that the night she'd disappeared I'd been completely wasted, and I'd blacked out. I had never regained my memories of that night.

Drake had accused me of lying, of knowing more than I was saying, but I didn't know more. I wished I did. And I wished I wasn't here right now, having to relive the worst night of my life.

But this night wasn't the same as that night, and I needed to focus on the differences. The Belle Haven Lodge had set up the bonfire with an eye to luxurious comfort. There were Adirondack chairs all around the fire pit with thick, colorful blankets hanging off the back of each chair. There were also beanbag chairs and fluffy towels on the sand for those who wanted to stretch out.

To the side of the fire pit were two long tables, one a cocktail and coffee bar, the other filled with snacks and all the makings for s'mores. Two waiters were moving through the crowd to deliver drinks. A musical trio was playing beachy music, and a few couples had already kicked off their shoes to dance in the sand.

This was definitely not the down and dirty Saturday night bonfire scene of ten years ago, where we'd filled soda cans with vodka, danced to loud, dirty music, and looked for someone to make out with under the shadows of the trees.

That there weren't a lot of trees here should have also made me feel better. There was nowhere to hide, no danger lurking in the shadows. This night would not end in disaster.

A waiter offered me a choice of champagne or wine. I waved him away, thinking once again how different everything was and yet how it was also the same. Alcohol had always played a role in our bonfires. And while I'd started out too scared to drink much, by the end of that last summer, I'd been doing shots.

That was partly Melanie's doing. She was younger than me, but so much more of a party girl. She was always telling me to stop taking pictures at our parties and start experiencing them.

I shouldn't have listened to her. Maybe if I had stayed in the shadows, looking at my life through my camera, I would have seen something that would have made a difference. But that last night, I'd put my camera down and picked up a drink, and I'd decided not to be the shy, good girl anymore.

What a mistake that had been.

I let out a sigh as I glanced around the group. My parents and the Chadwicks were sitting by the fire along with the Connellys and the Hamiltons. The younger generation was mostly standing or flopped on blankets on the sand. Kelsey and Gage got up from one of those blankets to dance, and they looked happy.

Kelsey wore a bright red slip of a dress under a white leather jacket. Gage wore dark jeans and a button-down shirt. They'd obviously gotten past whatever had been bothering them. Now they were smiling and laughing. It felt like the old days, but this time in a good way.

"Willow?"

I turned to see Jenny Nolan, who was not only Kelsey's wedding planner, but a long-time friend. We embraced, and for the first time since I'd arrived on the island, I lost the chill that had clung to my skin. But that was Jenny. She'd always been a great hugger, an empathetic soul. As we broke apart, she gave me a warm smile.

"It's good to see you, Willow."

"You, too. How are you?"

"Busy," she said with a laugh. "Your mom and Kelsey are keeping me on my toes."

"I don't doubt that."

"What do you think of the bonfire?"

"It's…different."

"That's a good thing, right? We host these bonfires for almost every wedding now. Kelsey was a little worried about having one, but I assured her it wouldn't feel like the old days."

"It's definitely more sophisticated than the ones we used to have."

"I'm glad you think so," Jenny said with relief. "I thought if anyone would care, it would be you."

"You were right. I'm trying to be positive and happy about all this, but it's difficult. It's the first time I've been back since Melanie…"

"I know. We've missed you."

"I've missed you, too. So, you're a wedding planner now. What's that like?" I was eager to change the subject.

"Busy. I don't just plan weddings; I also do corporate events."

"I'm surprised you're working for a competitor to your parents' hotel." Jenny's parents ran the Baker Street Hotel downtown, which had been in their family for generations.

"Their hotel only hosts small private dinner parties, so the Belle Haven Lodge is not in competition. My parents are happy I left Seattle to come back to the island to work, so it's all good. Anyway, I need to check on things, make sure everyone is happy. I hope we can catch up later, Willow. I'd love to know about your life in San Francisco."

"Sure, let's talk," I said, although I didn't really think it would happen. Despite Jenny's warm embrace and genuine smile, I didn't get the feeling she wanted to go too deep with me, and that was fine, because I didn't want to go too deep with her, either.

Melanie's disappearance had put a huge wedge between all my relationships, especially those with the local kids. Jenny might not have blamed me for anything, but the accusations flying around, and my inability to remember anything about the night, had made things awkward.

As Jenny left, I decided I'd done my duty. I'd made an appearance. I didn't need to stay. It wasn't like anyone would miss me. I walked toward the lodge, hoping to grab a cab and head home. As I reached the restrooms, which were housed in an exterior building, a man stumbled out the door. It was James Connelly. James's brown hair was mussed. His tailored shirt was halfway out of his pants, and it looked like he'd spilled a drink on himself.

He gave me a confused look and then said, "Hey, babe. I was wondering where you were."

As James drew closer, I realized there was a serious stench of alcohol coming off him. He had so much vodka in him. If I lit a match, he would go up in flames.

"You're much prettier than you used to be," James slurred. "What do you say we do what we did before?"

"We never did anything, James."

"Sure, we did. Remember the back seat of my car? Your bedroom?"

"We were never in your car or my bedroom. You're thinking about Brooklyn. I'm Willow."

His hand came around my waist, sliding down to my ass. I quickly removed it.

"No, it was you," he insisted. "You were too young for me, but you wanted it. You begged me for it, so why not?" He took a step closer.

I put a hand against his chest. "James, stop. You're drunk, and I'm leaving."

"I was drunk the first time. That didn't matter to you."

I frowned, wondering who he was confusing me with. It didn't sound like he was talking about Brooklyn, but that was odd. They'd started dating when they were seventeen, and they were together for years.

"I can make it good for you," he said, his eyes completely dazed.

"You couldn't make it good for anyone." As I tried to leave, he put both arms around me, and I struggled against him, surprised by his strength. "Let me go."

"Just a kiss, and you'll remember."

"No." I shoved him away so hard he hit the wall of the building and then sank down to the ground.

James put his head in his hands. I turned to leave and came face-to-face with Drake Maddox.

His sharp gaze swept the scene. "Are you all right, Willow?"

"I'm fine. James is drunk."

"Clearly. I didn't know the two of you were...together." He gave me a speculative look. "Isn't he Brooklyn's boyfriend?"

"James and Brooklyn broke up years ago, and James and I are not together."

"He just tried to kiss you."

"He's out of his mind." I frowned. "If you saw him try to kiss me, you could have stopped him."

"I didn't know if you wanted him to kiss you."

"Wasn't that obvious?" I turned my head and saw that James had rolled over onto his side, his eyes closed. Most everyone was down at the bonfire, but someone would walk by soon, and that would not be good. "We need to get him up and out of here."

"That sounds like a job for the Connellys, or the Chadwicks, or your family. Hide away the mess before anyone sees it, before anyone can blame you, and then plead complete ignorance," he said with a bitter note in his voice.

"I opened myself up for that one, didn't I? Do you feel better now?"

"Not really."

"What are you doing here, Drake?"

"I want answers."

"After all these years? No one is going to suddenly remember something. No one is suddenly going to talk."

"Is that what has been decided?" he challenged.

"It's just the truth. If someone knew something ten years ago and said nothing, they're not talking now." I paused. "I want answers, too. Everyone who loved Melanie wants those answers, but they're not coming."

"They might come with the right inducement."

"What does that mean?" I asked, his answer concerning.

He shrugged. "Memory is a funny thing, especially when you're back in the place where it happened."

"You really think someone in our group hurt your sister?"

He met my gaze. "I've asked myself that question a million times. In the beginning, I couldn't imagine it was someone in our group. I was friends with everyone. So was Melanie. But the more people couldn't remember, the more they clammed up, the way they quickly exited the island changed that answer to a yes."

My pulse leapt at his words. "It's impossible," I whispered.

"Is it, Willow? You don't remember that night. So how do you know for sure that it isn't extremely possible?"

"Because there's no motive. Everyone loved Melanie."

"It might not have been about that. Maybe Melanie saw something she wasn't supposed to see, or she threatened to tell on someone."

"You're speculating."

"Yes. I've been speculating for ten years."

"It could have been a complete stranger. If she was alone, it could have been anyone. It was August. The island was packed with tourists. Hundreds came and went on the ferry each day," I argued. "You've zeroed in on one small group of people because it's easier, but you're wrong."

"I don't think I am."

The anger sparked gold lights in his dark-blue eyes, and those sparks reminded me of other emotions I'd seen in his gaze, emotions he'd given into once and then quickly denounced, leaving me heartbroken, confused and feeling like a fool. But I wouldn't be a fool again. I wouldn't believe Drake, because he'd already proven to me he could lie, that he was untrustworthy.

"Willow?" His sharp voice dragged me back to the present.

"What?"

"I said I'm not wrong. And you shouldn't fight me. You should help me. Melanie was your best friend."

"I can't help you; I don't know anything."

"I think you do. Maybe you're scared. Maybe you're protecting someone's secret. Hell, maybe it's yourself you're protecting."

My jaw dropped in shock. "You seriously think I had something to do with Melanie's disappearance?"

"You were supposed to meet her that night. You didn't. And you claim to remember nothing. You don't know where you went after Ben's party. You don't know if you were at the bonfire. You have no idea how you got home."

"That's all true. If I knew something, I would have told the sheriff. I held nothing back. I didn't protect anyone, including myself." I shook my head in frustration. "You are so off base, it's ridiculous. But you won't believe me, so it doesn't matter what I say. Just like it won't matter what anyone else has to say. You have your theory, and nothing will change it."

"The truth might change it. But I have heard nothing close to the truth."

"Just because you don't believe people doesn't mean they're lying. If the sheriff had found evidence against anyone in our group, he would have pursued it."

"I don't know about that. Money is power, and on this island, the rich families at Chambers' Point wield all the power." He tipped his head toward James. "He should have had a DUI ten years ago, but Sheriff Ryan gave him a warning. You know why? Because the Connellys donated money to renovate the police station."

I couldn't argue with that one, because I knew it was true. I'd overheard Brooklyn and Kelsey talking about how lucky James was to have gotten off.

"Nothing to say?" Drake challenged.

"I heard that happened. It was wrong. He should have paid a price for driving drunk."

"You didn't say anything then."

"I didn't find out about it until weeks later."

"How convenient."

"I'm not the person you should be mad at, Drake. I loved Melanie. She was like my sister."

"You let her down."

The words hurt as much this time as they had the first time he'd said them. "Maybe I let her down, but I hope that wasn't the reason she disappeared. Now I need to get someone to help James." As I turned to leave, he grabbed my arm. I was surprised by the tightness of his grip. "Let me go, Drake."

"I want you to know something, Willow."

"What?"

"I will find out what happened to Melanie, and I will get justice for her. If that ruins Kelsey's wedding, then that's what happens. It might be for the best, anyway."

"How could it be for the best?" I challenged.

"Kelsey is way too good for Gage."

"You don't know that. You don't know any of us anymore." I pulled my arm free. "When did you get to be so cold, so ruthless?"

His lips tightened. "Ten years ago—August 19th." He let that sink in, then added, "I don't think anyone has changed as much as you think they have."

A chill ran down my spine as he walked away. He was going to do something. *But what?*

CHAPTER SIX

I NEEDED TO WARN KELSEY. Maybe she could talk to Drake. Perhaps he would relent if Kelsey asked him to back off, although I wondered again when they had gotten to be such good friends. *Had something gone down between them all those years ago that I'd never known about?* That thought was a little sickening.

As James stirred, I hurried back to the bonfire. I didn't want another encounter with him. Brooklyn, Carter, and Rachel were standing together on the periphery of the group. Since Rachel was James's sister, she could deal with him.

"James is passed out by the restrooms," I told them.

"Oh, man," Rachel groaned. "I knew he was drinking too much. Will you help me, Carter?"

"Sure," Carter said. "What the hell is wrong with him? He's been drinking since we got on the ferry. I thought he was supposed to have that under control."

"I don't think he wants to be here," Rachel said shortly, sending Brooklyn a pointed look.

"His drinking has nothing to do with me," Brooklyn said defiantly, folding her arms across her chest.

"That's not true," Rachel argued. "It has a lot to do with you. He's hurting. Can't you see that?"

"You should get James back to your parents' house, Rachel," Brooklyn replied, her lips tight, her tone cold.

Rachel shook her head. "I'm definitely not taking him there. They'll flip out. I'll take him to a hotel so he can sleep it off."

As Rachel and Carter left, I moved closer to Brooklyn. "We have a problem."

"James is not my problem," she said sharply. "He hasn't been for years. I don't know why everyone suddenly thinks I'm going to take care of him."

"Brooklyn—"

"Did James say something about me?" she interrupted.

"No. And the problem isn't James. Well, he might be a problem, but he's not the one I'm talking about. It's Drake. He just told me he's determined to find out what happened to Melanie. I think he's going to screw up Kelsey's wedding."

"He said that?"

"Yes. He believes someone in our circle of family and friends has withheld information all these years, but now that everyone is back on the island where it happened, someone might remember something and be willing to talk."

"Why would they suddenly do that now?"

"He said something about inducement, whatever that means."

"That's not good."

"No, it's not. Drake also can't stand Gage. He said Kelsey would be better off if her wedding was ruined, because she's too good for Gage. I tried to shut him down, but he wasn't listening to me."

"I'll talk to Kelsey tomorrow."

"Maybe we should do it tonight."

Brooklyn hesitated, then shook her head. "Gage and Kelsey are having fun, and there are too many people around. I'll talk to her later tonight or tomorrow morning. I don't really think Drake can ruin the wedding, but we need to figure out how to defuse him."

"The only way to do that is for someone to tell him something they didn't tell the sheriff."

"Well, we're going to have to find another way, because that won't happen. Let's keep this between us for now. No need to worry anyone else. I'll talk to you later."

As Brooklyn moved toward our parents, I walked back to the restrooms. There was no sign of Rachel, Carter, or James. One problem averted. I blew out a breath, debating what I wanted to do next. I didn't want to stay here, but I also didn't feel like going home.

Impulsively, I headed toward the street. The lodge was only about a mile from downtown, and it felt good to walk. I needed to burn off the stress and worry that had been weighing me down ever since I'd gotten on the ferry this morning. It hadn't even been twenty-four hours yet, and I was already feeling desperate to get off the island.

As I walked down the road, I drew my jacket more tightly around me. Luckily, I had found a heavier coat in my closet at the house. I hadn't come prepared for this weather; it was summer after all. But today was colder than any I could remember, with a series of storms threatening the next few days, although the weather report still suggested that Saturday could be dry. That was the most important day.

A big gust of wind lifted my hair off the back of my neck, and I shivered, feeling uneasy now that I was away from the lodge. I'd forgotten how deserted this stretch of road was. The path along the bluff had excellent ocean views in the daylight, but there were few streetlights, and with the cloud cover, the night felt very dark.

I picked up my pace, feeling more tension as a car came up behind me and appeared to slow down. I didn't recognize the vehicle or the man behind the wheel. He gave me a look and then sped up, disappearing down the road.

It was nothing, I told myself, but an odd memory flitted through my head. *Had I been on this road before?* I couldn't remember walking it at night. But I had walked somewhere that last night. My memories were splintered and cloudy, but I remembered a road—and headlights. *Had they come up behind me or toward me?*

My breath came faster as sudden panic gripped me. I could feel myself getting pulled back into the past. I shouldn't try to fight it. Because Drake might be right. I might know more than I had ever said. But maybe what I knew was too terrifying to remember.

I stopped and drew in a breath, trying to calm myself down. I looked toward the sea as the clouds parted and moonlight lit up the crashing waves below.

This scene also felt eerily familiar. *I remembered being on a bluff overlooking the ocean, afraid I was too close to the edge. I didn't want to fall into that churning water.*

I had fallen, but not into the sea. I knew that because I'd had abrasions on my hand and blood on my knee where my jeans had ripped when I woke up in the early hours of the morning on a chaise lounge on the patio, with no idea of how I'd gotten there. I'd gone upstairs in the dawn light and fallen into bed, feeling sick, dizzy, and confused.

When I'd woken up, it had only gotten worse. Melanie was missing.

Another car came down the road now, and for a split second, the headlights blinded me. Another flash of memory. *Had I felt blinded before?*

Maybe Drake was right. Coming back to the island might be loosening something up in my brain.

As another car passed by, I started walking again. I needed to get off this road. I needed people, lights, and noise. I broke into a light jog, the darkness of the past propelling me forward. I was running away from something, but I didn't know what, and I was afraid to find out.

What if I had seen something?

What if I could have saved Melanie?

What if I was the reason she was gone?

Each question brought pain and panic. By the time I hit the outskirts of town, I was sweating and panting. I stopped at the first traffic light, relieved when a crowd of tourists surrounded me as they waited to cross the street.

Their mere presence made me feel better. A mom was laughing with her kid. Two teenage girls were talking about some hot guy they were hoping to run into. A man was telling his friend about the big fish he'd caught earlier that day. People were living their lives. It wasn't ten years ago. It was now. I don't think any of these people had even heard of Melanie. That was a little sad. She'd loved when the tourists came to town. New faces were always exciting to her.

The light changed, and I crossed the street. With my pulse slowing down, I ambled through the downtown, letting the crowd carry me aimlessly along. Things had changed and yet were still very much the same. The bookstore brought back happy memories of hours spent sitting on the fluffy chairs in the window, reading the latest beach book.

Some restaurants and clothing boutiques were new, but the big hardware store on the corner of Main and Winston looked exactly the same, including the two electronic horses that sat out front. A quarter would give a three-minute ride. They were supposed to be for small kids, but Melanie and I had ended up on them at least twice a summer, usually with ice cream cones in our hands.

My gaze moved across the street to the ice cream parlor owned by Gabby's family. It had a line halfway down the block, despite the wintry feeling of the night. I could smell the sugar as I passed by. I definitely needed to get a triple scoop of mocha almond fudge on a waffle cone before I went home. But I'd come back when it was warmer.

For the next thirty minutes, I made my way around town. Now that I was around people and action, I wasn't desperate to get home. It actually felt good to walk, to breathe fresh air, to hear laughter and music. I'd built up the island to be this dark, dangerous place in my mind, but it had never felt that way to me when I was a kid.

Back then, I'd loved the hundreds of trails that ran through the woods, the beautiful beaches that encircled the island, the town events—everything from a cornhole championship on the Fourth of July, to the summer sailing races, and the art festivals. I'd loved warm summer nights, endless amounts of ice cream, the predictable crash of the waves as I'd drift to sleep each night, dreaming of the adventures Melanie and I would go on the next day.

Melanie came back into my head. Her big dark eyes gleamed with excitement, her shimmery black hair falling loose about her shoulders as we ran down hills or dove into the ocean. Her unrestrained, wholehearted laugh came from down deep and was so contagious, I always laughed, too, even if I didn't know what we were laughing at. An intense sadness ran through me.

I knew there were people in this town who still loved and remembered Melanie, but there were so many who had never known her or who had mostly forgotten her, and that bothered me. Melanie had never wanted to be forgettable. But while I'd never forget her, remembering her was emotionally exhausting.

I shivered as the breeze kicked up, and I moved a little faster. It would be easier to get a ride from the heart of downtown, so I made my way toward a cluster of bars and restaurants on Ocean Avenue.

Raley's had a rooftop deck, and I could hear the music pumping from above my head. The Island Brewery also had an outdoor patio, and it was packed as well. The Road House still had a dive look to it. I'd never gone there, but Brooklyn, James, and Gage had snuck in there a few times that last summer. They were only twenty, but they'd had fake IDs, and the old man who owned the place didn't look at anything too closely.

I frowned, thinking about what Drake had said earlier about James's DUI. James should have been arrested. And judging by James's condition tonight, maybe he wouldn't be such a drunk now if he had suffered a consequence for his actions back then.

Or maybe it would have made no difference. I'd never really liked James. I'd always thought he was arrogant and condescending to me. It was unbelievable that he'd ever told Brooklyn I liked him. It was even more unbelievable that he thought we'd made out in his car or my bedroom. Clearly, that had not been me. But he'd also said that the person was too young for him, which made me wonder if he'd been talking about Kelsey. That would be disgusting. Kelsey wouldn't have hooked up with Brooklyn's boyfriend. *Would she?*

Kelsey could be a little selfish. *No.* I shook my head. Kelsey wouldn't have hurt Brooklyn like that. James had just made the whole thing up. Or he'd been talking about someone else.

When I got to the corner by the liquor store, I pulled out my phone and checked one of the ride apps. This was a busy part of downtown, and it looked like a car would arrive in fifteen minutes. That was doable. After confirming, I moved back toward the building to get protection from the wind. A man came rushing around the corner, almost knocking me over. At first, all I saw was the shiny gleam of his badge. But as he grabbed my arms to steady me, our gazes met.

"Willow?" he asked in surprise.

I smiled into his familiar brown eyes. "Hello, Ben. I guess you still don't look where you're going."

He grinned. "That's right. The first time we met, I knocked you off your bike."

"Because you were speeding down Mountain View."

"I wasn't speeding; I just wasn't braking."

I laughed at the old excuse. "Same old story."

"It was the truth then, and the truth now." He dropped his hands from my arms and stepped back, his gaze moving down my body. "You look good."

"You look official," I said, noting his uniform. "I heard you took over for your dad."

"Two months ago," he said with a nod.

I shook my head in bemusement. "I never thought you'd follow in your father's footsteps. You were always a rule breaker, not a rule follower. And you said you wanted to live far away from here."

"I lived far away from here for a long time. I was gone nine years before I came back. I was in Portland, Los Angeles, and San Diego. But when my dad retired, he urged me to come home. I had no intention of taking his old job, but the island worked its magic, and here I am."

"Enforcing the law instead of breaking it. How ironic. You rebelled so hard against your dad."

"I did. But it turns out he always wanted what was best for me. I finally realized he was trying to protect me, not just ruin my fun. I grew up."

He had grown up, and he was even more attractive than I remembered with his sandy-brown hair and boy-next-door looks. He'd always had a warm, friendly, persuasive smile. He'd talked me and Melanie into doing a lot of things we shouldn't have done, just because he always made everything sound fun. Not that we'd ever done anything that bad, but we'd certainly broken a few laws back in the day. Luckily, Ben had always known how to avoid trouble.

"So, what are you up to these days, Willow?" Ben asked.

"I sell real estate in San Francisco."

"You don't do photography?"

"No. It wasn't something I wanted to do after Melanie vanished."

He nodded, a somber expression entering his gaze. "I get that. We all grow out of things. And you shouldn't do anything you don't want to do. If real estate is your new passion, that's cool."

"I don't think I have a passion anymore. I just have a job. Is the law your passion?"

"It is," he said with a laugh. "Hard to believe, I know."

"It's unexpected. What do you like about being the sheriff?"

He thought for a moment. "I enjoy taking care of the people on this island the way my dad did for over thirty years. I like having the power to make a difference in someone's life."

"That must feel good. I have little power over my life."

"You always have power. Even if it's just the power to not take control."

"When did you get to be so philosophical?" I asked with a smile.

"Probably about ten years ago."

I met his gaze, feeling the old connection between us grow stronger. "It was hard for me to come back here."

"I know. You loved Melanie so much."

"I really did. But I let her down. I left her on her own that night. That might have been the reason she—"

"You don't know that. I've looked at Melanie's file. No one saw her after four o'clock that day. You weren't supposed to meet her until eight. We have no idea where she was or what time she disappeared. Her mom didn't notify the sheriff until the next morning when she realized Melanie hadn't come home the night before."

"I just don't see how anyone could have taken her from the bonfire or a crowded location. It had to have happened when she went to meet me at Five Falls, but I never got there, because I was drinking." I paused. "With you."

"I shouldn't have let you get that drunk." A regretful look entered his eyes.

"You didn't force it down my throat. You just invited me to a party, and I wanted to be there." Ben probably thought I'd wanted to party with him, but I'd really gone because I knew Drake was going to be there.

"You weren't used to doing shots. I should have looked out for you. But I wasn't very good at even looking out for myself. I made some poor decisions."

"Me, too."

"It's another reason I wanted to go into law enforcement," he added. "I wanted to save some other stupid kids from doing stupid things."

"How's that going?"

He gave me a small smile. "Not particularly well. Now, I know what my dad was up against. Off season is a hell of a lot easier than summer. The more tourists, the more trouble."

"Speaking of trouble, I think Drake is going to ruin Kelsey's wedding. He still believes one of us knows something. Now that we're all back in the same place, he thinks he's going to get someone to talk. How he intends to do that worries me."

"I know Drake is still searching for the truth, but he always liked Kelsey. He wouldn't want to hurt her."

"I'm not sure he cares if she's collateral damage. Can you talk to him, Ben? You've known him a long time. Can you tell him to leave it alone? Or maybe arrest him until after the wedding?"

He smiled. "I can't arrest him, but I can talk to him. Drake is a good guy, Willow. He might try to grill you and your friends, but it won't go beyond that."

"I hope not." I paused as a motorcycle roared down the street, then parked in the loading zone in front of me. A guy got off, pulling off his helmet and shaking out his long blond hair. As he hit the sidewalk and came under the streetlight, he paused, and then a sheepish expression ran across Dillon Petrie's face.

"Uh-oh," he said. "I didn't see you there, Ben."

"Dammit, Dillon, how many tickets do you want this week? I already pulled you over for speeding," Ben said. "You know you can't park there."

"I'm going to be one second. I'm just grabbing something from the liquor store. I'll be in and out, and there's no other parking."

"Move the bike."

"Come on, dude. We've been friends forever."

"And we're still friends, but I'm on duty."

"Fine. I'll move it." Dillon's gaze moved to me, and then a startled gleam entered his eyes. "Wait, a second. I know you." He snapped his fingers. "Willow Kent. Wow, you look awesome."

I smiled. "Thanks. How are you, Dillon?"

"I was doing better until I ran into this guy," Dillon drawled. "Can you believe he turned on us and became a cop?"

"It surprised me."

"And you're stalling, Dillon," Ben interrupted.

"Just hold on one second. Is your sister really going to marry Gage Chadwick? What is Kelsey thinking?"

"That she loves him."

Dillon shook his head in bemusement. "She could do so much better."

"Gage is a very successful man," I said.

"Gage might be successful, but he's always been a prick," Dillon said. "Tell her Ben."

"I don't know Gage anymore. Neither do you." Ben's words were guarded. "He could be a different person now."

"Guys like Gage don't change."

"Some people change," Ben argued. "Maybe not you, but other people do. You need to move your bike, Dillon."

"Fine, I'll move it. I'm really missing your old man. He wasn't such a hard-ass with little things." Dillon put on his helmet and headed back to his motorcycle. A moment later, he roared away.

"So, Dillon is still breaking the rules," I said.

Ben's expression was tense. "Yes. And everyone I grew up with seems to think they get a pass on unacceptable behavior."

"They're probably testing you."

"They're definitely testing me."

"What does Dillon do now?"

"An assortment of jobs. He still works for Party Planet, setting up events. He also works for his uncle, delivering fresh fish to the local restaurants. He plays guitar, gets high, goes surfing, gets high, same as always…"

I laughed. "Got it."

"I wish he'd left the island, done something else," Ben continued. "But Dillon says when he figures out what else he wants to do, he'll go. Sometimes, I envy how unstressed he is."

"I think getting high has a lot to do with that," I said dryly.

"Probably." A car pulled up to the curb, and I started. "This is my ride. It was nice to see you, Ben."

"I'm sure we'll see each other again before you go."

"I hope so."

I opened the car door, then paused. "Do you think Gage is a bad choice for Kelsey?"

"I wouldn't presume to tell anyone what to do. Frankly, I'm not surprised Gage and Kelsey got together. They're the perfect match —a star athlete and a supermodel. Obviously, Kelsey loves him," Ben added, with an edge to his voice. "She loves him, right?"

"I don't think she'd be marrying him otherwise."

"I guess not. I'll see you around, Willow."

As Ben left, I got into the car, thinking about what both Dillon and Ben had said. Their knowledge of Gage was ten years old. They could be completely wrong now.

A niggling doubt pricked at the back of my mind.

What if they weren't wrong? What if Kelsey was making a big mistake?

I could try to talk to her again, but it was her life, and I knew very little about her relationship with Gage. I had to trust that Kelsey knew the man she was going to marry.

Melanie's Diary–June 28th

Ben and I won a sailing race today. It was so cool. There were about a dozen boats competing. I was supposed to race with Drake and my dad, but my father went on one of his walkabouts, and Drake got sucked into some story he's pitching to the newspaper and bailed on me. So, Ben and Dillon reluctantly agreed to come with me, and we came in first place.

It felt amazing. The wind was fierce. We practically flew across the water. And the best part is that we beat the Chadwick brothers: Preston, Gage and Carter.

It's the first time the Chadwicks haven't won that race in like three years. Gage blamed Carter for the loss. He said he moved too slow. I don't think Carter was too thrilled about Gage's comment. He looked like he wanted to punch him.

Ben and Dillon thought their fight was hilarious. They love it when the Chadwick brothers turn on each other. I don't think they like any of them too much, although they spend a lot of time with those boys. That's the thing about living on the island. Even if you don't like some of the rich kids, they still make your life more interesting when they're in town.

Anyway, I'm a winner, and I don't care why the Chadwicks think they lost. It's not like Dillon was moving fast. He basically just came along for the ride because this race required a three-person crew. Ben and I did all the work. I didn't actually know that

Ben could sail that well. The last few years, he has gotten into heavy partying, and he's never out on the water.

Sometimes I worry about Ben. I worry about Dillon, too. They're fun-loving guys, but they both suffered losses when they were young. Ben was ten when his mom died. Dillon was only four when he lost his mother. Then his dad took off, and he ended up living with an uncle who seemed pretty mean. I think that's why Ben and Dillon became such close friends. It's probably also why they don't like the Chadwicks, who have the perfect family. Sometimes those beautiful families at Chambers' Point are really annoying.

Anyway, we all had a good time. Sheriff Ryan, my parents, and Ben and Dillon all met up for pizza later. We put our trophy in the middle of the table. The sheriff was cool. He likes to tell stories and be the center of attention, but that's okay. My dad is so quiet. Sometimes, it's nice to go out with people who talk more.

Maybe I can convince Ben to sail again. It would be a lot better for him than all the partying. I'm sure he won't listen to me, though. But he should. I know he'd be happier if he did.

Gotta go. I want to call Willow before it gets too late. We're going to hike up to the summit tomorrow. We should be able to get some amazing pictures. Willow will probably complain about the long hike. She's not really into hiking, but she'll do anything to get the perfect shot. In the end, it will be worth it.

CHAPTER SEVEN

WHEN I GOT BACK to the house, it was after nine. I'd spent more time wandering around town than I'd realized. The lights were on and as I let myself in, I heard a clash of voices coming from the living room.

I peeked in and saw my parents with the Chadwicks and the Connellys. The men were gathered by the bar, the women seated on the couch and love seat in front of the fireplace.

I didn't feel like making conversation, so I headed into the kitchen to see what I could find to eat. The refrigerator was packed with healthy snacks, plenty of veggies, and leftovers from lunch, but I felt like something more decadent.

I walked into the adjacent large pantry and found the sweets I was looking for. While my mother was always watching her weight, my dad still had his stash of candy in the back corner. As I poked through the large variety bag, I heard people come into the kitchen.

Before I could make my presence known, I heard my mother say, "Drake is out to ruin Kelsey's wedding. He's probably the one who broke the sculpture."

"There's no way Drake got into the house with no one seeing him," Sean Chadwick said.

"Then he paid the caterer to do it."

"Why would he?"

"He wants to shake us all up. Brooklyn said that Drake thinks one of us knows something about Melanie's disappearance, and he's going to find out what it is."

I was surprised that Brooklyn had expressed that concern to my mother. She must be more worried than she'd let on to me.

"There's nothing to find out, Monica," Sean said, a firm note in his voice.

"Are you sure?"

I stiffened. How could my mother even ask that question?

"Am I sure? Hell, yes, I'm sure," he retorted.

"Don't snap at me."

"Then don't be stupid."

I was shocked by their words. I'd never heard them talk that way to each other before. It was the way my mom talked to my dad, or my dad talked to my mom. But Sean and my mother? *Where had the boundaries of politeness gone?*

"I'm not being stupid, Sean. I am never stupid. I am the one who is thinking ahead," my mother continued. "I need to protect Kelsey. I'm going to speak to Drake's mother tomorrow. I'll tell Sylvie that he's not welcome and if he tries to come to the wedding, security will escort him out. I don't think they'll want that to happen. I'll also make sure she knows we won't be patronizing the restaurant in the future if she allows her son to ruin the wedding."

"I don't think you should involve Sylvie. You'll make this bigger than it is. Besides, didn't I hear that Kelsey invited him to the wedding?"

"She's so naïve. She just wants to let bygones be bygones. But I cannot go along with that. Nor can I stand by and do nothing."

"Don't talk to Sylvie. She can't control Drake, and it will just upset her."

"Why do you care if she's upset?" my mother asked sharply.

"She's a nice woman who lost her daughter a long time ago. I have compassion."

"So do I. But that doesn't mean my compassion will allow Drake to drop some bomb on us."

"Monica, there is no bomb to drop. If Drake knew something, we'd all know it. He's just desperately trying to find answers that will never come. If he tries anything, we'll shut him down, like we did the last time."

Shut him down like we did the last time? What did that mean? Had there been some sort of cover-up?

"I should never have let Kelsey have the wedding here," my mother continued. "But there really wasn't any other choice, not in the time frame in which she wanted to have it. And Gage liked the idea, which, I have to say, surprised me."

"Gage loves the island. It didn't surprise me at all. You're spinning out, Monica. I'm sure the caterer knocked over the sculpture by accident. And Drake can talk all he wants, but he has no evidence to prove anyone in our circle was connected to his sister's disappearance. We protected our kids. You need to calm down."

I winced. My mother's least favorite words were: *calm down.* Whenever my dad expressed that wish, her rage only increased, not decreased.

"Don't tell me to calm down," she said hotly. "And I am not spinning out. Drake may not find out what happened to his sister, but there are other secrets he could stumble upon."

I tensed. *What other secrets was my mom talking about?*

To my surprise, Sean laughed. I couldn't imagine my dad laughing in the face of my mom's wrath; he always caved. But Sean Chadwick apparently didn't take my mother so seriously.

"No one cares about our secrets, Monica."

"I care. You should, too. Some days I really don't like you, Sean."

"But other days…" His voice fell away

"Stop it, Sean. We should go back to the living room."

"So soon?" he challenged. "I thought you asked me to help you get drinks for a reason."

I felt sick as the tenor of their voices changed from anger and worry to seductive innuendo. I didn't want to believe what I was hearing. I didn't want to believe that my mother was having an affair with Sean Chadwick. *How long had that been going on?*

"I just wanted to talk to you, Sean. That's it," Monica said firmly. "Let's get the drinks and go back to the group."

I heard the fridge open and close, then footsteps fading into silence. My stomach churned as I thought about what I'd overheard. My poor dad and poor Eileen.

Did they have any idea that their spouses were cheating on them?

I ripped open the chocolate bar in my hand and stuffed the mini Three Musketeers bar into my mouth, feeling a desperate need for sugar. Leaning against the wall, I thought about what else they'd said.

Sean's words rang through my head. *If Drake tries to cause trouble, we'll shut him down, just like we did before.*

What did that mean?

Did Sean and my mother know something about Melanie's disappearance that no one else knew? And what had Sean meant when he'd said they'd protected their kids? Was he talking about his boys?

But he'd said *we.* That made little sense. My parents hadn't had to protect any of us.

That wasn't true, I realized. They'd had to protect me. I couldn't remember anything about that night, and they'd told me to say that every time I was asked a question. They didn't want me trying to bring up random details to the sheriff because those details might be misconstrued.

Had they thought I'd had something to do with Melanie's disappearance?

That seemed unimaginable. I had loved Melanie more than anyone.

What about Brooklyn and Kelsey? What instructions had they been given when they spoke to the sheriff?

As the questions ran around in my head, I heard someone else enter the kitchen. The water turned on. The refrigerator opened, then closed. I didn't hear voices, so the person must be alone. I grabbed another chocolate and walked out of the pantry.

Brooklyn jumped in alarm. "Willow, you scared me."

"Sorry. I needed some candy." I held up the bar in my hand. "I found Dad's stash."

"He still has a sweet tooth," she said as she filled a glass with iced tea. "Did James get home all right?"

"I don't know. When I went by the bathroom, he was gone. I assume Rachel and Carter took him to a hotel."

"Good. Hopefully, he can hold it together the rest of the week."

"I hope so. Is Kelsey back?"

"I haven't seen her. I think she and Gage wanted to be alone for a bit. They left the bonfire before we did."

"That makes sense. She said he's been really busy lately." I paused. "Has Kelsey seemed off to you?"

"Maybe she's a little tense, but there's a lot to do, and Mom always stresses her out."

"That's true." I leaned against the counter, debating if I wanted to share what I'd just heard.

"What?" Brooklyn asked, giving me a searching look. "You seem like you want to say something."

"Are the Chadwicks still here?"

"No. Everyone just left. Why?"

"Just wondered."

Brooklyn gave me a considering look as she sipped her tea. "What exactly are you wondering about?"

"Mom and Dad. Do you think they're happily married?"

"That's a weird question," she replied, not quite meeting my eye.

"And that's not an answer."

"I don't know. They're still together. That's something."

"But do you think they're happy?"

"No one has said otherwise to me," Brooklyn said shortly. "I'm going to take my tea upstairs."

"You suddenly seem in a hurry to leave."

She shot me an irritated look. "I don't want to talk about our parents' marriage."

"And you don't want to talk about Melanie or James. What do you want to talk about?"

"Nothing. It's not like we're close, Willow. You don't talk to me. I don't talk to you. That's the way it is with some sisters."

"We used to be closer when we were kids."

"That was a long time ago. You barely see anyone in the family these days, so whatever your sudden concern is, I'm sure it will pass when you get on the plane to go home."

She was right about me missing family events. I had missed quite a few over the last several years. "I haven't come home because I've been busy, and it's not like I'm the center of the family. It never occurred to me that anyone cared if I wasn't there."

"That's ridiculous. Of course, we care."

Her reply was automatic, but not sincere. "Good to know."

She let out a sigh. "You say you don't fit in, but it's not like you try, Willow. I'm close to Mom because I work for her. And I'm close to Dad because I took an interest in golf. I knew if I did, I'd get to spend more time with him. Kelsey will shop all day to make Mom happy. And she'll watch one of Dad's boring documentaries just to hang out with him. What do you do?"

The challenging question stiffened my spine. "I've tried to connect to everyone. But Mom doesn't like my taste. She stopped wanting to shop with me a while ago. She also never thought I was smart enough to work for her. I'm terrible at golf. The two times I tried, I hit every ball in the sand or in the water. Dad was embarrassed to have me at his club. And I've watched plenty of boring documentaries with him. But he has always adored Kelsey, and Mom has always adored you. Unfortunately, there are only two parents and three kids."

"And you're the poor, pitiful middle child. You need to find another label, Willow. You've worn that one out."

"I'm not imagining things. You guys forget about me all the time. I got left behind at Disneyland when I was eight."

"It was crowded. And I've heard that story a million times. If you want to be noticed more, do something that merits attention. But you don't like to do that. You like to stay in the background, and then you're shocked when no one notices you're missing." She shook her head. "This is a pointless conversation."

"I agree," I said, knowing she wasn't completely wrong. Melanie had said the same thing to me. She'd told me I needed to take part in life, not just photograph it. Well, I wasn't photographing anything anymore. I was participating. I was living. I was hearing things. "Okay. You want me to say something that gets your attention—here you go. Tonight, I heard Sean Chadwick and Mom having a flirtatious and inappropriate conversation. It sounded like they were having an affair."

Brooklyn's face paled. "That's absurd. You must have heard wrong."

"I didn't hear wrong, Brooklyn. Sometimes when people don't know you're around, they tell the truth."

"What did they say?"

"Mom said sometimes she hates him, and he said not all the time. Sometimes she really likes him. It sounded like they kissed."

"Where were you?"

"In the pantry."

"So that's where you eavesdrop?"

"Don't turn this around, Brooklyn. Did you know they were involved?"

Brooklyn stared back at me, and I could see the wheels turning in her head. She clearly knew something. "You can't say anything about this to anyone, Willow. You didn't tell Kelsey, did you?"

"No, I haven't seen Kelsey. But I can't promise that I won't say something."

"Just stay quiet until after the wedding. If you say something now, it will be a disaster. Do you want to hurt Kelsey? Because this will."

"I don't want to hurt Kelsey, so I won't say anything before the wedding." I paused. "But it's weird that you're more worried about Kelsey than about Dad."

Her lips tightened. "I think if Mom went to Sean, then Dad has a lot to answer for."

"You're blaming him?" While I wasn't particularly close to either of my parents, I definitely had a warmer relationship with my father than with my mother. "Why is Dad responsible for Mom's inappropriate behavior?"

"He's not the perfect husband. Neither of them is perfect. But they're our parents, and it's not our business. So, let's pretend you heard nothing, and this conversation never happened."

I felt like there was something significant that she wasn't telling me, something about our father.

"Was Dad cheating, too?" I asked.

"I have nothing more to say. Just leave it alone, Willow. In a few days, you'll be back to your life, and none of this will matter. We'll see each other for the occasional holiday or birthday. It won't be any different than it is now. You have your life. Let everyone else have theirs. And don't say anything to anyone."

Brooklyn's persistent demand that I stay silent made me wonder what else people had stayed silent about.

"I'm going to bed," Brooklyn said, as the silence lengthened between us. "You should do the same. You look tired."

I felt exhausted, but that was more emotional than physical. I didn't think I could sleep with so many questions buzzing around in my head. But I had several busy days to get through, and I doubted they were going to be any easier than this one. "I'll be up in a minute."

Brooklyn's gaze softened. "I know it's difficult for you to be back here, Willow. Believe it or not, it's not that easy for me, either."

"Because of James. Or are you going to continue to deny that?"

She tipped her head in concession. "I will admit that seeing him again has brought back a lot of feelings, but not in the way you think. I don't want to live in the past. And I don't think you do, either. So let's move forward. Stop looking over our shoulders. Mom and Dad will be fine. They'll be who they've always been.

They'll love us and we'll love them. Don't make things more complicated than they need to be."

Brooklyn was the fixer in the family and, clearly, she could see that I needed to be fixed. Unfortunately, when you refuse to acknowledge the truth of a problem, it can't really be repaired. "It's not that simple, Brooklyn."

"It really is, Willow. Do you think some revelation from you is going to make anyone feel better?"

"I get why you don't want me to tell Dad. But why can't you just talk to me—sister to sister?"

Brooklyn hesitated, then her gaze moved toward the door as our dad came into the kitchen.

"Someone got into my chocolate, I see," he said, tipping his head toward the candy bar in my hand.

"Caught me," I replied with a guilty smile. "But there's still plenty left."

"Don't tell your mother that."

"I think she knows, Dad." I wondered if there really were any secrets between my parents. Maybe my dad knew everything about my mom, the way she knew everything about him.

He chuckled. "Perhaps. I'm not the best at keeping secrets."

I saw a pained expression cross Brooklyn's face.

"Where's Kelsey?" my father asked.

"She and Gage wanted to spend time alone together," Brooklyn said. "They know how busy the next few days will be."

"That's true. Good for them. I was just thinking it might be fun to make some popcorn and watch a movie together, the way we used to when you girls were little."

"We can still do that," I said.

"That sounds fun, Dad," Brooklyn said. "But I think we should wait for Kelsey. She'd be so disappointed if we did it without her. Let's do it tomorrow night. I'm sure Willow is tired from all the traveling."

"Oh, of course. Sure. Another night," he said.

"I'm not that tired," I protested.

"We'll wait for Kelsey," he said decisively. "Now I'm going to get some chocolate. Sleep well, girls."

As he went into the pantry, I followed Brooklyn out of the kitchen. "I wasn't going to say anything," I told her.

"Well, now you won't be tempted. And it would be more fun to do it with Kelsey. I think she'd feel left out."

"Well, we wouldn't want her to feel left out."

My sarcasm only made Brooklyn roll her eyes. Then she jogged up the stairs in front of me, closing her door as I hit the upstairs hallway.

I entered my room and flopped on the bed, feeling like my life had turned upside down again. My mom was cheating on my dad. Maybe he was cheating on her, too. I didn't know how to feel about it all. I felt sad and angry, and also somewhat unsure why it was bothering me so much. I rarely saw them, and I wasn't a child. It was their relationship, their business, but it still made me unhappy. It made me feel like the ground had shifted beneath my feet once more.

Brooklyn hadn't been upset at all. But she was very much like our mother. She liked to gloss over bad news. It was distasteful, annoying, and not worth her attention. She'd just put it away and not think about it.

Maybe that's why everyone else could come back here and not be haunted by tragedy.

As Melanie came back into my mind, Sean's comment about Drake rang through my head again.

We'll shut him down just like we did the last time.

What had they done the last time?

Maybe their affair wasn't the only secret they were keeping.

CHAPTER EIGHT

ON WEDNESDAY MORNING, I woke up feeling groggy, exhausted, and still in my clothes. Even though I hadn't been able to fall asleep with all the questions running through my mind, I also hadn't found the energy to dig into my suitcase for my PJs. I sat up in bed. I could see that it was still cloudy, but it didn't appear to be raining. That was good. The groomsmen were supposed to play golf today while the bridesmaids were getting massages and having lunch downtown.

My gaze moved to the clock. It was almost ten. I needed to get up, get dressed, and get my head together, so that I could be the cheerleading, supportive, happy bridesmaid I was supposed to be. God, this week was going to be tiring. I should have been good at faking happiness. I'd done it enough as a kid. But for the past decade, I hadn't had to pretend nearly as much, and I'd gotten out of practice.

Maybe this wedding would help reconnect me to the family. Last night, when my father had mentioned watching a movie and having popcorn, I'd been reminded of happier times, and it had felt good. Even talking to Brooklyn about James had broken through the barrier of polite nothingness that had existed between us for so long. It was like we were sisters again.

I told myself not to get too excited. I'd gone down that road as a kid, yearning to be included, wanting to feel the love, and then being left behind or completely ignored. It was easier to expect nothing than to get my hopes up and be disappointed. Nothing this week was about me. I needed to remember that.

As the sound of loud voices rang through the house, I frowned. It sounded like something was wrong. I heard cars in the driveway, more voices outside the house. Rolling out of bed, I hurried to the window. My eyes widened as I saw Ben step out of a police vehicle and join another officer, who was talking to Gage and Carter. They were all involved in an animated, tense conversation.

My stomach tightened. I felt a terrible sense of déjà vu.

Ten years ago, I'd heard cars pulling into the drive. I'd heard shouting and didn't know what was going on. I'd slept in my clothes that night, too.

And then Brooklyn had pounded on my door before throwing it open. She'd told me something bad had happened to Melanie, and I had to come downstairs.

My breath came a little faster with that terrible memory.

And then my heart jumped into my throat when I heard the sharp rap at the door. It opened before I could say come in.

Brooklyn was standing in the doorway again, her face strained, her eyes worried.

"What's wrong?" I asked, wondering if I was dreaming…if I was just reliving the morning from ten years ago.

"It's Kelsey."

Kelsey—not Melanie? This couldn't be a dream, which only made it worse.

"Is Kelsey all right?"

"I don't know," Brooklyn said tersely. "She's missing."

"What does that mean? How can she be missing?"

"Gage said he dropped Kelsey off here last night around eleven, but she hasn't answered his texts since then. They were supposed to have breakfast with some of his extended family this morning, but she didn't show up. Nor has she answered her phone. She also didn't sleep in her bed. You need to come downstairs."

Brooklyn's impatience was tinged with fear. "Mom and Dad called the sheriff. The Chadwicks are here, too."

"I don't understand."

"Neither do I. Just come now."

"I'm coming. Kelsey has to be all right."

God! Had I said those words the last time, too?

Melanie hadn't been all right. Melanie had never been seen again. That couldn't be true for Kelsey. Kelsey would be found. She would be fine. There was no other option I could handle.

I followed Brooklyn down the stairs. Everyone was now gathered in the living room. Ben stood in front of the fireplace, his deputy hovering near the archway to the dining room. Ben looked extremely somber and very official. Sean and Eileen Chadwick were seated on the couch, my parents on the love seat. Gage was pacing by the window looking nothing like the calm, confident man who was always in control, while Carter stood nearby, his arms across his chest, worry written in every line of his face.

"Now that you're all here, let's go over what we know," Ben said.

"I already told you what happened," Gage said, turning to face Ben. "This isn't getting us anywhere. We need to find Kelsey."

"Let's take a few minutes to compare notes. One more time."

Gage gave Ben a frustrated look. "Are you really the one who's in charge now? You?"

Ben didn't react to Gage's dismissive words. "Tell me again when you last saw Kelsey."

"I saw her when I dropped her off here a little before eleven," Gage bit out.

"Did you walk her into the house? Did you wait to see if she got inside?" Ben asked.

"No. She was almost at the front door. I didn't think I needed to wait."

"So, you didn't see her enter the house?"

"I said no, Ben."

"You also said you texted her after you got home?"

"Yes, around eleven thirty. I said good night, told her I loved her, and I'd see her for breakfast in the morning. She didn't answer, but I didn't think anything about it. I figured she was in bed or talking to her family. We were supposed to meet my parents, my aunt and uncle, and cousins in town for breakfast at eight thirty. When Kelsey didn't show, I called her and texted her. There was no answer. So, I came here. Brooklyn let me in. We went upstairs together, but it was clear Kelsey hadn't been in her room or slept in her bed. We both tried calling her again. Her parents tried, too. But her phone was shut off. That's when I called you."

"Okay," Ben said, turning to my sister. "Brooklyn, do you want to add anything?"

"No. Gage said exactly what happened."

"Where were you, Mrs. Kent?" Ben's gaze swung to my mother.

"I was in the shower when Brooklyn came to my room. I quickly got dressed and grabbed my phone."

"And you, Mr. Kent?"

"I was working out in our gym in the basement. I didn't see anyone this morning until Monica came downstairs, shouting that something was wrong."

"And no one saw Kelsey last night after the bonfire?" Ben asked.

"Monica and I went to bed early. It was a long day," my father replied.

"I was also in my room," Brooklyn added.

"Same for me," I said.

"What about the doorbell camera?" Ben asked.

At his question, my father reached for his phone, muttering, "I should have checked that first thing." He took a moment to open the app, then said, "Gage's car turns into the drive at ten-fifty-six."

My mother moved closed to my dad. "Is that her?"

"Kelsey gets out of the car," my dad said. "Gage backs out. Kelsey doesn't come in the house. She walks to the left and then I can't see her." He looked up from his phone with extreme worry in his eyes. "I can't see her anymore. I don't know what happens next."

"Do you have any other security cameras?"

"One by the patio door," Brooklyn answered, drawing everyone's attention to her. "I'm pulling it up now. The camera doesn't pick her up. It doesn't show anyone coming near the back door."

"Well, at least we know she was at the front of the house," Ben said.

"We already knew that. I told you that," Gage said impatiently. "But where did she go?"

"That's what we have to figure out." Ben turned to Sean and Eileen. "I assume neither of you spoke to Kelsey after she was dropped off last night. Did anyone see Gage last night after eleven?"

"Why the hell are you asking them that?" Gage demanded.

"Just trying to get a timeline. Mr. and Mrs. Chadwick? Carter?" he added.

Sean's lips tightened. "Eileen and I were in bed."

"I heard Gage go into his room," Carter said. "But I didn't see him or speak to him."

"What time was that?"

"I wasn't looking at the clock," Carter replied.

"This is ridiculous, Ben," Gage interrupted. "We need to search for Kelsey."

Gage's words were another echo from the past, but there had been different people in our living room ten years ago. Drake and his parents and Sheriff Tom Ryan, Ben's father, had come to the house to see me, to find out what I knew, but I knew nothing.

Ben's father had failed to find Melanie. His son couldn't fail us now.

"We will look for Kelsey," Ben said with an air of calm that I appreciated, because panic was ripping through me. "She hasn't been missing very long. Is it possible she went to see a friend last night and just hasn't come home yet?"

"I called Trina, Dahlia, and Rachel," Carter said. "They haven't talked to her since the bonfire."

"I also called Jenny, Gabby, and Preston," Gage added. "They haven't heard from her, either. Nor have any of my friends."

"Maybe Kelsey wanted some space," I said. "She seemed tense about the wedding yesterday."

Everyone's gaze turned on me, some of their expressions accusatory, as if I'd said something damning.

"What are you talking about, Willow?" Brooklyn demanded. "Kelsey was happy about everything."

"I agree," my mother said. "She's been giddy since she got to the island. Did she say something to you, Willow?"

"Not specifically. It was just a feeling I had." I turned to Carter. "You and Kelsey had an argument on the ferry yesterday morning. What was that about?"

Carter stiffened with surprise. "We weren't arguing. We were just talking."

"About what?" Gage asked. "Was Kelsey upset about something, Carter?"

"Yeah, she was pissed off that you missed the morning ferry. I had to calm her down. Once you got here, that changed. She seemed fine to me at lunch and at the bonfire."

"She was fine," my mom said forcefully, as if she needed to believe that. "When she was dancing with Gage on the beach last night, she was glowing. You misread her, Willow."

"Maybe I did. Or maybe I'd rather believe that Kelsey just took a walk or went to stay at the hotel or something, because the alternative is too…frightening."

A hush descended over the room at my words. They'd suddenly realized my suggestion that Kelsey just needed a break was actually the best idea, not the worst.

"This isn't like before," Brooklyn said desperately. "It can't be."

"Let's take it one step at a time," Ben said. "We'll ping her phone. See if we can track down her movements. I'll have deputies check the beaches and trails around this property. We'll also check the ferry. A boat left the island this morning at eight a.m. It's possible Kelsey was on it."

"She didn't leave. She wouldn't run out on our wedding," Gage said. But there was an uncertainty in his eyes now.

"No, she wouldn't do that," Eileen Chadwick told her son. "She

loves you, honey. There has to be an explanation. I think she must
have a friend you haven't thought about yet. Someone she went to
see last night or early this morning. Maybe one of the local girls
she used to see when she was here in the summer."

I couldn't imagine who else Kelsey would have gone to see. I'd
rather think she got on the morning ferry. If she had run out on the
wedding, then maybe we could all get off this damn island.

"Are there any vehicles missing?" Ben asked.

"No," my father replied. "I already checked the garage."

"All right. If you hear from Kelsey or think of anything else,
call me," Ben said.

Gage was shaking his head impatiently before Ben finished
speaking. "Dammit, Ben. You're as slow talking and acting as your
father. You need to move faster."

"We'll do everything we can to find her," Ben said evenly.

"What about a search party?"

"We'll get into that when I get back to the station. I'll be in
touch."

As Ben and the other officer left the room, there was a chilling
silence, and then everyone started talking at once. Carter and Gage
were going to check the paths down to the nearest beaches themselves. My father and Sean would drive around town. My mom
and Eileen would talk to the neighbors. Brooklyn would start
making calls to form a volunteer search party, since no one wanted
to wait for what was probably an understaffed sheriff's office to
take charge of all that.

Within minutes, I was left alone in the living room, wondering
what I should be doing. As usual, I'd been left out of the plans. I
should join in some search. I should call someone. But I couldn't
seem to move. I still wanted to believe I was dreaming. I pinched
my arm as hard as I could, and the pain drove away that foolish
idea. I wasn't asleep. I was awake, and my reality now was as bad
as it had been ten years ago.

Back then, I hadn't known what to do, either. I'd spent most of
my time crying and feeling helpless. That had done nothing to help

Melanie. Nor had it helped me. Falling apart wouldn't get me anywhere. It certainly wouldn't save my sister.

I went back upstairs. Kelsey's bedroom door was open. I walked into her room. Her open suitcase was on a bench at the end of the bed. It was still at least semi-packed. I could see her wedding dress hanging in the closet in a white garment bag.

The bed was perfectly made, with a half-dozen pillows on it. She definitely had not slept in this bed. There was a box marked favors on the desk and the big wedding binder that my mom had made with all the wedding information in it. I'd seen them going through it yesterday afternoon.

But there was nothing in this room that gave me a clue where Kelsey might be or what state of mind she was in.

I had to do something else. *What?*

A lot of the bases were covered, except one, and it suddenly seemed to be the most obvious one—Drake Maddox.

Ben had asked if Kelsey would go to anyone else on the island.

Would she have gone to Drake? Had Drake taken Kelsey to get someone in our circle to talk about Melanie?

Remembering how friendly Kelsey had been to Drake, it wasn't difficult to believe she'd get in his car, that she'd accept an invitation to hang out or get a drink. Maybe Drake had picked Kelsey up after Gage had dropped her off in front of the house.

I needed to find Drake. I couldn't think of anyone who had a better motive for keeping Kelsey away from her family.

CHAPTER NINE

I ARRIVED at Drake's parent's house a little before noon on Wednesday. The two-story house sat at the top of a hill overlooking the harbor and their restaurant, which was only a five-minute drive from their home.

As I got out of the car, I paused on the sidewalk, looking up at the second-story window where Melanie would watch for me to arrive. She'd give me a wave and then run out of the house a few minutes later.

When we were younger, we spent a lot of time in her house, but that last summer, I was usually picking her up to go somewhere, because I had more access to a car than she did.

It wasn't just about the ride, though. Melanie hadn't wanted to spend time at home anymore. She'd been itching to get away any chance she could. Her dad ragged on her a lot. He was always questioning her, and if I walked in, I usually got interrogated, too. Her mom would step in with a smile and tell her dad to leave us alone, that we were good girls.

Maybe her dad had been right to be so worried. We'd always thought he was super overprotective. But look what had happened…

Drawing in a breath, I made my way to the front door. I hoped that Melanie's parents were at the restaurant. I didn't really want to talk to them. I just needed to see Drake's face when I told him Kelsey was missing. I might be able to tell if he'd had something to do with it.

Oh, who was I kidding?

I'd never been able to read Drake. When I thought he hated me, I found out he liked me. When I thought he liked me, I found out he hated me. The guy had always been a mystery.

I rang the bell. A moment later, the door opened, and I found myself looking at an older version of Melanie. Sylvie Maddox had black hair, brown eyes, and olive skin. She was a short woman with a few extra pounds around her waist that had always given her a soft, nurturing appearance. Melanie had shared the same features, although her face had been more square, her extra five inches and stubborn chin a throwback to her father, Holt Maddox.

Sylvie's gaze widened in surprise. "Willow? Is that you?"

"It's me, Mrs. Maddox."

"Yes, it is, you sweet girl. You look just the same."

"So, do you."

"Well, thank you, even though that's not true."

It wasn't true. There was gray in Sylvie's hair now, and there were dark shadows under her eyes that had probably been there for ten years.

"Come in." Sylvie waved me into the house.

"I'm actually looking for Drake."

"Well, you're in luck, because he's on his way over. Can I get you some coffee? I guess I'm allowed to offer that to you now that you're all grown-up."

I gave her a faint, sad smile as I remembered the times Melanie and I used to beg for coffee, but Sylvie had insisted on making us hot chocolate. She'd add a dollop of whipped cream to make sure we were still happy. A part of me wanted that hot chocolate again, but that would remind me too much of Melanie. "Coffee sounds wonderful."

As I followed her into the house and down the hall to the kitchen, I knew I was making a huge mistake. There were memories of Melanie everywhere in this house, especially in the line of photos along the wall. The family photo of Melanie as a five-year-old, with her dog, Josie, and a young Drake, brought a wave of stabbing pain. It only got worse with a Christmas photo taken probably only a few months before she vanished forever.

I felt a knot growing in my stomach, and a desperate urge to flee. But I reminded myself that I wasn't here for Melanie; I was here for Kelsey. I had to focus on the present.

"Why don't you sit down?" Sylvie said, as we entered the kitchen.

"I hope I'm not keeping you from anything. I really just wanted a few minutes with Drake."

"He'll be here soon. Have a seat."

"Okay." I pulled out a chair at the table and sat down.

"How are the wedding plans coming along?" Sylvie asked, as she set down a mug of coffee in front of me and then took the seat across from me. "I ran into your mother last week. She was so excited about the wedding, about Kelsey and Gage falling in love. They do seem well-suited."

I took a sip of coffee, needing the hit of caffeine. "I don't know about the wedding now…" I stopped, not sure what to say, but it might as well be the truth. "Kelsey is missing. We're not sure if she got cold feet or…" I couldn't bring myself to finish the sentence.

Sylvie sat back in her chair, her jaw dropping in shock. "What do you mean—missing?"

"Gage dropped her off at my parents' house last night around eleven, but Kelsey didn't sleep in her bed, and no one has seen or heard from her since. It hasn't been that long. She might have gone to see someone, but we're worried."

"This is terrible news, Willow. I'm—I'm stunned."

"Me, too."

The back door opened, and Drake stepped into the kitchen. He wore a sweatshirt and jeans, and he looked…wet. I frowned, thinking that was odd. It wasn't raining, but Drake's hair was damp, and there were beads of water clinging to his cheeks. The bottom of his jeans also appeared to be soaked.

"What are you doing here, Willow?" he asked sharply.

I jumped to my feet. "I was looking for you. Where were you? Why are you so wet?"

"I was at the beach. A wave caught me by surprise."

That seemed like a lie. "Really? You were a lifeguard, and a wave took you by surprise?"

"It can happen."

"I'll get you a towel," Sylvie said, getting to her feet. "You're dripping all over my floor, Drake."

"Sorry about that. Here's the package you asked me to get." He put a small box on the table.

"Thank you," she said, as she moved into the laundry room.

"So, what are you doing here?" he asked me again.

"Kelsey didn't sleep in her bed last night."

"I'm sure she was with Gage. Why would you come here to tell me that?"

"She wasn't with Gage. He dropped her off at our house after the bonfire. No one has seen her since then."

"I'm sure there's an explanation."

"Are you sure?"

"Why did you come here, Willow?"

"I thought you might help me. Kelsey was happy to see you yesterday. She wanted to catch up with you. I wondered if she saw you last night, after Gage dropped her off. Did you meet up with her?"

"No." He paused as his mother came back and handed him a towel. "Thanks, Mom."

I was surprised by the sweet smile he gave his mother. I hadn't seen him be anything but harsh and angry in years. I'd forgotten that he had a charming side, one he'd often shown to his mom.

Sylvie had always had a soft spot for Drake. Even when she tried to be stern, he'd give her a smile, and she'd crumble. Melanie would get so frustrated by that. When it came to her parents, Drake could do no wrong, whereas she could never charm her way out of trouble.

"I need to go to the restaurant," Sylvie said. "Thank you for getting the package, Drake. Your father is out…somewhere, so you'll have to talk to him later."

"All right. Is he okay?"

"I don't know." She exchanged a poignant look with her son. Then Sylvie turned to me. "Willow, if there's anything I can do to help, please let me know. I hope… No, I'm sure Kelsey is fine."

"Thanks."

Sylvie grabbed her purse from the counter and headed out the back door.

Drake ran the towel through his hair. Then he tossed it on the table and sat down. He waved me back to my chair. "Tell me again what's going on."

"Kelsey is missing." I sat on the edge of the chair, not liking the fact that Drake and I were alone. But that was ridiculous. He wasn't dangerous. He was just angry because his heart had been broken a long time ago, and he couldn't get over it. I shouldn't be nervous; I should be compassionate.

"Maybe she went to stay with one of her girlfriends," he suggested.

"No one in our group saw her or spoke to her after she left the bonfire with Gage."

"So, Gage drove her home."

"Yes—around eleven. We were all in our rooms by then. None of us saw her come in or heard him drop her off."

"Where did he and Kelsey go after the bonfire? They left there around nine thirty."

I stared back at him. "How do you know that?"

"I saw them leave. Where did they go between nine thirty and eleven?"

"I don't know. I didn't ask where they went."

"Seems like a good question."

"It's not a good question," I retorted. "Kelsey disappeared after Gage dropped her at the house."

"That's his story. No one can corroborate that, can they?"

"Actually, the doorbell camera recorded Gage dropping off

Kelsey. He didn't lie. Gage loves Kelsey. He's going to marry her on Saturday."

Drake gave me a mocking smile. "Maybe Gage didn't lie about dropping off Kelsey, but he is a liar."

"You don't even know Gage anymore. Maybe he told a few lies when he was a kid—"

"People don't change. At his core, Gage is a liar. He told Sheriff Ryan that he never saw Melanie the day she disappeared. It wasn't until someone reported seeing them together that he admitted he'd forgotten seeing her at the beach. How do you forget seeing someone a few hours before they go missing?"

"You're still really angry," I said, noting the sparks in his blue eyes.

"I am," he admitted.

I knew his anger included me, too. But I didn't want to get into that. "I'm sorry. I know you're hurting."

"This isn't about me."

"No. And it's not about Melanie. It's about Kelsey. I don't believe Gage would hurt Kelsey."

"You didn't believe he would hurt Melanie, either."

"You have no proof that he did."

"You have no proof that he didn't."

"He had no motive. Everyone liked Melanie, Drake. She was really popular in my circle of friends, more popular than I was."

"She was well-liked, but she wasn't one of you. And when something happened to her, that became obvious. Suddenly, no one remembered anything. No one was available to talk. Lawyers were called in. Vacations were cut short. The families at Chambers' Point circled their wagons, and they got off this island as fast as possible. You left five days after your best friend disappeared."

"I had no choice. My parents made me leave. They said I'd done everything I could do, and I had. I talked to the police. I searched with the other volunteers for three days."

"Three days," he scoffed. "I've been searching for ten years. I've been battling to get past the walls your family and friends erected, with no help from the one person who should have been willing to break down those walls with me."

"With you?" I challenged. "You weren't even talking to me unless you were accusing me of horrible things. The one person who should have believed me when I said I'd done everything I could to remember, thought I was lying. I don't know how you could have believed that, Drake."

"And I don't know how you couldn't remember an entire night."

"I was drunk. I was wasted. And you know why I was drinking so much that night."

He stared back at me. "Don't blame me for what you poured down your throat."

I couldn't get over how cold he was being. "You are so mean now. What happened to you?"

"You know what happened. My sister disappeared. She's gone because you got drunk and you didn't meet her like you were supposed to."

I caught my breath at his punishing words, but I could see the guilt in his eyes, too. "All that is true. But it's also true that I got drunk because you hurt me. I thought we had something, Drake."

"We had sex one time. And it was a mistake," he said harshly. "You just didn't want to accept that."

"Oh, I knew it was a mistake. Believe me, I knew. You didn't have to shove it down my throat by making out with someone else. You came to Ben's that night just to throw that girl in front of me. Tell me that's not true."

He paled at my words, his jaw tightening. I waited for him to defend himself, but there was only silence.

"Nothing to say?" I challenged. "You're suddenly speechless?"

"That was a bad move," he admitted.

Now I was shocked. "You're admitting it?"

"I was wrong."

"Wow." I was so stunned I didn't know what to say.

"Look, I didn't want to hurt you, Willow. We shouldn't have

messed around. It meant too much to you, and I knew that. I needed to push you away."

"Well, you did a great job. But you hurt me, and you didn't have to. I was leaving for college in a few weeks, and you were going back to school in another state. It's not like I was trying to march you down the aisle."

"I know. I overreacted."

"And you hurt me even more when you told me Melanie's disappearance was my fault."

"I can't apologize for that," he said, shaking his head. "You were supposed to meet her at Five Falls. And you didn't go."

"You're right. That was my fault. But we don't know if she ever went to the waterfalls. We don't know what happened to her or when it happened. The last time anyone saw her was four o'clock in the afternoon. I wasn't supposed to meet her until eight. So, where was she after four?"

"I don't know. That's what I can't figure out." He paused. "I don't just blame you; I also blame myself. I should have been paying more attention to Melanie. I should have been watching out for her."

"Melanie didn't want you hovering around her, scaring off the cute boys, which you often did without even trying. She hated when some guy would tell her he couldn't ask her out because she was your sister."

"Who said that?"

"A bunch of guys. It happened a lot. No one wanted to mess with your little sister."

"Maybe that was good." He took a breath. "But I never knew she felt that way. I wish she would have told me."

We stared at each other for a long minute, having both finally spoken words that had been running around in our heads for the last ten years. I wished I felt relieved, but I didn't. There could be no resolution until we knew what happened to Melanie, and I doubted we ever would.

"We've gotten off track," I said. "I came here to talk about Kelsey. I need you to be honest with me."

"About what?"

"Did you convince Kelsey to help you get information from our family and friends?"

His brow arched in surprise. "What does that mean? You think I took Kelsey?"

"It would be a great way to get someone to talk to you, someone like Gage."

"Are you out of your mind, Willow?"

"I saw the way she hugged you when we got off the ferry yesterday. You might have played on her affection, on her sympathy. Maybe you asked her to disappear for a day. What better way to get people to talk than to have another disappearance to worry about? We're all thinking about the past now—the past and the present."

"That's quite an idea. I wish I'd thought of it, but I didn't. You're giving me too much credit."

"Am I?"

"Yes. I don't know what happened to Kelsey—if anything happened. It hasn't been that long."

"My gut says it's been too long."

He frowned and let out a breath. "Well, I can relate to that feeling. I can see that you're scared, Willow."

"I'm terrified."

"And it's easier to believe I got Kelsey to hide out for a day than to consider the alternative. You want me to say that Kelsey is okay and that she'll be back as soon as someone tells me the truth."

"I really do want that. This can't be like before, Drake. You might not believe me, but losing Melanie almost killed me. I loved her so much. It was like losing a piece of myself. I know that my relationship with her was nowhere near as close as yours was, but it was real, and it meant a lot to me."

At my words, the rest of the wall between us crumbled. His gaze softened. The anger faded. He was just Drake again, the Drake who had starred in so many of my teenage dreams. That Drake had been handsome, kind, and funny. We'd connected at the local newspaper office where I'd tried to convince them to publish my photographs, and Drake had tried to convince them to publish whatever article he'd come up with. That Drake had been the one I'd fallen for. Of course, that Drake had also stabbed me in the heart. Maybe I'd never really known him the way I thought I did. I certainly wouldn't make the mistake of trusting him again.

"I didn't take Kelsey," he said. "I didn't convince her to hide away. I'm not part of this, whatever it is."

Disappointment ran through me. "Did you talk to Kelsey at all last night?"

"I did—at the bonfire, but it was only for a few minutes while Gage was getting her a drink."

"What did she say?"

"That I shouldn't come to the wedding. Gage wasn't happy about her invite. She apologized, and I told her not to worry about it."

"That's it? You backed off without an argument? That seems a little too easy."

"I knew he'd make her take the invitation back. I never thought I'd go to the wedding. I was more interested in talking to everyone before the big day. I was hoping being back on the island would trigger a memory." He paused. "Has it triggered any for you?"

I thought about last night when I was walking from the lodge into town. "As a matter of fact, yes. I remembered walking on a road. Headlights blinded me. I also felt like I was at the edge of a cliff at some point."

"When did you remember that?" he asked with excitement in his voice.

"I walked from the lodge into town last night. I got a weird feeling, like I'd been alone on a deserted road once before, but it wouldn't have been that road. The lodge isn't around any place I would have been that night."

"How do you know? You don't remember."

"Well, it just doesn't make sense. I was on the other side of town at Ben's house when I started drinking. Everyone said I just wandered away. One minute I was there, and the next I was gone, so it would be logical to assume I walked from there to my house."

"Which would have been a couple of miles. I've gone over your possible route home a million times."

"You have? Why?"

"Because it might contain a clue."

"You're really obsessed with this, aren't you?"

"Yes," he admitted. "In fact, I've been thinking about writing a book about my sister's disappearance. In gathering notes for that, I've done a lot of research. Last year, I asked Sheriff Ryan to reopen Melanie's case. That was before Ben came back to the island. His father refused, but he did give me a copy of the police reports. What I realized then was how thin the original investigation had been. I got a private investigator to help me dig into the details. Unfortunately, we ran into the same roadblock as the sheriff."

"What roadblock?"

"The wall of silence. My investigator tried to speak to the Chadwicks, but they refused and referred him to their attorney. Your parents did the same, as well as the Connellys and the Hamiltons."

"I never heard that."

"Does that surprise you?"

After the way Sean and my mother had spoken last night in the kitchen, I couldn't say no. "I guess not."

"I realized I needed to find a different way into the case. When Ben took over for his dad, he agreed to work with me, but in the weeks since then, he has come up with little information. I think he's stonewalling me, too."

"Why would he do that?"

"Because I pointed out some contradictions in the police report between various people's statements, including Ben's."

"I don't understand."

"Ben said he never left his house that night. After our party, he stayed home while others went to the bonfire. But I know he met with a Road House bartender by the name of Rick Hodges at nine. Did you ever meet Rick?"

"No. Why is he important?"

"Because Rick claims he sold Ben some opioids that night. When I related that story to Ben, he admitted that he'd lied to his dad because he didn't want to get into trouble. That he'd just bought a few pills to get a buzz. He didn't think his lie mattered, because he'd never seen Melanie that night."

"Maybe that's true."

"It's still a lie. And now he seems to be reluctant to dive deeper into her case. I'm not sure he isn't covering something else up."

I wasn't sure, either. I didn't really know what to make of what he'd just told me. Ben had never been a liar. At least, I'd never thought of him that way. But he had been a big partier, and I could see him buying drugs. He and Dillon were best friends, after all, and they liked to get high. But I didn't think Ben was lying about Melanie. He'd loved her.

Still, a lie was a lie, and I could see why it raised questions in Drake's mind. I could also see why Ben might be avoiding Drake. But Ben had been willing to cop to the truth, so maybe there was another side to the story.

Drake leaned forward, resting his arms on the table, bringing my attention back to him. "If neither Ben nor his father will help me, then I need to get my own answers."

"I have to believe that Ben will help you."

"I can't waste more time waiting."

"Okay, but how are you going to find answers? If someone lied before, why would they tell the truth now?"

"Maybe it's not that simplistic or even that dramatic. I'm looking for any tiny detail that can start unraveling a longer thread. You just said you had a flash of memory last night. Perhaps you'll remember something else. Or someone else will be triggered in the same way."

"I really hope that happens. But getting back to Kelsey. Did you say anything to Kelsey about Melanie, about wanting to get information again?"

"Yes. I asked her to help me. She said she would try, but she didn't know what she could do, because Gage doesn't like to talk about Melanie."

"A lot of people don't like to talk about her. I was speaking to Gabby about Melanie earlier, and she said Preston always shuts her down, too."

"That's interesting. I've tried to talk to Gabby, but she said she wished she could help, but she's a Chadwick now, and her in-laws had asked her not to speak to me."

I could see why he was frustrated, and I was a little surprised that Gabby didn't feel more of a loyalty to Drake, but I couldn't think about that now. "Did you and Kelsey discuss anything else?"

"I told Kelsey if she couldn't talk to the man she was going to marry about anything she wanted to talk about, maybe she shouldn't marry him. I also told her it wasn't too late to change her mind, and I didn't think Gage was good enough for her."

"Really? What did she say to that?"

"She gave me an odd, kind of sad look. Then she pulled herself together, put a smile on her face and said she was the luckiest girl in the world, and that marrying Gage was exactly right. Then Gage interrupted us and whisked her off for a dance. That was it."

"Did Gage speak to you?"

"Nope. He just gave me an annoyed look."

"Kelsey seemed a little sad to me yesterday, too. But she assured me everything was fine."

"Maybe she ran away from Gage and the wedding."

"I would love it if that was the reason, but I'm not sure I can believe it. Kelsey would have to know how worried we'd all be. And to not tell anyone—that's not like Kelsey. She's not a loner. She likes people. She's always surrounded by friends. To go off by herself like this, it doesn't feel right."

"Well, you know her better than me."

His words made me frown. "I would think so, but I have to say I was surprised at how affectionate Kelsey was with you yesterday." I paused. "Did you two…" I didn't have the guts to finish that sentence.

"No," he said flatly, his gaze meeting mine. "Nothing ever happened between me and your sister."

Finally, some actual relief ran through me. "Okay, good. It just seemed weird that she invited you to her wedding. I guess she was just being her usual impulsive self."

"I don't know about that. But I know you should work with me, Willow."

"I'm not working against you."

"That's different than proactively helping. You can get to people I can't get to. They trust you. They'll let down their guard with you."

"I'm not sure that's true. I'm not close to anyone in my family or in our group."

"You're closer than I am. And if you loved Melanie as much as you say, then you can't tell me no."

He was right. I couldn't say no. I wanted to get the truth as much as he did, but I was a little afraid of where his pursuit of justice would take me, especially after the conversation I'd overheard the night before.

"Well?" he prodded.

I couldn't worry about my mother's secrets right now. I gave a nod. "Okay, I'm in. But first, help me find Kelsey. You can talk to the locals. They might be more open with you than with anyone else. Once Kelsey is safe at home, then I'll help you with the people in my circle."

"I can talk to the locals, but I think the answer to Kelsey's disappearance will be found closer to your home. It could be the same person, Willow."

His words brought a tidal wave of fear with them. I lost my breath for a second. Then I murmured, "It can't be the same."

"Just because you don't want to believe it doesn't mean it isn't true. I learned that the hard way."

"I need to go. I have to stay positive. Ben will get everyone in the sheriff's office involved in this, and Gage is putting together a search party. We'll find Kelsey."

"I hope so. I also hope Gage doesn't steer the search party in the wrong direction."

CHAPTER TEN

MY STOMACH CHURNED as I left Drake's house. I wanted to believe that Kelsey was a runaway bride, but it made little sense to me.

As I got into my car, my phone buzzed. I didn't recognize the number. "Hello?" I said warily, hoping I wasn't about to hear more bad news.

"Willow? It's Jenny. I just heard about Kelsey. Is she okay?"

"I don't know. I'm not home right now, but she wasn't there when I left, and she apparently didn't sleep at the house or with Gage."

"This is awful."

The panic in Jenny's voice echoed the feeling running through me. "It is very scary."

There was a pause on the other end of the phone, then Jenny said, "Can we talk, Willow? Just you and me?"

My gut twisted at the edge in her voice. *Why did Jenny want to meet with me in private? Did she know something?* "Of course. Are you at the lodge?"

"No. I'm staying at my parents' house while my mom is recovering from hip replacement surgery. Why don't I meet you in the treehouse?"

"The treehouse is still there?"

"Yes, and it's the most private place I can think of. If we talk anywhere in the house, my mom will overhear, and she's the biggest gossip in this town."

"All right. But why do we need privacy?"

"We just do. The backyard gate code is three-four-six-ten. I'll be there in fifteen minutes."

I didn't want to go back to the treehouse. There would be lots of memories of Melanie there. But if Jenny knew something that could help me find Kelsey, then I didn't have another option. I just didn't understand why she needed to meet in private, why she couldn't tell me whatever she had to say on the phone.

My questions only tripled on the ride across town. Something was up, and I was afraid to find out what it was. Jenny was not only tied to Kelsey; she was also tied to Melanie. I didn't want to believe that the two disappearances were connected, but they could be.

Jenny had also been talking to Kelsey a lot the past few weeks as they'd worked on the wedding plans. She might know something about Kelsey's emotional state or her feelings about the wedding and her upcoming marriage to Gage.

Ten minutes later, I pulled up in front of the Baker Street Hotel, which was owned by Jenny's parents. The four-story main building housed a dozen guestrooms. Behind the hotel was the small home where Jenny had grown up, and beyond that, in a huge backyard, was a treehouse that her grandfather had built thirty years ago.

It had been our favorite place to go when we were kids. Hidden away in the trees, the treehouse had felt like our own private space. Since Jenny was an only child, there had been no other siblings to deal with, and the treehouse was too remote for any other kids to wander into.

At first, we'd played kid games, and it had just been the local girls: Melanie, Jenny, Gabby, and me. As we'd gotten older, the group of girls had expanded to include Kelsey, Brooklyn, Rachel, and other girls. They'd snuck in alcohol, and we'd spent hours playing Truth or Dare or Never Have I Ever.

I had hated both games. The truth made me look naïve and

inexperienced, and the dare made me look like a wimp. As for Never Have I Ever…well, I'd never done anything, so once again I felt like a fool. Not that anyone had paid much attention to me, not when my sisters were around. Their stars burned bright, and it had been easy to hide in the background.

Melanie had gotten really pissed off at me one night for letting them take over. But she didn't understand what it was like to have sisters who were prettier and smarter. It was different having an older brother. There was no competition between her and Drake. Although Melanie had shared that she often thought Drake was the favorite, which was something I could relate to. It was another feeling that had bonded us as friends.

I let out a sigh. Before coming to the island, I'd vowed not to let myself travel back to the past. Now, I was literally doing just that.

I'd been to Jenny's house a million times in my youth, and the side path to the backyard was as familiar as my own hand. I put in the code for the gate and walked into the yard, moving through the trees with a growing feeling of trepidation.

When I got to the treehouse, I climbed up the ladder and crawled inside. The memories were even worse here. I had to draw in several deep breaths to quell the panic running through me. It was just a treehouse. Nothing to fear. But it wasn't the house that was bothering me, it was all the memories.

My gaze ran around the room, which had a roof and plastic windows. Gone were the throw rugs, blankets, and colorful pillows that I remembered. There was, however, an old bookshelf filled with some of our favorite books. I ran my finger along the dusty volumes and smiled a little. We had had some good times in this treehouse.

Looking away from the books, I saw the quotes we'd written on the walls, the love hearts with our names intertwined with boys' names, most of which had been scratched out whenever one of our romantic fantasies ended.

My breath came quicker as I saw my name matched up with Ben. I'd just put Ben's name there so no one would realize my obsession with Drake. I think that Melanie might have suspected, but she'd said nothing, and neither had I.

Melanie had several hearts on the wall—which wasn't surprising. Melanie, Jenny, and Gabby spent time in the treehouse all year long, while I'd only been here in the summers.

I remembered most of Melanie's crushes. At one point, she'd also liked Ben, but then it had been all about Dillon. When summer came, she'd turned her fantasies to the Chadwicks—to Gage and Carter. There was even a heart featuring her and James.

But none of those hearts had become relationships. They'd just been crushes.

It was a little surprising that Alex's name had never appeared in any of the hearts, because he'd definitely had a crush on Melanie. That was a little odd. *Had Melanie ever liked Alex?* I couldn't remember. But I remembered how broken up Alex had been after she disappeared. He'd shed tears for her. I didn't think any of the other guys had done that.

I heard someone coming up the ladder, and Jenny crawled through the open door a moment later, scuffing her dark-blue pants on the dusty floor. She had a cardigan sweater over a silk blouse, and her hair was pulled back in a low ponytail. There was tension in her eyes, in the taut line of her mouth.

"Thanks for coming," she said.

"No problem." We sat cross-legged on the floor as we'd done a million times before. "This is weird. We're too old to be in here."

"But it still feels safe, doesn't it?"

That seemed like an odd choice of words, but I couldn't dispute that being here felt safe, like we were kids again, like we were hidden away from the world. "What's going on, Jenny?"

"I'm worried about Kelsey."

"So am I. But why did you want to talk to me in private?"

"I need you to tell me if I'm crazy."

"About what?"

"Kelsey asked me to meet her in Seattle about a month ago to go over the wedding plans. The wedding is a significant amount of money for our venue, so my boss was fine with me going to

Kelsey. I met her and your mom at a restaurant. After our meeting, your mom left, but Kelsey stayed behind to take a phone call. I went out to my car to head home, but then realized I'd forgotten my phone. When I returned to the restaurant, I saw Kelsey cross the street with Carter. He had his arm around her, and they walked into the Halcyon Hotel together." Jenny let out a breath after the rush of words. "It looked…odd."

"Are you saying that Kelsey and Carter were having an affair?" I couldn't believe it. *Or could I?* I'd witnessed an intense conversation between them on the ferry. But Carter was Gage's brother. The idea made me nauseous.

"I'm just telling you what I saw," Jenny said. "What do you think?"

"I—I have no idea what I think," I stuttered. "Carter and Kelsey? Are you sure?"

"I'm sure they walked into a hotel together. I'm not certain of anything else." Jenny paused. "I don't want to think that Kelsey was messing around with Gage's brother, but she wasn't one to worry about stealing someone else's boyfriend."

Now Jenny sounded angry, and my gaze narrowed. "Kelsey stepped on your toes, didn't she?" I looked at the heart on the wall that had Jenny and Carter together. "With Carter?"

She followed my gaze, then shrugged. "I liked him for a while. But we were never together. Have you spoken to Carter since Kelsey disappeared?"

"He came to the house with Gage this morning. He looked upset and anxious." I paused. "Why did you want to tell me this story?"

"I'm…afraid."

My body tightened. "Of what?"

"I don't want to say. It's too ridiculous."

I could read the truth in her eyes. "You think Carter had something to do with Kelsey's disappearance?"

"Do you?"

"No."

"Okay, good. Then I'm just adding two plus two and coming up with five."

My mind raced. *Was she on to something?* "Maybe you're not being crazy," I said with a frown. "If Carter liked Kelsey, maybe he wanted to force her to rethink her decision to marry Gage?"

"How could he force her? By holding her against her will? That doesn't sound like Carter. And where would he even put her? He's staying at his parents' house."

"I don't know. You're the one who came up with this idea," I said.

"Not *that* idea. If Carter and Kelsey were involved, maybe she ran away or went to one of her friends. Maybe she just needed time to think about whether she was marrying the wrong brother. That's the theory I came up with."

"I like your idea better, but when Gage called her friends this morning, they said they hadn't seen her."

"Maybe they wouldn't tell Gage."

"I suppose that's possible. Have you talked to Gabby about this? Does she know you saw Carter and Kelsey together in Seattle? She's married to Carter's brother. Maybe she would have some insight."

"No. I can't talk to Gabby. She and I are not close anymore."

I was surprised by that piece of news. "Why not? You've been friends forever, and you both live here now. The island isn't that big."

"Big enough. There have always been two parts to this island, and Gabby is now ensconced at Chambers' Point in a house her husband designed just for her. She's not the girl who used to work at the ice cream store, even if she is the manager now. She's changed. There's an enclave of wealthier families who don't just come in the summer anymore. They live here year-round and work remote, like Gabby's husband, Preston. She's part of that crowd. Anyway, that doesn't matter. I also didn't tell Gabby because she's a Chadwick. She's Carter's sister-in-law. I didn't want to put her in the middle."

"So, you put me in the middle."

"I had to tell someone."

"Why would Kelsey marry Gage if she was with Carter?" The question had been rolling around in my head ever since Jenny started talking.

"Gage is much more successful than Carter. He has money, fame, and he's better looking. Maybe Kelsey just got caught up in the idea of being Gage's wife. They're the golden couple. Everywhere they go, cameras follow. Kelsey might not have felt she could walk away from all that."

"Maybe." I drew in a tight breath and slowly let it out, trying to calm my racing pulse. But it didn't help. Panic was surging through me. "This is feeling like the last time."

"It's not," Jenny said forcefully. "It can't be. There's no sign that anything bad happened to Kelsey."

"We didn't think anything bad had happened to Melanie, either, but no one found her, and no one ever knew what happened to her."

Jenny bit down on her lip, an old habit that also reminded me of the past. "The year after Melanie disappeared, I used to think I'd see her in the woods. Sometimes, I'd run after what I saw. I even accosted a stranger once. It was never her. Still, I kept hoping. I'm sorry. I'm not making this better."

"Nothing will make this better until Kelsey comes home."

"You're right. I wish we weren't having this conversation, that we were just old friends catching up, Willow. When Kelsey is back, I hope we'll have a chance to do that." She gave me an uncertain look. "Unless you'd rather not."

I looked at her in surprise. "Why wouldn't I want to catch up?"

"When you left ten years ago, you never looked back. You didn't keep in touch with any of us. I know Melanie was your best friend, but I thought we were close, too."

Guilt ran through me. "We were close, Jenny. You were just a huge reminder of the worst night of my life. I couldn't handle it."

"I told myself it was something like that, but it was still sad."

"I'm sorry."

"You wouldn't have come back at all, if it hadn't been for this wedding, would you? Your parents still come here almost every year, sometimes for a month at a time. Brooklyn and Kelsey have been back, but not you."

"It's different for me. I let Melanie down. I was too flattered by Ben inviting me to party with him and his friends that I turned my back on my best friend. I drank too much, and I didn't meet her when I was supposed to. She was alone and vulnerable because of me."

"We all made bad choices when we were teenagers. No one blames you, Willow."

"Drake does."

"Well, he blames everyone, most of all himself. I have some guilt, too. You weren't the only one drinking and being stupid that night. I never even noticed that Melanie wasn't at the bonfire. What kind of friend does that make me?"

Her words made me realize that the burden I'd been carrying wasn't mine alone. Maybe it would have been better if I'd kept in touch, if I'd shared my grief with the girls who'd also loved Melanie. I certainly hadn't been able to share it with anyone in my family.

"Anyway," Jenny said. "I should get back to work."

We left the treehouse and walked down the path together. "You said your mom had a hip replacement?" I asked as we passed by Jenny's mom's house.

"Yes. It was a relief when she finally got it. She could hardly walk for a couple of years. It got so bad my dad needed help, which was why I left Seattle and took the job at the lodge last year."

"I'm sure your parents appreciated that."

"They did. And I felt better being able to help them. Plus, I have to say it was nice to be back on the island. I thought I would miss the city. I'd been in Seattle since I graduated from college, but when I stepped off the ferry fourteen months ago, I realized I was home."

"I didn't know you lived in Seattle that long."

"Yep. Far enough away to be away, but close enough that I could get home easily."

"You don't find the island too quiet now that you're here full time?"

"It's just the right amount of quiet." She gave me a small smile. "I know what you're thinking. How are you going to meet a man on this godforsaken island?"

I smiled as the familiar words resonated within me. "You, Melanie, and Gabby said that a lot."

"It's probably something I'll ask myself down the road. But right before I left Seattle, I had gotten out of a tricky, not-so-great relationship that went on far too long, and I'm not looking to rush into another one."

"I can understand that." I hesitated, then plowed ahead, needing information that Jenny might have. "Did you see Drake much when you were in Seattle?"

"I wouldn't say a lot, but we went out now and then, usually when one of our mutual friends was in town."

"Were you surprised that Drake came back to the island this week?"

She let out a long sigh as she gave me a troubled look. "No. He's obsessed with getting justice for Melanie. I wish he would have stayed away, but he's still desperate for answers."

"I'm afraid he's going to ruin the wedding."

"He won't do that. Drake is a good guy, Willow. His anger is just a cover for his broken heart and his tremendous guilt. He always saw himself as Melanie's protector, and he failed her. He has trouble living with that." Jenny's phone rang. She looked at the number and then sighed. "Another Bridezilla gone amok. I will call her back later." She slipped her phone into her bag. "What about you, Willow? Is there a man in your life?"

"No one serious."

"But you're dating?"

"I've had a lot of first dates."

"Been there," she said with a commiserating glance. Then her expression turned serious. "I hope Kelsey is back by the time you get home, and we can forget we ever had this conversation. I would never have said anything about Carter and Kelsey otherwise. I just kept thinking about it after I heard she was missing. Are you going to say anything to Carter?"

"I don't know."

"You don't need to mention I told you... Oh, never mind." She waved her hand. "Do what you need to do."

"I will. Jenny, I think you should tell Ben this story."

She immediately shook her head. "I don't know for sure they were doing anything more intimate than walking into a hotel together. Let's give it a little time. I can't imagine that Carter would hurt her, and we don't want to point Ben in the wrong direction. I also don't want Kelsey to think I betrayed her."

"You're trying to help her."

"She might not see it that way if her secret gets out—if she even has a secret. I feel like the worst gossip right now. Anyway, I'll be praying for Kelsey," Jenny added. Then she turned and hurried to her car.

As she pulled away from the curb, I felt uneasy about our entire conversation. Jenny seemed genuinely upset about Kelsey's disappearance, but it also felt like she had a hidden agenda for telling me about seeing Carter and Kelsey together at a hotel. I couldn't imagine what that could be, but I also couldn't shake the feeling that I'd only gotten part of the story.

Melanie's Diary—June 30th

I surprised Jenny yesterday with a birthday party at the beach. I got all our friends to come. We had two dozen chocolate cupcakes, three huge balloons, and a hot guy singing Happy Birthday. It was amazing. Willow took a ton of photos. I can't wait to see them.

I was happy that so many kids came. Jenny is lucky because her birthday is in the summer, so there are always more people around to party. Even the Chadwick boys showed up.

Carter seemed like he was flirting with Jenny. Maybe she'll be able to put his name on a heart on our treehouse wall. Maybe she'll be able to do more than that, like have an actual relationship. I know she wants one. She's as boy crazy as I am.

Anyway, Jenny was super happy that I made her birthday so special. She said I was her best friend in the world. She was exaggerating, but it felt good. I know Jenny has been a little jealous of Willow, but she doesn't have to be. I love Jenny, too. We'll be friends forever.

Gotta run. It's Saturday night—bonfire night. They're usually fun, but they're starting to feel a little like musical chairs. You never know who anyone is going to end up with by the end of the night. I know who I'd like to end up with, but I'm not going to say. I don't want to jinx it. It's early in the summer. Who knows what will happen? Fingers crossed, it's something good.

CHAPTER ELEVEN

AFTER LEAVING JENNY'S HOUSE, I went home to check in. My mother was on the phone, and after listening for a moment, it appeared she was talking to my aunt. Not wanting to bother her, I moved into the kitchen and found Gage's mother, Eileen Chadwick, making tea.

Eileen's blonde hair was pulled back in a low ponytail, and she looked thinner than I remembered in loose-fitting designer jeans and a white cardigan sweater. It felt weird to see her and think about the fact that her husband and my mother probably had an affair or might even still be having one. I told myself not to think about that. My mother's infidelity was a problem for later—much, much later.

"Willow, are you hungry? I made sandwiches and a Chinese chicken salad. I also have tea with some calming herbs from my garden," Eileen said. "I know you'll probably say you don't want to eat. Your mother told me not to bother, but I needed something to do, and I thought at some point, we'll all be hungry."

"That's very nice of you. Is there any news?"

"They found Kelsey's phone."

My pulse leapt. "Where was it?"

"It was in the grass by a deck chair in the backyard."

"The backyard?" I echoed, not sure what to think about that. "It doesn't make sense that Kelsey would leave her phone there. She's never without her phone."

"Maybe it fell out of her pocket or something," Eileen offered. "There's also no evidence that Kelsey got on the morning ferry, or any ferry since then."

"So, she's still on the island."

"Or she left by private boat."

"But we can't track her location through her phone, because she doesn't have it." That realization hit me hard.

"No, Willow. I'm sorry. I was also hoping her phone would lead us to her."

"Did Kelsey talk to anyone on the phone after eleven last night? Were there any text messages?"

"Only the one from Gage."

I felt sick knowing that Kelsey didn't have her phone. It made everything about this situation even worse.

"Ben has everyone in the department looking for Kelsey. No one is giving up, Willow. Sean, your dad and my boys, everyone in the wedding party—they're all out there searching. Hopefully, there will be some good news soon."

"Hopefully," I echoed. "But some of the hilly areas on the island are steep and difficult to access."

"I doubt Kelsey would take herself somewhere remote."

"If she took herself…"

Eileen gave me a reassuring look. "You have to stay positive."

"I don't see how I can. Kelsey doesn't have her phone. She wouldn't have voluntarily left without it."

"She could have dropped her phone when she went off with a friend. She might not have realized she didn't have it until she got somewhere else, and she wasn't ready to come back for it." Despite Eileen's upbeat words, I could see the tension in her mouth and eyes. She didn't believe her explanation any more than I did, but she was trying hard to make me feel better.

"Thanks for saying that."

"I really believe Kelsey will come home, and she'll be fine."

"I want to believe that, too."

As the kettle went off, Eileen said, "How about some tea?"

"I guess, thank you." I sat down at the kitchen table. As Eileen made my tea, I said, "I'm surprised Lorraine isn't in here, making tea for you." Lorraine was a local woman who worked part-time as a chef and housekeeper when my family was in residence.

"She'll be in this afternoon. Your mother had told her she wasn't needed today because the bridesmaids were going to the spa and the guys were golfing, so Lorraine had already scheduled something else for this morning." Eileen brought two mugs to the table. She pushed one in my direction and then took the seat across from me. "This tea always clears my head and makes me feel less anxious."

I took a sip and the warm liquid slid down my throat with a smooth swallow. "It's delicious. What is it?"

"A mix of herbs from my greenhouse: lavender, mint, and a few others."

"You should sell this. It's very good."

She gave me a small smile. "The last thing I need is a business. I'm trying to get Sean to retire, so we can have more time for ourselves."

"That makes sense."

"But the man likes to work. I doubt he'll ever quit." Eileen sipped her tea. "Gage is a lot like Sean. He loves his job. Whenever he does anything, he does it with every ounce of energy that he has. That's why he has always been so successful. First with football, then as an agent." She stopped. "Sorry, I'm rambling."

"It's fine. It's a distraction."

"Yes." Eileen gave me a thoughtful look. "Did Kelsey talk to you about Gage?"

"Uh, what do you mean?"

"Well…this is awkward, but I don't know who else to ask. Your mother says Kelsey adores Gage. Brooklyn won't say anything to contradict your mother. But if Kelsey ran away, then she must have doubts about getting married. Did she talk to you about any concerns she might have?"

"No. She never expressed concern."

"I think Gage and Kelsey are a perfect fit. They both love to work, to travel, and they'll have beautiful children together. Or maybe they won't. Perhaps Kelsey changed her mind." Eileen shook her head. "If that's the case, Gage will be devastated. I've never seen him so in love. Now, he's beating himself up for not watching Kelsey walk into this house last night. But who could imagine that someone would hide in the shadows?"

"I wouldn't have thought that, either."

"Kelsey must have had a panic attack or something. Your mom said that Kelsey has been having a lot of anxiety the last few years, the pressure of looking perfect, the late nights, and the constant travel. Monica said she was looking forward to Kelsey slowing down a bit and having Gage watch over her." Eileen sat back in her seat. "I wish I could do more than make tea and sandwiches. I don't think I'm being much comfort to your mother. She's barely spoken to me since the men left. I know she must be scared. I just don't know what to say. Everything I come up with is wrong."

"No one knows what to say." I wondered if my mother's distance wasn't also because she'd had an affair with Eileen's husband. "It's nice that you and my mom have stayed close all these years."

"We're not as close as we used to be when you were all kids, and we were in and out of each other's houses all summer long. Now, we only see each other for a week or two at a time, if that. But I always enjoy your parents. We've had some idyllic summers here on the island."

"We had some good times," I agreed. "For a while…"

Eileen's smile faded. "Yes, that was tragic. But this isn't the same, Willow. Kelsey will turn up."

"I hope so, but I'm scared."

"I know." Eileen reached across the table and put her hand on my arm. "Don't give up hope, Willow. Only good thoughts."

"I'm trying," I said as my mother entered the kitchen.

Her eyes and nose were red from crying, her skin pale and splotchy. I'd never seen her look so scared, and that terrified me.

My mom was always confident, always in control of every situation. That she wasn't now made everything seem worse.

Eileen got to her feet. "Monica, how are you doing?"

"Terrible," my mother snapped. "Ben just called. They found a shoe that looks like the one Kelsey was wearing last night."

I jumped to my feet. "What? Where?"

"At the harbor." My mother held up the phone in her hand, showing us the screen. There was a photo of a bright-red, wedge-heeled sandal, the same shoe I'd seen my sister kick off at the bonfire when she was dancing with Gage. "It's hers, isn't it?" my mom asked.

"I think so," I murmured, my heart pounding so hard against my chest I felt breathless and light-headed. "Was this by the ferry?"

"No. Ben said it was on the other side of the harbor, by the smaller boats."

"I don't understand."

"What don't you understand?" my mother yelled. "Someone took Kelsey. She didn't run away. She didn't leave of her own volition. She certainly didn't walk off without her shoe or her phone. Dammit, Willow, why are you being so dense?"

"Monica!" Eileen stepped between us. "Willow is just trying to help. Why don't you sit down? We'll talk."

"I don't want to sit down, Eileen. I don't want to talk. I don't want to drink tea. I want to find my daughter. I can't stand here and do nothing."

"You're not doing nothing. You're waiting here, so when Kelsey comes home, you'll be here," Eileen said calmly.

"What if she doesn't come back?" my mother asked, her voice breaking.

"She will come back." Eileen put her arm around my mother's shoulders and moved her toward a kitchen chair. "Sit down, Monica."

As Eileen almost forcibly pushed my mother into a chair, I left the kitchen, telling myself that my mother hadn't been yelling at me, she'd just been yelling at the situation. She was terrified for Kelsey, and so was I.

My brain spun with new questions. If Kelsey had gone to the docks, then someone might have seen her. I needed to get more information. I needed to talk to Ben.

CHAPTER TWELVE

I FOUND Ben in the middle of a hectic scene at the sheriff's department. He looked stressed and worried as he barked out orders to his deputies. I barely recognized this man. He was no longer the kid with the unruly, tangled brown hair, scruffy cheeks, ripped jeans, and a chill, easygoing vibe. This man was commanding, sharp-edged, and harsh. Maybe that was a good thing. I felt more confident in this version of Ben.

When the crowd around Ben dispersed, he waved me into his small office, which comprised a desk, a couple of filing cabinets, and walls covered with framed photographs, all of which appeared to be pictures of Ben's father, Tom Ryan.

The previous sheriff was pictured cutting the ribbon at the opening of the new medical clinic, passing out food to seniors at Thanksgiving, and showing a group of kids around the office. There were also photos of Sheriff Ryan holding up the large fish he'd caught, winning a poker tournament, and coaching a youth baseball team.

The only photo I saw of Ben was one with his dad when Ben was probably about eleven years old. They'd been photographed after coming in second in a father-son kayak race. I couldn't remember how long Ben had been working in this office, but he had definitely not made his mark.

"Do you want to sit?" Ben asked shortly, as he grabbed a box of files off the chair and set it on the ground.

I didn't want to sit in that chair. I could still remember being perched on the edge as the sheriff questioned me about Melanie. My dad had been with me. He'd stood behind me, his hand on my shoulder, and I remembered feeling thankful for that steady, reassuring weight. But I couldn't wait to get up, to leave, to get out of the nightmare I'd been trapped in. The only good thing was that Ben's father had been kind to me. Tom Ryan had seen how upset I was, and after taking my statement, which was basically worthless since I remembered nothing, he'd allowed me to go home.

I frowned, wondering now if he shouldn't have questioned me further. Drake's words echoed through my head, his criticism of how thin the investigation had been.

"Willow?" Ben asked, drawing my attention back to him.

"I don't need to sit. My mom showed me the photo of the shoe you found. I'm pretty sure it's Kelsey's shoe."

"That's what Brooklyn said. Gage wasn't sure. But I don't know a lot of men who notice shoes."

"Where was it found?"

"By the fish and bait shop."

"Aren't there security cameras in that area that would have caught Kelsey on the dock?"

"There are two cameras. One doesn't appear to be working. The other didn't cover that location."

"That's crazy. Why isn't there more security?"

"This is an island, Willow, with very little crime. But we're doing everything we can to find your sister."

I stared back at him, feeling like I was in a time warp. "Your dad said that same thing to me when Melanie disappeared. It's strange that in the last ten years, no one thought it might be a good idea to make sure there were more cameras around town and that they all work."

"I don't disagree, but I only came back two months ago. I'm working on making changes."

"Not fast enough."

His jaw tightened. "I understand your frustration. The best thing you can do is go home and let me get back to work."

Before I could reply, the office door opened, and an older man entered the room. He was fifty pounds heavier than Ben, with a round face, a balding head, and a thick middle, but his brown eyes were the same as his son's. It was strange to see Tom Ryan in regular clothes. Every memory I had of Ben's father was him in a uniform, with some sort of stain on it—spaghetti, mustard, or beer. But tonight, he wore jeans and a zipped-up windbreaker.

"Sheriff Ryan," I muttered, as his gaze swept across my face.

At first, he didn't appear to recognize me. Then awareness entered his gaze. "I know you. You're one of the Kent girls. The one with the name like a tree."

"Willow."

"That's it, Willow. I'm sorry about Kelsey. Terrible business. Am I interrupting?"

"I'll be with you in a minute, Dad," Ben said briskly.

"I want to help. I have experience in this area."

"I understand, but for now, if you don't mind stepping outside…"

Tom Ryan frowned, as if he wasn't used to being dismissed by his son or waved out of the office that had been his for thirty years. "Okay," he muttered. "But we need to talk."

"We will." As his father left, Ben turned back to her. "Sorry about that."

"It must be difficult for your dad to see you doing his job."

"He wanted me to have the job, so he's going to have to deal with that. I need to get back to the search, Willow."

"Do you have any other leads?"

"We're working on some theories."

"We have to find Kelsey."

"That's what I intend to do. I've got everyone in the department and half the town looking for your sister."

"Your dad had everyone on Melanie's disappearance, too," I reminded him.

"Let's focus on the present. Did Kelsey say anything to you about not wanting to get married?"

"No. She was tense, but it's a big week for her."

"Was she drinking last night?"

"I don't know. Gage could tell you that."

"He said she was sober when he dropped her off."

"Do you believe him?" I asked, searching his eyes for the truth. "Last night, you and Dillon both told me that Gage was a liar. Is he lying about Kelsey?"

"I'm not ruling anything out," Ben said carefully.

My gut twisted at his words. "Really? You're not ruling Gage out?"

"No."

"Do you think Gage had something to do with Melanie going missing?"

"Willow, I can't talk about Melanie right now." I knew he was right, even though part of me wanted to ask him about the lie he'd told the night she disappeared. But I couldn't risk upsetting Ben. I needed him focused on the present.

"You need to go home, Willow. Please."

I thought about sharing what Jenny had told me about Carter and Kelsey, but Ben had already opened the door. Maybe it was just as well. I needed to get more information. I only had Jenny's gossip to go on. I needed to talk to Brooklyn. She would know if Kelsey and Carter had gotten together. Kelsey told Brooklyn everything.

As I stepped into the hall, I saw Ben's father leaning against the opposite wall, tapping his foot impatiently on the floor. "About time," Tom complained.

"I'll be with you in a minute, Dad," Ben told his father, then shut the door in his face.

The sheriff swore under his breath. "My son can be a damn fool sometimes. He won't accept help when he needs it the most.

He was always this way. I had to save him from himself more than once."

"What do you mean?" I asked curiously.

"Oh, you know, kid stuff," he said with a wave of his hand, as if he regretted his words. "How are your parents holding up?"

"They're trying to stay positive." That was a vast understatement. My mom was falling apart, and I hadn't seen my father since he'd left the house this morning.

"They should be positive. We'll find her."

"You sound confident, but I don't know why. When Melanie disappeared, no one found her."

His face paled. "I worked that case damn hard. We just couldn't catch a break."

"Do you have a theory on what happened to Melanie, something you couldn't prove but stuck with you?"

"What are you asking?" A wary note entered his voice. "You think I let something fall through the cracks? Because I didn't. I was on it."

"I didn't mean to imply that. I just wondered what you thought happened to her."

"Well, there are a couple of scenarios that we explored."

"Like?"

"Melanie slipped and fell off a cliff, ended up in the water, and got swept out to sea. She was supposed to be meeting you to shoot some pictures, right? You two were always exploring. And Melanie was adventurous, fearless. She loved to hike, rock climb. It's not impossible to see her getting herself into trouble."

"What else could have happened?"

"She hitched a ride on someone's boat and ran away."

"Without contacting her family? She loved them."

"She had problems with her father. I suspected him at one point, too. His behavior could be erratic, but like I said, I couldn't prove anything."

"Drake thinks someone from Chambers' Point knew something."

"Drake has been grasping at any straw he can find, but there was nothing pointing to the Chadwick boys or anyone else."

"What about now? What about the fact that Kelsey, who is marrying Gage, is now missing? Does that make Gage a suspect in both cases?"

"Gage was seen by a dozen people ten years ago. He had all kinds of folks vouching for him. And he seems to love your sister, so, no, I don't think he's a suspect in either case."

"I hope not. But I'm concerned."

Tom tilted his head, giving me a speculative look. "I'm surprised you came back here. You couldn't stop beating yourself up ten years ago. I thought you were going to have a breakdown."

"It was the worst time of my life," I admitted. "If my sister hadn't decided to get married here, I wouldn't have returned."

"I don't understand why she made that choice."

"Apparently, the island holds better memories for her than for me."

"Well, I guess she held her alcohol better than you did."

I frowned. "I only had a problem that one night. I was a lightweight. I barely drank before that."

"You're lucky that you didn't get hurt. Someone must have been looking out for you."

"What do you mean?"

"Well, somehow you got home. Seems like you probably had a little help."

"No one ever said they helped me."

"Then I guess you had a guardian angel. Someone was looking out for you. Someone tried to protect you."

The way he was looking at me made it sound like he was that someone. But that was crazy. The sheriff had never protected me.

Ben opened the door, interrupting our conversation. "Dad. I'm ready."

"Finally," Tom grumbled.

Ben gave me a questioning look. "Was there something else, Willow? Were you waiting for me?"

"No, I was just talking to your father. I'm heading home now."

"I'll be in touch. Try not to worry." As Ben waved his father into his office, I heard him say, "You shouldn't have come down here, Dad. I told you to let me handle this."

"You need me, Ben. You just hate to admit it."

As the door shut, I wondered why Ben wouldn't want his father's help. Maybe it was just a competitive father-son thing. Ben was doing his dad's old job. That had to be uncomfortable for both of them.

Turning, I walked down the hall and out of the building. The sky had grown darker, and I couldn't stand the thought of Kelsey being alone somewhere. This island could be beautiful but also terrifying.

The sheriff had told me I was lucky ten years ago, that I must have had a guardian angel. I wondered again how I'd gotten home that night.

Had someone helped me? But why wouldn't that person have said anything?

I pushed the questions out of my mind and got into my car. I couldn't keep going back into the past. I needed to be Kelsey's guardian angel. I needed to bring her home.

CHAPTER THIRTEEN

I GOT BACK TO MY PARENTS' house a little before four. I couldn't believe how quickly the day had flown by. My parents were in the living room with the Chadwicks. The atmosphere was quiet and somber. My mother was pacing by the patio doors. Sean and my father were both on their phones, and Eileen was sipping more tea.

As I walked into the room. Eileen gave me a worried smile. No one else seemed to notice my presence.

I cleared my throat. "Any updates?" I asked.

Finally, I had their attention. My dad gave me a bemused look. "What?"

"Is there any news, Dad?"

"No. We just got back from searching the beaches on this side of the island. Gage and Carter are still out there. They won't quit until it's dark. Hopefully, she'll be back by then." My father gave me a sorrowful look. He was trying to stay hopeful, but time was taking a toll on him.

"Where have you been, Willow?" my mom asked sharply.

"I just spoke to Ben. He doesn't have any new information."

"He's as worthless as his father," my mother muttered.

"Tom Ryan wasn't worthless," Sean Chadwick put in. "He did a lot to keep this island safe."

My mother shot Sean an irritated look, which he sent right back at her, making me wonder again what was going on between them. Despite the animosity I could see now, I had not misheard them the night before. They had had an inappropriate relationship at some point, but maybe it was over. *Did that make it better?*

"We should get some food going for dinner," Eileen said. "Everyone will be tired and hungry when they get back. I have some fresh vegetables in my garden. I know it's summer, but with this wintry weather, maybe some soup would be good."

"Would you stop with the food, Eileen?" my mother snapped. "Or go home and make it at your own house. The thought of soup cooking in my kitchen turns my stomach."

"Monica," my father said sharply. "That was rude. Eileen is just trying to help."

My mother bit down on her lip. "I'm sorry, Eileen. I'm just frustrated and scared."

"Which is completely understandable," Eileen said. Although her words were kind, I could see that her patience was wearing thin. She'd been babysitting my mom all day.

"We appreciate your support, Eileen," my father added.

"Well, Kelsey is going to be my daughter-in-law. She's family. Just as you all are. We need to stick together and support each other." Eileen got to her feet. "I don't want to make things more difficult. I'll go home and make some food there. I can bring it by later, or you can all come over if you get hungry."

"That sounds like a plan," my father said.

"I'll go with you," Sean said.

"Could you wait?" my mother asked Sean. "I need to speak to you for a moment, if you don't mind."

"Uh, sure," Sean said, giving my mother a puzzled and wary look.

"I'll see you at home," Eileen told her husband.

My father also stood up. "I'm going to make some calls. I want to see if I can get more resources to the island to help in the search."

Realizing that I was going to be left alone with Sean and my mother, I quickly got up and followed my dad down the hallway to his study. Before he stepped inside, I said, "Dad, is there anything you know that you haven't wanted to say in front of Mom?"

He shook his head. "I don't know more than you do, Willow. I can't imagine Kelsey running off and letting us worry like this, but the alternative is unthinkable."

"This is awful."

His gaze filled with compassion. "How are you doing, Willow? Are you all right?"

"No. I'm terrified. I don't want to lose Kelsey."

"We're not going to lose her," he said forcefully.

"They couldn't find Melanie. And they searched just as hard."

"That's why I want to bring in additional resources. Ben is a smart kid, but I don't know if he has the manpower to cover this entire island and all the boats going in and out of the harbor."

"What can I do to help?"

"Look out for your mom. She needs support."

"I will," I said, as my father moved into his study and shut the door.

Despite my promise, I didn't return to the living room. My mother was with Sean, and she would find me more of an annoyance than a support, so I headed up the stairs. I wanted to look in Kelsey's room again. Maybe she had left some clue behind.

I entered the room and closed the door behind me. After setting my bag down on the desk, I took off my jacket, hanging it over the back of a chair. I then picked up a few items of clothing that Kelsey had left on the bed and hung them in the closet. As my gaze caught on the garment bag, I impulsively unzipped it. She'd sent me a photo of her wedding dress months ago, but the gown was even more stunning than I remembered.

One of the fashion designers Kelsey modeled for had made the dress, and it was exquisite, with lace, beads, plunging cleavage, and a sexy low back. Kelsey would be beautiful in this dress. But now I wondered if she would ever wear it.

Even if she came back, would she still marry Gage?

If she'd run away, then she had serious doubts about Gage. If she hadn't run away...

I zipped the bag back up and rifled through the two large suitcases she'd brought with her. As I moved clothes around, I found myself simply unpacking. When I was done, Kelsey's clothes were neatly hung in the closet or put away in the dresser. I had found absolutely no clue as to why she wasn't here to do this for herself. Not that she would have unpacked. She'd probably have waited for our housekeeper, Lorraine, to do it for her. In fact, I was a little surprised that my mom hadn't ordered that done already.

With Kelsey's room now clean and waiting for her, I sank down on the bed. The soft mattress enveloped me, and I stretched out on the thick, fluffy comforter. I could smell Kelsey's perfume in the air, and it was oddly comforting.

Closing my eyes, I savored her scent with several long, deep breaths. I felt suddenly exhausted. Maybe I'd just take a little nap.

I woke up, confused about where I was and why it was so dark. A quick look at the clock told me it was almost nine. I was in Kelsey's bedroom, and I'd slept for several hours.

I wondered why no one had woken me up. Although, the door was closed. Maybe they hadn't realized where I was. I suddenly heard voices coming from the room next door, which belonged to Brooklyn. I wondered if something had happened. I got up from the bed and moved closer to the vent. My sister was speaking to someone, and she was angry.

"I don't want to talk to you about any of this," Brooklyn said loudly. "I can't do this right now, James."

"We have to talk. You can't keep avoiding me," James said.

"This is the worst possible time. My sister is missing. And you can't help me find her, because once again you remember nothing about last night."

"I had too much to drink, and you know why I was pounding it down so hard."

"Don't blame your drinking on me. You're an alcoholic, James. You can pretty it up by calling yourself a heavy partier or a social drinker, but you have a problem. You've had a problem for years, and someday, I worry…"

"You worry?" James prodded when Brooklyn didn't finish her statement. "You actually worry about me?"

"It's a bad habit," she said harshly. "You should go home. Unless you know where Kelsey is, we have nothing to talk about."

"I don't know where Kelsey is. I wish I did."

"Then you're of no use to me."

"But there is one thing," James said.

"What? What is the one thing?"

"It might mean nothing."

"You're stalling."

"I got on the ferry early yesterday. It was just me and Kelsey for a few minutes. She was practically having a panic attack. She asked me if she was making a mistake marrying Gage."

"You're lying. She wouldn't have said that."

I pressed my ear closer to the vent, as shocked as Brooklyn was by James's words.

"I'm not lying," James returned. "Why would I?"

"Well, what did you tell her?"

"That it wasn't too late to back out if that was what she needed to do."

"You're Gage's friend. You're one of his groomsmen, for God's sake. And you're telling the bride to back out of your best friend's wedding?"

"I'm Kelsey's friend, too."

"Is that all you are?" Brooklyn asked, a bitter, scathing note in her voice.

I stiffened at the question. I really hoped that Kelsey hadn't hooked up with James, too.

"God, yes!" James declared. "How can you ask me that?"

"Because there are so many things you don't remember. And you know what I'm talking about."

There was a momentary silence. Then James said, "I had nothing to do with Melanie's disappearance. I told you that before."

My gut tightened once more. *What did Brooklyn know that I didn't?*

"But you don't know that for sure, do you?" she challenged.

"Hey, Willow couldn't remember what she did that night, either. We were all drinking. Memories were muddled."

"But Willow didn't ask me to lie for her; you did."

I sucked in a breath at her words. *Brooklyn had lied for James?*

"You know why I asked you to do that. I couldn't let myself get caught in the interrogation just because I'd blacked out. I was already on thin ice with my parents. They were threatening to stop paying for college because of my alcohol issues. I would have had to leave school. You agreed to do it. You thought it was a good idea."

"I thought you were a good idea," Brooklyn retorted. "I was wrong. And if you had anything to do with Kelsey going missing, I will make you pay."

"Kelsey must have run away, because she doesn't want to marry Gage."

"Of course she wants to marry him. She has been in love with him for years. He was always her dream guy. When he asked her to marry him, she was over the moon."

Hearing Brooklyn call Gage Kelsey's dream guy reminded me I'd looked at Drake the same way.

If Drake had suddenly seen me, wanted to date me, love me, marry me, would I have been so caught up in my fantasy coming true that I might not have seen the real man? Was that what had happened with Kelsey?

"Then what do you think happened?" James challenged.

"I don't know, but I don't believe Kelsey ran away," Brooklyn continued. "Her shoe was found on the dock. That terrifies me, James."

"She could have gotten on someone's boat. They gave her a ride back to the mainland."

"Or something awful happened. If she doesn't come back, I don't know what I'll do. She's my sister, my best friend. I love her so much," Brooklyn said, her voice shaking. "I don't think I could survive without her."

I heard a sob rip from Brooklyn's throat and then James's soothing words of comfort. Brooklyn let him reassure her for a moment, and then she snapped back.

"I don't need you to tell me it will be all right," she said. "You don't know that. And you're a liar, so why would I believe you?"

I wasn't surprised at Brooklyn's attack. Whenever she accidentally let herself appear vulnerable, she overcompensated by going on offense.

"I'm not a liar, Brooklyn."

"Yes, you are, James. You lie about everything, and then you pretend not to remember. You're never going to stop drinking until you can tell the truth, if only to yourself."

"I don't pretend not to remember; my mind is blank."

I could relate to his frustration. My one horrible blackout still drove me crazy.

"You need to go, James. We are done," Brooklyn said with a finality in her voice.

But James couldn't accept that. "We're never going to be done," he said defiantly. "There's too much history between us. And I want to help you now."

"You can't help me. Just leave."

"I might know something else."

"What? What do you suddenly know? Something else Kelsey told you at the ferry?"

"No. But I need to talk to Carter first."

"About what?"

"I think Carter is closer to Kelsey than we might think," James said.

My pulse leapt once more.

"What are you talking about?" Brooklyn asked.

"I think Carter and Kelsey got together last year in Paris."

"Kelsey said she barely saw him."

"That's not what I heard."

"No way. You're lying again. Why are you doing this, James?

Are you trying to hurt me?"

"I'm trying to help you."

"Kelsey did not cheat on Gage with his brother. There's no way. And if she had, she would have told me."

"You're pretty judgmental, Brooklyn. I don't think Kelsey tells you everything."

"Get out of my room, James. I mean it. Go."

"I'll go, but I still love you, Brooklyn. You might hate me now, but I still love you."

"No, you don't. You're just afraid. Every time you think you might have crossed a line, you come running to me for reassurance or an alibi. But I will never cover for you again. And I will never love you again. This is the last conversation we ever need to have."

"It won't be the last conversation. I'll be back when I have more information."

"I won't hold my breath."

I heard Brooklyn's door open and close. I moved to the door of Kelsey's room. As I opened it, I saw James heading down the stairs. I grabbed my bag and jacket and impulsively ran after him.

When I left the house, James was already in his car. The vehicle I'd used earlier was still in the driveway. I jumped inside and started the engine, following James down the street.

I didn't really have a plan. James might just drive the few blocks to his parents' house, but he didn't. He headed toward town, maybe to get that information he needed to make Brooklyn like him again.

Wherever he was going, I was going, too. At the very least, I could talk to him about what I'd just overheard. He seemed to be relatively sober for the first time since he'd arrived on the island, so maybe I could get something out of him. I probably had a better chance with him than with Brooklyn.

As James drove across town, I kept some distance between our cars, feeling both excited and concerned that I was making a mistake. But at least I was doing something, and that was better than sitting around and waiting. Hopefully, James would lead me to a clue that would help me find my sister.

CHAPTER FOURTEEN

JAMES DROVE TOWARD THE HARBOR, eventually parking in a lot next to a dive bar called Willie's. The bar was frequented mostly by fishermen and locals. It didn't seem like a place James would spend time in, but he was an alcoholic, so maybe he preferred to drink in bars his friends didn't patronize.

I pulled into a parking spot on the other side of a large truck and shut off my lights. I was across the lot from James, and I could see him in the rearview mirror. He was sitting in his car, and he appeared to be on his phone. Five minutes or more passed before he got out of the car and walked into the bar.

I was about to follow him inside when another car pulled into the lot. Carter Chadwick jumped out. My pulse leapt. James had told Brooklyn he was going to find out what was going on between Carter and Kelsey.

It made me sick to think anything had gone on between them. I knew Kelsey had few boundaries when it came to dating men who were involved with other women. She'd always said it wasn't on her to keep anyone faithful. But this was different. Carter was Gage's brother. That would be crossing a line that should not be crossed.

After Carter entered the bar, I stepped out of the car and headed inside.

The bar was small, dark, and smelled like beer and sweat. Looking around, I noted about eight tables and a long bar, at which every stool was filled. There were probably twenty people in the room and eighteen of them were men. This was definitely not my scene, but I was here, and I wasn't going home, not until I got some answers.

I moved through the crowd, ignoring a few rude male comments and offers to buy me a drink. I dragged a chair from a nearby table over to where James and Carter were sitting and took a seat.

They stared at me in surprise.

"Willow," James said, getting his mouth to work first. "What are you doing here?"

"I want to talk to both of you."

"This is not the kind of place you should be in," he told me.

"Don't worry about it. I'm fine."

"How did you know we were here?" Carter asked, giving me an unhappy look.

"I heard James talking to Brooklyn, and I followed him here."

Both of them looked at me with astonishment.

"What the hell?" James said. "You followed me. Why?"

"I have questions about your conversation with my sister."

"You were eavesdropping?"

"Not intentionally. You weren't that quiet. I want to know why Brooklyn lied for you ten years ago."

James turned pale at my question. "I—I have nothing to say to you."

"Maybe I should leave you two—" Carter began.

"No," I said, waving him back into his seat. "Sit down. I want to speak to you as well, Carter."

He looked shocked at my tone. "You're different. When did you turn bossy like Brooklyn?"

"About the time Kelsey disappeared," I snapped.

"Well, I don't know what James and Brooklyn were lying about ten years ago," Carter said. "So, I'm not sure why you need to talk to me."

"I'll get to you, Carter, but first I need James to answer my question."

"It was nothing," James said quickly.

"Be more specific. I'm not leaving until you tell me the truth."

"Maybe you aren't, but I am," James said.

"Sit down," I ordered as he started to get up. "If you don't talk to me now, I'll talk to Ben. And then I'll fill Drake in on what I heard. Believe me, you would rather talk to me than either of them."

He gave me a long, assessing look and then settled back down in his chair. "Carter is right. You are different."

"We're not talking about me. What happened the night Melanie disappeared?"

"I passed out on the beach, but I didn't want that fact to get back to my parents, so I asked Brooklyn to tell the police I was with her. That's it."

"And you didn't think Melanie's disappearance was more important than your parents getting mad at you?" I challenged.

"I never saw Melanie, so I couldn't have helped. And it wasn't just about my parents. Everyone in our circle needed an alibi," James said. "Drake was gunning for us."

"He's right," Carter said. "Drake is still convinced one of us is guilty of something horrific. I don't know how he can think that. We used to be his friends."

"My little lie wasn't a big deal," James added. "Don't make it one now, Willow. There's no point in dredging up the past."

"The past is here, James. We're reliving it right now. Kelsey is gone."

"This is completely different."

"Is it?"

"Yes," Carter interjected. "Kelsey must have left the island without anyone knowing. She must have arranged for someone to pick her up. That's probably why her shoe was on the dock."

"She just fell out of her shoe and left it there?" I asked.

"I don't know. Maybe she changed shoes," he suggested.

"Okay, let's go with that," I said. "If you think Kelsey left the island, then you must have some ideas why she would do that."

"She must have changed her mind about the wedding," he replied. "That's the only logical explanation." His gaze wandered toward the door as he finished speaking.

"Carter," I said sharply. "Look at me."

"What?" he demanded. "What do you want from me?"

"The truth. Did Kelsey bail on the wedding because she hooked up with you?" I asked.

Carter's jaw tightened, anger running through his gaze. He turned on James. "Did you tell her that? Did you tell Brooklyn that?"

"I might have said something to Brooklyn," James admitted. "Kelsey is missing, and I want to help find her. So, answer Willow's question. Did Kelsey change her mind about marrying Gage because of you?"

"I—I don't know." Carter sat back in his chair, his anger fading as his shoulders slumped. "She didn't give me any sign that she didn't want to go through with the wedding. But when she disappeared, I wondered."

"You were arguing with Kelsey on the ferry yesterday," I said to Carter. "She told me it was about Gage missing the boat, but that wasn't what you were discussing, was it?"

"She was angry about that," Carter returned.

"Were you also arguing about the wedding? Did you want her to call it off?"

"I don't know where she is, Willow."

"I didn't ask you that. Did you want her to call off the wedding?" I repeated.

"Yes, but she said she was committed to marrying Gage."

"What is between you two? Are you in love with her?" When he didn't answer, I pressed harder. "Is she in love with you? Dammit, Carter, tell me the truth."

"When I was in Paris, we got close," Carter said.

"But she was dating Gage when you were in Paris. And she got engaged a few weeks after she came home."

"I know when everything happened," he said bitterly.

"Why didn't she break it off with Gage?"

"She said…" Carter drew in a breath. "Gage was the one she wanted. I told her I would treat her so much better than he would. But she wouldn't hear me."

"Did you talk to her last night after Gage brought her home?"

"No. After I got James settled at the hotel, I went home."

My gaze returned to James, who stiffened when he realized my attention was back on him. It felt a little strange to have the power to make these two men uncomfortable. When we were younger, they'd had all the power. They'd been handsome, popular, in demand, and I had not been any of those things. They'd barely seen me back then, but they were seeing me now.

"What about you, James?" I asked, even though I already knew the answer. James had been in no condition to do anything with Kelsey. "Did you see Kelsey after eleven last night?"

"I don't even remember leaving the bonfire," he said.

"Do you remember talking to me?"

"Were you by the bathroom?"

"Yes. You thought that you and I made out in your car and my bedroom when we were teenagers. But that never happened."

"I was obviously wasted, Willow."

"Obviously. But I want to know who you were remembering. You said the girl was too young for you, so it wasn't Brooklyn. That got me wondering. Was it Melanie? Did you and Melanie get together ten years ago?"

"No."

"I don't know if I believe you."

"Well, you should, because I'm telling the truth."

"Knowing that you lied once before, it's difficult to believe you."

"I had nothing to do with Melanie's disappearance," he reiterated.

I ignored him, turning back to Carter. "And you—you were

sleeping with Kelsey while she was sleeping with your brother. Does Gage know?"

"Of course not. And you will not tell him," Carter said sharply. "It would kill him. It would destroy everyone in my family, and it doesn't matter. It's over now."

His words had a finality to them that scared me even more.

Was it over because Kelsey was gone? Had Carter hurt my sister?

"You need to leave this alone, Willow," Carter said. "This information will only splinter everyone apart when we need to pull together to find Kelsey."

"I won't protect you."

"Then protect your sister," Carter snapped. "I wasn't in the bed alone. Do you think Kelsey wants everyone in our families to know what happened between us? Do you think she wants her future in-laws to know what she did?"

As much as I hated to admit it, he had a point.

"I love Kelsey," Carter added. "I love her more than I ever imagined and more than I should. I would never hurt her. I would never want her to be hurt. I just want her to come home, and if that means marrying Gage, then I'll make peace with it."

He was very convincing, and I wanted to believe him. *But how could I?* Every time I turned around a new secret came out.

"How can you be so sure that Gage doesn't know?" I asked. "James obviously had some idea, which probably means Rachel knows." I didn't bother to mention Jenny because I didn't need to bring her into it.

"If Gage knew, he would have beaten the crap out of me," Carter said.

I stared at him. "Would he have gone after you or gone after Kelsey?"

Carter's face turned to stone, his eyes burning with anger. "No way. My brother did not hurt Kelsey."

"He's right," James agreed. "Gage wouldn't hurt Kelsey. I still think she just took off. This whole situation got too complicated, and Kelsey doesn't like complicated."

That was true. Kelsey preferred to keep things simple, and if she didn't want to be bothered by something or someone, she just cut them out of her life. But while I could see her cutting both Gage and Carter out of her life, she wouldn't have done it like this.

"Gage and I have been looking for Kelsey all day. We've walked miles around this island," Carter continued. "We're doing everything we can to find her."

"I appreciate that, but if you really want to help, go to Ben and tell him everything."

"None of this will help him find Kelsey. And I won't destroy Kelsey's life for no reason," Carter said.

"Her life *is* the reason," I said in frustration.

"My relationship with Kelsey has nothing to do with why she's gone."

"You don't know that, Carter."

"I do know it. Let it be for tonight, Willow. If Kelsey doesn't come home in the morning, then I'll talk to Ben and whoever else I need to speak to. Let's just give her a chance to come home."

I knew they expected me to agree because I'd always run from conflict in the past, but I didn't want to run now. I glanced at my watch. It was after ten. There wasn't much I could do tonight anyway. "All right. I'll leave it alone until the morning, and then everyone needs to start talking. That includes you, James."

"If I come clean about my lie, I'll be throwing Brooklyn into the fire, Willow. Are you willing to destroy your sister for a lie that won't make one bit of difference now?"

"So, you both want me to stay quiet to protect my sisters?"

"Why hurt them if you don't have to?" James asked.

"Drake was right," I said. "Everyone I know has more to hide than I ever imagined."

"Drake was not right," Carter said harshly. "None of us hurt Melanie."

"And none of us have hurt Kelsey," James added. "You need to drop it, Willow. Go back in the shadows where you belong."

"That won't happen," I said, fired up again by his snide tone.

As I got to my feet, Carter gave me an apologetic look. "Willow, we're on the same side."

"I really hope that's true, Carter."

When I left the bar, I drew in a deep breath of salty sea air. There was too much adrenaline running through me to just get into my car and go home. I needed to burn it off. I needed to think about everything I knew and decide what to do next.

I'd promised Carter to wait until morning to do anything. *Was that a mistake?*

With that question rolling around in my head, I started walking. The wind was gusting now, but it felt invigorating. I moved out of the parking lot and across the street to the harbor. Fifteen minutes later, I realized I was nearing the location where Kelsey's shoe had been found.

This part of the harbor was deserted. The only two businesses around were a bait and tackle shop and a boat rental kiosk, both of which were closed. The dozen or so boats bobbing in the nearby slips were completely dark.

Had Kelsey found someone to give her a ride off the island? But why would she have left after eleven at night? It would have been dangerous. The seas had been rough yesterday. It didn't make sense.

Unless Kelsey had just spent the night on one of these boats and then...

Then what?

I blew out a breath. I had no good answers.

"Where are you, Kelsey?" I whispered, struggling to hold back a rush of overwhelming fear.

I was losing hope, and I didn't want to do that. I didn't want to let Kelsey down. I didn't want to give up on her. We might not have been close in recent years, but she was my sister. We'd grown up together. Despite the distance that had grown between us, I loved her, and my heart broke for her. This should have been the happiest time of her life.

The pain swamped me, and tears streamed out of my eyes. As I wiped them away, I heard footsteps behind me. They were coming hard and fast. Before I could turn around, someone barreled into me, propelling me forward, knocking me off my feet. I flew into the air, flailing my arms and my legs, trying to stay on the dock, but it was no use.

I hit the icy cold water and my heart stopped. I went under. Everything was dark, and I couldn't breathe. I tried to fight my way to the surface, but my shoes, my clothes, were weighing me down.

A new panic swept over me.

Someone had pushed me into the water.

Were they waiting for me to come to the surface? Was a bullet coming next?

Silent screams rang through my head. I didn't know what was waiting for me, but I had no choice. I needed air.

I kicked as hard as I could, desperately searching for light, for life…

CHAPTER FIFTEEN

MY HEAD finally broke the surface. I gasped for air, immediately choking as the swirling sea dumped more water over my head. I tried to swim, but my arms were entrapped in my heavy, now waterlogged jacket. I could see the dock, but it was twenty feet away, and the ocean current was dragging me toward the sea. I tried to swim toward the dock, but I was getting nowhere fast, and my body was already tiring.

Then I heard a splash. I stared in alarm at the dark figure coming toward me.

Was this the person who had pushed me into the water? Had they come back to finish the job?

The alarm gave me new energy. I turned and started kicking toward the nearest boat, which still seemed too far away. Then I heard my name on the wind.

"Willow, stop!"

I knew that voice. I treaded water as I looked over my shoulder. A man swam toward me. I couldn't see his face yet, but I knew that voice.

He drew nearer, his words louder. "You're going the wrong way, Willow."

I wanted to cry with relief. "Drake. I didn't know it was you."

He moved through the water like the powerful swimmer and lifeguard he'd once been. "I've got you. Take my hand."

"We'll both go under."

"We won't. Trust me."

I didn't trust him at all, but I was struggling to stay afloat, so I grabbed his hand. I was surprised by the sudden blast of warmth even as my body shook with the cold. I hung onto that warmth as hard as I could.

Drake swam toward the dock, pulling me along with him.

His strength was amazing. I didn't know how he was fighting the current so successfully. I felt heavy, clumsy, exhausted, and frozen from the cold, but he dragged me along as if I weighed nothing at all.

Eventually, we got to a ladder, and he pushed me onto it. I wrapped my fingers around the rails as my feet hit the bottom rung. There were only about eight steps to the dock, but I wasn't sure I could find the strength.

What the hell was wrong with me? I needed to fight.

"You can do it, Willow. I'm right behind you. I won't let you fall," Drake said.

I didn't bother wasting energy to answer him. Instead, I lifted one leg and took a step. It was slow going, the water wanting to suck me back in every time I faltered. But I could feel Drake right behind me, and it kept me going.

Finally, I crawled onto the dock and sprawled across it, gasping for air.

Drake came off the ladder. He squatted down next to me, his sharp gaze sweeping across my face. "Are you all right?"

"I—I think so," I mumbled, the words barely getting through my chattering teeth.

"How did you fall in?"

"I didn't fall. Someone pushed me in the water."

He gave me a shocked look. "Someone pushed you in? Who? Why?"

"I don't know. I was standing on the dock, and someone ran up behind me and hit me with tremendous force. The next thing I knew, I was in the water." I paused, wondering how he'd been so close by. "What are you doing down here?"

"I wanted to see where Kelsey's shoe was found. I saw you in the water, and you were in trouble. Do you feel any pain?"

I slowly shook my head. "No, although I can't feel much at all at the moment." I licked my cold lips. "I couldn't swim. I felt so heavy with all these clothes on, and the water was so cold. If you hadn't come along—"

"Well, I did. And this is probably the first time you've been happy to see me in ten years," he said dryly.

"I'd say so."

Was it just a coincidence that he'd arrived to save me? I really wanted to believe it was. I shivered as the wind hit the water on my face.

"You need to dry off and warm up. Let's get out of here."

I watched as Drake grabbed his shoes off the dock and put them on. Then he picked up his keys, a phone, and a wallet, which made me realize my bag was gone.

"My purse," I said, sitting up straight. "It was on my shoulder when I went in the water."

Drake flashed a light from his phone on the surrounding dock and water. "I don't see anything. Wait." He moved several feet away. "I've got your phone."

I was relieved to see my case in his hand. "Do you see my bag? My keys? Wallet?"

His light swept the dock once more. "Sorry. Your phone must have fallen out before the bag went into the water."

That made sense, since it had been in the outer pocket of my bag, but I wasn't thrilled to have lost everything else. "Damn! I won't be able to drive home."

"Where's your car?" he asked, looking around once more.

"It's in the lot by Willie's," I said as he handed me my phone. "I walked over here from there."

"Willie's? That doesn't seem like your scene."

"It's a long story."

"You can tell it to me when you get warm. Since you can't

access your car, we'll go to the restaurant. It's not far. Can you walk?"

"Yes, of course I can walk," I said, but I was grateful for his hand as he helped me to my feet. "I don't know why I'm so unsteady. I'm not hurt."

"You're in shock."

"That's true."

He let go of my hand and put his arm around me. He was as wet and cold as I was, but I still felt a warmth coming from the shelter of his body as we walked to the restaurant.

Drake used a key to open the front door to the Crab Pot, which closed at nine during the week, eleven on weekend nights. The interior of the restaurant felt deliciously warm. I wanted to sink down into one of the plush booths, but Drake was pushing me toward the upstairs apartment. Once again, I felt like I was step-ping back in time.

As I entered the apartment, images from the past flew through my mind, and they didn't just involve me and Melanie hanging out here when she was taking a break from working the restaurant. No, my brain took me back to another cold night, the time Drake and I had waited out a summer storm and then ended up creating a storm of our own.

"I don't want to be here." I turned toward the door, but Drake was in my way.

He gave me a determined look. "You need to get warm, Willow."

I shook my head. "I'll call for a ride if you don't want to take me home."

"What are you afraid of?" he challenged.

"Nothing."

"You're remembering the last time we were in this apartment. We got drenched running down the pier, because you wanted a photo of the monster yacht in the harbor, the *Carolina*."

"And you wanted to interview the owner, a reclusive billionaire."

"You got your photo, but I couldn't get even one foot on board," he said.

"The first time I saw your charm not work."

He smiled dryly. "I don't think it was the first time."

"The paper never ran the photo I took. They said they had plenty of pictures of that yacht. Getting caught in the storm was definitely not worth it, not for either of us."

"Well, I wouldn't say it was all bad."

I licked my lips at the very adult male look in his eyes. I wasn't seventeen anymore, and I certainly wasn't in love with Drake, but I was still very aware of him and of the reckless flow of desire that always seemed to surge when I was with him. "We don't need to talk about that night."

"Agreed. Look, I'll make sure you get home safely, but we need to talk first, and you need to dry off. Why don't you take a shower? There's a robe on the door in the bathroom. Throw your clothes out, and I'll put them in the dryer."

"I'd really rather just go home," I said desperately.

"My plan is better. I'm not trying to get you naked for any other reason than your own health." He looked into my eyes. "You can trust me, Willow. I just saved your life. Doesn't that mean something?"

"As long as you didn't push me in so you could save me and gain my trust."

He shook his head in amazement. "You really think I'm that nefarious?"

"Let's just say I hope you're not."

"All right." He paused. "You should take the shower, Willow. You were in the water longer than me. But do what you want. I'm going to change." He walked over to the closet.

"Wait a second. You're staying here?" I suddenly became aware of the clothes hanging in the open closet, the suitcase by the couch. "I thought you were at your parents' house."

"No. I prefer to stay here when I visit now. If you want to watch me take my clothes off, feel free, but I'm not waiting another second."

As he pulled his shirt over his head, I ran into the bathroom, flushing at the ridiculous thoughts running through my head. I could not still have a thing for Drake, not after everything that had happened. But there was no denying that my heart was racing, and my body was tingling with memories.

A knock came at the door, and I jumped.

"Don't forget to throw your clothes out," Drake said.

I stripped down, shivering so hard my teeth were chattering. Then I turned on the shower and wrapped myself in a towel before tossing my clothes out of the bathroom. When that was done, I closed the door and locked it before stepping under the hot spray. It took a few minutes for the heat to drive away the cold.

Once I was able to stop shaking, I felt better, and my brain started working again. I finally got a grip on my runaway emotions. I didn't need to think about my one night of passion with Drake; I needed to stay in the present. Someone had pushed me into the water. *Why? To kill me? To scare me?*

I'd been standing right by the spot where Kelsey's shoe had been found. *Was that a coincidence? Had she met the same fate? Had someone come out of nowhere and shoved her into the rough water?*

It didn't seem likely. It also didn't seem like the most efficient way to kill someone. I could swim, and I was in the harbor, not the open sea. I might have made it to the dock even without Drake, although I wasn't completely sure of that.

If someone hadn't thought the shove would kill me, had it just been an impulsive crime of opportunity?

If I was scared enough, I might stop asking questions, I might leave the island, and I could think of at least two people who would probably like that: Carter Chadwick and James Connelly. I'd been stupid to tell them both what I knew. I just hadn't thought confronting them would be dangerous. I'd known them forever. I'd grown up with them. They weren't violent people. *Were they?*

That question rolled around in my head as the water went from hot to lukewarm. I stepped out of the shower, drying off with a thick gray towel. I used a comb on the vanity to run through my hair and then picked up the hair dryer. There were signs of Drake all over this bathroom: the shaving case on the counter, the cologne, and the toothbrush. It felt oddly intimate to be using his bathroom.

He was a man now, not the boy I'd fallen for. In the past decade he'd lived a life I knew nothing about, and I'd lived a life he'd known nothing about. Whatever had driven us to be together for that one crazy night certainly hadn't lasted much longer than the sex, at least not for him.

I'd made a mistake with him once; I wouldn't make the same one again.

When I finished drying my hair, I put on the robe, tying it tightly around me, as I was acutely aware of my naked state. Then I moved back into the living room. Drake was standing in the small kitchen, making coffee. He'd changed into jeans and a navy sweatshirt. The dryer was rumbling nearby. Hopefully, my clothes would soon be wearable again.

"Feel better?" he asked, giving me a quick look.

"Yes."

"Coffee?" He held out a mug.

"Thanks." I took a grateful sip. "It's good."

"I brought my favorite blend from Seattle. I can do without a lot of things when I'm on the island, but not my coffee."

It was weird to hear him say something so prosaic, so normal, so undramatic. "It sounds like you have an addiction."

"To caffeine, absolutely," he said with a dry smile. "What about you?"

"I love coffee, too. Your mom would never serve it to Melanie and me when we were young."

"Oh, I know. She kept trying to drown us in hot chocolate."

"With marshmallows. It might have made us feel like kids, but it was tasty."

"It was. It's funny the things we remember, isn't it? Random moments that often seemed meaningless, but they stick with us."

I nodded, sensing we were getting a little too personal. I almost liked it better when we were yelling at each other. Oddly, that seemed a little less dangerous. "Are my clothes dry?"

"They need a few more minutes. Why don't you sit down, Willow?"

Since I couldn't go anywhere without my clothes, I took a seat in the chair while he sat on the futon, setting his coffee on the table in front of him.

"So, why were you at Willie's?" he asked.

"I followed James there. I overheard a conversation between him and Brooklyn that bothered me, so I followed him. He met Carter in the bar, which was good because I had questions for Carter, too."

"Let's start with James. What bothered you about the conversation he had with Brooklyn?" Drake asked, giving me a speculative look.

I hesitated. If I told him, I could get Brooklyn into trouble. James's lie was tied to hers. "Just some stuff," I said vaguely.

Disappointment and annoyance ran through his eyes. "You're always protecting someone, aren't you?"

He had a point. "All right. James and Brooklyn were talking about the night Melanie vanished. It didn't sound like James was with Brooklyn the entire night, the way he said he was."

"And the way she said he was. Why were they even talking about that night?"

"Kelsey's disappearance has brought the memories back for everyone, not just me. I believe the lie festered between them. It might have even led to their breakup years later."

"Interesting. Well, don't worry, Willow. You're not blowing the case wide open. I already figured out that James lied. I just don't know why or where he was."

"James said he was passed out on the beach, and his parents were going to take him out of school if he had another problem with alcohol, so Brooklyn covered for him. He insisted he did not see Melanie that night, so his lie didn't matter."

"But he doesn't remember the entire night, does he?"

"No. How did you figure out he lied?"

"Someone saw his car at ten p.m. in the downtown area. He sped through a stop sign."

"Someone saw him?" I asked in surprise. "I don't understand. Did the sheriff question him about that?"

"No. Or if he did, it wasn't in the file. The information was buried in a witness statement from Mrs. Wiggins, who ran the Corner Market. She rambled on about a lot of irrelevant things, including the fact that teenagers were speeding down her street at all hours of the night. That's when she mentioned a red Audi running the stop sign in front of her store. She'd just locked up around ten. She didn't say it was James, but that was the car he drove, and I doubt there were two of them on the island."

"Have you talked to Ben about it?"

"I was going to speak to him today, but he's been busy looking for Kelsey."

"What about reaching out to Mrs. Wiggins?"

"She passed away three years ago."

"Oh, that's sad." I paused. "So, you think James was in town that night?"

"I do. I don't believe he was passed out on the beach."

"Why would he lie to Brooklyn?"

"Probably the reason any guy lies to his girlfriend. He was with someone else. Or he was doing something he didn't want her to know about."

"Who would he have been with?"

"No idea. Maybe Brooklyn knows. Could you ask her?"

"I don't know that she'd tell me the truth."

"But you did say you would try to help me get answers," he reminded me.

"I will ask her about it. But not right this second. She's really worried about Kelsey. It's not the best time."

Frustration entered his eyes. "It is the best time, Willow. It's past the best time."

He had a point. "All right. I will talk to her tomorrow. I'm sure James will probably tell her I followed him to Willie's anyway." I let out a breath. "I've never liked James, and I like him even less now. But I need your honest opinion—is James someone who would shove me in the sea and hope I died?"

Drake stared back at me. "Was he drunk?"

"He was actually sober tonight. But he was angry with me for eavesdropping, for following him, for threatening to tell Ben about his lie, if he didn't do it himself."

"You told him that?" Drake asked with surprise.

"Yes. It was probably stupid, but I wanted them both to know I was serious. Which brings me to Carter."

"What did he have to say about James's lie?"

"Not much. He didn't think it concerned him. I didn't pressure him for an opinion, because I was more interested in learning about his relationship with Kelsey."

Drake raised a brow. "What kind of relationship are you suggesting?"

"Apparently, Carter and Kelsey got together when they were both in Paris last year. It was a few weeks before she got engaged to Gage. She ended the affair at some point, but Carter is still in love with her. He tried to talk her out of marrying Gage."

Drake sat back on the couch, folding his arms across his chest. "I was not expecting you to say that." He tilted his head, giving me a speculative look. "Does Carter think Kelsey ran away?"

"He's holding onto that hope. Carter begged me not to say anything about their affair. He said it would ruin Kelsey's reputation. I could hurt her if she is just taking time to think."

"They found her shoe on the dock. I don't believe she's just thinking somewhere."

"She might have been in a hurry to get on a boat. Maybe she was running barefoot, and she had the shoe in her hand, and she dropped it."

"Okay. That could have happened," he said carefully.

I saw the doubt in his gaze. "But you don't really think so."

"I told myself a lot of stories about where Melanie might be when she disappeared. I understand why you need the stories. It helps you get through the night."

"I can't let them go," I admitted.

"I understand."

He did understand, probably better than anyone.

"You need to let Ben know about Carter and Kelsey," Drake continued. "Maybe Carter got desperate and stopped her from getting married. Or Gage found out and got angry."

"If that happened, Gage would have just called off the wedding." I felt desperate to believe that. "No one is killing anyone over this affair."

He leaned forward, giving me a hard look. "Don't underestimate anyone. You talked to two men about their secrets and then someone shoved you into the water. You could have drowned tonight. Your silence would have been assured. You need to call Ben. If James and Carter are innocent of everything, that will become clear. But if they're not, and you don't say something..."

"You're right. I don't need to protect them. I don't want to protect them. I just want Kelsey back. But I don't have Ben's number anymore. I deleted everyone's phone number a long time ago. I couldn't look at the names."

Drake pulled out his phone and read me the number.

I punched it in, then waited. Unfortunately, Ben didn't pick up, and the call went to voicemail. I left a message. "Ben. This is Willow. I got into a dicey situation tonight. I'm okay, but I need to talk to you about it. I also have some other information I need to discuss with you. Call me back as soon as you can."

As I was about to set down my phone, a text came in. I gave Drake a dry smile. "You just sent me your number."

"You may need to call me sometime, and I'm sure I was one of the names you deleted."

"First one," I admitted. "I'm surprised you kept my number."

"I have everyone's number. I just can't seem to get anyone to answer."

"You've never called me."

"I was thinking about it recently," he admitted.

"What stopped you?"

He let out a sigh. "A lot of things. Would you have taken my call?"

"I don't know." I sat back in my chair, propping my feet on the coffee table. "I never thought I'd have to live through this kind of situation ever again, but here I am. I had a bad feeling about the wedding being rescheduled here, but I never thought anything like this would happen. When I arrived, I thought my biggest problem might be you standing up in the ceremony and making some dramatic proclamation."

"Not my style."

"Maybe not. But I don't know you anymore."

"Fair enough. I have to say that you've changed, Willow. You're not the shy girl. You're much more direct. You don't look away. You don't chew on the end of your braid."

"I haven't worn a braid in a very long time."

"It was cute."

I sighed. "Just what I wanted to be around my best friend's sexy older brother—cute."

He laughed. "It's not a bad word."

"I didn't want to be cute or the shy girl, but I couldn't find the courage to be more than that, except when I was with Melanie. She brought me out of my shell. She gave me confidence. Sometimes I think our relationship was very one-sided. She pushed me to be better, but she was already great, so I didn't add to her life."

"That's not true. Every night at dinner, she'd talk about some adventure the two of you had had. It was weird. She grew up on the island, but when she was with you, she saw it with fresh eyes. You made her look at the details. She was always amazed at the pictures you'd take, the tiny drops of dew on a flower that you would notice, that you would immortalize in a photograph."

I was touched by his words. "Really? She used to get impatient when I took too long to get a shot."

"Well, she was impressed with the end result."

"I'm glad. Thanks for telling me that."

"Now I have a question for you. What did Melanie think about me?"

His question surprised me. "What do you mean?"

"Melanie and I got into a fight a couple of days before she

vanished. She'd been irritated with me most of that summer. Everything I did annoyed her. I'm not sure why we weren't getting along. We always had in the past, but not those last few weeks."

It was impossible not to hear the pain in his voice. I didn't know what to think about Drake, but I knew that his love for his sister had been very real.

"Did she say anything to you?" he continued.

"She loved you, Drake."

"That's not what I asked."

"Whatever she said to me reflected what she was feeling about herself, not about you."

"And you're being very careful in your choice of words. Just tell me what she said."

"It changed often. Sometimes, she thought you were amazing. Other times, she thought your parents favored you. She was happy to have you home but also frustrated that you were treated like a god by your mother—her words, not mine. She was jealous that you were living a life away from the island. She wanted to be in your shoes. She wanted to be the one coming home and talking about her adventures. She just wanted to be an adult, like you."

A mix of emotions ran through his gaze. "I knew she was feeling restless. I should have invited her to visit me at college. I should have taken her on vacation. Instead of coming back here that summer, I could have taken her to Europe, Hawaii, one of the places she wanted to go. But I just wanted to come home and see my friends and hang out."

"You weren't wrong to want that, Drake. Like I said, it wasn't about you. It was just Melanie, feeling frustrated that she wasn't old enough to do what she wanted. Your dad was hard on her, too. The older she got, the more he seemed to treat her like a child. He even followed us once when we went to a party to make sure we weren't lying about where we were going."

"Are you serious?"

"Yes. He made up a story when Melanie confronted him. He said he thought she'd forgotten her wallet, but it was her mom's wallet in his hand, and I'm pretty sure he knew that. It's so tragically ironic that he wasn't watching her the one time he needed to be."

"And that thought has been slowly destroying him."

"How is he doing now? Melanie told me he heard voices in his head, and noises could trigger flashbacks to his military experience. She said he rarely slept well, and sometimes he'd pace the perimeter of the property late at night as if he was waiting for a foreign army to attack. As time went on, it didn't feel like he was protecting her from the outside world. It felt like he was her jailer."

"I didn't think it was that bad."

"Would you know if it was? You were gone most of the year."

"That's true," he said with a frown. "But we talked."

"Did you ever find her diary?"

"No. We looked everywhere for it."

"She said she didn't like the diary at first. It felt weird to write about her feelings, but then she started loving it. She took the diary everywhere we went. Sometimes when I was setting up a shot, she was writing in the diary. I never asked her what she wrote. I felt like we were so close. I knew what was going on with her. But later…after…I wondered if I did know what was going on. But that's because I'm looking for a reason for Melanie to vanish, and maybe the only reason is a terrible, tragic crime of opportunity."

A darkness entered his gaze. "It could have been that, but my gut tells me it was more personal. I think somewhere in your head you know that. I need your help, Willow."

"I told you I can't remember anything."

"Maybe you will if you try."

Anger ran through me. "You don't think I've tried, Drake?"

"I think you ran away and stopped thinking about Melanie because it was too painful. But I need you to think about her now. I need you to help me find out what happened to her because Melanie and Kelsey are connected."

"These are two completely different situations."

"They're not, Willow. All the same people are involved. Whoever took Melanie probably took Kelsey."

"Why? Why?" I practically shouted.

"That's what we have to figure out. The best way, maybe the only way, to save your sister is to find out what happened to Melanie."

"That will take too long. It has been almost ten years."

"Then we better start now. Before someone else disappears—someone like you."

His words reminded me of how close I'd come to drowning, to vanishing in the dark of the night, with no one around to know what had happened to me.

If James or Carter had pushed me into the water, how could I say for sure that one or both of them hadn't hurt Kelsey, hadn't hurt Melanie? I'd already discovered two secrets. *How many more were there?*

The idea of digging deep into the past terrified me. I was afraid of the pain, of what I couldn't remember, but I couldn't keep running away. Kelsey's life was at stake, and maybe so was mine.

"Well?" Drake asked.

CHAPTER SIXTEEN

"ALL RIGHT," I said. "I'm in. I'll help you."

Relief flooded his gaze. "Good." Drake got up and walked over to the closet. He grabbed a big box, brought it over, and set it on the coffee table. "This is everything I know about Melanie. I've read it all a million times, but I need your eye for detail. I need you to look at everything and tell me what I'm missing."

He lifted the lid, and I saw about ten file folders stuffed with paper. "Are those the police files?"

He pulled out one folder. "This is the police report." He set it on the table and grabbed another file. "This is from a private investigator I hired. The rest are my notes on the case."

"You have all this, and you need me?" I asked in bewilderment.

"Yes, because there are more questions here than answers. And you are on the inside. You know at least a certain subset of players better than I do."

"I'm not an investigator. Ben will be a better ally for you."

"Well, Ben is otherwise engaged. And I told you that he backed off even before Kelsey disappeared."

"What about Ben's father? Have you tried to sit down and talk to him since you got back this week?"

"No. The sheriff made his thoughts clear on many other occasions. He'd given me the file, and he was done discussing the case. I think he regrets now that he gave me any information at all, because small inconsistencies and comments are what led me to two lies, the one told by Ben, and the other by James."

"Do you think the sheriff was just incompetent, or that he didn't want to solve the case?"

"Could be either or a combination of both. The rich summer tourists donated to the sheriff's benevolent fund and contributed to some of his other charities. Sheriff Ryan was in tight with your parents and their circle of friends."

"I can't believe he would let donations get in the way of justice, especially for a local girl."

"Something got in the way."

"Maybe he was just incompetent. Ben always said his dad didn't like to work that much. That's why he was happy to stay on the island and be a small-town sheriff."

"Like I said, the sheriff could have been bad at his job, but he also could have been protecting someone, maybe even his son. If the sheriff thought Ben might be involved in Melanie's disappearance, it would explain why the investigation sputtered out so quickly. He wanted the case to be over. He wanted people to forget. And for the most part, that's exactly what happened."

I frowned, thinking back to my conversation with Ben's dad at the station. "Sheriff Ryan said something to me earlier today. He was annoyed that Ben was keeping him waiting in the hall. He told me he'd always looked out for his son, and that Ben had never appreciated everything he had done to protect him. After what you just said, it makes me wonder. But am I reading something into an innocent comment? A lot of parents don't think their kids are grateful for what they've done for them."

"Did he say anything else?"

"He said I must have had a guardian angel the night I blacked out. That someone must have been trying to protect me. The way he looked at me was weird, almost like he was implying that he'd been the one to do that, but that's impossible. He never protected me from anything. And after Melanie died, I had to sit in his office and answer questions for a long time. Did you read my statement?"

"I did. It was one paragraph long."

"What? I talked to Sheriff Ryan for at least an hour."

"Well, when he wrote it up, it boiled down to a paragraph."

"I guess that's because I didn't remember anything. There was nothing to put in the report except I didn't know where I was the night before or what happened to Melanie."

"That sums it up. Maybe Sheriff Ryan was protecting you by not bringing you back for questioning."

"He would have had no reason to protect me. I was a…nobody."

"You're a Kent. You're hardly a nobody," he said dryly.

"I may have the last name, but I never fit in my family."

"Did you try? Melanie told me you liked to be in the shadows. You were uncomfortable with the spotlight."

"She said that to me, too, that I needed to stop being invisible, stop being the one taking pictures and watching life through my lens. She wanted me to be living, not spectating. I wanted the same." I bit down on my lip as memories swamped me. "Melanie and I had plans to go to Italy after she got out of high school. She wanted to eat pizza in Rome, and I wanted to photograph everything: the monuments, the food, the people, and the landscape. She got a book on basic Italian words, and we'd practice them when we were at the beach. We had a couple of phrases we were sure we would need."

"Like what?"

"Where's the restroom? How much does this cost? And the most important one—where do we meet the cute boys?" I smiled at the memory. "Of course, we weren't really going to say that." I shook my head again. "We probably wouldn't have even gone. Your parents wouldn't have permitted it."

"Probably not."

"But it was a nice dream. Life can be so cruel."

"Did you go to Italy without her?"

"No. I haven't gone anywhere. We talked about so many

places, but I thought it would be too lonely to go on my own. It would feel wrong. If Melanie couldn't go, I shouldn't go."

"Is that your penance for not remembering the night?"

I hadn't really looked at it that way, but he was right. "Yes, I think it is." I met his gaze. "What's your penance, Drake?"

"I can't move on with my life until I know what happened to her, and I get justice."

"What if neither of those things happen?"

"I don't know, but I'm not ready to stop trying." He tipped his head toward the files. "Somewhere in there is a clue. I just have to find it. I've looked at everything so many times, I'm probably missing something."

"I will help you, but it's after midnight, and I'm exhausted. I'll come back tomorrow. I'm going to join one of the search parties in the morning, but I can stop by after that." I got to my feet. "I'm going to dress and then I'll need you to give me a ride home."

"No problem," he said as he rose. "I just hope you don't change your mind between now and tomorrow."

"I won't. This isn't just about Melanie, it's also about Kelsey," I said. "I can't lose another person I love. I'm also not willing to let someone get away with almost killing me. I'm ready to step up and do what needs to be done." I lifted my chin in the air as I squared my shoulders. I'd never considered myself a particularly brave person. But I needed to be that person for my sister and for Melanie.

Melanie's Diary—July 28th

Boys suck! Instead of hanging out with us on Friday nights, some of the guys have started having poker parties, no girls allowed.

I blame Drake for this. Ever since he came home from college, he's been into poker. He likes the competition and the mind games. He says there's nothing better than a good bluff.

I think there are a lot of things that are better, but the guys love to follow Drake. It's funny how popular he is with both the rich kids and the locals. They all love him. The guys want to be his bro and the girls want to make out with him. I think part of his appeal is that he just doesn't care if he's popular. He's so confident in who he is. He knows exactly what he wants in life. He's going to be a reporter. He's going to break big news stories. He's going to change the world.

I'm sure all that will happen, because Drake is stubborn. He won't quit, no matter what. Sometimes, that's a real drag. If he can't do something he thinks he can do, he'll just keep trying over and over again. We once stayed at the batting cage for over an hour because he couldn't believe he couldn't hit the ball over the homerun line when he was such a good hitter. I bet some of the girls who like him would not like him so much if they knew how annoying he can be.

Mom says I should be glad I have a popular big brother. It hasn't helped me at all. Most of his friends treat me like a kid, and I am not a kid. I'm sixteen. I'm practically a woman. With a woman's needs. Okay, even I'm laughing now. I don't know about a woman's needs, but I do know what desire feels like, that tingly feeling you get when something amazing is about to happen. My heart flutters and my stomach jumps around, and I get this restless, reckless feeling. It's actually amazing.

Except it doesn't happen all that often. Especially now that the guys are into poker.

Tonight, Willow, Jenny, and I spied on them while they were playing in Ben's garage. There were seven of them in the garage: Ben, Dillon and Drake representing the locals, and Gage, James, Alex, and Carter from Chambers' Point. They had the door open because it's so hot. They were drinking beers and burping, which was disgusting, and then James started talking about sex.

That was interesting. It sounds like he and Brooklyn get into some weird stuff. Although Gage asked him if he really did that shit with Brooklyn, and James just laughed.

I think James is kind of a pig. I bet he's not faithful to Brooklyn. He's too slimy. He's good-looking, but I don't trust him.

When everyone started asking Drake about his sex life, I made Jenny and Willow leave. I do not want to hear about who my brother is hooking up with. That is too gross.

To get back at the boys, we went down to the beach and tried to pick up some new guys. They don't live up at Chamber's Point. These guys are from the new development by Moss Landing. New-money kids. I thought a couple of them were cute, but Jenny and Willow weren't interested. I think they both wished they were still spying on the game in Ben's garage. Willow is still into Drake. They've been meeting at the newspaper office. I don't know what's going on there. I think Drake is going to break her heart, but she won't talk to me about him. I don't know who Jenny is into. I think it might be Carter or Alex. She seems to flip-flop between them.

I was right to make them leave. We can't keep hoping certain guys take interest in us. There are plenty of fish in the sea, as my mom likes to say. I'm thinking we need some new fish. We're halfway through the summer and none of us are that happy about our love lives, mostly because we don't have love lives. Maybe that will change. Fingers crossed!

CHAPTER SEVENTEEN

AFTER A FEW HOURS OF SLEEP, I got up early on Thursday morning, meeting Brooklyn downstairs at eight.

"I was just about to leave," Brooklyn said, giving me an impatient look. "Where's the Lexus? I didn't see it in the garage."

"I lost my key, so I left it downtown. I'll get it later."

"That's great. You need to get it as soon as we come back. What if Mom and Dad want to go somewhere?"

"I'll get it right after we return. Are Mom and Dad joining the search party?" I asked, as I put on my jacket.

"No. They're staying here."

Which meant they probably didn't care that I'd left the Lexus at Willie's. Brooklyn just liked to remind me of how careless I could be, not that she had any idea what had actually happened.

As Brooklyn drove us across town, I wondered if I should tell her about James and Carter and our conversation at Willie's, or whether I should tell her about getting shoved into the harbor and almost drowning, but she wasn't making it easy to say anything. She'd turned on the radio and amped up the volume. Speaking over the music would not be easy. Clearly, she didn't want to talk to me. But I wanted to talk to her.

I turned down the music. "Brooklyn, I overheard you and James talking in your room last night."

She shot me a dark, wary look. "This morning is about Kelsey. It's about finding our sister."

"Yes, it is, but last night you were talking about Melanie, about covering up for James. Why did you lie for him?"

A long minute passed before Brooklyn said, "I loved him. I wanted to protect him."

It was such a simple answer, and yet there were so many complicated consequences to her decision. "That was wrong."

"Yes, it was." She glanced over at me. "You're surprised I know that?"

"I am. I'm also surprised you told me the truth."

"James had nothing to do with Melanie's disappearance. He got drunk, and he passed out on the beach. When he woke up, he came to our house and begged me to sneak him inside. He couldn't go home. He didn't remember the code. He didn't want to wake up his parents. They'd threatened to take him out of college if he had another bad incident with alcohol. He was already on probation. He promised me he'd go to rehab if I just let him stay there. When I said yes, I didn't know Melanie was going to disappear. I didn't find out until the next morning. And then James asked me to say he'd been with me all night and had left shortly before the police arrived at our house."

"Did you wonder why he needed you to be his alibi if he was innocent?"

"No, because he was trying to keep his drinking a secret from his parents. I knew where he was."

"You knew where he told you he was," I corrected.

"I know James. He's not a violent person. He couldn't hurt anyone, except himself."

I wasn't so sure of that. I remembered the way he'd grabbed me at the bonfire, the way his fingers had ground into my arms. He'd been out of control, and he'd felt strong and overpowering until the alcohol caught up to him and took him down. Before that happened, I'd felt very uneasy.

"It bothered me, though," Brooklyn said. "That lie was always between us."

"So you had some doubts about where he was?"

She stopped at a light and turned her gaze on me. "Yes, but the doubts weren't about Melanie. I thought he might have cheated on me."

"With who?"

"I don't know."

"Did you ever ask him?"

"Not directly."

"Why the hell not? You're always direct. You like to ask the hard questions."

"Not when I'm afraid of the truth. We danced around the subject, but I never asked him flat out. I should have, but I didn't."

"Is that why you broke up?"

"It was part of it. He went to rehab when we got back to college, and for a couple of years after that, he was better. But then he started slipping. There were more weird nights where he would disappear and then show up with no recollection of where he'd been. I couldn't take it anymore. I had to walk away."

"That makes sense."

"Does it?" she asked, an uncertain gleam in her eyes. "Mom thought I should have given him more support. She liked us together."

"She wasn't in the relationship; you were. I think you made the right decision in the break-up, but you made a huge mistake when you covered for James, and you need to clean that slate."

"It won't matter now," she said, as she drove through the inter-section. "And even if I don't care about James, the lie will hurt Rachel and her parents. What's the point? James didn't see Melanie."

"You keep saying that, but you don't know if it's true," I argued. "He could have cheated on you with Melanie."

Her jaw dropped at that piece of information. She flung me a quick look. "Why would you say that? Do you know something? Were they together?"

"You need to ask James who he was with, and you need to tell Ben that you lied."

Brooklyn didn't answer, as she slowed the car down and turned into the parking lot by the nature trail. The lot was crowded with volunteers who had come out for the search, and there was only one spot left.

She turned off the engine and then faced me. "I hear you, Willow, but we need to focus on finding Kelsey right now. That's why we're here."

"You're right. But when we're done searching, you know what you have to do. If you don't, I will."

"You're threatening me, Willow?"

I met her gaze head-on. She flinched a little, as if she wasn't used to my fighting back, which, of course, she wasn't, since I'd rarely fought back when I was a kid. It had been so much easier to just let her have her way, but I couldn't do that anymore. The stakes were too high. "I'm telling you what's going to happen."

"James will be furious if I go to Ben, if I reveal his secret after so many years."

"He already knows the secret is out. I told James I overheard your conversation."

"You did what?"

"I followed James to Willie's last night where he met with Carter, and we had a discussion about James's lies and Carter's secret affair with Kelsey."

She shook her head in disbelief. "I can't believe you did that." Despite her words, there was a gleam of respect in her gaze. "What did they say?"

"James told the same story to me he told you. Carter admitted to the affair and said he was in love with Kelsey but that she'd chosen Gage. He'd tried to get her to call off the wedding, but she refused. He begged me not to say anything to anyone about their relationship, because I would hurt her, and when she came back, she'd be humiliated. But I can't worry more about possible humiliation than getting Kelsey back safely. That's all that matters."

"I can't believe he told you all that. I also can't believe Kelsey was with him. Are you sure they actually slept together?"

"Yes. Carter confirmed it."

Brooklyn gave me a bewildered look. "Kelsey never told me. I thought we were so close. Did Carter say anything else?"

"No. But there's something else you should know. After I left James and Carter in the bar, I went to the dock to see where Kelsey's shoe had been found. Someone came up behind me and shoved me into the water. I almost drowned."

Brooklyn gave me another shocked look. "Do you think Carter or James pushed you in?"

"I don't know. They didn't like our conversation."

"This is…crazy," Brooklyn said, waving a confused hand in the air. "I don't understand anything that's going on. Did you go to the police? Did you tell them what happened?"

"I called Ben last night and left him a message, but he hasn't gotten back to me. I was going to call again this morning, but I didn't want to distract him or any of the other deputies from looking for Kelsey, so I haven't gotten into it, but I will."

"You made the right choice. The focus has to be on Kelsey." Brooklyn paused. "Are you all right, Willow?"

I was surprised she'd taken a moment to ask. "Yes, I'm still shaken, but physically I'm fine. When I was flailing in the water, I thought I might disappear without a trace, like Melanie, like Kelsey. It was terrifying."

"But you can swim. You were able to get out."

"Drake rescued me. I was struggling with the weight of my clothes."

"Drake? What was he doing down there? Was he at Willie's too?"

"No. He went down to the dock for the same reason I did, to see where Kelsey's shoe had been found."

"Or he went there to hurt you."

I shook my head. "He didn't push me in."

"You don't know that for sure, do you?"

"He saved my life."

Brooklyn didn't look convinced, and I didn't have time to explain further. "The volunteers are gathering for instructions. We should go."

"Let's not say anything to the others about any of this," Brooklyn said.

I wasn't surprised she wanted me to be silent, but at the moment I was willing to do that.

We got out of the car and made our way to the back of the group. Rachel, Dahlia, and Trina were already there, as were Alex, Peter, Gage, Carter, and Preston. I wondered where James was, but there was no time for questions. A deputy gave us quick instructions and then passed out maps for the area.

Brooklyn, Trina, Dahlia, Rachel, and I formed one group, while the guys were ahead of us and a dozen or so other volunteers behind us.

As we moved through the thick trees and foliage, I remembered the last time I'd done this, the second day after Melanie disappeared. I'd thought with every step that we'd find her, but we never had, and that memory brought a heavy weight of hopelessness down on my shoulders. I could tell myself it was different this time, but it felt very much the same.

We walked through the woods for over two hours. With each passing minute, I felt more anxious and more panicky, afraid we would find something and terrified we would not. Brooklyn, Trina, and Rachel were also more subdued than they normally were. They didn't include me in their conversation, but that wasn't unusual. I'd gone back into my shell, staying in the background, and they were happy to leave me there.

It was almost noon when we ended up back in the parking lot, having found absolutely nothing. An additional group would start in a different area at one, but I was done. I'd promised to meet up with Drake, and I didn't think I could stand another few hours in the woods, worrying about whether I was going to trip over the body of my sister. I didn't want her to be out in some forsaken part of the island. I wanted her to be safe somewhere. I wanted there to be a happy ending.

Brooklyn and I didn't talk on the way home. When she turned on the radio, I was fine to just let the music roll through me and try to relax.

When Brooklyn and I walked into the house, our parents were in the dining room. There was a plentiful buffet of food set out on the side table, as well as a coffee and tea service.

My mother was listlessly stirring her tea, a full plate of salad untouched in front of her. My father was on his phone while he worked his way through some pasta.

When we entered the room, my mom looked up, new light entering her eyes. "Did you find anything?"

"No. Sorry, Mom," Brooklyn said.

"Well, I didn't think Kelsey was out there, anyway. She's probably hiding out in a luxury hotel room."

My mother was definitely clinging to that narrative.

"I'm going upstairs to shower," Brooklyn said. "I can't seem to get warm."

I could relate to that. I was shivering, too, but I was more interested in coffee and food than in a shower. I needed some energy. There was still a lot to do. I filled a mug with coffee and then put a couple of sandwiches on a plate and took it to the table.

"Did Lorraine make all the food?" I asked as I sat down.

"What?" My mother gave me a confused look.

"The food." I tipped my head toward the buffet. "There's a lot."

"Oh. People keep dropping things off. Marie came by with a salad. Eileen sent over pasta and sandwiches. Not that anyone feels like eating."

I felt a little guilty that I'd just taken a big bite of a turkey pesto sandwich, but I needed to eat. I needed energy to get through the rest of the day.

The doorbell suddenly rang, and my father immediately stood up. "I'll get it." He waved us back into our seats.

I had a feeling my father wanted to protect my mother in case someone had arrived to deliver bad news. A moment later, I heard a woman's voice, and then my dad and Jenny walked into the dining room. Relief ran through me.

"Oh, it's you, Jenny," my mother said in a less than welcoming tone.

"I'm sorry to bother you," Jenny said. "I just wanted to check in."

"Of course," my father said. "Have a seat. Would you like some lunch?"

"No, thanks." Jenny sat down at the table, giving us a wary look. "I wanted to talk about the wedding."

"No." My mother shook her head, giving Jenny a warning look. "We're not calling off the wedding. We're not changing anything. The rehearsal is still tomorrow at four and the wedding will be Saturday at five. That's what's happening. Kelsey will be back, and she'll want everything to be the way she planned it."

My mother's declaration was met with silence. I didn't agree with her. My father probably didn't, either, but neither one of us wanted to upset my mother any more than she already was.

Jenny tucked her hair behind her ears, then said, "Okay, that's good to know."

"Monica," my father began.

My mother quickly cut him off. "I said no, Larry."

"But I'm sure there are food orders, staff..." My father's voice trailed at the stubborn glint in my mother's eyes. "All right. We'll leave everything as it is."

"Is that all, Jenny?" my mother asked.

"Is there anything I can do to help?" Jenny asked.

"You can help by making sure my daughter has the perfect wedding. She'll be home soon, and I want to tell her that every-thing is set."

My mother was barely holding it together. We could all hear the quiver in her voice.

"It's all set," Jenny reassured her.

"Good." My mother pushed back her chair and left the room.

"Dad," I began.

He stood up. "I'll talk to her, but it doesn't really matter at this point. We'll pay for everything, whether or not it happens."

"I'm sorry. Maybe I shouldn't have come," Jenny said, as my

father left the dining room. "My boss asked me to find out what I could. But I didn't mean to be insensitive."

"You did nothing wrong. You had to ask the question. There's just not a good answer."

"I was really hoping that Kelsey would be back by now."

"Me, too. I went on a search this morning. It was nice to see so many people looking for her, but it was also difficult. It reminded me of the times we searched for Melanie."

"Those were hard, wanting to find something, but not wanting to at the same time."

"That's exactly how I felt all morning. Can I get you some coffee, food? There's enough to feed an army."

"I'm not hungry, but coffee would be great. I can get it myself."

"No worries." I got up, filled a mug, and brought it back to the table.

"Thanks." Jenny took a sip. "Did you speak to Carter?"

I suddenly had the feeling that this was the real reason she'd come by. "I did. He confirmed that he was in love with Kelsey and that he didn't want her to marry Gage."

"Really? He actually said that?"

"He did."

She blew out a breath. "Well, if Carter loved her, he didn't hurt her."

"I hope not. But if Gage found out…"

"Right. But Willow we are leaping to a lot of conclusions."

"I know, and I don't like any of the conclusions. But I can't overlook the fact that Melanie's disappearance and Kelsey's disappearance involve a lot of the same people."

Jenny frowned. "You really think Kelsey's disappearance is connected to Melanie?"

"I'm leaning that way. I had a long talk with Drake last night. He is absolutely convinced that they're related. And he has a huge box of files on Melanie's case. He's digging deep. He has already found some discrepancies in statements."

"Whose statements?"

"Gage, James…who knows who else?"

"I know Gage lied, but James? What did he lie about?"

"Where he was the night Melanie disappeared. His car was spotted in town, but he was supposedly on the beach. Brooklyn covered for him."

"Wow, I can't believe that. Is James a suspect?"

"I don't know. Maybe down the road, he will be. Right now, we have to focus on Kelsey, and James was too drunk on Tuesday night to do anything to her."

"I heard he was drunk at the bonfire. I didn't see him, though."

"Carter and Rachel got him out of there fast. Anyway, I'm continually being surprised with lies. Drake was right about our group. Not everyone was telling the truth."

"That's true. And Drake is determined to uncover every last lie. He even wants to write a book about Melanie, but I think that's a bad idea. It feels like an invasion of her privacy. She's not here to say if she wants a book to be written about her. And..." Jenny licked her lips as she gazed at me with indecision.

"What?" I asked.

"It's not something I'm sure about, and I've never told anyone, not even Drake, because I don't know if it's true. Or if I saw what I thought I saw."

"What are you talking about? What do you think you saw?"

"I shouldn't say."

"Why not? It's way past time to be keeping secrets."

"Will you promise not to tell anyone?"

"No," I said flatly. "I can't make any promises, so tell me or don't tell me. It's up to you."

"All right. I know you loved Melanie, so you won't want to do anything that will hurt her."

"That's true."

"About a week before Melanie vanished, I saw her at the pharmacy looking at pregnancy tests."

Shock ran through me. "Are you sure?"

"Well, when she saw me, she dropped the test and grabbed a box of condoms off the shelf."

Pregnancy test? Condoms? My mind whirled with the implication. "She never told me she had sex with anyone. I know she made out with some guys, but she never said anything went further than that. Did she buy the condoms?"

"No. She made some joke about the different sizes, then she put the box back, and walked across the aisle to get tampons. I told her if she wanted to buy condoms, I wasn't going to judge. She said she'd never buy condoms in town, because her father would probably find out and kill her. I said I'd buy them if she wanted them. She just laughed and said she was good, and she was just kidding."

"And you told no one this?"

"I didn't. When Sheriff Ryan asked me if Melanie had a boyfriend, I said no, because I didn't think she did. And it wasn't like I saw her buy the condoms or the pregnancy test. She could have just been goofing around."

"The sheriff asked me about Melanie's love life, too. I said the same thing you did, that I wasn't aware of anyone serious, but she'd kissed a few boys that summer, including Ben."

"I'm sure Sheriff Ryan didn't want to hear that."

"He didn't really react. Did Ben ever say if he and Melanie hooked up?"

"No. He never said that. And she liked other guys, too: Carter, Alex, that red-haired kid, Joshua."

"I don't remember him."

"He only came one summer."

I sighed. "I can't imagine Melanie having sex and not telling me. We were so close." My words felt like an echo of what Brooklyn had said when she'd found out that Kelsey had slept with Carter. Maybe we were never as close with people as we thought.

"This is why I'm worried about Drake writing a book," Jenny continued. "Melanie's private life should stay private."

"Well, that's between Drake and his parents."

"It sounds like you're getting involved with Drake."

"Not in the writing of a book. But if there is a connection between Melanie and Kelsey, then I have to find out what it is."

"Be careful around Drake, Willow. His obsession knows no

bounds. If you get on that ride with him, you may never get off. I don't think that's good for either of you."

"Unfortunately, I don't have a choice. Until Kelsey comes home, I have to chase every lead."

"I understand. I should go. I hope there's good news soon."

"Me, too."

After Jenny left, I finished my lunch, grabbed the emergency credit card from the kitchen drawer as well as an extra car key, and called a cab. I probably could have asked Jenny for a ride to Willie's, but then I would have had to explain why I'd gone there and who I was with, and I couldn't go through all that again.

Despite Jenny's warning about Drake, I had already promised to help him, and I intended to do that. First, I wanted to get my car.

I arrived at Willie's a little before two. The bar was open, but there were only a few cars in the lot. I slid behind the wheel quickly, feeling nervous about being in the area by myself. Then I drove a few blocks to the public parking lot across from the restaurant.

When I entered the Crab Pot, I didn't see Sylvie in the dining room, just a hostess and a couple of servers I didn't recognize. I jogged up the stairs to the apartment. The door was partly open, so I knocked, then walked in.

"Drake?" I called out.

The man standing by the coffee table whirled around, but it wasn't Drake; it was his father, Holt Maddox.

Holt stared at me in shock, his eyes oddly unfocused. He was still a big man, but he looked much older than I remembered, and his hair had turned completely white. He was holding a photograph in his hand. I could see it was one of Melanie, the same one that had been on the missing posters that had been all around town ten years ago.

"You," he said, his expression shifting. "Where is she? Where did you leave her?"

"What?" I asked, surprised by his questions, by his aggressive tone.

He stalked forward, and I instinctively backed up. But I hit the wall, and there was nowhere else to go.

"Melanie. You know where she is. Tell me. I have to get to her."

"I—I don't know where she is," I stuttered.

He moved so close I could feel his breath on my cheek.

"It's going to rain again," he said. "She'll be cold and scared. Tell me where she is. You know."

"I don't know."

"You do." The photo dropped as he put his hands on my shoulders, pressing me against the wall. "Tell me now."

I saw the desperation and anger in his gaze. His hands were gripping me so tightly, I could feel the bruises forming.

"I'm sorry. I can't. Please let me go."

"Tell me where my little girl is," he ordered again. "Or I will make you very sorry."

There was murderous intent in his eyes. I needed to get away. "Mr. Maddox, please. It's me, Willow. I'm Melanie's friend. I love her."

"No. You did this to her. You need to talk."

He pressed me harder against the wall and a terrible fear ran through me.

CHAPTER EIGHTEEN

"You need to stop lying," Holt said. "Tell me where she is."

"I—I can't."

The door suddenly flew open with a bang, and Drake rushed into the room.

"Dad! Let her go." When his father didn't immediately release me, Drake grabbed his arm. "Let her go, Dad," he repeated.

Holt Maddox didn't take his eyes off me. "She knows something. She has to tell us."

"She knows nothing, and you need to let her go. You're hurting her. You don't want to do that, Dad. This is Willow. This is Melanie's friend."

Mr. Maddox's grip on my shoulders finally eased as Drake's words sank into his consciousness. His gaze refocused on my face, no longer murky or panicked. He dropped his hands and stood back, his breathing short and ragged. "I—I'm...sorry."

"What happened?" Drake asked, his worried gaze moving from his father to me and then back to his dad.

"I'm not sure," Holt said in confusion. Then he suddenly gathered himself together. He leaned down and picked the photo up off the floor. "Why do you have this photo and all those files?" He waved his hand toward the files on the table. "What are you doing with the police report?"

Before Drake could answer, Sylvie appeared in the doorway. "What's going on?" she asked with concern. "I heard shouting."

"Do you know what Drake is doing up here?" Holt demanded. "He's got a box of files on Melanie."

"I'm taking another look at the investigation," Drake said. "I still want answers. You know that."

"You're writing that damn book you mentioned earlier. This is about you, not about her. You want to use your sister's disappearance to make money."

I was surprised by Holt's words, by his anger toward Drake.

"It's about Melanie, Dad," Drake said quietly, seeming to take no offense to his father's accusation. "And now it might also be about another missing woman—Kelsey Kent."

"Don't bring my sister into this," I said. "Don't use Kelsey."

"I'm not using her. I'm not using Melanie, either. I'm just saying that it's even more important than ever that we get answers soon."

"Drake is right," Sylvie interjected. "Come on, Holt, let's go downstairs. I'll make you something to eat." She put her hand on her husband's arm, but he shrugged it away.

"I don't want food," he said. "I don't want…anything." He walked out of the apartment without giving me another look.

Sylvie gave me an apologetic smile. "I hope he didn't say something upsetting to you, Willow. He has been really distracted since he heard about Kelsey. It triggered a lot of bad memories."

"I understand."

"I better check on him," Sylvie said, then left the room.

Drake turned to me. "Are you all right, Willow?"

I was hugging my arms around my body, still shaking from Holt's shocking attack. "Your dad looked like he wanted to kill me."

Drake paled. "He wouldn't have done that."

"I don't think you have any idea what he would have done if you hadn't come in. He wasn't all there. His eyes were glazed. Now I know why Melanie said she was sometimes scared of her father."

"She wasn't scared of him."

"Yes, she was. She always said he would never hurt her. But she'd say that repeatedly, like she was trying to convince herself."

"He never touched her."

"How do you know?" I challenged.

"Because I asked her," he admitted. "A few times. I just wanted to make sure. She swore he had never touched her. My mother said the same thing."

"But you had doubts."

Drake ran a hand through his hair. "I didn't want to have doubts, but I worried about her after I left home. My mom told me my father was hard on her. I didn't realize how hard until you told me last night about him following you and Melanie. That surprised me." Drake paused. "But you just said that Melanie told you he never hurt her, so I have to believe her."

"She did say that, but maybe she wouldn't have told me."

"I think she would have. Or she would have told my mom."

"That's true. Where was your dad the night Melanie disappeared?"

"He took a walk like he did every night after dinner. Usually, he was gone an hour or two, but that night he didn't come back until about ten. He mostly went to the beach nearest our house. The ocean waves would calm him down, so he could sleep."

"Did anyone see him that night?"

"Yes. Our neighbor, Frank Young, was walking his dog on the beach at eight thirty. He spoke to my dad for a few minutes, then they parted ways. Frank told the police that my dad seemed the same as always, not particularly friendly, not particularly talkative. But he wasn't agitated. He didn't look stressed." Drake paused. "My father didn't hurt Melanie. He couldn't."

I could see how much he wanted to believe that, and I wanted to believe it, too, because I knew Melanie had loved her dad, despite their problems.

Drake walked over to the couch and sat down, giving me a weary look. "Damn, I don't know long I can keep doing this."

The man I'd been angry with for so many years suddenly

looked broken. There was so much emotion and vulnerability in his eyes that my heart ached for him. What he'd done, whatever he was doing, it was all for Melanie.

I sat on the chair across from him. "Maybe you should stop all this, Drake. It won't bring Melanie back, and clearly, your father doesn't want you to write a book about her."

"It's not about the book. That never has to happen, but I can't stop looking for justice. My sister deserves that. Whoever took her away from us needs to pay. And it's not just about Melanie anymore. It's about Kelsey, too. How did the search go?"

"It was unsuccessful."

"Did Ben ever call you back?"

"No, and I need to talk to him. He needs to know that I was attacked last night, and that Carter and Kelsey had an affair. I should have tried to reach him before now, but when I saw Gage and Carter stomping through the woods for hours on end this morning, it made me wonder how I could think either of them was guilty of something."

"Looking for Kelsey could just be a cover."

"I know. I want to help you, Drake, but I need to talk to Ben first. I'll have a better chance if I just go down to the station than if I try to call him again."

"I'll go with you."

"I don't need you to go with me."

"We'll get farther faster if we work together. Isn't that what you want?"

"What I want is for this nightmare to be over."

He jumped to his feet. "Then let's make that happen."

I was impressed by the renewed energy n his gaze. "You don't stay down for long, do you?"

"No time for that."

Drake had his cocky, confident, relentless fire back, and it made me feel more hopeful. I was going to cling to that feeling as long as I could.

I drove Drake to the station, needing to be in control of at least one thing in my life. When we arrived, we were told Ben was in a meeting, so we waited in the lobby. Drake seemed to get lost in the display case, his gaze focused on the photographs, awards, and mementos displayed there. Those items probably meant more to him than they did to me, since Drake had grown up on the island. I suspected he had a lot of love/hate feelings for his hometown, and for the former sheriff, who was featured extensively in the case.

As the front door opened, I turned to see Dillon come in, wearing ripped jeans and a long-sleeve T-shirt under a navy windbreaker.

"Willow! I've been thinking about you since I heard the bad news. Has Kelsey been found yet?" Dillon asked.

I shook my head. "No. We're waiting to speak to Ben. He's in a meeting."

"I was hoping she was back home by now. I ran into Gage and Carter yesterday down at the beach and joined the search party for as long as I could, but we didn't have any luck."

"Thanks for trying, Dillon."

"I wish I could do more. Kelsey was a cool girl."

I nodded, hating that he'd used past tense. "She'll still be a cool girl when she comes back."

He gave me an apologetic look. "Oh, sorry. I always say the wrong thing."

"You didn't. There is no right thing to say."

Dillon's gaze swung to Drake. "How are you doing, Drake? This has to be rough on you and your family."

"It's triggering a lot of terrible memories," Drake admitted. "How was Gage acting during the search?"

"Uh, I don't know," Dillon said with a shrug. "He was quiet, tense, angry. He didn't speak to me. He and his brothers mostly stayed together." Dillon paused. "Is Ben looking into Gage?"

"Do you think he should?" I asked.

"I always thought the golden boy had a lot of secrets," Dillon muttered.

"Care to be more specific?"

"Gage was always looking out for himself. If he got into trouble, he made sure he didn't take the blame. Drake knows."

"I'm not a fan of Gage," Drake said. "But I also don't want to focus on him so much we miss something or someone else."

"That's true." Dillon glanced down at his watch. "I gotta go. I have to set up a fortieth birthday party at the Rec Center."

"You still work for Party Planet?" I asked him.

"Yep," he said with a shrug. "It's an easy job. You know me, I like easy." He turned to go, then paused. "After I set up the party, I'm going to join another search group this afternoon, the one heading over to the east shore. Will I see you out there?"

"I'm not sure," I said. "But thanks for doing that, Dillon. I really appreciate it."

"I always liked your sister, and I can't stand the thought of another girl never coming back," he said heavily.

"Me, either."

"Drake, if you want to get a beer sometime after we get Kelsey home, let me know," Dillon added. "It's been too long."

"Sounds good."

As Dillon left, the receptionist told us we could go back to Ben's office.

"Looks like we're not the only ones who want to point Ben in Gage's direction," Drake said as he opened the lobby door, and we walked down the hall.

"Dillon definitely doesn't like Gage. But I also wonder if Dillon has a hidden agenda."

Drake gave me a questioning look. "What do you mean?"

"That drug buy Ben went on the night Melanie disappeared... Is it possible Dillon was with him? He was more of a druggie than Ben."

"Rick told me Ben was alone, but Dillon could have been in the car. I don't know. That's a question for Ben."

"But not today's question," I reminded him. "I don't want to take Ben's focus away from Kelsey. If he thinks he has to cover his ass for something he did ten years ago, he may not do what he needs to do now. Let's stick with the information we have on Carter and Kelsey and how that might impact the case."

"I agree." He knocked on Ben's office door, then pushed it open. Ben wasn't alone. His father was there, too. That was disappointing. I wanted to talk to Ben alone.

"What's going on?" Ben asked.

"We need to speak to you," I said, adding, "Alone, if that's possible."

Tom Ryan bristled. "Alone? I'm working on this case with Ben. I'm trying to save your sister, Willow. If you know something, you can tell us both."

"Why don't you give us a minute, Dad?" Ben suggested.

The former sheriff's cheeks turned bright red, his eyes gleaming with anger. "I know more about Melanie's case than any of you, and if you think Kelsey's disappearance is tied to Melanie, than you need me in on everything. Unless you have something you want to say about me?" he asked. "Do you want to accuse me of trying to protect someone again, Drake?"

"Are you protecting someone again?" Drake countered.

Tom shook his head. "I never did that. And I've done everything I can to help you and your family, Drake. I even turned over all my files to show you that the department has got nothing to hide, but you're still here stirring the pot. You want to blame the people who are trying to help you." Tom's gaze pivoted toward me. "And you're letting him. He's going to derail the investigation. If anyone needs to leave this room, it's him. The rest of us want to find your sister, not retrace a ten-year-old investigation."

"Dad, stop!" Ben put up his hand. "I need your help to do what we just talked about. Can you do that now? And let me deal with Drake and Willow?"

Tom looked like he wanted to tell Ben to go to hell, but finally he said, "Fine. I'll go. Because I know what's important."

When the door closed behind him, I blew out a breath, then turned back to Ben.

"What do you want to talk to me about?" Ben asked wearily.

He had dark shadows under his eyes and looked nothing like the carefree kid I'd grown up with. But then, I might not have really known that carefree kid the way I thought I did.

"I have some information that might impact the investigation."

"Tell me. I could use a lead."

"Carter was having an affair with Kelsey."

Surprise raised his brows and widened his eyes. "Are you sure?"

"Yes."

"How do you know this?"

"Carter told me last night. He admitted that he's in love with Kelsey and that he didn't want her to marry his brother."

"Well, this would have been helpful information to have yesterday."

"I called you last night and left a message."

"You should have left that on the message. But sorry for not calling you back. I've been working nonstop since your sister disappeared. Does Gage know about his brother and Kelsey? If so, he would have a motive to hurt Kelsey. And he was the last one to see her before she vanished."

"I don't want to believe Gage would hurt Kelsey. Carter implied that it was a secret, but you need to talk to both of them," I replied. "I also want you to know that Carter begged me not to come forward with the information. He thought it was an invasion of Kelsey's privacy."

"You made the right decision," Ben said. "And if Carter wanted the wedding to be called off, he also had a motive to get Kelsey away from his brother, which is exactly what happened. Was there anything else?"

I frowned, thinking I would just be adding another distraction. "It can wait."

"No, it can't," Drake said firmly.

"Well, someone tell me," Ben said, his gaze moving between us.

"Someone shoved Willow into the harbor last night," Drake

said. "She could have drowned if I hadn't come by at the right moment."

"Damn! You should have called 911, Willow, instead of my personal number. They would have gotten an officer to you immediately."

"I was fine. Drake pulled me out of the water."

"Did you see the person who attacked you?"

"No. They came up behind me. I had gone to look at the location where Kelsey's shoe was found."

He sighed. "You already know we don't have cameras in that location."

"I do, but here's the thing. I had been at Willie's speaking to Carter and James right before I went down to the dock. They were both angry with me for digging into their personal business."

"I get why Carter was angry. But James?" Ben gave me a questioning look.

"That's a story for another time."

"You're here. Get it out," Ben ordered.

"It turns out that James lied about being with Brooklyn the night Melanie disappeared. He said he was passed out on the beach, but there are conflicting stories."

"Conflicting stories?"

I looked to Drake. "Do you want to fill him in?"

"A witness saw James's red Audi in town around ten o'clock that night, so he wasn't on the beach, and he wasn't with Brooklyn at that point," Drake said.

"Brooklyn covered for him," I added. "But we don't want to derail your investigation into Kelsey's disappearance with all this right now."

"Got it." Ben gave Drake a speculative look. "That was in the police report? I never saw that."

"It was buried in a long witness statement made by Mrs. Wiggins."

"Oh. Right. Mrs. Wiggins went on for three pages about how Hawk Island was becoming riddled with crime," Ben said. "I guess I missed the mention of James."

"It was a mention of his car, which I'm sure the deputy taking the statement wouldn't have known had any significance to any of the other witness statements."

I was surprised Drake wasn't expressing anger about the missed detail, but maybe he was trying to stay on Ben's good side now.

"James did confirm that he lied about being with Brooklyn all night," I put in. "But he told me he was passed out on the beach and that he didn't want his parents to know. That's why he lied. Anyway, we can deal with that later."

"Is that it?" Ben asked.

"Yes."

"You need to be careful, Willow." Ben gave me a pointed look. "I'd say the same thing to Drake, but he's not going to listen. You should. You could have died last night."

His words sent a chill through me. "I know. I'm going to be more careful."

As I finished speaking, Ben's desk phone rang.

"Hold on a sec." He picked up the phone. "Yes? What?"

My stomach turned over. Ben was getting news and judging by his expression, it wasn't good. My body trembled as panic ran through me. I moved closer to Drake, impulsively slipping my hand into his. He squeezed my fingers as we waited for Ben to get off the phone.

"All right," Ben said. "I'll be there as soon as I can."

"Kelsey?" I bit out as he hung up the phone.

"No." He gave us a grim look. "Carter Chadwick overdosed. He's on his way to the medical center."

I gasped in shock. I was extremely glad I was hanging onto Drake, as I felt like the ground had just shifted beneath me once more. "Is Carter going to be all right?"

"I don't know. I have to go."

"We're going, too," Drake said. "We'll meet you at the medical center."

"I don't think any of the Chadwicks will want to see you there," Ben said.

"Well, I don't think I care," Drake said. "And you don't want to waste time arguing with me, Ben."

"Or me," I added.

Ben shrugged at our united front. "Fine. But let me do the talking."

CHAPTER NINETEEN

THE HAWK ISLAND MEDICAL CENTER was in a two-story building about two miles from the sheriff's department. It had been built twelve years ago, funded by many of the generous summer residents, including my parents. They'd become concerned about the level and quality of medical care on the island when Brooklyn had broken her hand while hiking. That concern had encouraged my mother to lead a fundraising campaign to build a new center. The other families at Chambers' Point had also been donors. It was a nice reminder that my circle of family and friends had done some good things on this island.

I wanted to keep that perspective, because watching secrets and lies unravel around me the past few days had colored my thinking. People I'd thought I could trust had become strangers and suspects in crimes too horrible to contemplate. My mind was probably exaggerating the feeling of evil lurking all around me. At least, I hoped it was. Because the alternative was terrifying.

Drake and I caught up to Ben as he entered the facility, and we accompanied him down the hall to the emergency department where the Chadwicks were waiting. Eileen and Sean were seated on a long bench. Eileen was crying, and Sean had his arms around her, trying to console her. Preston was talking to a nurse while Gage was pacing.

Gage looked like he'd aged ten years since he'd first arrived on the island. He was normally very put together in expensive clothes, with blond hair styled, and face shaven. But his hair was wind-blown, and there were dark shadows under his blue eyes, a growth of beard on his face. His clothes were wrinkled. It didn't look like he'd slept in a very long time.

Ben walked over to Gage. "What happened?"

"My father found Carter on the floor of his bathroom. There was an empty bottle of Vicodin next to him," Gage said tightly.

"We don't know if the bottle was full to start," Sean put in. "It's possible Carter had a heart attack, and the pills had nothing to do with it."

Sean was already putting together a narrative he could live with. I couldn't fault him for that. He was desperate to believe his son had not tried to take his own life. That thought hit me hard. I'd been thinking accidental overdose all the way over here, but perhaps it had been deliberate.

"I'm sorry," Ben said. "When was the last time any of you spoke to Carter?"

"We searched together for Kelsey this morning," Gage replied. "He left at lunchtime. I haven't seen him since then."

"What about the rest of you?" Ben asked.

"What does it matter when any of us talked to Carter?" Sean asked. He set Eileen to the side and got to his feet. "This isn't a crime scene, Ben. Our son…he had a medical emergency. We don't need you here. We need you looking for Kelsey." Sean's gaze moved to Drake. "What the hell is he doing here?"

"Drake is with me," Ben said before Drake could reply.

"Then you should both leave," Sean said coldly.

"I need a word with Gage," Ben said, ignoring Sean's comment.

I was surprised at the look of determination on Ben's face. I thought he might back down from wanting to talk to Gage with

Carter's life hanging on the line. But he was in sheriff mode, direct and decisive.

"No." Sean shook his head. "Don't talk to him, Gage."

"Dad, it's fine. I want to talk to Ben. I can't do anything here, but Kelsey is still out there, and I need to find her."

Gage's words hit exactly the right note for a man who was desperate to find the woman he loved and wasn't scared to talk to the sheriff about her. I'd started to think he was guilty of something, but maybe he wasn't.

As Ben and Gage moved down the hall, Drake followed. Before I joined them, I turned to Eileen. "I'm so sorry. I pray Carter will be all right."

"He has to be. He's my baby boy."

I felt so sad for her. She looked completely devastated, and I had no words to comfort her, so I told her what she'd told me earlier in the week. "Don't give up hope. Carter is young and strong. He can recover from this."

"Will you tell your parents, Willow?"

"Yes, of course."

As Eileen started crying again, Sean sat back down and pulled her into his arms. I was glad to see that. She needed her husband, even if he was a cheater.

I hurried down the hall and through the lobby. I caught up with the men by the large fountain in front of the medical center.

"I'm sorry about the timing, but this can't wait," Ben said.

"What do you need?" Gage asked, his gaze more wary now.

"I've heard that Carter and Kelsey were romantically involved," Ben replied. "Is that true?"

Gage's eyes widened in disbelief. "No, it's not true. Who told you that? One of these two?" He waved an angry hand in our direction. "You can't believe anything Drake says. And Willow—what the fuck? What are you trying to do? Are you that jealous of your sister that you'd try to destroy her reputation?"

I shivered at the angry glare in his eyes, but I refused to let his fury intimidate me. "Carter told me last night," I said evenly. "They got together in Paris."

"You're lying."

"I'm telling you exactly what Carter told me. He also said he was in love with Kelsey, and he didn't want her to marry you."

Gage shook his head in bewilderment. "Why are you saying this? Are you trying to get some reaction out of me? Shake me up? Shake me down?" He refocused on Drake. "Brooklyn told me you were going to cause problems for me, for Kelsey, for the wedding, because you still think I had something to do with Melanie's disappearance."

"I do believe that, but we're talking about Kelsey and Carter," Drake said. "Willow is only repeating what Carter told her."

"She's lying."

"James was there," I said, drawing Gage's attention back to me. "We were at Willie's last night. James heard the same thing I did. You can ask him."

"No way. This isn't true. Kelsey loves me." He choked on his words. "She loves me," he repeated, but his voice wasn't as strong this time. His anger was slowly replaced by pain.

"I'm sorry, Gage," I said. "I didn't want to believe it, either."

"You're talking about my fiancée and my brother, the two people I trust the most in this world."

"I guess it's safe to assume you had no idea," Ben said quietly.

"No. I didn't have a clue." Gage took a quick breath. "But Carter has been acting weird for weeks. I thought he was jealous. I've got my life together, and he doesn't. He acted like an ass at my bachelor party last month, but I figured he was just feeling sorry for himself."

"He probably was feeling sorry for himself," Drake said. "You were marrying the girl he wanted."

"But Kelsey chose you in the end, Gage," I put in. "She wanted to marry you, not Carter."

He gave me a sorrowful look. "Maybe she wasn't sure. Everyone has been saying how Kelsey probably just got the jitters and needed to think before the wedding. That made little sense to me. We were both ready to get married. But maybe she wasn't…

God! Maybe she was in love with Carter. Maybe that's why she ran away. She couldn't face me."

I wanted to believe his narrative. It made me think Kelsey was alive and well and just in hiding. But deep down, I knew it wasn't true.

"With what you know now, Gage," Ben began. "Do you think Carter tried to kill himself? Was it an accidental OD? Or was it deliberate?"

"I don't know. But then I didn't know my brother was fucking my girlfriend," Gage snapped. "So, maybe I'm not the best person to ask." He shook his head again, as if he were trying to force away some other bad thought.

"Gage?" Ben pressed. "What do you want to say?"

"Nothing."

"Are you sure?" Ben challenged. "Is it possible Carter made sure that Kelsey didn't marry you?"

Gage shook his head, his lips tight. "Impossible."

"Did you see Carter in your house after you went home Tuesday night, after you dropped off Kelsey?" Ben continued.

"No. I told you before. I didn't see anyone. I just went to my room and went to bed."

"So Carter might not have been home?"

"I have no idea, and we may never know now," he said heavily. "Carter is in terrible shape. They don't know if he's going to make it." Gage sucked in another breath. "I can't believe any of this is happening. My fiancée is gone. My brother might be…dying." Gage sank down on the cement bench that ran around the fountain, looking defeated. "I can't…I can't do this."

Gage's emotions seemed raw and honest, but he could be acting. If he'd had something to do with Kelsey's disappearance, we'd just given him a good story to tell, a way to blame his brother, to be the distraught, innocent fiancé who had no idea what was going on. I was a little surprised at my cynicism, but this week was taking its toll. I couldn't take anyone at face value anymore.

Even though I didn't trust Gage, I knew we needed him to keep talking. I sat down next to him. "You can't give up, Gage. We need to find Kelsey. Once she's back with us, the two of you can work everything out. If you love her, you can't give up on her."

Gage lifted his gaze to mine. "I'm not going to give up on her. I know you don't like me, Willow, but I love your sister. I didn't hurt her." He turned to Drake. "I didn't hurt Melanie, either. I still don't know how you could think I did something to her, Drake. We were friends. And Melanie was a sweet girl."

"You lied about seeing her and then you stopped talking to me, to the sheriff, to everyone," Drake said sharply. "You left town as fast as you could."

"I regret that. But I had parents and lawyers on my back. They insisted I follow along. I did what they told me." He paused, giving Drake a regretful look. "Now I know what you went through. How terrifying it must have been to lose your sister, to have no idea what happened to her. Because right now, with Kelsey missing, I feel overwhelmed with fear." His gaze moved back to me. "I'm doing everything I can to find Kelsey, Willow. I hope you can believe that."

He seemed sincere, but Gage had always been smooth, and I didn't know if I could trust him. "I want to believe you. But if you found out Kelsey betrayed you, I'm sure you would have been furious."

He straightened at my words, anger moving back into his eyes now. "So that's where this is going. I'm the suspect once again." He stood up. "I would never hurt Kelsey. I would never hurt a woman. We're done."

"Wait," Ben said. "Did Carter have his phone on him when he was admitted?"

"I don't think so, but I wasn't in the house when my father found him. My dad called me on the way to the hospital. I can check when I go back inside. Otherwise, the phone will be at the house. Our housekeeper, Gloria, is there. She'll let you in if you want to take a look. Believe it or not, Ben, my family has nothing to hide."

I found his words ironic, considering what Carter had been hiding from him.

Gage frowned, perhaps coming to the same conclusion. He gave me a questioning look. "Did Brooklyn know about Carter and Kelsey?"

"Not until a few hours ago. She didn't want to believe it, either."

"I guess I should be happy she didn't lie to me, too," he murmured. "I have to get back inside. Ben, get what you need to get from my house, but please don't slow down on the search for Kelsey. I'm increasing the reward to $50,000. That will go on the local news this afternoon. Hopefully, it will encourage someone to talk."

"Sometimes you need more than money to make people talk," Drake said.

Gage gave him a long look, then a nod. "You're right. I understand now why you punched me. I'd like to do the same."

For a moment, I thought Gage might take a swing at Drake, but his clenched hands stayed at his side as he walked back into the hospital. I looked at Drake and Ben. "What do you both think?"

"I'm leaning toward believing him," Ben said. "If he didn't know Kelsey was cheating on him, he had no motive to make her disappear. Carter, on the other hand, did have a motive to stop her from marrying his brother."

"And he tried to kill himself because..." I struggled to get through the sentence, but I couldn't run from my fear; I had to face it. "Because he hurt Kelsey?"

"I don't know," Ben said. "Maybe. He might have also been the one who shoved you in the water, Willow. That could have sat on his conscience, too."

"He saw me this morning. He knew I was fine." I turned to Drake. "Do you believe Carter's OD was deliberate?"

"It could have been an accident. Carter has been upset since Kelsey went missing. He's made it clear he's in love with her, that he tried to talk her out of marrying his brother. Maybe the last time they spoke, there was anger between them. He could have felt guilty about pressuring her. He might think he was responsible for her disappearance, which could have led him to take too many pills. He might have been just trying to escape the anxiety."

"Thanks," I said. "That was the story I wanted to hear." I put up a hand as he opened his mouth again. "Don't tell me the other version of that story."

"I'll go by the Chadwick house and get Carter's phone and computer," Ben said. "Maybe there's something on his devices that will give us a clue, not only about him but also about Kelsey."

"Can we come with you?" I asked.

"No. Let me handle this. I appreciate the information you brought me, but I need to take it from here."

"You wouldn't be here without us," Drake pointed out.

Ben ignored that comment. "If you find out anything else, let me know."

As Ben left, Drake turned to me. "What do you want to do?"

I thought for a moment. "I need to go home, talk to my parents and Brooklyn. They have a right to know what we've discovered about Carter and Kelsey. It may not be what they want to hear, but I feel like I should tell them."

"You should. It's better than being left in the dark, wondering if anyone is even looking for the person you love."

"You must have felt so alone," I murmured. "Your mom was probably tending to your dad, leaving you on your own."

"She did what she had to do," he said tersely.

"Which doesn't make it better. It's the same with my family. My dad is busy watching over my mom, and Brooklyn is trying to be so strong she can't let anyone else share her pain. But each person is living on an island of pain."

"Especially you."

"Well, I'm not exactly alone. I can't seem to get rid of you."

He gave me a faint smile. "Better than nothing?"

"I'm still undecided," I said dryly.

"Fair enough."

"So, talking to Gage was illuminating," I added as we walked toward the car. "I wasn't expecting him to apologize to you."

"That was surprising. But I'm not sure it wasn't an act. Gage's back is against the wall. He and his brother are suddenly suspects in Kelsey's disappearance. He needs to look like he wants to cooperate. Gage is smart, Willow. Probably smarter now than he was ten years ago."

"You're right." I paused as we reached my car. "I can drop you off before I go home."

He met my gaze. "I think we should stick together."

"Why?"

"Why not?"

"It will be awkward. Plus, my parents and Brooklyn are under a lot of stress right now. Seeing you won't help."

"I won't say anything to bother anyone. Let me be there for you, Willow."

I wanted to believe that Drake cared about me and wanted to be there for me. But I was afraid to let myself believe in the fantasy of Drake again. That might lead to the same painful place I'd been once before.

"If you come with me, you can't bring up the lie Brooklyn told. I can't let you create more stress for my parents or my sister. Not now. Not when everything is so terrifying."

He nodded. "I understand. I won't bring it up. I will just be your silent support."

I was too tired to argue, and there was a part of me that wanted Drake by my side. "All right. Don't make me sorry. I don't think I can handle another crushing disappointment right now."

CHAPTER TWENTY

WHEN WE GOT TO MY PARENTS' house, we found Brooklyn and Rachel in the living room. Rachel was sobbing, and Brooklyn was trying to comfort her.

"Did you hear about Carter?" I asked.

"Preston called and told us," Brooklyn replied, a sad note in her voice. "Mom and Dad just left to go to the clinic. I don't know what good Mom will be. She was a mess before this happened. She's barely holding it together. But she said she wanted to be there for Eileen."

I had a feeling my mother was more interested in being there for Sean, but I kept that thought to myself.

"What are you doing here, Drake?" Brooklyn asked, her gaze catching on the man behind me.

"He's with me," I said quickly. "He wants to help us find Kelsey."

"Or accuse us of doing something horrible," Rachel said with an angry sniff.

"That's not why I'm here," Drake said. "I'm sorry about Carter."

"It's awful," Rachel said. "I had a long talk with Carter on Tuesday night, after we took James to the hotel, and I never imagined this would happen two days later. He must have been so upset over Kelsey that he just didn't realize how many pills he'd taken."

"Or Carter knew exactly what he was doing," I said.

Rachel shook her head. "He wasn't trying to kill himself, Willow. This was an accident. It had to be."

"What did you and Carter talk about the other night?"

"Our lives. Where we were, what we wanted. He helped me weigh some career options." Rachel paused. "Carter didn't seem depressed. He was a little off, but I think he was just tired of being in Gage's shadow. He was saying how Gage always gets forgiven for everything, even minor stuff, like missing the ferry. Kelsey gets mad at Gage, but once he comes in and gives her a smile, everything is instantly better. It was just brother stuff."

"He didn't mention that he was in love with Kelsey?" I asked.

Rachel stared back at me, the truth in her eyes. "Why would you ask me that?"

"It's out, Rachel. I know Carter and Kelsey had an affair. Brooklyn knows, too. Oh, and so does Gage, by the way. We just told him."

"You told him?" Brooklyn asked in shock. "Why would you tell him that now?"

"Because Carter and Kelsey's affair could be tied to her disappearance."

"What did Gage say?" Brooklyn asked. "Was he devastated?"

"He was stunned. He felt betrayed by both Kelsey and Carter. How could he not?"

"This is awful," Rachel murmured. "I warned Carter it might come out, but he said he'd deal with it when he had to, but he wasn't really thinking about Gage. He couldn't get Kelsey off his mind. She definitely has that effect on men."

"Why didn't you tell me, Rachel?" Brooklyn demanded. "You're one of my best friends. Why didn't you tell me as soon as you knew?"

"I didn't have a chance, and then Kelsey disappeared. I didn't want to add to anyone's stress. I'm surprised Kelsey didn't tell you. I assumed you knew but just hadn't said anything."

"I didn't know," Brooklyn snapped, anger in her voice.

I could understand why she was upset. Brooklyn had always prided herself on being Kelsey's big sis, her confidante, the one she looked up to, trusted in. Kelsey's silence about her affair made a mockery of their supposedly close relationship. For me, it wasn't a surprise that I'd been left out. Kelsey had never shared her secrets with me.

Drake cleared his throat, then said, "Rachel, did you speak to Carter after Kelsey disappeared?"

"Yes, of course. He was desperate to find her. If you're thinking that Carter hurt Kelsey, you are way off. He really loved her."

"But she didn't want him," Drake said. "She rejected him for his brother. That had to hurt."

"Carter wouldn't have done anything to Kelsey."

"Maybe he just wanted to stop the wedding," I interjected. "Put Kelsey somewhere so she could reconsider her decision."

"He could have done that." Brooklyn latched onto my theory with enthusiasm. "Carter might have thought he could change Kelsey's mind."

"No," Drake said, his single harsh word erasing our momentary hope. "If Carter had done that, he wouldn't have overdosed. He would have been with Kelsey when he wasn't putting on a show by searching for her." He gave me a compassionate look. "I'm sorry, Willow. I'd love to tell you what you want to hear, but that won't get you closer to the truth."

"I don't even know what's true anymore," I murmured. "I never thought so many people would have so many secrets, would tell so many lies."

"Don't," Brooklyn warned, sending me a sharp look.

"Don't what?" Rachel asked. "What am I missing?"

I hesitated. "It's going to come out, Brooklyn." I turned to Rachel. "Your brother lied about where he was the night Melanie disappeared. He wasn't with Brooklyn all night. She covered for him."

"Because he was passed out on the beach. James told me," Rachel said. "He had nothing to do with Melanie going missing."

"So he says," Drake drawled.

"Can't you two find other suspects for these horrific incidents without looking at your friends, at people you're supposed to care about?" Rachel demanded. "And why are we even talking about Melanie right now? I'm sorry, but she's gone, and she's not coming back. Whoever took her is probably a million miles away."

"Or not," Drake said evenly. "The reason we're talking about Melanie now is because her disappearance is connected to Kelsey."

"You don't know that," Rachel argued. "That's a huge leap. And my brother would never hurt anyone. He's too…weak, if you want to know the truth. He's a drunk, yes, but he's not violent. And if you believe that Melanie and Kelsey are connected, then James is completely in the clear, because he was passed out at the Baker Hotel on Tuesday night. You know that, Willow. You saw him."

"I don't believe James was in any condition to grab Kelsey," I admitted.

"Finally," Rachel said. "Then can we leave James out of this?"

"He'll have to answer for the lie he told at some point," I said. "But he didn't take Kelsey. Whether he knows something about her disappearance is another question."

"Oh, please, this is ridiculous." Rachel turned to Brooklyn. "Why aren't you saying anything? Why aren't you defending James?"

"Because I don't do that anymore," Brooklyn said. "He'll have to defend himself."

"If you lied for him, then you'll go down with him. You should be more concerned."

Brooklyn gave a weary shrug. "I don't care anymore. My only concern now is Kelsey. She was never alone Tuesday night. She was always with someone she knew. There's no way some stranger was lurking in the shadows of our house waiting to grab her when Gage dropped her off. It doesn't make sense. Kelsey met up with someone else, someone she knew, someone she wasn't afraid of, because she wouldn't have gone off with just anyone. That could have been Carter." Brooklyn paused, her gaze sliding to Drake. "Or it could have been you, Drake. Maybe you lured Kelsey away. She was friendly to you. She would have gone to meet you if you asked."

"Willow suggested the same thing two days ago, but I didn't meet Kelsey," Drake replied.

"Why should we believe you?" Rachel asked. "When you don't believe us? And why are you on his side, Willow? You know he was trying to ruin the wedding."

"We're past that, Rachel."

"You should be with us, not with him."

"There's no us versus him," I said.

"Of course there is," Rachel said, acting like I was an idiot. "There always has been. The locals versus the rich kids. Sure, we hung out together, but there was always a difference. Drake hated that we had money, and he had to work all summer. All the local kids hated that, including Melanie. She bitched every day about having to work at the restaurant."

Rachel wasn't completely wrong, but I didn't know what point she was trying to make. "Where are you going with this?"

"Drake has always had a grudge against us. You shouldn't be buying into his theories."

"They're not just his theories; they're mine, too."

"Well, I'm done talking," Rachel proclaimed as she got to her feet. "I'm going to the hospital to see how my friends are doing. Brooklyn, are you coming?"

For a split second, I thought Brooklyn might say no, that she might want to stay and work with me and Drake, that she might pick me instead of them.

But Brooklyn slowly rose. "I'll go with you, Rachel." She gave me a hard look. "You should be careful, Willow. You may not like where Drake's search for the truth takes you."

"What are you talking about?"

"You can't remember where you were that night. Maybe that's because you don't want to remember. The truth you're looking for could destroy you, Willow. Are you prepared for that?" Brooklyn challenged.

My heart leapt against my chest. "If the truth helps me find

Kelsey or learn what happened to Melanie, then it will be worth it."

"I hope that's true."

As they left the room, I sank down on a chair, feeling like I'd just run a marathon.

Drake took the seat across from me. "Are you okay?"

"Not really. That didn't go well," I replied.

"It went as well as it could. It was nice to have you on my side. Unless, Rachel and Brooklyn put doubts back in your head?"

"No. I'm committed to getting answers, whatever they are, whatever the cost. But sometimes I do worry about what I can't remember."

"Which might be why your memories aren't coming back." He gave me a long look. "You didn't hurt Melanie. You can't be afraid that you did."

"You suddenly sound so sure."

"I never thought you hurt her. I just thought you might have seen something."

"I might have," I said, meeting his gaze. "But the memory may never come back."

"Then we'll get our answers another way. What's next?"

Before I could tell him I had no idea what to do next, our housekeeper, Lorraine, came into the room.

"Willow, you're here. Could I ask you a favor? Your mother wants someone to take the food we've received over to the Chadwicks' house. I have it all boxed up."

"Sure," I said. "We can do that."

"Great. Whenever you're ready."

"We'll be right there."

"That was a fortuitous request," Drake said as we got up.

I met his gaze. "Ben might still be at the Chadwick's house. He told us to stay away."

"Or he came and went. He wanted to get Carter's phone and computer, but there could be other clues."

"I can't imagine there will be anything to find, Drake."

"Maybe not, but it's worth looking. This might be our only chance to get into that house."

I was impressed with his never-ending energy and unflagging resolve. It's probably what made him a good journalist. "Don't you ever get tired of being disappointed?"

He shook his head. "I don't allow myself to wallow in feelings that don't get me anywhere. When it comes to Melanie, I have to keep going. There's no other option. I'm not giving up, Willow."

"Me, either." I threw my shoulders back and lifted my chin. "No matter how many lies I have to uncover, no matter how many people come to hate my guts."

A gleam of appreciation entered his gaze. "You're stronger than I thought."

"I'm stronger than I thought," I admitted, hoping my words would withstand the test of whatever was coming next.

CHAPTER TWENTY-ONE

THE CHADWICK'S three-story luxury home sat on a bluff next to forestland, with the closest neighbor a quarter mile away. The house had a pool, a multi-use basketball court, a greenhouse where Eileen grew an array of amazing herbs and vegetables, as well as two decks with stunning ocean views. The Chadwicks also had their own private access to the beach below. My house was nice, but this home was in another stratosphere.

Sean Chadwick had made his money in tech and was also the grandson of a billionaire. Despite their massive bank account, I had always appreciated the fact that both Sean and Eileen were down-to-earth people who didn't brag a lot, although their three sons had often acted with a sense of entitlement.

After parking in the driveway, we headed to the front door. Drake carried a box of food with an assorted variety of casserole dishes, cold meats, and cheeses, while I brought a tote bag filled to the brim with crackers, cookies, and breads. I had a feeling the food would probably go to waste at the Chadwick house, too. But it was something to show concern.

The housekeeper, Gloria, a widow in her late fifties, opened the door and greeted us with a worried look. Gloria and our house-keeper, Lorraine, were friends, and she sometimes came by our house to give Lorraine a ride home, so I'd gotten to know her a little bit. Like Lorraine, Gloria worked at the Chadwick house whenever they were in residence. In the off-season, she cleaned houses for the locals and helped her sister at the fabric store.

"Hi Gloria. We have food," I said.

"Lorraine said you were coming by. This is very nice of your family."

"I'll bring it inside for you," Drake offered. "It's heavy."

"Thank you." She waved us into the house. "This is such an awful day. I'm not sure anyone will feel like eating, but I don't feel like cooking, either, so it will be good to have something here." Gloria led us down the hall to the kitchen, adding, "I'm so sorry about Kelsey, Willow. I've been praying for her to be found as soon as possible. How is your family holding up?"

"Everyone is trying to stay positive."

"I spoke to Ben earlier. He said there's still plenty of reason to hope. But we're running short of hope around here."

"We saw everyone at the hospital," I said. "I feel terrible for Carter."

"The family is blaming themselves for not seeing this coming, but everyone has been so distracted with Kelsey missing that I don't see how they could have foreseen such a tragedy."

"It's no one's fault."

"That won't stop them from feeling guilty," Gloria said. "Mrs. Chadwick, especially. She'll blame herself for worrying so much about Kelsey that she didn't see how upset Carter was. Carter was always the most emotional of the boys. Preston was all about his books, his drawings. Gage was the social, brilliantly athletic super-star, and Carter was the one who cared too much."

It was interesting how Gloria had summed them up. She had them spot-on. It made me wonder how she saw me and my sisters, another trio of siblings, with probably similar differences.

Drake set the food on the counter. "Do you mind if I use the restroom?" he asked Gloria.

"Sure. Go ahead. It's down the hall."

"I know where it is."

"That's right. You and the Chadwick boys were friends at one time."

"At one time," Drake echoed, then left the kitchen.

"Were you here when Sean found Carter?" I asked Gloria as she took the dishes out of the box.

"I was in the greenhouse helping Eileen. We were picking herbs for a dish I was going to make tonight. And then Mr. Chadwick started shouting. Eileen ran inside, and I followed her. There was more yelling. Gage came rushing down the stairs, his phone in his hand. He told me that Carter had passed out, and an ambulance was on the way. I guess Carter took too many pills." She paused. "I saw a bottle of prescription pills the other day when I was cleaning Carter's room. I didn't think much about it. Maybe I should have told Eileen. But Carter is a grown man, and I didn't want to intrude on his privacy."

"I can understand that."

"Sometimes it's difficult to think of him as an adult, though. When I started working for the family, Carter was about ten. Now he's in his late twenties. He was the sweetest boy. He used to draw pictures for me for my birthday and Christmas. He had a very soft heart." Gloria shook her head. "And now I'm talking about him in the past tense. He's going to make it; I know he is. He has more to do in life."

"Did Carter tell you anything about his personal life, his romantic life?" I asked curiously.

Gloria hesitated. "Uh—no."

I gave her a questioning look. "That actually sounds like a yes."

"He didn't tell me anything, but I saw some photos in his suitcase of a beautiful blonde woman. They were just fun photos, nothing X-rated or anything like that. But I was surprised to see the pictures in Carter's suitcase and not in Gage's bag."

"Because the girl was Kelsey?"

"Yes," she said, meeting my gaze. "I shouldn't have said anything. They're just friends."

"They were more than friends. Carter had feelings for Kelsey."

"Really? Well, that must have been difficult for him, loving a woman who was in love with his brother. He's been a wreck since she disappeared. Now I understand a little better why he was so distraught. That must have been why he took so many pills. He wanted to stop feeling the pain."

"Did you tell Ben about the photos?"

"Yes. I went up to Carter's room with him. He wanted to get the phone and computer, and he mentioned he thought Carter and Kelsey had an especially close friendship, and that's when I showed him the photos. Perhaps I shouldn't have done that."

I saw the worry in her eyes. "Carter's secret is out. You don't need to be concerned."

"It's out? Does that mean Gage knows?"

I nodded. "He does now."

Her gaze filled with concern. "Oh, dear, that's not good. Gage will be even more upset than he already was. And poor Eileen. Her loyalties will be split between her boys. Sean will have his hands full trying to keep everyone together, and it will be even worse if Carter doesn't..." Her voice trailed away. "I know I'm just a house-keeper, and I shouldn't be so invested, but I feel like the Chadwicks are part of my family."

"I'm sure they feel the same way about you. Did Ben say anything else while he was here?"

"He assured me he's going to find Kelsey, and I liked his deter-mination. He's already proving himself to be a better sheriff than his father."

"How so?"

"Ben pays better attention, and he doesn't play favorites. He doesn't care about schmoozing with the rich folks. He's loyal to his friends, to the locals. He has respect for the people who work here year round."

"And that's different from his father?"

"Oh, yes. Tom Ryan always had favorites. If you were his buddy, you could get away with anything. And if you could do something for him, you could get away with even more. The man was on a power trip. He thought he owned this island. I was happy when he finally retired. I think it's going to be better for all of us."

I appreciated her candor. " I hope that's true. Drake thinks that the former sheriff's investigation into Melanie's disappearance was not very thorough."

"I don't know about that. Tom spent a lot of time here asking questions. He must have come over three or four times. It made me nervous that he was putting so much energy into talking to the Chadwicks, especially after Drake accused Gage of lying, but nothing ever came of the sheriff's interviews."

"I didn't realize he'd talked to them more than once."

"I believe he really tried to solve the case. Melanie was a popular kid, so outgoing and friendly. Everyone knew her. Everyone loved her, including Tom. She was a big part of this community. She used to read to my grandkids after school. She helped clean houses for any of the crews that needed an extra hand. She worked in the family restaurant with her sweet mom, Sylvie. Tom wanted to bring her home."

"I wish he'd been able to do that."

"Me, too. I always felt so bad for Sylvie, losing her daughter like that. And Holt, too, of course, but he's a harder man to connect with. There was so much pain on this island during the awful weeks that followed that night. The ones that could leave, left. The ones who couldn't had to deal with months of uncertainty and worry that there was a killer amongst us."

"But there wasn't. Nothing happened."

"Until now."

I shivered at her words.

"I'm sorry," Gloria said quickly, putting up an apologetic hand. "That was thoughtless. I shouldn't have said that."

"It's okay. It's not like I haven't thought it." I paused as Drake returned to the kitchen.

"Sorry about that," he said. "I got a call after I left the bathroom, and I had to take it."

"Everything all right?" I asked.

"Yes. Just my mom checking in. Are you ready to go?"

"I am." As I finished speaking, Gloria's phone rang.

She picked it up from the nearby counter. "It's Mr. Chadwick. Hello?" She gripped her phone tightly as she listened to whatever Sean had to say. I couldn't tell if it was bad or good or something in between. "That's terrible," she said a moment later. "I'm so sorry." She paused. "I understand. Willow just brought some food over to the house. It will be here whenever you get back." She listened for another moment, then said, "I'll be praying for Carter. Please let me know if anything changes."

As she ended the call, she let out a breath. "Poor Carter is in a coma. He's still critical, but there's hope."

"That's good."

"Mr. Chadwick said they'll be back soon. I guess there's no point in staying at the hospital any longer. The doctors said Carter will be unconscious for a while. They asked me to make sure no one came in the house or went into Carter's room. It's probably best if you two leave now."

"Of course. We won't say anything," I assured her. "You can tell them we dropped the food off on the porch."

"Well, I'm sure they wouldn't care that you're here, Willow." Her gaze drifted to Drake, a suspicious gleam coming into her eyes, as if she'd just realized how long Drake had been gone. "You didn't go into Carter's room, did you?"

"No," he said.

"Okay, good." She waved us out of the kitchen, and we hurried down the hall and out the door.

I didn't say anything to Drake until we were back in the car. "You lied to Gloria."

He gazed back at me unapologetically. "There was no point in telling her the truth. The less she knew, the better."

"Did you find anything?"

"Why don't you drive down the road and then pull over? We don't want to be sitting here when the Chadwicks get home. But I have something to show you."

"You're making me very curious." I backed out of the driveway. "Start talking."

"I'd rather show you than tell you."

"Fine." I drove onto the main highway, going about a half mile, before turning down a road that led to Pope Beach. With the cold weather, there were no beachgoers around. I pulled over to the side of the road and turned to face him. "Well?"

Drake handed me a piece of paper. "This was in the pocket of a pair of jeans that were flung over the chair in Carter's closet."

I took the piece of stationery, my stomach churning as I unfolded the paper and saw the familiar handwriting. The note had been written on stationery from a hotel in New York. I knew Kelsey had been in Manhattan a week prior to returning to Hawk Island.

"Carter," I read aloud. "I'm writing you this letter because I can't email you, I can't text you. Too many people have access to my phone. I know you don't want to hear this, but I have to say it, and you have to believe me this time. I'm going to marry Gage. I'm sorry for hurting you. I've made some bad decisions, but I want to move forward, and I want you to move on as well. We'll always have Paris, but my life is with Gage. Contracts have been signed. There's a lot of money on the table. I know you don't care about money or fame, but it's part of who I am. Gage understands that because it's who he is, too. You're the romantic one, Carter. You have so much more heart than I do. I want to say you made me a better person, but the sad truth is that I made you a worse person. I'm sorry for that. I hope you can forgive me, that we can be friends and in-laws, that we can prevent our terrible secret from ruining the lives of everyone we care about. Please don't fight me on this. I need you to wish me well at my wedding. Can you do that, Carter? It's the last thing I'll ask of you."

I blew out a breath as I finished reading. Kelsey hadn't signed the note, but she hadn't needed to. It was obviously from her. And it was clearly a goodbye letter.

"She broke his heart," Drake said.

"How could she think he'd want to go to her wedding and wish her well? Everyone used to say I was the kid who lived in a dream-world. I think it was Kelsey. She had a vision for herself, and Gage became part of that. She couldn't let him go because she needed him to complete the fantasy. They were going to take that fantasy to a reality TV show. I think the production company was sending someone out here tomorrow to cover the rehearsal dinner and wedding in case they needed the film for later."

"That would have increased her public exposure and her bank account."

"Gage's, too. We need to give this to Ben. I'm surprised he didn't find it when he went into the room."

"I doubt he went looking through Carter's pockets."

"Well, he should have. You did. What kind of investigator is he?"

"I don't know what to think about Ben," he said candidly. "Sometimes, it feels like he wants what I want. Other times, it doesn't."

"I know. I have the same mixed feelings about him." I looked down at the note again, my sister's handwriting making me feel more emotional. "I hope this isn't the last time I'm going to see her handwriting."

"I hope so, too," he said heavily.

"I'm still surprised that Kelsey didn't tell Brooklyn about her affair with Carter. She usually liked to share the juicy details of her life. She wasn't that private. And I know Brooklyn is hurt that she was left in the dark."

"Her affair with Carter had to be private because of Gage."

"I wonder what other secrets are still to be found." I gazed out the window at the road. I could see the parking lot for Pope's Beach a half mile away and the wild waves of the ocean just beyond that. As the sky continued to darken, I felt a cold chill. I could also feel a memory tugging at my mind. It was closer than it had ever been.

But what was it?

"Willow?"

I heard the question in Drake's voice. I put up a hand. "Don't say anything. I might… remember something."

"What?" he asked sharply.

I got out of the car and stood on the road, looking toward the ocean, then back toward the highway. There was nothing much around me, just trees, shadows, dirt, and the crashing sound of the waves.

That sound echoed through my head. I closed my eyes. I could hear the waves even louder now.

I could feel the ground shifting beneath my feet. I was stumbling, running, feeling like I needed to get away, and then I tripped and went down on my knees. Pain shot through me. I felt dizzy, confused. Where was I?

As the past receded from my mind, I opened my eyes again. I could see Drake standing next to the car, but he wasn't moving. He was letting me have the moment. I looked back toward the beach, then closed my eyes once more.

Someone was coming down the road. The headlights were blinding. I tried to move toward the side, but my legs felt too heavy.

The car stopped. The door opened. Someone got out.

I couldn't see his face. The spinning lights made me dizzy.

"Damn," I swore, shaking my head in anger and frustration as I opened my eyes again. I sank to the ground, feeling weak and overwhelmed.

"Willow?" Drake asked as he walked toward me.

As I looked up at him, I had another flash of memory.

A man stood over me. He was so big. Fear ran through me. Was he going to hurt me? How was I going to protect myself? I couldn't even move.

Drake squatted down, and as our eyes met, the connection with the past slipped away.

"Did you remember something?" he asked.

"Yes. I was on this road. I was running toward the ocean. I tripped and fell. Then I heard a car. It was coming right at me. Someone got out—I think it was a man. He seemed big, but I can't remember seeing his face. I can't see his damn face."

Drake put a hand on my shoulder. "It's okay."

"It's not okay. What if I do know what happened to Melanie? If

I can't remember, we may never know. And if I could remember, we might be able to save Kelsey. I feel so frustrated. I don't know what to do."

I expected Drake to rail at me in anger and disappointment, but his gaze was steady. "Don't push it."

I was shocked at his answer. "Don't push it? I have to push it. We don't have time to spare. Every second counts."

"Pushing it might just bury the memory deeper in your head. We have a couple of new facts. You were on this road. There's not much around here. So why were you here?"

"I don't know why."

"It's close to the Chadwick house. It's also near to your house. Maybe you got lost trying to get home."

"Someone stopped to help me. But I don't know who, and no one ever came forward saying they'd found me on the side of the road and taken me home."

"Okay, take a breath."

"How can you be so calm, Drake?"

"Because one of us has to be. This is as close as we've ever been to your memories. Don't get angry with yourself. Don't fight your own brain."

"I don't know how to do that."

"Let's focus on details. Do you remember anything about the car?"

"I couldn't see it clearly. The spinning lights were blinding me."

"The lights were spinning? Like the lights on a police car or a fire engine?"

I stared back at him. "Maybe so. But if one of those official vehicles had stopped to help me, wouldn't there be a record of it? Wouldn't they have taken me home? Rung the doorbell? Made sure I got inside, okay?"

"Those are good questions."

"I need answers, not more questions."

"Someone wanted to help you by taking you home, but they didn't want anyone to know they'd done that," Drake mused.

I thought about that, remembering my earlier encounter with Ben's father. "Tom Ryan told me he'd always protected everyone, including me. What if he was the one who stopped? But why would he hide the fact that he helped me get home? Why would he have questioned me as if he knew nothing about my whereabouts the previous night?"

Drake stared back at me. "What if it was Ben? He used to take his dad's cruiser out sometimes. He wasn't supposed to, but he did."

"Oh, my God. You're right. I forgot about that. But he went to meet Rick to buy drugs. He wouldn't have done that in his father's police car, would he? And wasn't his dad working that night?"

"Tom wasn't working. He had dinner with a friend. He got home around eleven."

"Who was the friend?"

"I don't know. There was no investigation into Tom's whereabouts that night, since he was the one running the investigation."

"So, what do we do now? Talk to Ben? Talk to his dad? But if we make one of them nervous about our questions, will they stop looking for Kelsey with every resource that they have?" I was torn between wanting to find out more about that night now that I had remembered something, but also needing law enforcement to stay focused on finding my sister.

Drake's jaw tightened. I could see the indecision in his eyes. He knew Kelsey was the priority, but he was finally getting some insight into the night his sister disappeared, and he didn't want to let that go. "I understand your concern," he said tightly.

"Then let's think about what we want to do. But let's do that in the car because it's starting to rain."

I got to my feet, and we jogged to the car. Once we got inside, I turned to him. "Ben and his dad are not going anywhere. Once Kelsey is found, we can go full force into the past." I caught his gaze and held on. "I promise you that, Drake. I won't leave this island again without doing everything I can to find out what happened to Melanie."

"I'm going to hold you to that, Willow."

"I know you will. And hopefully, I'll remember more." I let out a heavy breath. "I am so angry with myself. If I had never gotten drunk that night..."

"I said the same thing about you a million times. I also said it about myself. I was partying hard that night, too, Willow. I might remember everything I did, but I also remember that I wasn't even thinking about my sister."

"You were more concerned with making sure I knew you didn't like me."

"Yes. That was my primary concern," he admitted.

"And I wanted to show you I didn't care, which was why I went to the party. Why I tried to awkwardly flirt with everyone while I got wasted. I was so stupid."

"I was worse."

"Well, I won't argue with that."

He gave me a dry smile. "I didn't think you would."

As the rain came down harder, my mind returned to the present. "I can't bear to think of Kelsey out in this storm. You must have had a million thoughts like that about Melanie."

"For a long, long time," he said heavily.

"When did you give up, Drake? How long before you couldn't lie to yourself anymore?"

"Years. Even now, I never say she's dead. I just say she's gone." He sucked in a breath and blew it out. "It feels like a betrayal to say the word, like I've given up. I don't want to give up."

"I understand. I can't say the word, either. About Melanie or about Kelsey." I licked my lips, seeing the pain in his eyes. "I'm sorry, Drake. I wish I'd stayed in touch with you, that I'd fought past your anger and my guilt. Maybe we could have helped each other. Maybe we could have gotten justice before now."

"I wasn't ready to let you help me, even if you'd wanted to. I didn't want to see you or talk to you, Willow. You left, and you didn't just leave Melanie, you left me."

"You pushed me away before I left," I argued. "That's on you."

"I know. I didn't say my feelings were right. I'm just saying how I felt." He paused as his phone buzzed. He took it out of his pocket and read the text. "My mom wants me to come by the restaurant and talk about my dad."

"Has something happened?"

"She says it's not an emergency. She just wants to check in."

"That's good."

"I guess. The bar is set low these days."

"Yes, it is. I'll take you back." I started the car and turned it around, then headed to the highway.

"Why don't you come inside with me?" Drake suggested a short time later, as I pulled into the restaurant parking lot. "My mom will want to feed me, and you must be hungry."

I hesitated. It was almost seven now and while there was plenty of food at my house, I wasn't in the mood to cook or reheat or even make a sandwich. I also needed to take a breather from my family. The Crab Pot looked warm and inviting. "I could eat something."

"Good. You don't have an umbrella, do you?"

"Nope."

"Well, it's not too far."

As we got out of the car and dashed through the rain to the restaurant, I was reminded again of that night ten years ago. But we were not going up to the apartment, we were going into the restaurant. I'd eat and then I'd go home. Nothing else was going to happen.

CHAPTER TWENTY-TWO

SYLVIE HAD a table waiting for us when we arrived. She seemed a little surprised that I was with Drake, but she covered it up with a cheerful smile. She said she would feed us first and then we could have a chat. I wasn't about to argue as the delicious smell of seafood and garlic set my stomach rumbling. We slid into a corner booth, and I had barely put a napkin in my lap when the server delivered a loaf of hot sourdough bread. I immediately reached for it, pulling off a chunk of bread and lathering it with butter.

"Amazing," I murmured with my mouth full.

Drake smiled in agreement. "I can never resist."

"Why would you want to? It's heavenly."

"It is," he agreed as he popped a piece of bread into his mouth.

The server returned with glasses of water and said, "Your mom is making all your favorites, Drake. She wants to know if that's all right."

"What do you think, Willow?" Drake asked.

"Fine with me."

"How about some wine?" the server asked.

"I'll just have the water," I replied. "But go ahead, Drake."

"I'll take a beer, whatever is on tap."

"Coming right up."

As the server left, Drake gave me a thoughtful look. "I'm surprised you don't want a drink. It's been a long day."

"It has, but I don't drink."

"Never?"

"Not since that night ten years ago."

He met my gaze. "Well, I guess I can understand that."

"I never want to be in a position where I've lost control, where I don't know what I'm doing or who I'm doing it with. I want to remember everything."

"That makes sense."

"Have you ever had a night you couldn't remember?"

"No. That's why it has been difficult to accept varying claims of blackouts and fractured memories. You're not the only one who doesn't remember or can't recall or has forgotten the details... Those answers run throughout the police report. So many vague and unreliable comments, many from our friends, or I should say, your friends."

"They were yours, too, at one point. In fact, they were probably better friends with you than with me. I might have been born into the circle, but you fit in better than I did. You were very popular."

"It was all superficial. That became very clear, very quickly."

"Maybe all teenage relationships are superficial, even in the best of times."

"I suspect you're right." He gave the server an appreciative nod as she set down his beer. Then he turned back to me. "It's good you remembered something today."

"I want to go back to the area tomorrow, see if it triggers another memory. I can't figure out why I would have been on that road. Why was I heading toward that beach? It wasn't where I was supposed to meet Melanie. The waterfalls were in the other direction. Maybe I was just trying to get home and got confused. I could have ended up in the ocean. A lot of terrible things could have happened to me; I was so vulnerable. I don't know how I got luckier than Melanie."

"I don't know, either, but I'm glad you didn't disappear, that you weren't hurt." He paused. "I was angry with you, but I never wished it were you and not Melanie."

"I don't believe that. You had to have wished that at some point."

"I didn't want it to be either of you. I wished I'd been the one to disappear." He took a long draught of his beer. "Getting back to the road you were on—it is close to the Chadwick house. Did being in the house trigger any memories?"

"No. It felt a little weird, but that's because of what happened with Carter. I still can't believe he might die. Even though I don't like what he and Kelsey did, I want him to live."

"The way you feel about Carter might change."

I read the meaning in his eyes, and I frowned, not wanting to go down that road. "Well, we'll have to see how this all plays out." I sipped my water, then added, "When I was talking to Gloria in the kitchen, she said something interesting. She told me that Sheriff Ryan came to the Chadwick house several times in the days after Melanie disappeared. It made her nervous to know he was questioning them so intently, which makes me think you weren't the only one who was suspicious of Gage. Obviously, the sheriff had some concerns."

"If he did, he didn't write them down. There was only one interview with Gage in the police report, and it was conducted in the sheriff's office."

"What about the other Chadwicks?"

"Carter and Preston both made brief statements, also in the sheriff's office. Eileen and Sean did a joint interview at their home, but they basically corroborated their kids' stories. There's barely a page devoted to the entire family and what they had to say. If he had numerous interviews with them, he didn't record their conversations."

"That's interesting. Gloria also said that she hopes Ben will be a better sheriff than his father, because Tom Ryan had a reputation for playing favorites. Anyone who was a rich tourist or who donated to one of his pet causes got special treatment."

"That was definitely true. All the locals were aware of his

favoritism. That's why I got so angry with the slow pace of the investigation. That's why I took matters into my own hands, why I barged into the Chadwick house and punched Gage in the face."

"You're lucky you weren't charged with assault."

"It would have been worth it." He paused. "Gloria should have told me and my parents that the sheriff was talking to the Chadwicks."

"I'm sure she thought he was filling you in. But I'm also sure she didn't want to risk losing her job."

"Loyalty breeds silence," he muttered. "Or maybe I should just say money."

"You can probably buy silence," I agreed. "But no one bought me off."

"No one suggested it was better if you didn't remember?"

I thought about his question. "Actually, my mother suggested that. She thought it would be better for my mental health if I could just forget and move on. Of course, I couldn't do that."

"Did you even get punished for getting wasted and blacking out?"

"I was grounded for two weeks when we went home. But that meant nothing to me. I didn't want to go out, anyway. I didn't want to do anything ever again. My parents forced me to go to college after that. It was a terrible time for me. I didn't have any friends. I couldn't stop thinking about Melanie. I didn't want to drink, which made me super unpopular, and I had no passion for anything anymore. I didn't want to take pictures, not even of the other girls in my dorm. I drifted along that first year, making just good enough grades to not get kicked out. While I didn't love school, I definitely didn't want to end up at home with my parents." I took a sip of water. "Did you go back to college that September?"

"No, I took the first quarter off. By the end of the year, my parents insisted I return to school. I was driving them crazy. I was driving myself crazy, too, so I left. Sometimes, I think that was a big mistake. I let the trail get too cold. By the time I got back to the investigation, too many years had gone by."

"You're investigating now, and you're getting further than you did before."

"I don't want the truth to come at Kelsey's expense, Willow. I really don't."

"I believe you. I don't want that to happen, either." I sat back as the server dropped off two steaming bowls of crab chowder as well as an appetizer of crab cakes. "This looks good."

"My mother is pulling out all the stops."

"She must be happy you're home."

"She would have preferred if my visit wasn't tied into the wedding. She didn't think it would be good for me to see all of you again."

"Or for us to see you," I said.

He tipped his head with a small smile. "Exactly."

I scooped up a spoonful of soup and blew on it before taking a taste. "It's wonderful—smooth and warm, exactly the way I like it. This chowder was one of Melanie's favorites."

"It was a family specialty. The recipe came down from my grandmother."

"Melanie said a lot of the restaurant recipes came from your mom's mom, that your grandmother had been a chef in a seafood restaurant in France a long time ago."

"She was very talented. She died when I was seven. I don't have a lot of memories of her, but I remember her food."

"Do you cook?" I asked curiously.

"Not really. I can make some basic meals, but that's about it."

"Too busy working?"

"I have been called a workaholic," he admitted. "Especially the last few years, when I became more obsessed with finding out what happened to Melanie and trying to do my job at the same time."

"It's cool that you became a reporter, the way you always thought you would. Not that I'm surprised. You were always ambitious and goal oriented. I remember that article you wrote for the Hawk Island Press about the scandal at the library."

He nodded. "The librarian embezzled money from the book sales and fundraisers to the tune of almost twenty-thousand dollars. It was my first exposé."

"I was impressed, even though your story bumped my incredible photo of a northern pintail off the front page."

His eyes filled with amusement. "You were so pissed about that. It was just a picture of a bird."

"A rare, elegant duck that had never been seen on Hawk Island, and I got a photo of it."

"It still ran in the paper. It just wasn't as important as the embezzlement."

"I suppose not, but it was still a great shot. It took me hours to get it. Melanie got so bored with me that day. She wanted to know when I'd gone from photographing cool stuff to dumb birds. But I have to give Melanie credit. She didn't leave; she stuck it out. She spent the afternoon writing in her diary while I was wading in and out of the pools by the grove." I shook my head. "She was a good friend."

"She thought you were a brilliant photographer. I can't believe you don't take pictures anymore. What's your passion now?"

"I don't have one. Not everyone has a passion. Some people just work and socialize, watch TV and stay alive."

"Is that what you do?"

"My life is too boring to talk about, Drake. Although now I miss some of that boredom." I took a breath. "So, this book you're writing on Melanie—what if you can't come up with an ending? Will you still write it?"

"I don't know. I want to tell her story. I want to write it down and get it out of my head. Beyond that, I'm not sure."

"Will you ever be able to let her go, Drake?"

"Let me ask you a question. If Kelsey isn't found, will you be able to let her go? Will you be able to move on?"

"Well, I haven't moved on from Melanie, so, no, I'll be stuck in another hellhole."

"Then you know my answer."

I set down my spoon as I sat back in my seat. "I'm tired, Drake, tired of spinning my wheels and getting nowhere, but then I feel guilty because the worst thing that's happened to me is being stuck. I don't know what Melanie went through. I don't know what my sister is going through. I'm sure it's awful. I can't feel sorry for myself. I can't be exhausted."

"Keep eating."

"You think that's going to help?"

He shrugged. "It won't hurt. Try the crab cake."

I put one of the crab cakes on my plate and then swirled a bite in a spicy sauce and popped it in my mouth. "Okay, that helped," I said as I swallowed. "I forgot how much I loved these. I like the little kick of pepper that your mother puts in. It always wakes me up."

"Good. I need you on your game."

"And I need you on your game, so you better eat, too."

"I will," he said, grabbing the other crab cake.

A few moments later, the server set down two plates of filet mignon with mashed potatoes and asparagus.

"Surf and turf," I said with appreciation. "Your mother is feeding us well."

"It's how she shows her love."

"She was always really nice to me. I wished she was my mom a million times." I took a breath, feeling a little emotional again. "I thought she probably came to hate me the way you did."

"Oh, no, Willow. My mother has a far more generous heart than I do. She never hated you. She knew you loved Melanie. She actually got angry with me for being so hard on you."

"I deserved it. If I'd been able to remember, it might have helped. If I'd never gotten so drunk, I might have been able to prevent what happened."

"I've played that 'if I'd done something different' game a lot. It doesn't get you anywhere. You should eat your steak before it gets cold."

I picked up my fork again, feeling surprisingly comfortable

with Drake. I don't know when we'd gone from enemies to friends, but it seemed like we'd gotten to a different point in our relationship. Not that we had a relationship, I reminded myself. We were just working together to bring Kelsey home and get justice for Melanie.

As we finished our meal, Sylvie slid into the booth and gave me a questioning smile. "How was your food?"

"It was delicious," I replied. "It's the first good meal I've had since I came back. Thank you."

"I'm glad you liked it. I think my husband scared you earlier today, Willow, and I'm sorry about that." Sylvie gave me a regretful smile.

"I know he can have difficult moments."

"Yes, he can. Holt has been really good the last couple of years, though. I was thinking he'd finally found some footing, but as soon as talk of the wedding came about, and all the families began arriving, he got jittery. When your sister went missing, something in him snapped. He has been having trouble determining what's now and what's in the past."

"I'm sorry."

"Oh, please, Willow, don't apologize to me. I know what you and your family are going through. It's horrific, and I wouldn't wish it on anyone."

"It is awful," I agreed. "I feel guilty just sitting here having a meal when I don't know where my sister is."

"I know that feeling. Just smiling felt like a betrayal." Sylvie blew out a breath. "I heard about Carter Chadwick. That was another shocking piece of bad news. Do you know how he's doing?"

"He's in critical condition."

"That's terrible. Such a young man with a long, bright future ahead of him."

"How's Dad doing?" Drake interjected.

"Mitch took him for a hike along the Bell Trail. They got back an hour ago. Your dad said he was going to stay home and rest, that he felt calmer since he'd walked five miles."

"I'm glad he's feeling better. I should talk to him."

"Wait until tomorrow, honey. Hopefully, there will be some good news by then. Also, if he asks you about the book again... well, I hate to tell you to lie..."

"But you want me to lie," Drake finished.

She gave her son an apologetic smile. "You could just say you're not writing it right now."

"And if I write it?"

"Then you will have changed your mind, but he won't have to think about it and worry incessantly for the next several months or years."

"All right. I can do that."

"I know you're fighting hard for Melanie, Drake, and I don't want to stop you. I just want to protect your father's fragile mental state."

"I understand."

"Now, can I bring you some dessert?" Sylvie asked.

"I'm full," I said. "But thank you again for an amazing dinner."

"I'm good, too, Mom," Drake added.

"Then I better get back to work." Sylvie slipped out of the booth. "Willow, please tell your mother I'm thinking about her."

"I will." As Sylvie left, I turned my head toward the nearby window where rain was streaming against the panes of glass. The storm had arrived in full force.

"That doesn't sound good," Drake commented.

"No, it doesn't."

"Why don't you give it a little time before you go home? You don't want to drive in that."

"There's a line at the hostess stand. I think they need the table."

"We can go upstairs. You can look through my notes, see if anything jumps out at you."

More time alone with Drake in the place where we'd once made love—had sex, I amended quickly—was probably not the best idea. But I couldn't find the desire to run through the rain, drive home, and then wander around my house all night with no one I really wanted to talk to. It wasn't like there was any support I could give my parents or Brooklyn. They were all locked in their own version of hell. I'd be more useful helping Drake.

At least, that was the reason I was going with. I didn't want to admit that I'd started feeling close to him again, that I wanted to keep talking to him, that being with him was bringing back a piece of me I thought I'd lost.

"Okay, I'll come up for a bit." I didn't want to psychoanalyze my decision any further.

He looked happy with my decision. "Good. Let's go."

We slid out of the booth and headed up the stairs. We got into the apartment, I took off my jacket and tossed it on the chair. Despite my best intentions to just look at the police reports and focus on Melanie, my heart started beating faster as Drake removed his coat.

It was how it had started before, only then we'd been dripping wet. We'd laughed as we'd thrown our wet coats to the side. I'd pulled the band out of my hair, running my hand through my braid to pull it apart, to shake out the raindrops. And that's when I saw the look of desire in Drake's eyes. My seventeen-year-old heart had melted.

I deliberately cleared my throat, turning away from Drake. I needed to stay in the present. The box of files was still sitting on the coffee table, and there was a lot of information to go through.

But I couldn't find the strength to pick up one of the folders. My brain was tired of the relentless circle of unending questions. And the sound of the rain on the windows, the steamy warmth of the room, was taking me back in time. I should fight that feeling, but I didn't want to.

"Willow?"

I slowly turned around.

Drake gave me an uncertain look, his gaze darkening. "Where do you want to start?"

"Where I shouldn't," I said helplessly, memories of a very similar conversation coming back into my head.

He'd asked me if he could kiss me. I'd never expected him to ask. I'd just thought he'd grab me and kiss me, and I'd be in heaven. But he'd given me a choice. And I'd said yes.

It had been a mistake. It had been the wrong time, the wrong place then, and it was the wrong time, the wrong place now. But my breath was coming fast, and my nerves were tingling.

"I should have learned my lesson," I added.

"Me, too," he replied, a husky rasp in his voice.

We stared at each other for a long minute.

"Willow? Tell me what you want."

I looked deep into his beautiful blue eyes. "I shouldn't want anything from you."

"I shouldn't want anything, either, but I do."

There was so much electricity between us, I could hear the sizzle. I'd always been drawn to him like a moth to the flame, knowing he could burn me, but yearning for all that heat.

There were so many reasons why being with him was a bad idea, but I couldn't remember any of them. I didn't want to think anymore. I just wanted to feel. I wanted to be with Drake. I wanted to lose myself in him.

I didn't care if I got hurt again. It would be better than feeling nothing. I'd shut down all my emotions ten years ago, to the point where I often felt dead inside, numb, cold. I didn't want to feel that way anymore. I wanted to burn. I wanted to fly.

"Drake?" I took a step forward.

"Are you sure? Because I'm not."

His words disappointed me, but they only made me want to fight harder for what I needed. "It doesn't have to mean anything. I'm not seventeen anymore. I don't have expectations. You don't have to worry about protecting me."

"You're vulnerable, scared for your sister, for your family."

"And I want to forget about all that. Let's not think about tomorrow or yesterday. Let's just be who we once were. Two people who had absolutely no problems, except a crazy, hot need for each other? We can't let the past go forever, but we can let it go for a little while. Can't we?"

Drake didn't answer. He just pulled me into his arms and

pressed his mouth on mine. We kissed with an unrestrained passion
fueled by emotion and desire.

They were the same hot, wild kisses I remembered. As we
stripped off our clothes, the barriers between us fell away.

This was Drake, the man I'd loved forever, even when I'd hated
him, even when he'd hated me.

CHAPTER TWENTY-THREE

"So that happened," I murmured, as I snuggled against Drake on the futon in his living room an hour later. "And comparatively speaking..."

He rolled onto his side and gave me a smile. "Are you going to finish that statement?"

"Way better," I said.

"Yeah," he agreed, tucking my hair behind my ear. "But just as unexpected."

"It must be the rain, this apartment, and your incredibly sexy blue eyes—a dangerous combination."

"I think it's you that brings the danger, Willow."

"The shy girl brings the danger?" I teased. "I don't think so."

"You weren't as shy as I thought you were when we started kissing."

"Tonight? Or ten years ago?"

"Both. You have a lot of hidden depths, Willow Kent."

"I never thought I did."

"You never saw yourself the way I saw you."

I thought about his words, then propped myself up on my elbow as I gazed into his eyes. "How did you see me back then?"

"At first, you were just my sister's friend, but when we started running into each other at the paper, I realized you weren't just this quiet, shadowy girl. You were creative and imaginative, and you had determination. You might have hidden behind your camera, but you were bold with your pictures. I became fascinated by you."

I was incredibly touched by his words. "I was fascinated by you, Drake. I couldn't stop looking at you, and when we got to know each other away from Melanie, away from anyone else, I felt like we had a connection. I loved how you wanted to shed light on the problems of the world. You were much more of a deep thinker than I'd first thought and an interesting mix of arrogance, intelligence, and charm. I enjoyed talking to you about things that mattered. All my other conversations with boys seemed so meaningless." I sighed. "And then it wasn't the talking that I wanted, it was the kissing, and everything else. I was glad my first time was with you."

"Until I fucked it up?" he asked.

"Until then," I agreed.

"You scared me, Willow. The way I felt about you took me by surprise. I didn't know how to handle that kind of emotion. I'm sorry I hurt you."

"Me, too. Did you sleep with that girl that you were parading in front of me the night Melanie disappeared?"

"No. After I realized you'd left Ben's house, we went to the bonfire. I was in a bad mood by then. She got bored with me and made out with someone else. I went home, locked myself in my room, pissed off at everyone but mostly myself. And then the next morning, my world was completely ripped apart."

I touched his face, seeing the anguish in his eyes. I felt an immense wave of compassion for him. "That morning, my world ripped apart, too. I thought it was bad the night before, when my biggest concern was why you didn't like me anymore. I had no idea how much worse everything would get. Or that the hurt would last so long." I paused. "I do want to help you, Drake."

"I know. After we find Kelsey."

"Yes." I gave him a regretful smile. "I should probably go home."

"It's still raining."

"Not as hard as it was, and I should check in with my family. I don't want anyone to think I've forgotten about Kelsey."

"Anyone or yourself?" he challenged.

"Both," I admitted. "This was fun, and I'm not sorry we got together. But I do feel a little selfish for taking pleasure when..."

He put his fingers against my mouth. "Don't. You didn't do anything wrong."

"I just feel like every minute should be spent on finding Kelsey."

"There's nothing you could be doing right this second, but I do understand where you're coming from. I'll walk you to your car."

"You don't have to do that," I said, as I slid off the futon and put on my clothes. "You'll get soaked for no reason."

"Then I'll get soaked, but I'm not letting you go to your car alone. In fact, I'm going to follow you home and watch you walk all the way into the house."

His words brought back fear and uncertainty. "I'll be okay," I said halfheartedly.

"You will be okay. I'll make sure of it."

"All right. Thanks."

We finished dressing and then met by the door. Before Drake opened it, he leaned in and gave me a long kiss. It felt like there was a promise in there somewhere, but he didn't verbalize it, and I didn't ask.

Then he grabbed an umbrella, and we went down the stairs. It was almost eleven now, and the restaurant had closed, but there was still a warmth to the building, and I was reluctant to leave it.

"Ready?" Drake asked as he opened the door.

"No, but let's do it."

He opened the umbrella and held it with one hand as he put his other arm around me. Together, we ran toward my car. Drake waited until I had the doors locked, then went back to retrieve his vehicle from behind the restaurant.

It felt good to see his lights behind me. It felt even better to know that he cared enough to worry about me. Not that I was going to let myself go down that road. I didn't know what the future would bring. I didn't know what tomorrow would bring, but for now, I was going to savor the first genuine connection I'd felt in the past ten years.

When I got home, I parked in the drive and ran up to the front door. I opened it and then gave Drake a wave. Closing the door, I locked it behind me.

There was a light on in the hall, but the house was silent. I went upstairs and saw the open door to Kelsey's dark room, which served as a cold, cruel reminder of reality. The other bedroom doors were closed, and I couldn't hear anyone talking.

It occurred to me that Kelsey was the one who'd always brought the life to our family. She'd been the most gregarious, the one with the loudest voice, and the longest laugh. If she'd been home, I would have heard music coming from her room. Or she might have been on the phone, talking to one of her friends. Or she and Brooklyn might have been sitting on her bed, discussing the wedding. But none of that was happening tonight, and without her, the house was very quiet, an ominous sign of a future I didn't want to contemplate.

I went into my room, shut the door, took off my clothes and crept into bed, suddenly exhausted. I wanted to sleep, and I wanted to wake up to happy news.

I closed my eyes, praying that would happen.

Despite my weary state, I had trouble falling asleep and when I did, disturbing dreams created terrifying images in my mind. I woke up as the morning light crept through the window, and it reminded me of the past, of waking up on the patio, chilled and dazed.

I squeezed my eyes shut, trying to go back in time before that. *How had I gotten onto that patio lounger?* I felt like someone had helped me. There had been a hand on my arm. Then it was gone.

Who had taken me home?

I'd been on the road. I'd seen flashing lights. A figure had come over me.

I struggled as the seat belt tightened around my body. I

couldn't sit upright. I felt dizzy and sick. I slumped down. My head banged against the console. There was a radio. Someone's arm. They were wearing a black jacket.

My gaze moved toward the back.

Was someone there?

There was something red on the floor.

My breath started coming fast. The red was swirling around in front of my eyes like a blob of paint taking different shapes. Was I just imagining it?

Finally, it settled down. It was a book.

A book?

Yes. A red-leather book.

My eyes flew open. I jerked up in the bed, confused as to where I was.

I wasn't in a car. I was in bed, and it was ten years later. I'd remembered something. *The book in the car.* I sucked in a desperate breath. I had to be wrong. It wasn't possible. *Was it?*

I got out of bed and paced around the room. It was lighter out now, almost eight o'clock in the morning. The rain had eased. I could hear people downstairs. The dream was fading from my mind, but it still felt very real. Because it wasn't a dream; it was a memory.

I needed to talk to Drake. I grabbed my phone from the nightstand and punched in his number.

"Willow?" he said. "Is everything all right?"

"Yes, but I remembered something."

"Hold on," he said.

I could hear a roaring sound in the background. "Where are you?" I asked.

"I'm on the beach looking for my dad."

"What do you mean? Where is he?"

"I don't know. My mom woke up around four in the morning, and he wasn't in bed. She waited until six to call me. She's worried about him."

I sank down on the edge of the bed. "I'm sorry."

"He's probably fine, Willow. He does this—a lot."

"But you're still concerned."

"Well, I'd like to find him, but he could be anywhere. What's going on with you?"

"I remembered something. That night on the road, I got in the car, the one that stopped. I was feeling dizzy and sick. Everything was blurry, like things were moving in front of my eyes. I saw something red on the floor. It was a book—a red book."

"What?" he asked more sharply. "Are you saying what I think you're saying?"

"Yes! I think it was Melanie's diary. It was in that car."

"Are you sure?"

"No, I'm not sure," I said in frustration. "My brain could be playing tricks on me, but I don't think so. I believe I saw her diary, but I don't know if she was there. I didn't see her. I just saw the book."

"We need to find out who picked you up. I'm coming over. I can be there in twenty minutes."

"Wait. Don't come here." I didn't want to upset Brooklyn and my parents, with Drake showing up at our door.

"Then where?"

I thought about that. "Tom Ryan's house. I want to ask him if he picked me up that night."

"If he had Melanie's diary in his vehicle, why would he tell you the truth?"

"Maybe he won't. But maybe whatever he says will tell us something. He said he protected me. He's the best lead I have. I can be at his house in an hour. I have to get dressed and make sure my parents and sister don't need anything from me before I head out. But I can go on my own if you need to find your father."

"If I don't find him before it's time to meet you, then I'll look for him later. He'll show up. This isn't like Melanie or Kelsey. This is just my dad needing to get out of the house. I'll see you soon. And Willow, this is good."

"I hope it's good," I said, but there was nothing but bad feelings running through me as I got up from the bed and went into the bathroom to take a shower.

CHAPTER TWENTY-FOUR

WHEN I WENT DOWNSTAIRS, Brooklyn and my parents were in the dining room talking to Sean Chadwick. The conversation paused when I entered the room.

"How's Carter?" I asked.

"He's…alive, barely," Sean said with an angry, sad grimace. He looked like he'd aged ten years in the last twenty-four hours. "Doctors think there's a chance he'll recover, but we don't know what condition his brain will be in if and when that happens."

"I'm so sorry," I murmured.

"Thanks. Gage told us about Carter and Kelsey last night. Now, I'm worried about him snapping, breaking…" Sean drew in a breath. "I can't believe what's happening to my family."

"I don't want to discuss Carter and Kelsey," my mother said flatly, her words a bit cold, considering the pain in Sean's gaze. "I don't even know that I believe it. I will wait to hear what Kelsey has to say when she comes home. Until then, it's all just speculation."

It was a lot more than speculation, but no one wanted to argue with my mother, including Sean.

He ran a weary hand through his thinning hair. "It's nothing we need to get into now. Gage would also prefer that we keep it private, which is one reason I'm here. I need to make sure we're on the same page."

"We are," my mother said, answering for all of us. "And that's all we need to say."

"The other reason I'm here is about the wedding," Sean continued. "I don't know what's happening with the plans, but we need to shut everything down."

"We could still get Kelsey back," my mother argued. "I don't want to cancel anything."

"The wedding is supposed to be tomorrow, Monica," Sean said with exasperation. "Carter is in the hospital fighting for his life. My family is in tatters. There is not going to be a wedding this weekend."

My mother bit down on her lip. "I'm sorry," she said. "Thinking about the beautiful wedding we planned has been the only thing keeping me sane."

"I understand, but it's not happening," Sean said.

"We'll take care of everything," my father interjected. "You don't need to worry about it, Sean. Neither does Gage. Just focus on Carter, and we'll concentrate on Kelsey. Now, if you'll excuse me, I need to check in with Ben. I have several investigators who can't get here because the ferry is not running. I need to see if we can get them out here by private boat."

"Boats aren't running, either," Brooklyn said. As all eyes turned to her, she added, "The Connelly's wanted to leave this morning, but Rachel told me they weren't able to go."

"Why would they leave?" my mother demanded.

"People are rattled, Mom," Brooklyn replied. "They're scared. They don't want to stay here anymore."

"They need to stay until we find Kelsey. No one should leave," my mother said. "We need everyone here."

"We left when Melanie was missing," I said. "We left five days after she disappeared. You forced me to get on the ferry when I wanted to stay, when I begged you to let us stay."

My mother gave me an annoyed look. "That was different."

"It wasn't different. It was exactly the same."

"I was protecting you, Willow. You were hysterical. I needed to get you away from here. I needed to get all my kids to safety. I did what I had to do."

"Well, maybe that's the way the Connelly's feel, too."

"Rachel and James are not kids."

"And they're not going," Brooklyn put in, trying to ease the tension in the room. "It was just an idea they had, but the ferry stopped running, and the private boats are saying it's too dangerous to leave right now." She turned to Sean. "How is Eileen? Does she need anything?"

"She needs her son to wake up," Sean said heavily. "Beyond that, there's not much anyone can do. Eileen is very upset. She can't eat or sleep. She was up all night and went back to the hospital this morning. I'm going to join her there shortly."

"We'll come by later," my mother said.

Sean shook his head. "There's no point. But I'm sure Eileen would appreciate a call or a text." He got to his feet. "Gage could use some support, too. He's spinning around in circles, wanting to look for Kelsey, wanting to stay with his brother. It's all a big mess."

"I'll reach out to him," Brooklyn said.

"Thank you."

"I'll walk you out, Sean." My mother got to her feet.

My father's gaze followed them out of the room and in that moment, I thought he knew about them. Whether he'd ever confronted my mother or Sean, I had no idea.

He cleared his throat, then stood up. "Brooklyn, can you talk to Jenny? Tell her everything is off."

"Yes, I'll take care of it," Brooklyn replied. "Don't worry about any of that, Dad."

"Thanks. I'm going to make some calls."

As Brooklyn and my dad left the room, I found myself once again standing alone in the middle of the room. But not for long.

This time, I knew what I needed to do. I grabbed my coat and an umbrella and headed out the door.

It was a short drive to the Ryan's house, which was in the foothills, not far from where Drake had grown up. The single-story home had three bedrooms and two baths. I'd never spent much time in the house, but the free-standing three-car garage on the property had been a big hangout. A third of the garage had been converted into a game room, with a pool table, darts, and an old pinball machine.

It was ironic that the sheriff's house had been the center of so much underage drinking, but because Ben's dad worked a lot, he'd had a lot of parties with no adult supervision. I'm sure the sheriff must have known, but he'd always been lenient with Ben. I think in some ways he'd been trying to make up for Ben losing his mom when he was so young.

The garage looked dark, but there were lights on in the house. It was ten o'clock in the morning, and there was smoke coming out of the chimney, so it looked like someone was home. I wondered if Ben lived with his dad, or if he'd gotten his own place. Even if he lived here, he was probably at work. I would prefer to talk to Tom when Ben wasn't there. The more I thought about the night Melanie disappeared, the more convinced I became he had picked me up, especially in view of what he'd said to me the other day about looking out for me. It all seemed to go together.

On the other hand, it made little sense that he would have just carried me out to the patio and let me sleep on a chaise lounge all night.

Why wouldn't he have rung the bell and notified my parents? They might have been angry with me. *But why would he care?*

I blew out a puzzled breath. I might be on the wrong track. Drake had reminded me that sometimes Ben drove his dad's cruiser. If Ben had seen me, he probably would have rescued me, too. But unlike his father, he would have been motivated to sneak me into the backyard of my house and leave. He wouldn't have wanted to answer to my parents about the condition I was in.

If it had been Ben, what would he have been doing out on that road? He'd supposedly been buying drugs behind the Road House. *What else had he been doing?*

I didn't want to believe Ben was guilty of anything more than lying about a drug buy. But I wouldn't have thought he'd do that, either.

I was relieved when I saw a car turn down the road. I needed to get out of my head and take action. As soon as Drake parked, I grabbed my umbrella and got out of the car. I didn't bother to open my umbrella. It was only drizzling, and the wind was so fierce, it would probably take the umbrella right out of my hand. I hurried down the street.

"Did you find your dad?" I asked, as Drake stepped out of the car.

"No, but hopefully he'll turn up soon. Any other news?"

"Carter is still clinging to life. My mother has finally agreed to cancel the wedding. The Chadwicks and my parents know about Carter and Kelsey, but no one wants to talk about it."

"Sounds about right."

"Brooklyn said the Connellys were trying to leave this morning, but the ferry isn't running. My mother was furious that they would try to leave in the middle of all this." I saw the cynical glint in his eyes. "Yes, I'm aware of the irony. In fact, I told her we left five days after Melanie disappeared. She said she wanted to protect me. I was in so much pain."

"She just wanted to get the hell away from the problem."

"She did. Anyway, no one is leaving the island any time soon, but that also means that the investigators and additional law enforcement resources my father has lined up cannot get here for another day."

"Maybe the wind will ease by this afternoon."

"I hope so. Listen, Drake. I think I should go in by myself."

"Why?"

"Tom might say more to me if I'm on my own, if it's just me and him. He won't see me as a threat. He might see you as one."

Indecision ran through his gaze, but in the end, he gave a reluctant nod. "All right. If you run into trouble, yell."

"I will."

Drake got back into his car, and I headed up to the porch. When I got to the front door, I was surprised to find it ajar. I could hear a television program coming from inside. I knocked on the door, then pushed it open.

"Tom?" I called out as I stepped into the living room.

The TV in the corner was playing an infomercial. As I came around the side of the couch, I looked toward the fireplace, and my breath stalled in my chest. Tom Ryan was lying on his side, gasping for air as blood streamed from a gash on the back of his head.

"Oh, my God."

"Help," he gasped.

"I'll get you help right now." I ran back to the front door and yelled for Drake. Then I pulled out my phone and called 911 as I returned to the sheriff's side.

Drake came running into the room as I was talking to the dispatcher.

"Shit!" he swore. Drake grabbed a blanket off the back of the couch and pressed it against the sheriff's head, while I finished talking to dispatch.

"They'll be here soon," I told Tom, trying to ignore the amount of blood on the floor. "You'll be okay."

"Should have told you the truth," the sheriff said slowly, each word taking a tremendous amount of effort.

"What truth?" I asked, but then I realized he was looking at Drake.

"It was too late when I got there, Drake," the sheriff said, a plea in his gaze. "You gotta believe me. Couldn't have saved her. Sorry. So sorry."

"You found Melanie?" Drake asked in shock. "Where was she? Who took her?"

The sheriff's eyes rolled back in his head.

"Stay with me," Drake yelled. "Tell me what happened to her. Tell me, dammit." He gave Tom's shoulder a shake. But Tom's eyes were now closed. "Wake up," Drake shouted. "You can't die on me now."

As Drake continued to try to bring Tom back to life, tears filled my eyes and ran down my cheeks. Tom was gone, and whatever he knew had died with him.

Drake looked at me in utter despair. "What else did he say?"

"Nothing. I'm sorry, Drake. He didn't say anything."

"He saw Melanie. He knew what happened to her and he kept it a secret." Drake jumped to his feet. "Why? Why would he do that?"

"I don't know," I whispered, seeing the agony in his eyes.

"And now he's dead," Drake said. "God damn him!"

I got to my feet as the sirens grew louder. A moment later, the door opened and a half-dozen people rushed into the room, including two paramedics, two firefighters, a deputy, and finally Ben.

Ben's face went white when he saw his father. He ran to his dad's side. "No, no," he said, shaking his head in disbelief.

The paramedics checked for breathing, for a pulse. But we all knew the truth.

"He's gone," the paramedic told Ben. "I'm sorry."

Ben ran a hand though his hair as he stared at his father in shock. I couldn't imagine what he was going through. It had just been him and his dad since he was ten.

"Dad," Ben said, his heart in his voice. He fell to his knees, putting his hand on his father's chest as the paramedics moved back to give him a little room. "Why?" he muttered, shaking his head in confusion. "Who would do this to you?"

His question was met with utter silence, the only sound in the room, the tick-tock of a big grandfather clock.

Then Ben suddenly jumped to his feet. His gaze swung to Drake. "What the fuck happened? What did you do to him?" He strode toward Drake as if he were going to deck him.

I grabbed his arm. "Ben, I found him," I said sharply. "He was like this when I got here. I swear to you that's the truth. Drake didn't hurt your dad."

He stared down at me. "I don't understand. What are you doing here, Willow?"

"I came to talk to your father. The front door was open. I walked inside, and he was lying on the floor. There was blood coming from the back of his head. I called 911 immediately. Drake tried to slow the bleeding, but he couldn't."

"Was he alive when you got here?"

"Yes."

"Did he say who did this?"

I shook my head. "No."

"He must have said something."

"Oh, he said something," Drake declared, anger in his voice.

"Drake, don't. This isn't the time," I begged.

He ignored me. "You want to know what he said, Ben? Your father said he was sorry, that he'd made a mistake, that he should have told me the truth."

"The truth about what?" Ben demanded.

"Your father said it was too late when he got there. That he couldn't have saved her. He was sorry. He was talking about Melanie, Ben. All these years, he knew what happened to her, and he covered it up."

Ben stared at Drake in shock. "You're crazy. You didn't hear him right. He didn't know what happened. He looked for Melanie. He looked everywhere for her."

"He didn't have to look. He knew where she was."

"But he didn't kill her," I said, bringing their attention to me. "Tom said he was too late when he arrived. That means he didn't do it. Someone else did. Someone he had to protect."

Ben stared back at me. "Who would that be?"

The words wouldn't come through my tight lips, but Drake didn't have the same problem.

"You, Ben," Drake said. "He was protecting you."

Ben's gaze hardened. "Outside now."

"Fine. We can have this conversation anywhere you want, but the truth will come out," Drake said.

"I'll make sure of that," Ben retorted. "I'll meet you out front. But first, I need to..." He glanced at his father and then at us. "I'll join you in a few minutes."

CHAPTER TWENTY-FIVE

As we left the house, Drake moved to the corner of the porch, gazing mindlessly at the street, which was crowded with emergency vehicles.

I moved to his side. "Are you all right?" It was a stupid question. Thankfully, Drake didn't appear to have heard it.

"Melanie is dead." He gazed at me with a raw, fresh pain.

I remembered how much he hated that word, how he'd never wanted to use it. But whatever last bit of impossible hope he'd had was gone. "I'm sorry, Drake." The words seemed meaningless. They couldn't begin to cut through his pain, but I didn't know what else to say.

"How could he keep the secret all these years? How could he watch my parents suffer? How could he look me in the eye and lie?" He gave me a bewildered look. "What kind of person does that?"

"He must have had something to hide or someone to protect."

"Like his son," Drake said caustically.

"I don't think Ben would have killed his father."

"Why are you defending him?"

"I'm not defending him. I'm looking at the facts. Someone hit Tom on the back of the head. Whoever Tom was protecting had to be the person who killed him, the person who killed Melanie. Don't you think?"

Drake frowned as he processed that thought. "Maybe. But why now? After so many years? Why would Tom be killed now? What's different?"

"Kelsey is missing now. That's what's different. Maybe Tom couldn't live with another girl disappearing. Instead of a protector, he became a threat. I just wish he'd told us who hurt Melanie." I paused. "I know you're bursting with rage, Drake. Maybe you should take a walk. Take a minute."

"No. I want to talk to Ben."

"And I want to talk to you," Ben said as he joined us on the porch.

Looking at the grim expression on Ben's face and knowing how close he had been to his father made it difficult for me to believe he could be the bad guy.

Was I being naïve? Was I letting Ben's easygoing, boy-next-door charm color my thinking?

"Tell me again what happened," Ben ordered. "And start with why you came here, Willow."

"I wanted to talk to your dad about the night Melanie disappeared," I replied. "I thought your father might be more open with me than with Drake, so I asked Drake to wait in his car. When I saw your dad on the floor. I yelled for Drake and then called 911. Drake came into the house and applied pressure to your father's wound, but we were too late. I'm really sorry we didn't get here in time." It was ironic that I was apologizing in the same way that the sheriff had just apologized to Drake. I could see by the stony expression on Drake's face that the irony was not lost on him, but he was letting me do the talking.

"What did you want to ask my father?"

I hesitated. If Ben was involved, was I about to give him too much information?

"Might as well tell him," Drake said. "Every last secret will come out one way or the other."

"He's right," Ben said. "Tell me everything, Willow."

"I remembered something about the night Melanie disap-peared. I was walking down Delaney Road to Pope Beach, and a car was coming toward me. I think it was a police vehicle. I could see the lights spinning. Everything else is a blur. Someone picked me up and took me home. While I was in the car, I saw Melanie's diary on the floor." I took a breath. "I think your father picked me up. He said something to me the other day about trying to protect me. But I didn't have a chance to ask him about it."

Confusion filled his gaze. "Why would my father hide the fact that he picked you up?"

"I don't know."

"Tell me again exactly what he said." As Drake opened his mouth, Ben shook his head. "I want Willow to tell me."

"It won't be any different," Drake snapped.

"It won't be," I said, holding Ben's gaze. "But here's what happened. Your father looked at Drake. He said, 'I should have told you the truth. It was too late when I got there. You gotta believe me. I couldn't have saved her. I'm sorry.'" I blew out a breath. The words would probably be imprinted on my brain forever.

"He didn't mention Melanie by name. He couldn't have been talking about Kelsey?"

"No, he didn't say her name, but he was talking directly to Drake, and he apologized to Drake. It was clear that he was talking about Melanie."

"He was talking about my sister, Ben," Drake said impatiently. "Clearly, he knew who had killed her, and he was protecting them."

"Well, he wasn't protecting me. I can't believe you would think for one second that I'd be involved," Ben said hotly. "Melanie was my friend. You were my friend, Drake. We grew up together."

"But you lied about where you were that night."

"I told you why I lied. It had nothing to do with Melanie."

"I asked you to reopen the case weeks ago, and you haven't done that, not since you found out I knew about your lie."

"I haven't had time. But I will help you get to the truth, Drake."

"I don't believe that, especially not now, not when we know

your father was involved. You'll try to cover for him the way he covered for someone else."

"No, I won't. I don't know how he could have done that. It doesn't make sense to me."

"He was corrupt," Drake said. "There's no doubt about what he said to us. Unless you're going to claim you don't believe us?"

"I'm going to investigate," Ben said. "I just need…a minute."

I knew he was going to need more than a minute. "I know you're in shock, Ben," I said. "Whatever your father did, you loved him."

"I did love him. But if he covered up a murder, the murder of a good friend of mine…" Ben shook his head. "Then I didn't know him at all."

"Can you think of anyone he would need to protect?" I asked.

"Or someone who had something on him?" Drake put in. "Maybe he was blackmailed into silence."

"I have no idea. He certainly never said anything to me." Ben blew out a breath. "I can't believe he's dead. I just talked to him an hour ago."

"What did you talk about?" I asked.

"He called to say he'd be in to help me later. He had something to do. I didn't ask him what. I should have asked him what. But frankly, I've been tripping all over him for the last couple of days. He wanted to be involved in every part of the search for Kelsey."

"Because he wanted to know what was going on?" I asked. "Or because he wanted to know if you were getting close to finding Kelsey? The same person who took Melanie could have taken Kelsey." I stopped abruptly, realizing what I'd just said. If that person had killed Melanie, and he had Kelsey… I put a hand to my mouth.

"Don't go there, Willow," Drake said, reading my expression.

"I can't stop myself. God! I feel sick."

"Drake is right," Ben said. "We don't have enough facts. We don't even know if the person who killed my father is the same person who killed Melanie. He didn't say that, did he?"

"No," I murmured.

"That attack on your dad looked personal," Drake said.

"Yes," Ben agreed. "There was no sign of forced entry. It didn't appear anything was taken. My father knew the person who came into his house."

"Who didn't like your father?" Drake asked.

"You and your dad come to mind," Ben retorted.

"You already know that I got here the same time as Willow."

"Did you?" Ben challenged. "I see two cars. You didn't come together?"

"No," I said. "Drake came after I did."

"Or he made it look like that."

"Sure, try to pin this on me," Drake said harshly. "It won't work."

"I'm just looking at facts. What about your father? Where was he this morning?"

I took a quick breath, wondering if Drake would tell the truth.

"I don't know," Drake said. "I'm staying at the apartment over the restaurant. I'm not at the house. But I can find out."

"I'll find out," Ben said. "I'll talk to your mother."

"I can think of someone else who might want to keep your father quiet," Drake said. "And that's you."

"I wouldn't hurt my own father."

"Maybe he didn't want to protect you anymore," Drake suggested. "Maybe he did that once before, and when Kelsey went missing, he didn't want to do it again. You had to shut him up."

"That's a complete fabrication," Ben said, shock in his gaze.

"It's no different from the story you're weaving about me or my dad."

"It is different," Ben said forcefully. "Your father was always a suspect in Melanie's disappearance. He was following her around that summer, showing up wherever she was to make sure she wasn't lying to him. He was losing it. Maybe he lost it again. Maybe he took Kelsey."

"He didn't lose it then or now," Drake ground out, his fists clenching.

As anger flowed through the air, I stepped between them. "Stop it, both of you. This speculation is getting us nowhere. And my sister is still missing. We need to find Kelsey. Then we'll deal with what happened to Melanie and with what happened to your father, Ben. I'm sorry if that's harsh, but that's the way it has to be."

Drake blew out a breath. "You're right, Willow."

"I am right." I turned to Ben. "You need to get one of your deputies to take over the investigation. You're too upset and emotionally involved."

Ben gave me a hard look. "No. I can be objective. And you need me on this because I'm extremely motivated to find who killed my father."

"If your dad was corrupt—"

Ben cut me off. "Then I'll deal with that. I will get to the truth about all of it. And I won't shy away from where the facts lead me." He looked at Drake. "Even if that takes me to your father."

"I'm not worried," Drake said. "I know my dad didn't kill my sister."

"I hope you're right."

"Why?" Drake challenged.

Ben gave him a long look. "Because that would crush you, and believe it or not, I don't want that for you. I made a mistake when I lied about that night. I could only live with the lie because I knew I hadn't hurt Melanie, that I hadn't seen her, that I had no information that could help you. But that was a rationalization, and I should have come clean when you first came to me to reopen the case." He paused. "If my father was involved, and it sounds like he was, then I'll figure it out. I owe that to you and to Melanie."

"I just want the truth, Ben. That's all I've ever wanted."

Ben nodded. "We'll get there." Then he went back into the house.

"I need to find my father," Drake said.

"You should go do that. I'm going to hang around here for a bit. If Tom had Melanie's diary, maybe it's in the house."

"If he had it, he probably got rid of it a long time ago."

"That might be true, but if I stay close, I might learn something else. Go find your father, Drake."

He frowned. "All right, but be careful, Willow. Don't turn your back on anyone, including Ben."

"I won't. Drake…" I put my arms around him and gave him a quick hug. "I'm sorry about Melanie."

"I knew she was gone. But it was hard to hear it."

"I know."

He hugged me once more and then ran to his car. I felt a chill run through me when he drove away. I missed him already.

Before I could go back inside, the paramedics brought Tom out on a stretcher and loaded him into the back of the ambulance. They'd placed a sheet over him, so I could no longer see his face, but I didn't think I'd ever forget what he'd looked like. The fear in his eyes as he realized he was dying. At least, he'd tried to confess. It was too little, too late, but it was something.

I moved back into the living room. Ben was talking to two deputies. When he saw me, he came over while the deputies moved into other parts of the house.

"You can go, Willow. I have all I need from you."

"I feel bad for you, Ben. I know it was just you and your dad for a long time."

His jaw tightened. "We were close, but we didn't always get along. He wasn't the easiest man to live with. But the longer I was away from him and from the island, the more I missed both. When he said he was going to retire, and he needed me to take over, I came home."

"Why do you think he was so intent on you taking over for him?"

"He couldn't imagine anyone but a Ryan watching over the island. Although once I came back, he didn't always appreciate what I was doing. He's been questioning every move I've made since Kelsey vanished. He didn't trust me to do it right."

"Or he was afraid you would do it too well, and you would find something that would lead back to him. Maybe he wanted a Ryan at the desk so he would always be protected."

"I can't believe he was that conniving, Willow. But maybe he was," Ben said heavily.

"I've been thinking about who might have felt like they had your father in their pocket, and I go back to the Chadwicks. They donated a lot of money to the sheriff's department. Is it possible your father would have tried to protect Gage?"

"It's not impossible," he said unhappily. "But aside from Drake's gut instinct, we don't have any evidence that Gage was involved. I honestly think a better suspect is Drake's dad. The man has serious issues. And you know he was on Melanie all the time. She called him her jailer."

"Why would he kill her when he was trying so hard to protect her?"

"Maybe he went too far. He thought she was disrespecting him, and he flipped out."

"But your dad wouldn't protect Mr. Maddox. If Holt was guilty, your father would have brought him in. It has to be someone else. And as much as I hate to admit it, I think it's someone in my circle, just like Drake always suspected. You need to find out where Gage was this morning."

"I need evidence, Willow, not theories."

"What about cameras? Is there a doorbell camera?"

"No. I told my dad we should install one, and he just laughed. Said no one was going to mess with him on this island." He paused. "I don't know if any of the neighbors have them. I've been encouraging people to install them as the island has grown since the days when everyone just left their door unlocked. But there's a good chance there's no camera within a mile of here."

"That's disheartening."

"Tell me about it."

"Can I look through the house, Ben?"

His gaze sharpened. "You really think my father has Melanie's diary?"

"I don't know."

"Well, I'll look for the diary. It was red, right?"

"You should have someone else do that."

"I can't protect him, Willow; he's dead," Ben said flatly.

"You can protect how people will think of him, whether he'll be known as a beloved sheriff who always looked out for everyone, or the man who thwarted an investigation into a teenage girl's death."

"If that's what he did, I won't stop the truth from coming out. I took an oath to uphold the law, and that's what I'll do."

"He's your father. You love him."

"I loved the man I thought I knew. If he wasn't that man, then I'll do what needs to be done." He paused. "I regret I lied about where I was that night. It didn't seem that important at the time."

"A lot of people told lies and also told themselves the exact same thing."

"You're right. There's no excuse. But now, I need to go to work." He urged me to the door, and I had no choice but to leave.

I walked out to my car, noting that the fire engine and ambulance had left, leaving only the police vehicles in front of the house. My phone vibrated, and I pulled it out of my pocket. "Hello? Drake?"

"My father is home," he said. "He's not in good shape. He said he fell when he was hiking on the headlands. He has some cuts and bruises."

"From falling?"

"I hope that's where they came from," Drake murmured. "Maybe Ben isn't the only one with a father who lies. I don't know what to do, Willow. I haven't told my parents what Tom said yet. My father is calm now, but that won't last when he hears what I have to say. I almost don't want to tell him, but I have to, because the police could knock on the door any minute."

My heart went out to him. "Are you at your parents' house?"

"Yes."

"I'll be right there. Don't say anything to your dad yet. I pointed out to Ben that your father and Tom never got along. Tom wouldn't have protected your dad if he'd been guilty. They didn't like each other at all."

"That's true," Drake said, his voice filling with a bit of hope. "If he'd had something on my dad, he would have used it. But I still need to know the truth."

"We'll find it. The sheriff might be dead, but whoever killed him is not, and we're going to find that person."

Melanie's Diary—August 6th
Everyone has a secret. At least that's the way it feels.
My dad has a lot of secrets. I don't know what happened to him when he was a Marine. Mom says he's better now, but sometimes he sinks back into another world, a dark place filled with explosions and violence, blood and death. At least, that's what I imagine. He doesn't talk about it.
Sometimes he scares me. I know he wouldn't hurt me, but it feels like he's not all there, and that makes me nervous.
This week has been pretty good, though. Dad and Drake hiked around the south shore of the island yesterday. Dad came back tired and hungry. He didn't even ask me where I'd been all day. That's a first. His favorite thing to do is interrogate me.
I might be sixteen, but I'm not an idiot. I know not to take a drink from someone I don't know. I know not to get in anyone's car who I don't know. I know that guys might not mean what they say. But sometimes guys do mean it. And I'm smart enough to know the difference. At least, I hope I am. The guy I want to talk to suddenly doesn't want to talk to me. I don't understand why. Maybe I am naïve.
I want to tell Willow how I'm feeling, but I'm not sure where to start. I've been keeping a big secret from her, and I feel bad about that. I wonder if Willow has any secrets from me. She probably doesn't. She's not very good at hiding how she feels.
Other people are much better. That's something else I've learned from Willow. People tell you all kinds of things with their eyes, their mouth, the way they move their bodies. She captures moments in her photos that show vulnerability, fear, and sometimes cockiness. When I look at her photos, the ones she takes of the other kids, I see them differently.
Sometimes I don't want to see who they really are. I just want to see them the way I want them to be.

CHAPTER TWENTY-SIX

I ARRIVED at the Maddox house just after noon. The wind had gotten worse, and so had the rain. I ran from the car to Drake's porch. He stepped out of the house, closing the front door behind him. He looked as worried as I'd ever seen him. I couldn't imagine having doubts about my own father, wondering if he could hurt my sibling, maybe even kill them.

"How's your dad doing?" I asked.

"He's all right. He was chilled from walking in this weather, and like I told you, he was beat-up from his fall. I haven't told my mother or my father anything about Tom, but news will get out fast. I don't have much time. I just wish my father wasn't bruised. That's only going to raise more suspicion, especially since no one saw him fall. He also said he didn't run into anyone on his walk."

"I don't believe he went to Tom's house. And it didn't look like Tom wrestled or fought with anyone. Someone hit him on the back of the head. Your dad's injuries wouldn't be consistent."

"That's true. I hate that I even have a small doubt. How can I doubt my own father? And if I think he's capable of killing Tom, then…" He ran his hands through his hair. "But I can't think that." He cleared his throat. "Did you look for the diary?"

"No. Ben kicked me out. He said he'd look for it."

"I hate to leave that to him."

"I didn't have a choice."

"Maybe we can get into the house later when they're done examining the scene. Ben isn't staying there. He has an apartment in town."

"I wondered where he was living. We definitely need to get into that house. But putting the diary aside, if the past is linked to the present, then I'm back to Gage. He lied about seeing Melanie when he had no reason to lie. And the sheriff spent a lot of time talking to the Chadwicks after Melanie disappeared. If Tom was protecting someone, I think Gage is a good bet."

"And Gage had a really good reason to be angry with Kelsey after she slept with his brother. Not that I think he did anything to hurt her," he quickly amended. "I'm sorry, Willow. I shouldn't have said that."

"I was already thinking it."

He met my gaze. "Don't think it. Not until there's no other option."

"Okay, so we focus on Gage. We need proof of something, and I don't know how we're going to get it." As I finished speaking, a car came down the street, pulling up in front of the house.

Jenny hopped out of the car and put a hood over her head to avoid the rain as she jogged up the steps. "Do you know what's going on?" she asked. "I just heard that Tom Ryan was killed."

"This morning," Drake said. "In his house."

"Who did it? Was it someone we know? Was it..." Her voice trailed away.

"Was it who?" I asked, seeing an odd look in Jenny's gaze.

"I don't know."

"You had a name in mind. You've been acting strange this entire week, Jenny."

"It's been a horrible week. Can you blame me?"

"You say you want to help," I continued, giving my old friend a speculative look. "But it seems like you mostly just want information. You always show up when something bad has happened. Who are you so worried about, Jenny?"

"I'm worried about Kelsey, about you, everyone. Why are you asking me these questions, Willow?"

I almost backed down, but there was something in Jenny's manner that wouldn't let me do that. Every conversation we'd had the past three days had been tinged with some hidden agenda I didn't understand. "Let's see. You've been very invested in the Gage, Carter, Kelsey triangle. Is it Gage you're worrying about? Carter? But you must have heard by now what happened to Carter."

"It's terrible," Jenny said. "And I'm not invested in their love triangle. I'm just concerned about my friends."

"Are they your friends?" I challenged shaking my head in confusion. "Something doesn't add up. If it's not Carter or Gage you're concerned about, who is it? Alex? James?" I caught the almost imperceptible shift in her gaze. "It's James."

"No. I'm not worried about James."

"Yes, you are," Drake said, his gaze narrowing on Jenny's face. "Why are you worried about him? What is James to you?"

"He's nothing to me."

"But you are worried about him," I said. "When I told you the other day that James lied about where he was the night Melanie died, you had a strange reaction then, too."

"You're imagining things," Jenny said. "I don't even know why we're talking about me. I came over to see what you knew about Tom's death. I should go."

"Wait," I ordered. "Come on, Jenny. It's too late for secrets. Kelsey is missing. Carter is fighting for his life, and Tom is dead. If you know something, anything, you need to tell us right now."

"Do you know where James was the night Melanie disappeared?" Drake asked.

She stared back at us with indecision in her brown eyes. "Yes," she said finally. "James was with me."

"What?" I hadn't thought I could keep being surprised, but I was. "You and James were together? Why would you keep that a secret all these years?"

"Because he was dating Brooklyn. I knew it was wrong. I just liked him, and he liked me. I made a poor decision."

"Where were you that night? On the beach?"

"No. We were in the treehouse."

"Are you serious? That's why his car was spotted in town?" I asked.

"But he wasn't driving it; I was. I ran into him at the beach, and he had been drinking. We got in his car and started making out, and then he wanted to keep going. So, I drove him to my house, and I parked the car around back in the alley. He wanted to leave after we had sex, but he was still drunk, so I didn't give him his keys. I drove him back to the beach. I left him in his car, and I got a ride back to my house. That's the last I saw of him until the next day. But neither of us saw Melanie. We didn't lie about that."

I shook my head, feeling a heavy weight of cynicism. "That's what everyone says when they explain their lie. It's unbelievable how many people didn't tell the truth." I looked at Drake. "You were right. Everyone was lying. Everyone knew more than they were saying."

"Unfortunately, we still don't know who took Melanie away from us," he said harshly. "I suspect it's because someone has only told us half of their secret lie."

"I'm telling you the entire truth," Jenny said. "It's been eating away at me for years, but it got worse when everyone came back. And when Kelsey disappeared, I couldn't stand knowing that I was keeping a secret, even though I couldn't imagine that James was involved in Kelsey's disappearance any more than he was involved in Melanie's."

I thought about what she'd said. "You drove James back to the beach. So, you don't know where he went after that."

"I assume he walked to your house to meet Brooklyn, or maybe he drove there. I don't know. James isn't guilty of anything but drinking too much and cheating on his girlfriend."

"Easy to say, but you have no proof." Drake gave Jenny a scathing look. "You and Melanie were friends from the time you were little kids. And you protected James Connelly over your best friend. How could you do that?"

"I talked to James the next day. He swore he just went to Brooklyn's house, and I believed him."

"Because you were in love with him," I said. "You were the girl he talked to me about at the bonfire the other night. He mistook me for you, the girl who was too young but wanted him bad. For a second, I almost thought he was speaking about Melanie, but it was you." I paused. "Or was he also messing around with Melanie? You said you saw her looking at condoms."

"What?" Drake interrupted. "When was that? Was Melanie having sex?"

"I don't know," I said as his gaze swung to me. "Melanie never told me she was with anyone. But Jenny said she saw her looking at condoms in the pharmacy."

"I never heard that." Drake gave Jenny a hard look. "Why didn't you tell me?"

"We were just joking about condoms. I don't know if she was sleeping with anyone or just thinking about it."

"If she was having sex, then that person should be questioned," Drake added. "Who would it have been?"

"I don't know," Jenny said. "I'm sorry. Sorry for everything."

"How can I believe you're sorry when you're a liar?" he challenged.

She stiffened. "I'm not the only one, Drake."

"That's clear. This island is riddled with liars."

"At least, I'm owning up to it now," she said defensively.

"Bravo." He gave her a mocking clap.

Jenny bristled with anger. "I know what I did then was wrong, but what I did for you was even worse. I did not have anything to do with Melanie's disappearance, but I feel somewhat responsible for what happened to Kelsey."

"What do you mean—what you did for Drake?" I asked, confused by her words and the sudden tension between them. "And why would you be partly responsible for Kelsey's disappearance?"

Jenny turned to me. "Drake asked me to contact Kelsey, to get her to bring her wedding to the island. He wanted to get everyone back together. He's the reason you all came back."

"It was your idea?" I asked Drake, stunned once more. "I thought you were just acting opportunistically after the wedding got rescheduled."

"It was more than that," Jenny said, before Drake could answer. "Drake is as big a liar as everyone else."

I waited for Drake to defend himself, but his silence was damning. "What is she talking about, Drake?"

He gave me a grim look. "A friend of mine is an event planner. She works for very wealthy corporate clients in Seattle. I asked her if she could move one of her events to the Worthington hotel on the date of Kelsey's wedding."

"But her wedding was already booked."

"My friend's client had an event that would pay double the price of the wedding, and she had a long relationship with the hotel. They bumped Kelsey's wedding, offering her other dates, but they weren't until next year. I had a feeling Kelsey wouldn't want to wait. I had heard she and Gage were thinking about doing the reality show together."

"In which they would have to be married," I said slowly.

"Yes. That's when I asked Jenny to help me. She called Kelsey and offered her the Belle Haven Lodge. You know the rest."

"You did all that on the off chance that Kelsey would bring the wedding here?"

"It was a long shot, but Jenny could offer incentives that your mom didn't want to refuse. I saw a chance to get everyone together, so I took it. I couldn't go another ten years without answers. I needed to shake things up."

His eyes pleaded with me to understand, but I didn't want to understand. I was pissed. "I don't care what you could or couldn't do. You're the reason Kelsey is missing. If you hadn't done what you did, she would be in Seattle right now. She'd be getting married tomorrow, far away from this island, from these liars, from whoever has her now."

"I never imagined someone would take Kelsey. You have to believe me, Willow."

"You weren't ever going to tell me, were you? I thought we'd gotten honest with each other, Drake. I thought everything was on the table. But it wasn't. You had a secret. How do I know there aren't more?"

"There aren't."

"Those are just words." His betrayal cut deep. The pain was so bad I could barely breathe. There were so many reasons to hate him right now, I couldn't even count them all. "I thought I could trust you, Drake. I thought I could count on you. But you were just working your plan."

"I stopped working on the plan the minute Kelsey went missing."

"I don't believe you."

Jenny cleared her throat. "I should go."

"You should go, Jenny, and please feel free not to talk to me again," I said sharply.

"I never meant to hurt anyone, Willow."

"You knew that having us all come back to this island was a bad idea, but that didn't stop you from doing it. And the secret you kept about James—despicable."

"That's why I helped Drake. I felt guilty about that lie," Jenny said. "And I could see how much pain Drake was still in, how much pain his whole family was dealing with. He said he just wanted a chance to talk to everyone in the same place. I didn't know all this was going to happen."

"Neither did I," Drake said. "I just wanted to unnerve everyone, hope someone would say something, and the lies would unravel. It wasn't the best plan. It was all I had."

"And I wanted Drake to find out what happened to Melanie," Jenny added. "I'm very sorry." She walked back to her car, started the engine, and drove away.

"Willow," Drake began.

I put up my hand. "Save it. I don't want to hear any more explanations or excuses."

"Then let's talk about what we should do next to find your sister."

"There is no *we*. There is no *next*. I'm done. Every time I think you and I have some special connection, I am proven wrong. You were just using me."

"I wasn't using you. I was trying to help you."

The hurt blurred my eyes with tears, but I furiously blinked them away. "You should have told me before what you did to get Kelsey here."

Guilt ran through his gaze. "I thought about it several times," he admitted. "But I knew it would end us, and I didn't want to end us. I was hoping once Kelsey came home, we could get past it."

"There's no *us*. Last night was just sex."

"It was more than that."

"No, it wasn't." I gave a bitter laugh. "The tables have turned, haven't they? That's what you said to me ten years ago, that it was just sex, and I said I thought it was more, and you told me I was wrong. Well, now you're wrong. And we're done."

"We can be done, but we still need to work together. We still need to find Kelsey."

"I don't need you to do that, Drake."

"You can't afford to turn away anyone's help," he argued. "Your sister's life is at stake."

"And you're the reason."

"I've hurt you, and I'm sorry, but I want to help get Kelsey home."

I bit down on my bottom lip as the tears slipped down my cheeks. "I can't do this again. I can't let myself believe you." I ran back to the car, jumped behind the wheel and tore down the street, not letting myself look in the rearview mirror. I didn't want to see Drake's pleading face. I didn't want to think about his pain. I wanted to wallow in my anger.

I drove for a good forty minutes before I realized I was just going around in circles. I was literally getting nowhere. So, I went home.

When I pulled into the drive behind several other cars, I saw

James and Rachel talking to Alex, Trina, Pete, and Dahlia in front of the house.

I got out and walked over to join them. "What's going on?" I asked.

"A lot," Rachel said. "Where have you been?"

"Just tell me what happened."

"Someone killed Tom Ryan, and Ben picked up Gage and took him to the station," Rachel said. "Ben seems to think Gage did it."

I sucked in a breath. I was surprised Ben had gone that far, but it was about time.

"The Chadwicks are furious," Rachel continued. "Carter is fighting for his life and now Gage has to fight with the sheriff. We're all leaving as soon as the ferry starts up again. It looks like it might go at four."

"You're going to leave with Kelsey missing, with Gage talking to the sheriff, with Carter in the hospital?" I asked.

"Yes," Rachel said flatly. "There's nothing we can do here."

My gaze swept the rest of the group. Trina and Dahlia wouldn't look at me. Alex gave me a grim nod. Pete was on his phone, and James was staring at the ground. "I used to think you were all the cool kids. I wanted to be like you. I wanted to be in your group, but I'm glad I was never one of you. You're all selfish and secretive."

"We are not selfish or secretive," Rachel declared. "We're scared. And you should be, too."

"I can't afford to be scared. I need to find my sister. You remember her, Rachel, your best friend."

"I love Kelsey, but I can't save her, if she's even still alive to be saved," Rachel bit out.

"Don't say that," I ordered. "She's still alive."

"Of course she is," Trina agreed. "There's just nothing we can do to help, Willow."

"Did you tell Brooklyn you're leaving?" I asked.

"We were just about to go inside," Trina said.

"Well, don't let me stop you." I turned to leave, not at all interested in following them into the house and having to hear all their lame excuses for a second time. But then I paused, remembering what else I'd learned. "By the way, James, I know about you and Jenny. About where you were the night Melanie died. I'm going to make sure Ben knows, too. So even if you leave, I'm sure he'll follow up with you."

"You and Jenny?" Rachel echoed. She turned to her brother. "You slept with Jenny?"

I almost laughed at the look of surprise on Rachel's face. "See what I mean, Rachel? Our group is filled with selfish people keeping selfish secrets."

"It was a mistake," James said.

"You make a lot of those," I said, holding his gaze. "Did you push me into the harbor the other night, after we spoke at Willie's?"

"What are you talking about?" he asked, but I could see the truth in his eyes.

I shook my head. "You're not at all convincing, James. You might want to work on some better stories before you talk to Ben. Oh, and you may not be leaving this island as soon as you think you are. Gage isn't the only one who will be questioned."

I ran back to my car, thinking it was probably stupid to threaten James after he most likely had tried to kill me once before. But at heart, I thought he was a coward. Pushing someone into the water whose back was turned was about the level of violence he could handle.

After I pulled out of the drive, I made a quick decision and drove back to the Ryan's house. If Ben had taken Gage to the station, then he wasn't at home. Maybe I could get into the house and look for the diary or some other clue that would tell me who Tom had been protecting.

As I drove, my phone buzzed with calls from Drake, but I ignored them all. I didn't know when I'd feel ready to talk to him again, but it wasn't going to be now.

CHAPTER TWENTY-SEVEN

THE EMERGENCY VEHICLES WERE GONE, but as I drew closer to Tom Ryan's house, I saw movement at the rear of the property. I pulled in behind a truck that was parked in front of the neighbor's house, not wanting to be seen.

I watched for a few minutes. It didn't appear that it was anyone from the sheriff's department. Then I realized it was Dillon in the backyard. He had something in his hand. It looked like a large manila envelope. He made his way to a van parked on the other side of the garage. I saw the logo for Party Planet, the company he'd worked for off and on since he was a teenager.

Dillon was probably pretty upset about Tom's death. He'd grown up in the Ryan house, and I knew that Tom had tried to look out for him over the years. But I couldn't help wondering why he was in the house now and what was in that envelope. I needed to find out.

As Dillon drove his van onto the street, I thought about getting out of the car and flagging him down, but then he flipped on the party lights on the top of the van, and I gasped.

The spinning lights...

I suddenly realized the truth. I hadn't been in a police car the night Melanie died. I'd been in that van.

Had Dillon been the one to rescue me?

I couldn't see his face in my head, but as I wrinkled my nose, I remembered the odd smell in the van. It had been the smell of weed.

And just like that, my memory came back. Dillon had picked me up on the side of the road. He'd driven me home and carried me out to the backyard and set me down on a lounger.

But why hadn't he told me? Everyone had known I was confused about my whereabouts. Why would he have kept that a secret?

As the van reached the end of the block, it turned the corner. I quickly started my car and made a U-turn.

I caught up with the van a few blocks later. A car moved in between us, but I could still see the flashing lights. I didn't know where Dillon was going, but I needed to talk to him, and I needed to know what he'd taken out of Tom's house.

A moment later, Dillon pulled into a fast-food drive-thru. I frowned. So much for me thinking he was acting suspicious, he was just picking up food. Maybe he'd been at the Ryan's house for a completely innocent reason. Although it was still weird considering that the sheriff had been killed there only hours ago, and Dillon hadn't just parked in the driveway.

I pulled into a parking lot across from the fast-food restaurant, wondering what the heck I was doing. But I didn't have a better idea, so I just waited. I'd follow Dillon to wherever he was going and then I'd talk to him.

A few minutes later, he picked up his food and got back on the road. He weaved his way through the city streets, eventually leaving the downtown area behind. When we reached a two-lane road, I slowed down, staying far enough away that hopefully he wouldn't notice I was following him. Not that I probably needed to worry. Dillon had never been a particularly observant guy. In fact, his usual expression was one of surprise and wonder.

Melanie used to say Dillon was a new soul. Everything amazed him. But I had thought it was the weed or whatever other drugs he was putting into his system that made him so awed by life.

Dillon suddenly turned down a narrow road that was barely visible in a thick crush of trees. There was a sign for Gold's Beach two miles ahead and a smattering of cabins tucked into the forest, some edging a rock-heavy stream.

Dillon stopped in front of a cabin about a half mile ahead of me. I turned into a driveway for what I hoped was an unoccupied home and watched as Dillon got out of the van and jogged up to the front door with a bag of food, a milkshake, and a large envelope—the same envelope he'd had in his hand when he'd left Tom's house.

I debated what I wanted to do. I could just go to the house and knock on the door, but something held me back. I was very aware of how isolated this area was. I'd never had reason not to trust Dillon, but I hadn't known him that well. With everything that was going on, I didn't want to be stupid.

If he had been the one to pick me up all those years ago, then Melanie's diary had been in his van, which sent a shiver down my spine. How would he have gotten her diary, unless…

Maybe Dillon was the one Tom Ryan had protected. Dillon had been like a second son to him.

While I was considering that, Dillon jogged out of the house and got in the van again. I ducked down in my car as he drove back toward the main highway.

Why had he left so soon? He'd just picked up food.

My stomach twisted with an uneasy feeling. I could follow Dillon or I could check out the cabin. I knew what was in the fast-food bags, but I was curious about the envelope.

My phone buzzed, startling me with the sound. It was Drake again. I hesitated. I was still furious, but I also wanted to talk to someone, and he was the best choice.

"Hello?"

"You picked up," he said in surprise.

"You've got thirty seconds."

"Gage disappeared from the police station. Ben was talking to him, but he went into his office to take a call and when he came back, Gage was gone. You need to be careful, Willow. I don't know what is happening, but if Gage is guilty, there's no telling what he'll do or who will be his next target."

"It might be you," I said, a sinking feeling in the pit of my stomach.

"Or you. We've both been asking uncomfortable questions."

"Okay, I appreciate the heads-up. But it might not be Gage."

"What are you talking about? Where are you, Willow? I know you're angry, but I don't think you should be alone right now. Are you at home?"

"No. I went to Tom's house. I was going to try to get in, but then I saw someone in the backyard. It was Dillon. He had a large envelope in his hand. But that's not the most important thing. When he drove down the street in the Party Planet van, he switched on the spinning lights."

"The spinning lights?" he echoed. "It was Dillon who picked you up?"

"I think so. It wasn't a police car. It was the party van."

"Are you still at Tom's house? I'll come to you."

"I'm not there. I followed Dillon. He went through a drive-thru, and then he brought food to a cabin in the woods."

"Willow, you need to be careful."

"I am being careful. I parked in front of a cabin a good distance away. He didn't see me. In fact, he just left the cabin, going back the way he came. But he didn't have the envelope in his hand anymore, and I need to see what was in it. Since he's gone, this is my best chance to find out what he needed to take out of Tom Ryan's house so soon after his death. It could be Melanie's diary. If Dillon picked me up in the van, then he might have had the diary. Tom could have been protecting Dillon all these years."

"It makes sense, but damn—Dillon? I can't imagine he would hurt Melanie."

"It's hard to believe. She really loved that kid. I'm going to check out the cabin."

"But you said Dillon dropped the food off. That means someone else is there."

"I was thinking that, too," I conceded. "But Dillon could have just eaten the food while he was driving and dropped off the trash and the envelope at the cabin before leaving again."

"Don't go in there without me. Where are you?"

"I'm not sure. There was a sign for Gold's Beach. I think I was there a long time ago, but this area doesn't seem that familiar."

"I know where you are. Just stay put. I'll be there as soon as I can."

I set down the phone and thought about staying put, but as minutes passed and there wasn't a soul or a car around, I got out of the car and moved through the trees, careful to stay in the shadows, not that there was anyone around to see me.

The motorcycle I'd seen Dillon on earlier in the week was parked by the garage. This had to be his home. But I had no idea if anyone else was in the cabin. I moved toward a nearby window and peeked inside.

My heart stopped. There was a woman in the cabin. She had her back to me, but the long, blonde hair was very familiar. My breath sped up. *Was it Kelsey?*

I wanted to tap on the window, to call out her name, but I didn't know if she was alone or if there was someone else in the cabin. I backed away and hid behind a tree. I pulled my phone out of my pocket and tried to call Drake, but there was no signal. I didn't want to take time to run back to the car. I could wait.

But what if Dillon came back? What if this was the only chance I had to save my sister?

I walked around the back of the cabin. There was a door that appeared to be off the kitchen. I twisted the knob, but it was locked. I moved around to the other side of the building and saw a window that was half open. It was about five feet off the ground. I looked around for something to climb on and saw a paint bucket by a shed. I dragged it over to the window, then climbed up. I shoved the window higher, cringing at the noise it made. It probably wasn't that loud, but it felt exceptionally loud to me. I waited, wondering if someone would come to investigate, but I didn't hear any movement.

I put my hands on the sill and lifted my body through the

window, landing on my feet in a small bathroom. There was a brush on the sink, blonde hair wrapped around the roller. I held my breath as I moved to the door. It was closed. That was a lucky break. I turned the knob and quietly opened it. I was in a hallway. I stepped out, now hearing a television in the background.

I crept down the hall and peeked into the room. My breath stalled in my chest. Sitting at the kitchen table was a blonde woman. She was sipping on a milkshake, her hair falling forward, covering her face. But I knew her. I'd known her from the minute she was born. I took another step forward.

She lifted her head, her startled gaze meeting mine.

"Oh, my God! Kelsey!" I cried. I had no idea if there was anyone else in the room, and at that moment, I didn't care. I just needed to get to her. I ran forward as she got to her feet. I threw my arms around her thin body. "You're alive. You're all right."

"Willow," she murmured in wonder.

As her shoulders start to shake, I stepped back to look at her, keeping my hands on her arms. That's when I realized she had a handcuff on her wrist that was attached to a long metal chain.

Tears of relief dripped from her blue eyes, her gaze exhausted and terrified. "Willow," she said again. "Is it really you? Where did you come from?"

"I climbed through the bathroom window." I knew that wasn't exactly what she had meant, but it was all that came to mind. "Are you hurt?" I didn't see bruises or blood, but her hair was dirty, and she didn't look like she'd slept in days. She was barefoot and still wearing the dress she'd put on for the bonfire three days ago, but she also had on an oversized gray sweatshirt.

"I'm okay. I just didn't think anyone was ever going to come." She cried harder and moved forward, wrapping her arms around my neck.

I wanted to hold her forever. This was my baby sister, the girl who'd once looked to me to take care of her. Over the years, we'd lost that. We hadn't hugged like this in forever. We'd been so different that Kelsey had turned to Brooklyn and not to me, but now it was just us again.

The heavy weight of the chain hitting my side reminded me we didn't have time for this. I gently disengaged from her. "I've got to get you out of here."

"You can't," Kelsey held up her arm. "I've tried to break the cuff open. Nothing works."

"Dillon did this to you?"

"Yes."

"I can't believe it."

"He said he's trying to save me. He has told me wild stories, Willow. I don't believe any of them. Dillon is crazy. He thinks Gage killed Melanie. That's why he kidnapped me so that Gage wouldn't kill me, too. Dillon is insane. Gage wouldn't hurt me; he loves me."

Her words took me back to my original thought—that Gage had killed Melanie. But then I'd started thinking it was Dillon. Now, I didn't know what to believe. "Maybe Dillon isn't crazy," I said slowly.

Shock widened her gaze. "What are you talking about? Gage is not a killer. He's a good man. I'm the bad one. I did so many bad things. You don't even know."

I knew more than she thought. "We can talk about it all later. I need to get you out of here before Dillon returns. Does he have a key to the handcuff? He must let you up to go to the bathroom."

"The chain is long enough I can reach the bathroom. He has never taken it off. He kept saying he was doing it for my own good and that one day I'd thank him. Even if I didn't, I'd still be alive."

I didn't know what to make of her story. Some of it made sense, but a lot of it didn't. I was considering our options when I heard an engine. I ran to the window and saw the van. "Damn. Dillon is back already."

"He just went to get me some ranch dressing. They forgot to put it in the bag. He knows I like it with my fries."

My gaze narrowed at her words. She'd just painted a picture of a very thoughtful kidnapper. "Dillon has been feeding you, taking care of you?"

"Yes."

"Did he...touch you?"

She shook her head. "No. Nothing like that. He's been okay. But I want to go home. I want my bed, my clothes, my phone. I really miss my phone."

Her plaintive cry for her phone was so very Kelsey I almost smiled. "I'm going to get you home, but we need to deal with Dillon."

"How? He keeps saying he loves me. He doesn't want me to be hurt. He's all twisted, Willow. I think it's the weed, the drugs. He told me he knows everything about Gage and Melanie, but he can't tell anyone, because Tom Ryan will put him in jail or make sure he disappears. He says Gage and the sheriff were in on it together. I don't understand."

I didn't understand, either, but I didn't have time to figure it out. I looked around for a weapon. Running over to the kitchen, I searched for a knife, but there were only plastic utensils in the drawers. Dammit! I ran back to my sister as the front door opened, jumping in front of her. If the only way to protect her was to put my body in front of her, I'd do it.

Dillon came into the room, then halted, his jaw dropping in shock. "Willow! What are you doing here?"

"Saving my sister," I snapped. Although, I didn't know how I was going to do that. Dillon was a big, tall guy, and I had no weapons.

"I'm saving her too," Dillon said, reaching into the pocket of his jacket.

I was afraid he was going to pull out a gun, but instead, he took out several packets of ranch dressing and dropped them on the table. The gesture was so innocent; it was disconcerting.

"I didn't hurt Kelsey, Willow. Did she tell you I did?"

"No, I didn't say that," Kelsey said. "I told her I want to go home, like I've been telling you for days."

"You need to let her go, Dillon," I implored.

"I will let her go as soon as I know she's safe."

"She is safe. Tom Ryan is dead. You know that because you just went to his house."

"You followed me?" he asked in surprise.

"I did."

Dillon shook his head. "I never saw you. It doesn't matter that Tom is dead. I mean, it matters, but Gage is still free. He's still walking around."

"He's not free. Ben took him to the station."

"And Gage got away," Dillon said. "I just talked to Ben. I was only going to keep Kelsey until Gage was in jail, but now he's out there, and I can't risk Kelsey getting hurt, not after all this. Gage has to pay for what he did to Melanie. He probably thinks he'll get away with it now that Tom is dead. That's why he killed him. I just wonder if he knew..."

"Knew what?" I asked in confusion.

Dillon stared back at me. "You're not going to believe it."

"You're not," Kelsey added. "It's absurd."

"Tell me."

"Tom Ryan was Gage's biological father," Dillon said. "Gage was his kid."

His words were stunning. "How can that be?"

Dillon picked up the envelope I'd seen him carrying earlier. He opened it and pulled out several photos and a piece of paper, tossing them on the table. "I got the DNA test and the photos to show to Kelsey, to prove to her I'm not lying."

"That's why you were in the house."

"I wanted to find them before Ben did. I didn't want him to accidentally stumble upon the truth," Dillon replied.

I moved closer to look at the pictures. They were photos of a blond boy, the first one taken when he was about thirteen, then sixteen, then twenty. They were all of Gage.

"Eileen sent them to the sheriff," Dillon said. "So he could have pictures of his other son."

"I told you Dillon was crazy," Kelsey interrupted. "There's no way Gage is Sheriff Ryan's son."

"Look at the test," Dillon said, pushing the paper over to me.

It was a DNA test, the results proving that Gage was the sheriff's son. "My God, you're right."

"Eileen and Tom had an affair," Dillon continued. "Thirty-one years ago, she came to the island with her son, Preston. She was having problems with her husband, and she was thinking about a divorce. She was here for several weeks, and that's when she and Tom got together. But Eileen's husband showed up and begged for forgiveness, I guess, and she went back to him."

"What about Tom? Was he married to Linda then?"

"Not yet. He met Linda a few weeks after the affair with Eileen. He said sometimes he wondered if he didn't use Linda to get Eileen out of his head, not that he didn't love Linda, but he told me Eileen put some kind of spell on him. He couldn't seem to forget her. But they never got together again."

"When did Eileen tell Tom about the baby?"

"Not until Gage was thirteen."

I was surprised again. "Why would she wait that long?"

"I think she would have waited forever if she hadn't been forced to do something."

"How was she forced?"

"When Gage was thirteen, he got caught for shoplifting here on the island. Tom wanted to make an example of him to the other kids by letting him sit in jail for a few hours and then do community service. It wasn't that big a deal, but Mrs. Chadwick couldn't stand the thought of her son having any kind of mark on his record. She told Tom that Gage was his son and he had to protect him."

"Wow. He must have been shocked."

"Tom said he couldn't believe it. But he also couldn't say no to her. He loved her and he felt sorry for her. Her husband was always cheating on her, but he understood why she couldn't leave Sean. Eileen grew up poor. She didn't have anything. And Sean was her knight in shining armor. He took her out of a bad situation and gave her a beautiful life. She couldn't let anyone see it wasn't as pretty as it looked. After the affair, she became obsessed with keeping up their image of a perfect family. She just didn't have it in her to choose love over security."

Having known Sean and Eileen for a long time, a lot of what he said made sense. "Okay, let's say I believe all that. Why would Gage kill Melanie?"

"Because she was pregnant with his baby."

I felt like I'd just gotten sucker punched. "No way," I breathed. "And he killed her?"

"Yes. And the sheriff covered it up, because Gage is his son, because he had to protect Gage, and he had to protect Eileen's perfect family."

"How do you know all this?" I demanded. "Why would Tom tell you?"

"Because I heard some of it, and I saw some of it, and I had enough pieces to put it together. Eventually, he told me the truth, but only because he needed to make sure I didn't talk."

"What did you hear? What did you see?"

"I found out about the pregnancy from Melanie. The night she disappeared, I went down to Pope Beach to smoke. Melanie was sitting on the sand, writing in her diary. She was crying. She was really upset. She had just come from seeing Gage. And he'd broken her heart. I offered to go beat him up for her. I was trying to make her smile, but it didn't work. She told me I couldn't hurt him because he was the father of her baby."

"She actually told you that?" I didn't think I could keep being amazed, but I was.

"Yes."

"That's impossible," Kelsey put in. "Gage never slept with Melanie. He told me he barely knew her."

"He was lying," Dillon said.

"Why should I believe you?" Kelsey asked.

"Because I'm telling the truth."

"No, you're not."

"Kelsey, stop," I said.

She looked at me in confusion. "You're buying into this? I know you're naïve, Willow. You don't read men very well, but he's clearly delusional."

"There are things you don't know," I told her. Turning back to Dillon, I said, "What else did Melanie tell you?"

"Melanie said Gage told her to get an abortion, but she wasn't going to do that. She would have the baby and raise it alone. Apparently, he just said good luck and walked away. She was devastated. I tried to comfort her. I tried to give her some weed, but she said it wouldn't be good for the baby. We sat on the beach for a while. She wrote in her diary until it got dark. Then she got a call and suddenly smiled. She said she thought things with Gage were going to work out after all. And she had to go to the house."

A shiver ran down my spine. "She just went to his house?"

"I was happy for her," Dillon said, his eyes darkening. "I sat on the beach for a while after that, but then I noticed she'd left her diary behind. I knew how much she loved writing in that book, so I picked it up and walked down the beach. I didn't think I could drive at that point. I went up the path behind the Chadwick house to return it to her. I was halfway up the hill when something went flying off the cliff and into the ocean. I thought someone had fallen, but I hadn't heard a scream, and I couldn't see what happened from where I was. I figured I was just stoned, and it was a big rock falling. When I got to the top, I ran into Tom. I asked him what fell, and he told me to go back to the beach. He practically shoved me down the path. He said I'd be arrested for trespassing if I didn't get off their property. I tried to tell him I was just looking for Melanie, but he wouldn't hear me. So, I left. I think I passed out for a while when I got back to the beach."

My heart was beating so fast I could barely breathe. "But you said Gage killed Melanie? It sounds like Tom pushed her off the cliff."

"I asked Tom the next day what happened. He said I was imagining stuff. He was never there. I was never there. It was just a dream. When I kept asking questions, he got more furious than I'd ever seen him. He shoved me up against the wall of his house. He said I needed to shut up that he was trying to protect me. If I didn't keep my mouth shut, I'd go to jail. Melanie's disappearance would be pinned on me. I'd end up in a cell, and he knew I couldn't take it because of what happened to me when I was a kid, when I was locked in a closet. I don't know if you ever knew about that."

"Ben said you had a rough childhood, but I didn't know that."

"Yeah, well, I couldn't take the chance that I'd go to jail. And it was easier to think it was just a weird dream that I'd had. I didn't want to believe the sheriff, the man who was like a father to me, could have done something bad. I also didn't want to think I'd done something bad that I couldn't remember. Years passed, and no one ever found Melanie. And then one night I was at the Ryan's house. Ben wasn't there. It was just me and Tom. The old man was drinking heavily. He was looking through a bunch of photos, and he started talking about making mistakes. He said he had a kid who didn't even know him. The worst part was that he was still in love with that woman, and he couldn't stop wanting to make her happy, wanting to protect her."

"Did he tell you that Gage was his kid?" I asked. "Did he actually say that?"

"Yes. I picked up the photos, and I said, this is Gage. He told me not to tell anyone. It was a secret he would take to his grave, along with the other secret."

"The other secret?"

"That's when I asked him what really happened at the Chadwick house that night. He gave me a weird look and said he'd done something he'd never thought he'd do. He'd covered up a crime. He'd wanted to come clean, but it wasn't just about love. Money had been exchanged. His hands had been dirtied. He couldn't speak the truth without it taking him down, too. He picked up the photo, and he looked right at Gage, and that's when it all clicked in. I said Gage killed Melanie, and you protected him. He got all shook up then. He shut down. Reminded me I'd spend the rest of my days in jail if I ever tried to say anything."

"So, you stayed silent. You let Drake and his family continue to suffer with the uncertainty of what happened to Melanie."

"He only came clean two years ago—eight years after Melanie disappeared," Dillon said defensively. "Drake had a life in Seattle. His family was happy again. And I didn't have any proof. It was just my word against the sheriff. Who was going to believe me?" He paused. "To be honest, I guess there was a part of me that didn't want to take down the sheriff. Tom took care of me when I was in trouble as a kid. And he was Ben's dad. I felt like I was part of their family." Dillon drew in a breath and let it out. "But when everyone came back to the island this week, all the memories returned. I felt like something bad was going to happen again. When I saw Kelsey arguing with Gage on the beach, I knew I had to do something."

"When were you arguing with Gage?" My gaze moved from Dillon to Kelsey.

"After the bonfire. We stopped at Pope Beach to talk. We wanted somewhere private. I guess that was a mistake. I didn't even see Dillon there."

"But I saw her, and I saw Gage grab her arm and yank it hard. Kelsey started crying. It reminded me of Melanie. They left the beach, and I followed them back to your house to make sure Kelsey got home."

I thought about that. "You didn't go in the house," I said to Kelsey. "Your phone was in the backyard."

She nodded. "I wanted to think. I'd just sat down on the deck chair by the bluff when Dillon came around the corner. He scared me to death. But then he was being sweet to me, and I was feeling sad and conflicted. I didn't know what to do about Gage, about my wedding. Dillon said he could make me feel better fast, that we could get high. And I really wanted to feel better. So, I went with him." Kelsey paused. "I guess I dropped my phone in the yard."

"Where did you go?"

"Dillon drove me here. We smoked some weed, and I told him what I was arguing with Gage about. I fell asleep at some point, and when I woke up, I had this on my wrist." She held up her arm. "That's when I realized Dillon was crazy. He was trying to convince me that Gage was a murderer. He wouldn't let me go, Willow. He took my shoes, too, my beautiful five-hundred-dollar heels from Matoni."

"I wanted to make it look like she'd gotten on a boat, so I dropped one of her shoes at the harbor," Dillon said. "I wanted Ben to look for her far away from here. I couldn't let her go, Willow.

Gage would have killed her as soon as he found out about her and Carter."

I looked at Kelsey again. "You told Gage about Carter?"

Her gaze widened. "Wait! What? How do you know about Carter?"

"Did you tell Gage that you and Carter hooked up?" I asked, ignoring her question.

"No. God, no! I told Gage I wanted to call off the wedding because it didn't feel right. He was angry. He said we had a lot of money on the line, that it wasn't just about love. We needed to get married for the show. We could divorce later." She paused. "But I told Dillon about Carter. And I said I needed to tell Gage, too, before we got married."

"Gage wasn't going to let her walk away before or after the wedding," Dillon said. "He would get rid of her the way he got rid of Melanie. That's why I had to protect her. This was for her own good. You have to believe me."

"How do you know about Carter?" Kelsey asked again.

"He told me he was in love with you. The secret is out."

"Oh, God! Everyone knows?" she groaned. "I feel so stupid. I didn't mean to hurt Carter. I liked him. But I think I was using him as a reason to walk away from Gage. I feel terrible, Willow."

I believed her. Kelsey had a heart. Unfortunately, her brain allowed her to do things before her heart realized that she was hurting someone.

"I just want to go home," Kelsey said with a plaintive cry. "Please, Dillon, let me go."

Dillon gave an adamant shake of his head. "You both need to stay here until Gage is in jail. He killed Tom today. He's going to come after you if you go home."

"Why would Gage have killed Tom now?" I asked. "Did he know that Tom was his father?"

"I'm not sure. But Tom was getting worried about Kelsey being gone for so long. He must have figured Gage had killed her, too, and he didn't know how he was going to cover up another murder, especially since Ben was now in charge. If Ben didn't bring Kelsey back, his career would probably be over."

"This is unbelievable," Kelsey said.

"Unfortunately, it's very believable," I said. "Dillon might be a little crazy, but he's not wrong about Gage. Gage killed Melanie. And finding out about you and Carter probably would have put him over the edge." I paused, looking back at Dillon. "You picked me up that night. You took me home. Didn't you?"

"Yeah, it was a couple hours later. I shouldn't have been driving, but it was getting cold. I saw you in the road, and you were really out of it. I took you home and put you in the backyard. I couldn't risk letting your parents see me."

"Why didn't you ever say anything? You must have heard I couldn't remember."

He gave a helpless shrug. "To be honest, I started to wonder if I'd imagined everything, if I'd just gone on a bad trip in my head. I didn't know what was real and what wasn't real until years later when Tom told me about Gage, about the coverup."

"You should have said something."

"I know. I was protecting myself. And then you left the island, and I never saw you again."

"It's not just me you should have told. You should have talked to Drake. You should have talked to Ben. I don't understand Dillon. Were you really that scared of Tom and his threats?"

He nodded grimly. "I have a lot of anxiety. I can't be locked up. That's why I live out here. I have to be free. I have to be, Willow."

I could see the pain and panic in his eyes, and I suspected there was a lot about Dillon's past that I didn't know. But I finally knew who had picked me up and taken me home. And that's what I needed to do for Kelsey.

"Okay," I said. "I need to take Kelsey home. It was good that you protected her, but my family will do that now. We won't let Gage near her. Please, take off the chain."

"I just wanted to save her," Dillon said again. "That's all I wanted."

"You did save her. But now you have to let her go."

Dillon pulled a key from his pocket and walked over to Kelsey. He unlocked the cuff and took it off her wrist.

She rubbed her wrist and started to cry again. Then she gave me another hug. "Take me home, Willow."

"I will," I said, giving her a reassuring smile. "You're going to be okay, Kelsey."

"I'm sorry, Kelsey," Dillon said, stepping back. "Maybe you'll never believe me, but I just wanted to save you, because I couldn't save Melanie."

The door behind Dillon suddenly flew open.

I stared in shock at the person who came into the room, gun in hand. "No," I said in disbelief. "Not you."

CHAPTER TWENTY-EIGHT

As I LOOKED down the barrel of a gun, I froze. It seemed impossible to believe that the woman who puttered in her garden all day long and made me herbal tea every time she saw me was holding a gun on us. Eileen Chadwick's eyes glittered with rage, with insanity, I realized. The Eileen I knew wasn't there anymore. She was gone.

"What are you doing, Eileen?" Kelsey asked.

"Shut up," Eileen ordered. "This is all your fault, Kelsey. You destroyed Carter and Gage. They will never be the same because of you."

Kelsey paled. "You know about Carter?"

"I know everything. And you will pay for your sins."

"My God, it was you," Dillon suddenly said, his dazed gaze snapping to attention. "I thought it was Gage who killed Melanie. I thought the sheriff was protecting Gage. But he was protecting you."

"I did what had to be done to protect my family," Eileen said, evil in her gaze.

As Eileen lifted her arm, Dillon rushed forward.

The gun went off with a thunderous blast. Kelsey screamed.

Dillon's body crumpled. He staggered forward, knocking Eileen to the ground, crushing her with his body.

I grabbed Kelsey's hand and pulled her to the door. When we got outside, we could hear a scream of rage coming from behind us. I wanted to run toward the car, down the road, but it was the obvious choice, and there was not as much cover as going the other way.

I made a quick decision and turned toward the trees, pulling Kelsey along with me. We ran as fast as we could, but the terrain was rocky, and the ground was slippery from the pouring rain. The storm had worsened in the last thirty minutes. It was in full force now.

Kelsey yelped as her bare feet hit a sharp rock, but I pulled her along, urging her to keep running.

Five minutes later, I heard crashing behind us, shouts of anger and promises of revenge. Eileen wasn't far behind us.

"Faster," I said.

Kelsey was panting, her eyes terrified. Then she stumbled and fell to her knees, almost dragging me down with her. I tried to help her up, but she squealed with pain and grabbed her ankle.

"I can't do it," she said, a grimace on her face. "I can't run."

For a split second, I panicked, but I didn't have time for that. I looked around, seeing a thick area of brush to the right. "Over there," I said, pulling her up. "We need to hide."

She stumbled with me into the brush. I pushed her behind a bush. "Lay down. I'm going to bury you with leaves."

"What?"

"Sh-sh." Eileen's voice was getting louder. "Stay here and be very quiet," I whispered, as I picked up piles of leaves and dumped them all over her.

"What about you?" Kelsey asked.

"I'm going to lure her away from here."

"She'll kill you."

"It's our only choice. Put your head down."

I covered her blonde hair with dirt and leaves and then I got up and ran in the other direction. I made as much noise as I could, wanting to get Eileen's attention. For several minutes, I wasn't sure it had worked. It seemed too quiet. I silently prayed that Eileen hadn't found Kelsey, that I wouldn't hear the gun go off again.

I felt a terror I'd never felt before, but I couldn't cry. Tears would only make it more difficult to escape. I ran through the tall trees, my heart pounding against my chest. I didn't know where I was going, and the thick foliage and dark skies confused me. If I'd been in this area before, I couldn't remember it. I hoped I'd run into someone who could help me, but there wasn't a soul around, except for the person who was after me.

The wind gusted as the rain pelted my head. My clothes were quickly drenched, the water on my face freezing with the cold wind. My foot slipped as I hit a rock. I stumbled, hitting my hand against a tree to steady myself. The wood left a deep scratch, and blood dripped down my fingers, but I couldn't stop.

My breath came hard and fast. A crack of thunder was so loud it almost knocked me off my feet. Seconds later, there was a flash of lightning. Maybe I could use the storm to my advantage. Perhaps the rain would make it more difficult to find me.

Then I heard someone crashing through the brush.

I sped up, but I feared I wouldn't be fast enough.

Crashing through the trees, I came to a terrifying, dizzying stop as I realized I was at the edge of a cliff. I looked down at the white-caps below, the dark, churning water ready to suck me under. I couldn't let the sea take me. I looked to the left, then to the right.

One impossible choice.

Would it be the right one?

I turned to the left and sprinted toward another thick grove of trees. I needed cover. My lungs strained from the pressure I was putting on them. Within minutes, I was running out of gas. Exhausted and disoriented, I didn't know which path to take, which trees to cut through. Every turn led into a deeper, thicker forest, paths that seemed untraveled by anyone.

Tears pricked my eyelids. The worst thought I'd ever imagined was raging around in my head. *Would I die tonight? Was this it?*

A voice rang through the trees. "There's nowhere to go. Give up."

"Never," I muttered, not daring to scream the words, because that would be stupid, and I'd done enough stupid things already. I broke through another thick patch of trees and found myself back out in the open, with only a few feet between me and the edge of a cliff. I'd run out of room.

I'd made the wrong choice.

Eileen stormed toward me, only slowing down when she realized she had her prey. But she also seemed confused.

"You aren't the one I want," she yelled. "Where is she? Where did Kelsey go?"

"You'll never find her. And you'll never get away with this."

"Of course, I will. I'm a Chadwick. No one takes us down."

There was nothing but confidence in her voice.

"Why did you kill Melanie?" I asked, wanting to get her talking until I could find a way out of this impossible situation. "Why did you do it, Eileen?"

"Because she was pregnant, and she wanted to have the baby. She was going to derail Gage's career, his chance at going pro. She was ruining everything."

"She didn't have to die. Gage could have just stayed away from her."

"He wouldn't have stayed away from her. The fool was in love with her."

"Then you should have killed him," I said bitterly. "I'm sure he forced Melanie to have sex with him."

"There was no force. They were stupid children thinking they were in love. She told me that herself."

Her words confused me. I'd never heard Melanie talk about Gage. Of all the Chadwicks, she'd mostly talked about Carter, but maybe that had been a cover. Carter had usually been where Gage was. Maybe she'd used Carter to get closer to Gage, the way I'd sometimes used Ben to get closer to Drake.

"I tried to pay her off," Eileen continued. "I offered her money. She threw it in my face. She disrespected me."

"So, you killed her? How did you even do that?" I asked in bewilderment.

"I told her we both needed to calm down, and I offered her some tea."

"You poisoned her tea?"

"It was so easy," Eileen said with a simple shrug. "Melanie just went to sleep. Then her heart stopped. It was quite peaceful after the yelling. All I had to do was get rid of her."

I felt sick to my stomach at what she'd done, but I couldn't give in to my emotions. I had to keep her talking. "The sheriff—Tom Ryan—he helped you, didn't he?"

"Tom had no choice. We dragged her to the cliff and pushed her over. She was already dead, Willow. She didn't feel anything."

"Why didn't Tom have a choice?"

She stared back at me. "I think you know already."

"Because he was Gage's father?"

"So, Dillon told you. Well, it doesn't matter. Tom is dead. Dillon is dead and you and Kelsey won't survive the day. I'll go back home. We'll all mourn you and then we'll go back to our lives far, far away from here."

A terrifying chill and a crushing hatred for Eileen ran through me. "Melanie was an innocent girl. How could you kill her? How could you throw her into the sea?"

"She would have destroyed my son's dreams." There wasn't even a hint of regret in her voice. "Now Kelsey has done the same thing. I will find her, and I will kill her, too. Gage will never recover from her betrayal. And Carter will never be the same man. Kelsey will die. Make no mistake about that, Willow, but you will no longer be a problem for me."

I was running out of time. I could rush her, but I'd seen what happened when Dillon did that. I searched desperately for some way out. Maybe jumping into the ocean was my best bet. But as I looked at the raging sea and saw all the jagged rocks, I knew I wouldn't survive.

"You have no options," Eileen said, an odd calm in her voice now. "But I'll kill you first. You won't feel the rocks or the cold. It will just hurt for a second."

"How can you kill me? You know my parents. You've practically been an aunt to me."

"Our family relationship is a joke. Your mother has been fucking my husband for years. I can't stand her."

"You've always pretended to be her friend."

"It was easier that way. I'm actually sorry that you're the one who got in my way, sweet Willow. You were the nicest one in your family. But now you know too much. You've asked too many questions. You used to be someone no one noticed. Now you have everyone's attention."

"What about Tom?" I asked, desperate to stall as long as I could. "Did you tell him Gage killed Melanie?"

"Yes. I told him he had to protect his son. He agreed. He had no idea that Gage was innocent."

"Was Gage innocent? What did he know?"

"Nothing. He knew nothing. He thought some stranger had abducted Melanie. I didn't realize that fool Dillon knew the whole story until this morning when I spoke to Tom. He said Dillon was asking a lot of questions. Tom was worried that Gage had done something to Kelsey, too. He said he couldn't help me hide another murder. That Ben was in charge now, and he would protect Ben over Gage."

"So, you killed Tom."

"I had no more use for him."

"When did you figure out Dillon had Kelsey?"

"After I talked to Tom. It's the only thing that made sense. It just took me a little longer than I thought to find his cabin. I'm done talking. If you need to say a prayer, say it now."

I made a sudden dive to the right as her gun went off, rolling on the ground, waiting for an explosion of pain, but none came. Then someone came flying through the trees. He tackled Eileen from behind. She fell forward, the gun flying out of her hand.

Drake smashed her head into the ground.

I scrambled to my feet. Then I ran over and picked up the gun, pointing it at them as they wrestled for control. I'd never even held a gun before, but I would pull the trigger if I needed to do that to save Drake's life, to save my own.

But I didn't need to shoot. Eileen was no match for Drake. He had her pinned face-down in the dirt, holding one arm behind her as he put a hard knee in the middle of her back. She twisted to get free, screaming like a trapped wild animal.

Drake looked at me with concern. "Are you all right?"

"Yes." I lowered the gun. "How did you find me?"

"I ran into Kelsey and Dillon at the cabin."

"Wait! Eileen said Dillon was dead."

"He's alive. He was shot in the shoulder. I don't think it's life-threatening."

"And Kelsey was with him?" I asked. "She went back to the cabin? I told her not to move. She never listens to me."

"She said you saved her life. I didn't take time to get the whole story. She told me you were in trouble and Eileen was going to kill you. I was afraid I wasn't going to get to you in time."

I drew in a shaky breath at his words. There was so much adrenaline running through me I hadn't had time to register just how close I'd come to dying. I couldn't let myself do that now. I had to tell him at least part of the story, the most important part.

"Drake, Eileen killed Melanie. It wasn't Gage. It was Eileen."

His face paled. "Why? Why would she do that?" He turned his attention to Eileen. "Why would you do that?"

"Because that bitch was pregnant," Eileen shouted.

"Shut up!" Drake pressed his knee harder on Eileen's back. "What the hell did you do to my sister?"

"I poisoned her with tea and threw her in the ocean," Eileen said, twisting her face to the right so she could show Drake how much she didn't care.

Drew pulled her arm up behind her back, and she yelped in pain.

"You killed her?" he asked in shock. "Because she was pregnant?"

"With Gage's child," Eileen said.

"That's impossible." He looked at me. "Did you know?"

I shook my head. "I had no idea, Drake. I swear it. I didn't know Melanie had sex with anyone, much less Gage. She never told me."

He turned back to Eileen. "You didn't have to kill her."

"She was going to ruin everything for my son, for my family."

Drake suddenly jumped up, dragging Eileen to her feet. He put his arm around her neck as he moved toward the edge of the cliff.

"What are you doing?" I shouted. Even though I knew exactly what he was going to do.

"She threw my sister into the ocean. She can see what that feels like."

I saw the murderous rage in his eyes. "Don't, Drake. You can't kill her."

"I can kill her. I can get justice for Melanie."

"That's not justice, it's murder."

"Go ahead," Eileen gasped. "Do it. Kill me. You know you want to."

"Please, Drake, don't," I begged. "You'll go to jail for her crimes."

"I don't care what happens to me. She killed my sister."

"Well, I care what happens to you. And Melanie would not want you to do this. She would not want your parents to lose another child. She would not want them to have to visit you in jail."

Doubt entered his gaze. "They'll be okay. I might not be free physically, but mentally I'll finally be able to let go."

"It's too easy," I argued. "Eileen needs to sit in a prison cell. She needs to see the pain her family and her kids will go through because of what she did. She needs to feel the shame, the embarrassment. Her family, her name, everything she loved so much, will slowly be destroyed right in front of her. That's the revenge, Drake. Watching her secrets get revealed one by one. The humiliation will kill her more slowly. All the ugliness of her pretty life will be revealed. The whole world will know who she really is. Her sons will hate her. Her husband will turn away. Her friends will act like they never knew her."

"No," Eileen cried. "Kill me now." She struggled again, pushing them both closer to the edge.

More fear ran through me. "Drake, let her go. She's going to take you over the side with her."

"No, she's not." He dragged Eileen away from the edge. "You're right. She needs to suffer, the way we all suffered. I want her to live every day for the rest of her life in the kind of pain she put us all through."

A rush of movement caught my eye, and I was relieved to see Ben and another deputy come crashing through the trees with guns drawn. *Thank God!*

Ben took in the scene with a sharp eye. "Everyone all right?"

"It was Eileen," Drake told Ben. "She killed Melanie."

"That's what Kelsey said." Ben's gaze hardened on Eileen. "Did you also kill my father?"

Eileen's answer was to spit on the ground. The refined woman I'd known was really just a mean alley cat. She might have married her way into a different life and become a different woman, but this was who she really was.

"She killed your dad, Ben," I said, answering for her. "And she shot Dillon, too."

Ben's eyes filled with rage, his entire body stiffening, but he fought for control. In the end, he just motioned to the deputy next to him. "Take her into custody."

"Let me die," Eileen begged, but no one was listening to her.

Drake released her into the custody of the deputy, who quickly handcuffed her. Eileen sank to the ground, refusing to move.

"We can drag you out of here," Ben told her. "It would actually be my pleasure to do that."

"Just shoot me. Pay me back for what I did to your father."

"Oh, I'll pay you back, but it won't be with a bullet." Ben walked over to her, grabbed her arm, and yanked her to her feet. Then he turned to us. "I want to hear the entire story. But I need to get her out of here. Kelsey and Dillon are both on their way to the medical center. Your parents and your sister are on their way there, too, Willow."

I blew out a breath of relief. "Thank you."

"Don't thank me. It looks like you and Drake did the heavy lifting."

"It was all Willow," Drake said. "I just came in at the end."

"Meet me down at the station."

"We will," Drake promised.

As Ben and the deputy moved Eileen toward the trees, Drake came over to me. He put his hands on my shoulders, giving me a long, searching look. I could see dozens of emotions in his dark-blue gaze, but there was one missing now—uncertainty. He had no more questions. But there was still anger and sadness. I didn't think those would go away soon. I'd gotten my sister back, but Drake had not. He would never see Melanie again, and neither would I.

Tears filled my eyes. "I'm sorry," I whispered. "I wish the truth could have brought her home."

"Me, too," he said gruffly.

I slid my arms around his waist and pulled him close. We stayed that way for several long minutes, an island of warmth and safety in a sea of drizzling rain and stormy emotions. It had taken us ten years to get back here. Closing my eyes, I breathed in and out, letting my heart slow down, letting my mind catch up with everything that had happened.

"We're getting soaked," Drake murmured, as he released me.

I smiled, keeping my hands on his waist, needing him to stay close. "We've always been good in the rain."

His lips curved upward. "That's very true. Are you really okay, Willow?"

"I am. How about you?"

"I'm trying to process it all. I feel like I came into the middle of a story."

"I know. I'll tell you everything. There were some unexpected twists."

He shook his head in bewilderment. "I can't believe Melanie was with Gage, that she was pregnant. She was sixteen. She must have been so scared when she found out she was going to have a baby, but she didn't tell you; she didn't tell me. Why couldn't she confide in us?"

His question brought me more pain. "I don't know. I wish she had. But I can't be angry at her for that. I never told her about you and me. It was too personal. Maybe Melanie felt the same way about Gage."

"I always had a bad feeling about him, about the lie he told. Now I understand why he didn't want anyone to know he'd seen her that day. He was afraid the secret about the baby would come out."

"Your instincts were right."

"I wish I could have protected her."

"I wish the same thing."

"But Kelsey is okay," he said. "You saved her life. She said you hid her in the woods and made noise so Eileen would follow you. That was brave and selfless."

"I just did what came to mind. But I was in trouble. Until you showed up." A knot came into my throat. "I thought for a minute there, I was going to die."

His gaze darkened. "When I heard the gunshot... Well, I don't think I've ever been that scared. I didn't know what I was going to find when I came through the trees."

"You were a sight to see. I dodged the first bullet, but I don't think she would have missed a second time. Thank you."

"You're more than welcome. I'm glad you told me where you were. I know I hurt you, Willow. I betrayed your trust by keeping a secret from you."

"I had thought we were being completely honest with each other," I admitted, still feeling the sting of his lie of omission.

"It was a mistake."

I let out a weary sigh. "Well, I don't want to talk about that now. I just want..."

As my voice trailed away, he gave me a searching look. "What? What do you want?"

"You asked me that before."

"Is your answer still the same?"

"I'm not sure," I said honestly. "I need to think about a lot of things. But I'm too tired and overwhelmed, so can I say what I want for the next minute?"

"You can say anything."

In the end, I didn't need words. I pulled him to me and took the kiss I both wanted and needed. Nothing else mattered. It was just me and him. But not even our heat was enough for the cold wind. I shivered, and Drake let me go.

"We should get out of the rain," Drake said.

"Yes. Everything else can wait."

CHAPTER TWENTY-NINE

I STRIPPED off my jacket when I got into Drake's car, grateful that it had provided some protection from the rain. We didn't want to split up, and I didn't feel like driving, so I'd get my car later.

Drake cranked up the heat as we headed to the medical center. My hair and jeans were still damp when we got there, but the chill had eased, and I didn't want to waste time going home to change.

When we arrived, Dillon was in surgery, but his prognosis was good. Kelsey had been checked over and had her ankle taped and was about to go home with Brooklyn and my parents. We had a short reunion with promises to talk later, and then Drake and I left the hospital and went to the sheriff's office to speak to Ben.

We'd no sooner sat down with him in a conference room when Gage burst through the door, a deputy following close behind.

Gage looked like a wild man. His blue eyes were lit up, his hair wet and windblown.

"What the hell is going on?" Gage demanded. "My dad just called me. He said Dillon kidnapped Kelsey, but you have my mother in custody? Are you crazy? First, you think it's me, Ben, then it's my mother? If you did this to get me to turn myself in, well, here I am," Gage said. "You need to let my mother go."

"Sit down," Ben told Gage. He nodded to the officer. "You can go."

The deputy left, closing the door behind him.

Gage remained on his feet, giving me and Drake a hard look. "What are they doing here?"

"They're going to fill me in," Ben replied. "Since you seem to be in the middle of this, you can stay, but you need to sit down."

Gage pulled out a chair and took a seat, giving Ben a hard look. "I want to get my mother out of jail and then I want to talk to Kelsey. Is she all right? Was she hurt?"

"No, she wasn't hurt. Dillon was protecting her from you. He thought you killed Melanie and would do the same to Kelsey. He didn't realize that it was your mother who took Melanie's life."

Gage's face turned white. "What are you talking about? That's absurd. My mother isn't a killer."

"I didn't think she was, either," I said, drawing Gage's attention to me. "But Eileen shot Dillon right in front of me. Then she told me why she had to kill Melanie, because she was pregnant with your child and was going to ruin your life."

Gage was shaking his head before I finished speaking. "That's impossible. She's not a murderer." Despite his words, there was now a shadow of doubt in his eyes.

"I don't think you know who she really is," I said. "Eileen was willing to do anything to protect her family, her image, her reputation."

"She just confessed this?"

"She was going to kill me, too. She believed the secret would die with me."

"I want to talk to her," Gage demanded, turning to Ben.

"You'll have a chance at some point, but not now," Ben replied. Then he turned to me. "I want to know how my father became a threat to Eileen."

I knew I was going to hurt Ben with this part of the story, but it had to be told. "Your father and Eileen had an affair years ago, Ben. There was a baby, a secret baby that she passed off as Sean's. That child was Gage."

Both Ben and Gage stared at me like I'd lost my mind.

"It's not true," Gage said.

"Gage," I said with a sigh. "You need to stop telling me things aren't true, because everything I'm going to tell you is the truth. You won't like any of it, but you have to hear it."

"Go on," Ben said shortly.

"Yes, let's hear about this secret baby," Gage added, anger written across his face.

"Eileen didn't tell Tom that he was your father until you were thirteen," I said, focusing solely on Gage. "That's when you got into trouble shoplifting. Tom wanted to teach you a lesson by putting you in jail. Eileen told him he couldn't because you were his son. She gave him DNA proof he was your father, along with photos of you."

"How do you know this?" Gage demanded.

"Dillon told me first, then your mother confirmed the story."

"Dillon knew?" Ben asked in shock.

"He found out two years ago," I said, meeting Ben's questioning gaze. "That part of the story, anyway. Your dad was drinking heavily one night. He was looking through the envelope with the DNA and the photos, and Dillon saw them."

"Why wouldn't Dillon have told me? We were like brothers," Ben said. "This doesn't add up."

"Because it's a lie," Gage put in. "I look just like everyone else in my family."

"You look like your mother," I corrected. "So do your brothers. But neither of you have to believe me. The evidence is in Dillon's cabin." I turned to Ben. "Did you see the manila envelope? It was on the kitchen table."

"My crime scene team is going through the cabin now. I still don't understand why Dillon didn't tell me."

"Because he couldn't. Your father threatened him."

"With what?"

"That's when we get to Melanie."

Drake sat up straighter in his chair. "Wait! Dillon knew what happened to Melanie?"

"Not exactly, but he knew some of what had happened. The day Melanie disappeared, Dillon ran into her at Pope Beach. She was writing in her diary and crying about Gage. She told Dillon about the baby, that Gage wanted her to get an abortion, but she refused. A short time later, Melanie got a call. She said Gage had changed his mind, and she had to go up to the house."

"I never called her," Gage said.

"There was an unknown number on Melanie's phone, but we couldn't trace it," Ben said.

"That's right," Drake interjected. "I had my investigator look into that number, too. He said it was probably to a burner phone."

"Which must have belonged to Eileen," I said.

"My mom had a burner phone?" More disbelief entered Gage's voice. "You're talking about a sweet woman who liked to putter in the garden all day."

"She was a lot more than that," I said.

"Keep going," Drake ordered.

"When Melanie got to the house, she and Eileen had a heated discussion. Eileen made Melanie some tea to calm her down. But it was spiked with some kind of poison. Melanie passed out, and her heart stopped." I bit down on my lip as emotion ran through me, but I had to push on. "Afterward, Eileen called Tom. She told him Gage killed Melanie, and he had to help her cover it up. They dragged Melanie to the edge of the bluff and tossed her into the sea."

Gage sucked in a sharp breath. "That's not possible."

"Unfortunately, it's what happened," I told him. "Tom was still standing on the bluff when Dillon came up the path from the beach that was behind your house. Melanie had left her diary behind, and he wanted to return it to her. Dillon told Tom he thought he saw someone fall. The sheriff told him he'd imagined it; he was high. He told him to go back to the beach and sleep it off. When news spread of Melanie's disappearance the next day, Dillon went back to the sheriff, asking him what happened the night before. Dillon thought Gage was involved because Melanie had gone to meet him. Tom told him again that he was imagining things, that he'd never been at the house, never seen Melanie, never seen him, and that if he said a word to anyone about anything, he'd be the one to end up in jail. Melanie's disappearance would be pinned on him. Apparently, Dillon suffers from severe claustrophobia. That threat scared him into silence. Plus, he had doubts about what he'd seen. He started to believe that Tom was right, that he'd just imagined it all."

"And he kept the secret all these years," Ben mused. "Unbelievable. I thought I knew Dillon as well as I know myself."

"I think Dillon was confused and also conflicted. The sheriff was trying to protect him, and he was doing the same. But he can tell you more about his motives."

"Oh, I intend to have a long talk with Dillon," Ben said grimly. "Why did Dillon kidnap Kelsey?"

"Ironically, Gage and Kelsey had a fight on Pope Beach after the bonfire, which is where Dillon still gets high. Dillon believed Gage had killed Melanie and now he was going to kill Kelsey. So, he followed them back to my house and convinced Kelsey to party with him. She was upset and wanted to escape her thoughts, so she said yes. Dillon took her to his cabin and after she fell asleep, he handcuffed her and chained her up. He told her everything, but she didn't believe him. She thought Dillon was delusional. But he wasn't. Ultimately, he jumped in front of a bullet for her. He saved her life." I let out a breath. "That's it. That's the story. Eileen killed your dad, Ben, because he was getting too worried about Kelsey. Tom wanted to protect you. He thought your career could be over if you didn't find Kelsey. He told Eileen that."

"So, he was done protecting me," Gage said bitterly. "I can't believe Tom is my father. How could my mother sleep with him?"

"You'll have to get the details from her."

"But I can't get the details from my father," Ben said heavily.

"Dillon knows more than I do," I told him. "But the affair with Eileen was before your dad married your mom. If that helps."

"I have a question," Drake said, his gaze narrowing on Gage. "Why didn't you tell anyone Melanie was pregnant when you were questioned?"

"I told Sheriff Ryan," Gage answered. "He instructed me not to say anything."

"Did he say why?"

"He certainly didn't say he was my father. He just said it wasn't pertinent to the case." Gage paused. "I made a mistake telling Melanie to get an abortion. I had changed my mind, but I didn't get a chance to tell her. She died not knowing that I would have stood up for her. Knowing that has eaten me alive, but I had no idea that my mother got involved, or that she did any of what you just said. It's like you're describing a stranger."

"Your mother is mentally ill, Gage," I said, drawing his gaze to mine. "I saw that tonight. She had an obsessive, fanatical desire to protect you."

"Protect me or her reputation?" Gage said cynically. "My God! She killed Melanie. She killed the girl I loved. I can't believe she had it in her."

"The girl you loved?" Drake questioned.

"Yes. Look, the pregnancy scared me. I was about to get drafted. I had my senior year of college coming up. My whole life was planned out, and having a baby wasn't part of the plan. But I told you, I changed my mind. I just wish I could have told Melanie," Gage said, regret in his voice.

I turned to Ben. "What's going to happen now?"

"Eileen will be charged with multiple homicides. I'm not sure what charges Dillon will face; he kidnapped Kelsey and held her against her will."

"What if Kelsey doesn't want to press charges?"

"Are you sure she feels that way?"

"I don't know," I admitted.

"We'll have to see," Ben said.

"And me?" Gage challenged.

"I'd like to talk to you for a few minutes, if you're willing." Ben paused. "I guess we're..." His voice trailed away. "It's hard to believe that we're brothers."

"Impossible," Gage muttered as he stared back at Ben. "I'm going to need to see the DNA test."

"Me, too," Ben returned. "But when I think about how often my dad stood up for you, it makes sense. I couldn't understand it before." He cleared his throat. "But you are free to go if you want."

Gage hesitated. "I can stick around."

Drake got to his feet. "I need to talk to my parents."

"Do you want me to go with you?" I asked.

"I need to do that on my own, but I'll give you a ride home."

"Okay." I stood up. "Ben? Do you need me for anything else?"

"Not right now. I'm glad you're okay, Willow."

"Thanks. I know this is a difficult day for you."

"Difficult isn't a big enough word to describe this day, but I am glad that I have the person in custody who took my dad's life."

I gave Ben a sympathetic smile and then followed Drake out of the room.

As I left the building, a ray of sun hit me in the face. "The storm is over," I said, as I got into his car.

"Nothing left but the cleanup," he muttered. "And there's a lot to clean up. Do you want me to take you home, or do you want to get your car from the cabin now?"

"I'll get the car later. I want to see Kelsey."

Drake started the engine but made no attempt to put the vehicle into drive. He was staring out the front window, lost in thought.

"Drake? Are you all right?" I questioned.

"No." He turned to look at me. "I wanted answers, and I got them, but they don't change anything. Telling my parents what happened will make it seem like Melanie is dying all over again."

"But they'll know the truth."

"The truth is horrific. Someone they knew killed their daughter, someone they trusted covered it up. A lot of people told lies to protect themselves. And in the end, Melanie is still gone."

"I know it won't be easy. Are you going to tell them she was pregnant?"

"I have to tell them everything. I don't want to hurt them, but that will be unavoidable."

"Maybe it will be some solace to know that she just fell asleep.

She wasn't afraid. Eileen had just made her tea. She didn't know what was going to happen."

"I wish that made me feel better, but it doesn't. The only thing I feel good about right now is that you're safe and that Kelsey is home. That's because of you, Willow. You figured everything out."

"I got lucky when I saw Dillon and the van, and my memory suddenly reappeared. I wish I'd remembered things earlier."

"Your memories would not have saved Melanie. We know that now. It's time to stop looking back. It's time to let go of the guilt."

"I could say the same to you." There were a lot of other things I wanted to say, too, but I wasn't ready to say them.

CHAPTER THIRTY

When I walked into my house, the atmosphere was completely different than it had been earlier in the day. I could hear the laughter, the high pitch of voices, the happy undertones of conversation coming from the living room. As I stepped into the room, I was relieved to see it was just us: my parents, Brooklyn, and Kelsey. I didn't want to see anyone else right now.

"Willow," Kelsey squealed, as she got up from the couch, hobbling on one foot as she opened her arms to me.

"Don't walk on that ankle," I said, moving across the room to give her a hug.

"Totally worth it." She gave me a radiant smile.

Kelsey looked a thousand times better. She wore leggings and a soft sweater and smelled like soap and lavender. Her hair was silky smooth. Even though shadows were under her eyes, her gaze was filled with gratitude.

"Come sit by me." Kelsey took my hand, and we sat down on the couch next to Brooklyn.

"Kelsey told us what you did, Willow," Brooklyn said, amazement in her gaze. "You were incredibly brave."

"We're very proud of you, Willow," my father added.

"Thanks." My gaze moved inevitably to my mother. I wasn't

looking for praise from her. Well, maybe I was, because old habits die hard.

"You brought Kelsey home," my mother said, her expression one of bemusement, as if she still couldn't quite believe it.

"Yes, I did. Where she belongs."

"How is Gage?" Kelsey asked, her bright eyes dimming. "Did you talk to him, Willow? Does he know everything?"

"Yes, but I'm not sure most of it has sunk in yet."

"Brooklyn told me about Carter's overdose. I feel so awful about that. I really made a mess of everything."

"Did you love either one of them?" I asked curiously.

"I liked both of them. Carter was sweet to me, but his love scared me. It felt too overwhelming, like it would carry me away. I also didn't think I could stay on the pedestal he'd put me on."

"And Gage?"

"Gage didn't love me as much as Carter did, but it was simpler. We had a lot in common, and we had fun. When we got engaged, our careers, our brands, grew like crazy, and everyone wanted us to be together. They wanted to put us on TV and follow our lives. I got caught up in all that. I had Carter in one ear telling me not to make the biggest mistake of my life by marrying a man I didn't love, and then I had Gage in the other ear telling me how exciting our lives were going to be."

"And what did you think, Kelsey?"

"I didn't let myself think. I just went along with things. I used to call you out for doing that. Willow always bends, never stands up for what she wants. But that's exactly what I did."

"I remember both of you saying that a lot," I said dryly, my gaze encompassing Brooklyn as well as Kelsey.

"We were wrong," Brooklyn said. "I have to admit that your actions over the last few days surprised me. I always thought you were weak, Willow, that you didn't have determination or ambition, but you were much stronger than I realized."

"I got stronger this week. I couldn't live in the shadows anymore. I couldn't wait for someone else to solve the problem. I couldn't lose another person I love."

"I don't think I realized you loved me that much," Kelsey said. I smiled. "I've loved you since the day you were born. We drifted apart over the years, but I hope we can forge a better relationship going forward." I looked around the room at my family. "I hope we can all be who we are now, and not who we used to be. Let's change the patterns. Let's change the way we see each other. We are far more complicated and three-dimensional than we give ourselves credit for."

"I agree." Brooklyn cleared her throat. "On that note, Mom, I'm going to be quitting the firm."

"What?" my mother asked in shock. "Why?"

"I'm not happy. I need to be on my own. I need to create a path for myself that doesn't follow in your footsteps. I'm sorry if that disappoints you," Brooklyn said.

"Well, I'm surprised," my mother replied. "I didn't know you were unhappy."

"I was afraid to tell you. You're not the easiest person to open up to."

"I'm beginning to realize that. I thought I had close relationships with at least you and Kelsey. I knew Willow wasn't confiding in me, but I believed you two were. The last few days have proven me wrong."

"You judge quite harshly, Mom," Kelsey said. "It's why we can't tell you things."

"Maybe I judge because you're wrong."

I had to smile at that response. My mother might be trying to be more self-aware, but she was still who she was.

"Mom," Brooklyn said sharply. "You just did it again. You judged what Kelsey said, and you got defensive."

"If I judge, it's because I always have my daughters' interests at heart. But I will try to do better. Now don't you all have anything to say to your father, perhaps something you want him to work on?"

My father laughed. "Don't turn this on me, Monica."

"Fine, you're perfect," she said, making a face at him.

"Not perfect, just trying my best. I'm so grateful to have all of you here. I feel like the luckiest man in the world." He looked at my mother. "How about we rustle up some dinner for our kids?"

"Lorraine can do that."

"I sent her home. I thought tonight it should just be us. Let's cook something, Monica, the way we used to when the girls were little."

I couldn't remember them cooking together, but apparently my mother could, because she smiled and got to her feet, following him into the kitchen.

"Now that it's just us," Brooklyn said, her gaze settling on me. "Did Gage know that Eileen killed Melanie?"

"No."

"Well, that's a relief. I wonder what Sean thinks. Did he know he was married to a murderer? Was he complicit?"

"There's no evidence Sean was involved."

"The Chadwicks will never be the same," Kelsey murmured. "But then I guess none of us will ever be the same."

"Probably not." My gaze moved from Kelsey to Brooklyn. "I know who James was with the night Melanie disappeared. It may come out in a more public way at some point. If you want to know, I can tell you."

"Wait! James was with someone else that night?" Kelsey put in. "I thought he was with you, Brooklyn."

"I lied for him," Brooklyn admitted. "Who was he with, Willow?"

"Jenny."

Brooklyn drew in a breath and slowly let it out. "I guess I'm not that shocked. I knew Jenny had a crush on him."

"Well, I'm stunned," Kelsey said, confusion in her gaze. "Not so much that he was cheating on you, Brooklyn, but that you lied for him."

"When I told the lie, when I backed up his alibi, I didn't realize the long-term repercussions," Brooklyn said. "But that lie festered within me. I could never trust him again. Eventually, I couldn't take it anymore, and I broke up with him."

"I had no idea," Kelsey muttered. "I wish you would have told me, Brooklyn."

"I was ashamed."

Kelsey nodded. "I understand. I couldn't tell you about Carter, because I was ashamed, too. We both messed up, me far more than you. I destroyed two men's lives because I was trying to have it all. I'm sorry about what I did." She paused. "Gage must be reeling. He finds out his mother is a murderer, and that his father isn't his father. I don't know how he's standing up right now. I was thinking I should call him, but I'm a little afraid."

"Is it over between you two?" I asked.

"It has to be, for a lot of reasons," Kelsey said. "I've been thinking about Gage and Melanie, about her getting pregnant, about the secret he kept for so many years. It makes sense to me now why Gage has a problem with intimacy. He never gets that close. He always holds something back. I didn't love Gage as much as I should. But he didn't love me that much, either. I wonder if that's tied to Melanie in some way."

Before I could comment, the doorbell rang.

Kelsey tensed. "I don't know if I want to see anyone."

"I'll send them away," Brooklyn said decisively, as she got to her feet.

A moment later, we heard Gage's voice, and despite Brooklyn telling him to go home, he rushed into the living room. He stopped when he saw Kelsey. I'm not sure he even noticed I was sitting on the couch next to her, because his gaze was fixed on my sister.

I expected anger, and I mentally prepped myself for another stormy scene. But when Gage opened his mouth, what came out was massive regret.

"I am so sorry, Kelsey. For everything," he said. "I should have seen what was going on with my mother. I should have known what happened to Melanie. I should have protected you."

I'd never seen Gage look so human or so vulnerable.

"Oh, Gage. You don't have to take the blame for your mother," Kelsey said. "And I'm sorry, too. I shouldn't have done what I did with Carter. I hurt both of you. And now Carter is...well, I heard it's bad."

"It is bad," he admitted. "If you were involved with him, why did you say yes to me?"

"You're a wonderful guy. I wanted to love you, Gage. I wanted us to be the couple everyone thought we were. But we weren't. Something was missing. We never got as deep as we should have."

"You're right. I loved you but not in the way a man should love a woman he's going to marry. The truth is my heart froze a long time ago. I didn't want to admit it, not even to myself. I didn't want to think that one sixteen-year-old girl could ruin me for everyone else. But maybe I deserved it. I told Melanie to get an abortion. I turned my back on her. And I'm the reason she's dead. My mother killed Melanie because I was scared of being a father. I never imagined that she could do something so horrible." His gaze finally swung to me. "I really thought it was a stranger, Willow."

I believed him. "It was easier to think that, Gage. We all told ourselves that no one we knew, no one we loved, could do something like that. But Drake knew all along that it was one of us. He just had the wrong person."

"He wasn't completely wrong. I just didn't know how involved I was." Gage turned back to Kelsey. "I'm glad you're all right. I searched for you, Kelsey. I did everything I could to bring you back. But I couldn't find you."

"I know. Brooklyn told me how hard everyone looked for me. I'm grateful. We were going to start a new life together tomorrow, Gage. But I think tomorrow you and I need to restart our own lives and be more authentic. We can't keep living for social media, for other people, for money, or fame. When I was stuck in that cabin, all I could think about was how meaningless my life had become. I want more. And you should want more, too. You need to find someone who can unfreeze your heart, and I need to find myself before I can find someone else. I've spent too many years going from guy to guy, defining myself by who I was with. I need to figure out who I am. I want you to be happy, Gage. And I hope one day Carter will wake up, and I can beg for his forgiveness, too."

"I hope that as well. I hate what he did behind my back, but he's brother, and I still love him," Gage said. "Now, I'm going to let you be with your family."

As Gage left the room, Brooklyn sat back down on the couch and grabbed Kelsey's hand. Then Kelsey smiled and grabbed my hand. I reached across for Brooklyn, and we formed a tight circle, the way we had when we were very small children, before we'd started competing for attention.

"I liked what you said about starting over tomorrow," I told Kelsey. "We should all do that. Let's not go back to the way we were. Let's remember that we're sisters before anything else. We don't need to criticize each other. We should celebrate our differences, not disdain them."

"I know you're talking mostly to me," Brooklyn said. "I've never given you enough credit, Willow. You slid into the shadows of our lives, and I let you stay there."

"And I thought you were too boring and not enough fun, Willow, so I turned to Brooklyn," Kelsey said with an apologetic smile.

I smiled back. "I was boring and not very much fun. But that was partly because you two shined so bright. No one saw me; they could only see the both of you. Melanie was the one who made me realize I had to find my own light. But after she died, I couldn't. Until I was forced to come back here and face all the horrible feelings. Then you went missing, and I knew I couldn't be that shy, boring girl who stayed in the shadows. You needed me, Kelsey."

"And you were there. You saved me, Willow. And Drake saved you. Where is he now?"

"Talking to his parents."

"That won't be easy," Brooklyn murmured. "I was too hard on Drake. He worried me, and you might not believe this, Willow, but most of my worry was about you. You couldn't remember what happened, and I thought that made you vulnerable. I told Mom we needed to get you off the island."

"Really? I didn't know that."

"Well, you are my sister."

"Speaking of sisters and sharing secrets," Kelsey said, a gleam in her eyes. "What's going on with you and Drake, Willow? When he came looking for you, he was shaken to the core when I told him you were running away from a murderer. There's something between you again, isn't there?"

"What do you mean again?"

Both Kelsey and Brooklyn rolled their eyes.

"We weren't blind," Brooklyn said. "We knew you liked him."

"Yeah, you had a big crush on him," Kelsey added. "I felt sorry for you. He was way out of your league."

I laughed. "He certainly was."

"Did something happen between you two back then? Or this week?" Kelsey pried.

"Maybe."

"So…"

"It's complicated."

"Well, that isn't a no," Kelsey said with a sly smile.

"It's also not a yes. Drake lied about some things, too. He's the reason your original venue got canceled, Kelsey."

Her jaw dropped. "Are you serious? How could he be the reason?"

"He wanted to get everyone back on the island. He had a friend with corporate clients booking events, and she made sure they wanted your date and your venue."

"That is incredibly devious," Kelsey said.

"And it turned out to be very dangerous," Brooklyn added, an unhappy look entering her eyes. "Maybe I don't feel that sorry for him."

"I don't like what Drake did. I like it even less that I didn't find out about it until earlier today, but he was desperate to get answers and we all stonewalled him."

"His actions could have gotten Kelsey killed," Brooklyn said.

"I told him the same thing," I replied.

"On the other hand," Kelsey said. "Maybe I would have always been in danger. I slept with Carter. As soon as Eileen found that out, she would have killed me for sure. And if it hadn't been that, it would have been something else. If I'd married Gage, if I'd offended Eileen, who's to say I wouldn't have faced the same danger? I'm not saying what Drake did was right, but he forced the issue, and Dillon, sweet, stoned, crazy Dillon, saved me."

"How can you call him sweet after he chained you up?" Brooklyn asked.

"He didn't hurt me. He gave me everything I needed except my freedom." Kelsey paused as my parents returned to the room with tacos and salad.

"Yum," Kelsey said. "Tacos are my favorite."

My mom smiled. "That's why we made them." She paused. "Will you help me with the drinks, Willow?"

"Sure," I said, getting up to follow her back into the kitchen. It quickly became obvious she wanted to speak to me alone. Apparently, getting drinks was a familiar ruse since it's what had brought Sean into the kitchen with her several days ago.

"Did Eileen say anything about Sean?" my mom asked, worry in her gaze.

"No. She never mentioned him. I don't think he knew anything."

"I can't believe she cheated on him with Tom Ryan, that she passed off Gage as Sean's son."

"You really can't believe that?" I challenged. "Didn't you have an affair with Sean?"

She paled at my question. "Did Eileen say that?"

"Is it true?" I countered.

"It was a long time ago. I was going through a rough patch in my marriage to your dad, and Sean was there. It was wrong. And I regret it."

There wasn't a lot of emotion behind her words, but that wasn't unusual. With the exception of this past week, when terror for Kelsey had taken down her defenses, my mother was always in control. "Does Dad know?"

She hesitated. "Yes, but that's between us. I hope you aren't going to make this a thing. There has been too much pain the last few days. I don't want there to be more. I know we haven't had the best relationship, Willow, and I'm sorry about that. You don't understand me, and I don't understand you, but I do love you. You might not believe that, but it's true. I just never imagined I'd have a child who was so different from me."

"We are different."

"You know I was jealous of Sylvie."

"Melanie's mother? Why would you be jealous of her?"

"You liked Melanie's family better than ours. You used to rave about Sylvie, how she made you soup and cookies, how kind she was. She was the mother you wanted, and Melanie was the sister you wanted. I think your sisters and I got a little upset about that. We turned away from you, because we felt like you were turning away from us."

"I had no idea you felt that way. I didn't think you cared that I was spending time with Melanie and her family."

"Well, of course, we cared."

She was rewriting history, but since this was the first honest conversation we'd had in decades, I went along with it. "I didn't like them better. But I did like myself better when I was with them. I could just be myself. When I was here, I wasn't as pretty as Kelsey or as smart as Brooklyn. You and Dad had your favorites. There were two of you and three of us, and I was left out."

"You never got over the time we left you behind at Disneyland."

"It was traumatic, Mom."

"I know. You were the middle child and sometimes you got lost or forgotten, but that was also because you were so quiet. You were always reading or playing with your camera."

"Now it's my fault?"

She sighed. "I'm being defensive."

"Yes, you are."

She gave me another sharp look. "You really have come all the way out of your shell."

"You should get used to it."

"I hope I'll see more of you so I can get used to it. I said some harsh things to you when Kelsey was missing. I'm sorry about that."

"We were all stressed out."

"You're a generous person, Willow. You get that from your father. Why don't you move back to Seattle? It would be nice to have you closer to home."

"I'll think about it. I'm not making any more decisions tonight. I just want to have dinner with my family." I couldn't remember the last time I'd wanted to do that, but now I couldn't wait.

CHAPTER THIRTY-ONE

I WOKE up to sunshine on Saturday morning. I blinked against the bright light, but I felt happier than I had in days. The long nightmare of my life was finally over. I remembered everything.

I sat up abruptly. I had remembered everything, but I'd also forgotten something important. In the madness of yesterday, I hadn't even thought about what else I'd seen in Dillon's van—Melanie's diary.

Dillon had confirmed that he'd picked it up on the beach. That's why he'd gone to the Chadwick's house, to take it back to Melanie. *Where was the diary now? Was it in Dillon's house?*

Scrambling out of bed, I opened my door and ran down the hall. Kelsey was in her bathroom, blow-drying her hair. She gave me a worried look.

"What's wrong now?" she asked. "I thought all the bad was behind us."

"Nothing is wrong. I just wondered if Dillon mentioned Melanie's diary. Did he have it in the cabin? Did he show it to you?"

"No. He never mentioned her diary. But I'm sure he'll tell you if you ask him."

"Right. I can just ask him." I ran back to my room and grabbed my phone. I looked up the number for the hospital, then called and asked for his room. A woman answered the phone, identifying herself as a nurse. "I'm trying to reach Dillon Petrie," I said.

"I'm sorry, he's still asleep. Visiting hours are at two. You can speak to him then."

I ended the call. As I was debating my options, my phone rang. It was Drake.

"Hi," I said. "How are you doing?"

"I'm okay. I had a thought, Willow."

"Melanie's diary."

"Yes," he said. "If Dillon had it, it might still be in his cabin."

"That's exactly what I was thinking. I just called Dillon. He's asleep. The nurse said I could see him at two."

"That's too long from now."

Drake and I were on the same page today. "I agree. I do need to pick up my car. If we're all the way out there, we could try to look for it."

"I can pick you up in ten minutes."

"Give me twenty. I need to get dressed."

"I'll see you soon."

Nineteen minutes later, I ran out the front door as Drake pulled into the drive. I hopped into his car as he came to a stop. I didn't want him to get out. I didn't want to delay our mission with conversation with my family.

"Still afraid to have me run into your parents?" he asked wryly.

"No. They would probably love to tell you how sorry they are. I'm more eager to get to the cabin and find that diary before someone else does."

"Who else would be interested?"

"I'm sure she wrote about Gage."

"Good point. But Gage has his hands full with his mother and with Carter. He's probably also trying to keep Preston and Sean from falling apart."

"You're right. I just feel like I need to get it back for Melanie, like it's the last thing I can do for her."

"I understand. I feel the same way." As he pulled away from the house, he added, "So, what are your parents sorry about?"

"A lot of things. Not being more supportive of you and your family when Melanie disappeared. Not being forthcoming with their answers. Leaving the island as soon as possible."

"They've come a long way around."

"Losing Kelsey for four days, not knowing if she was dead or alive, made them realize what your parents went through. They know they're lucky they didn't have to experience the same terrible outcome."

"Because of you, Willow."

"And you."

His brow shot up with a questioning look. "You're giving me credit when my moves put Kelsey's life in danger?"

"I'm not giving you credit for that. I have a lot of problems with what you did, Drake. But I also know that we wouldn't have gotten to the truth without your stubborn persistence and refusal to give up. You convinced me that Kelsey's disappearance was tied to Melanie's, and you were right."

"When I got the venue to cancel, I told myself the means justified the end. All I could think about was getting justice for Melanie before the ten-year anniversary of her disappearance. Kelsey's happiness didn't factor in," he said honestly. "All I saw was an opportunity to get everyone back on the island at the same time. I wasn't really going to stop the wedding or try to ruin it. And I never imagined Dillon would kidnap Kelsey."

"How could you? I never imagined there were so many secrets, so many lies. I really was blind to what was going on right under my nose. I wish you would have told me about switching the venue a few days ago, though. It hurt that you kept that from me. Especially after we got close."

"I know. It was a bad decision. I just didn't want to put a wedge between us. It was nice to have you working with me. You cared as much as I did about finding the truth, and you were willing to risk your life to get justice for my sister. It felt good to have you on my side."

"I was always on your side, Drake."

"I realize that now. My actions put you in danger, as well as Kelsey. You have a lot of reasons to be angry."

"I do have reasons, but you didn't put me in danger. I did that by myself."

"Not all by yourself," he said. "But speaking of danger, there's something I've been wondering about, Willow. Who pushed you in the water? It couldn't have been Eileen. She wouldn't have been on the dock that late at night."

"No. I'm pretty sure it was James. I saw him yesterday when he was trying to get off the island. I asked him flat out if he did it. He didn't admit it, but I could see the truth in his eyes. And it makes sense that it was him and not Carter. James has always been a sleazy asshole. It doesn't matter. He's long gone now. And I have no energy for going after him." I took a breath. "There's something I've been wondering about, too. Did you pay someone to break the ice sculpture for Kelsey's wedding?"

He shook his head. "No, I did not do that. I didn't even know there was an ice sculpture."

"I guess it was just an accident, probably the caterer or one of the servers. I'm glad it wasn't you, but I did wonder if it was part of your plan to shake everyone up."

"My plan wasn't that detailed," he said with a small smile. "I was winging it."

"Well, I'm glad you didn't do it. How did it go with your parents?"

His smile faded. "It was painful and exhausting. My mom cried for hours. My father barely said two words. In the end, he just got up and walked out of the house. But he didn't go far. He just went out to the old swing set and sat on the swing the way Melanie used to do. He must have sat there for two hours while my mom and I watched him from the window. When he finally came in, he said, 'I hope you can let this go now. I hope you can live your own life.'"

"That's a little surprising."

"He seemed calmer than he had in years. Maybe the truth set him free, even though it was a terrible truth."

"Did you tell him about the pregnancy?"

"Yes, and you know what? He already knew. He saw the pregnancy test in the trash, and he talked to Melanie about it. He told her that he'd support her in whatever she wanted to do."

"Wow. That shocks me. He was always so worried about her doing the right thing and instead of blowing up at her, he actually supports her?"

"He really did love her. He's a complicated man."

"What did your mom say? Had he told her about the pregnancy?"

"No, and she was stunned. She was angry that he'd kept that information from her. He said he had promised Melanie to stay silent until she could tell my mom herself. After she disappeared, he didn't want to add to my mom's grief. He didn't want her to feel guilty that she hadn't known what her daughter was doing or sad that she'd also lost a grandchild."

"That makes sense. Your dad must have thought that the father of Melanie's baby killed her."

"That's exactly what he thought, but he didn't know who it was. All of Melanie's girlfriends, including you, her best friend, said you weren't aware that she had a boyfriend. He didn't know if you were all trying to protect her, but he couldn't get any information."

"Did he tell the sheriff about the pregnancy?"

"Yes, but Tom didn't put it in the police file. My father also told me that Tom started turning things around every time he pressed about the secret boyfriend. Tom suggested that my father was trying to cover up his own involvement."

I shook my head in disgust. "Tom did everything he could to protect Gage."

"Yes, he did."

"I have to say, I never would have guessed Melanie was with Gage. But you always had suspicions about him."

"Not because I thought they'd slept together. I didn't understand his lie, but I couldn't quite get to a motive."

"If I'd known Melanie was pregnant when she disappeared, I probably would have guessed Carter or even Dillon," I said. "Well, I'm glad your father was there for Melanie when she needed him. Is he still worried you might write a book about Melanie's death?"

Drake shook his head. "I told him I wouldn't. But he said that if I felt it was important to tell my sister's story one day, I had his blessing. He'd been worried about a story without an ending. That was what bothered him the most. He didn't want me to make something up. But now that the truth is out there, he trusts me to know what to do with it."

"Your parents had to have been shocked to know it was Eileen who killed Melanie."

"They had trouble believing it."

"I don't blame them. I heard her confess, and I still have trouble believing she did it. You were right when you told me that everyone had a secret—even Melanie."

"Some of those secrets were worse than others. How is Kelsey feeling?"

"Grateful. She had an epiphany about herself, the shallowness of her life up until now, the mistakes she's made. She wants to change. Everyone in my family got a brutal wake-up call when she disappeared. But I think this entire experience might end up being good for us. Our lives got stripped down to the bare bones. The stories we told ourselves, the pretenses we lived under, the secrets we held, all stopped us from living meaningful lives. And with that gone, we saw each other for the first time in a long time."

"They saw a different you, I'm sure. No more hiding in the shadows, Willow."

"Nope. I found the light, just like Melanie always told me I would. She said when something was important to me, I'd step up. I really miss her, Drake."

"Me, too."

He held out his right hand to me and I wrapped my fingers around his. We stayed that way until we got to the cabin.

When we arrived, the place was deserted. There was no crime scene tape, but the door was locked.

"How did you get in before?" Drake asked.

"Through the bathroom window, but surely that would be locked now, too."

"Let's find out."

They walked around the small cabin and sure enough, the window was still open and the bucket I'd moved over yesterday was under the window. "I guess no one cared to close the window."

"It's Hawk Island," he said with a shrug. "And there's no one around." He turned back toward the small window. "I think I can fit."

I eyed the narrow opening and his muscular body and shook my head. "I'll do it."

"You sure?"

"Yes. There's no more danger inside this cabin."

I jumped onto the bucket and then pulled myself through the window once more. Despite my confident words, it felt surreal to land in that bathroom again, and the silence in the cabin was eerie. I pushed past the uneasy feeling as I walked down the hall and into the living room. I tried not to look at the bloody stain on the wood floor as I opened the front door and let Drake in.

"It feels weird to be back here," I said. Someone had done a little cleanup. The food wrappers from the table were gone. So were the chain and the handcuff that had kept Kelsey in the house. They had probably taken that into evidence. "Who owns this cabin?"

"Dillon does. I asked Ben about it this morning. He said when Dillon's uncle died, he left him a little money, which was surprising since his uncle had been abusive to him for years. But I guess there was no one else to leave his money to, so, Dillon bought this place. He preferred living far away from everyone. He could do his own thing, and no one would bother him."

"No one suspected him of taking Kelsey. He joined the search parties for her. He was talking to Ben at the station. He wasn't acting like someone who had anything to hide," I said.

"He wanted to be visible so he wouldn't look suspicious," Drake agreed.

"But he also wanted to find out what was happening with the search so he could make sure no one was getting close to him." I shook my head in bemusement. "I don't know what to think about Dillon. On one hand, he did it all to protect Kelsey, but he put us through hell and, ultimately, he put her in danger. Is he a villain or is he a hero?"

"Maybe he's a little of both."

"I guess none of us are just one thing. Where do you think he would have kept the diary all these years, if he even kept it?" There weren't a lot of hiding places. The furniture was minimal: a couch, an armchair, two guitars, a keyboard, and an old bookcase filled with what appeared to be music books. I walked over to the bookcase. "This is too obvious."

"I don't see a red spine," Drake said. "But let's take a look."

We stripped the bookshelf in record time. At the end, we just had a pile of books and no diary. I let out a groan of disappointment. "It's not here."

"Let's keep looking," Drake said with his usual stubborn determination. He pulled the cushions off the couch while I moved into the kitchen, opening drawers and cupboards.

We made our way into the bedroom, which was a total mess, clothes all over the floor, as well as dozens of cigarette butts, a collection of bongs, and the distinct smell of weed.

Drake went through the closet while I looked through the bedside drawer. After digging through too many bottles of pills, I pulled out a padded envelope. It was sealed and addressed, but it had never been sent—to me.

"What's that?" Drake asked.

I held up the envelope. "It looks like Dillon was going to send me something." My pulse raced as I fumbled with the seal. I finally got the envelope open. I pulled out the red-leather journal. There was a sticky note on the top.

I read it aloud. "I think Melanie would want you to have this, Willow, but I don't know if I'll ever have the courage to send it to you, because then I would have to explain what I can't explain.

Until then, I'll protect what she left behind. I'm sorry I couldn't save her."

I looked at Drake. His eyes had filled with sadness, Dillon's message was another reminder of the loss.

Drake swallowed hard, then cleared his throat. "Well, we found it."

"We did." I looked at the book. I wanted to open it. I wanted to see her handwriting. I wanted to hear her words. I lifted my gaze to his. "Should we?"

"I don't know, Willow. What do you think?"

I thought for a long moment. "She never let me read anything she wrote. She said one day she might. When she got rich and famous, someone would want to write a book about her and then she'd pull out her diary and it would be part of her story." I suddenly knew what had to happen. "You have to write the book, Drake. You have to tell Melanie's story." I stopped abruptly. "And all my photos…all the ones I took of Melanie—they can be in the book. It can be a story not just about her death but about her life, her sixteen beautiful years of life."

"I don't know if I can do her justice," he said worriedly.

"If anyone can, you can. We should read her diary. But not here. Let's go down to the beach. That's where she loved to write the most."

Melanie's Diary—August 19th

It has been a crazy day. So many emotions. I haven't written in a few days. I was afraid to put the truth down on paper. Not because I thought someone might read what I wrote, but because I was afraid to face what I've done. What I have to do going forward.

All my dreams have changed. Yesterday, I found out I was pregnant. I couldn't believe it. We used a condom. Well, we did the first time. The second time was sort of fast and we got carried away. I was stupid. I was even more dumb when I threw the pregnancy test away in the garbage can at my house. I didn't think my dad would go through the outside trash. But he's been looking for evidence against me all summer. I shouldn't have been surprised.

But I was surprised when he took me aside and told me he'd help me raise the baby. I couldn't believe he wasn't yelling. He wasn't threatening to lock me up. He wasn't even that angry. He was just worried. That's when I started to cry. And he hugged me. I can't remember when he last hugged me. It felt so good. It felt like he was my dad again. He loved me. He wanted to protect me. He wanted to take away my pain. He said he'd help me get through it. He even said he wouldn't tell my mom until I was ready.

Of course, he also wanted to know who the father was. I told him I'd tell him after I told the guy, after I knew what I wanted to do. He wasn't happy about that, but he said he'd wait.

So, today I saw Gage. He got really upset. And now I'm crying. I can't seem to stop.

Gage told me to get an abortion. He couldn't be a dad. We couldn't be together. He was worried he was going to get charged for rape because I'm sixteen. He was totally panicked. I told him I wouldn't let that happen, but he ran off. He was so scared. I always thought he was this big, strong, confident guy, but he seemed like a kid today.

I'm sad that he doesn't want the baby. But I don't feel that afraid. Maybe it's having this baby inside of me. It's like I'm suddenly not restless anymore. I know what I'm going to do. I'm going to have a child. My dreams will have to change, but that's okay. I can still be a mom and have dreams. I can still leave my mark on the world. Maybe my baby and I will do it together.

I'm sitting on the beach now with Dillon. I was really sad when he got here. I told him about Gage. I probably shouldn't have, but I had to tell someone, and he was here. Dillon is playing music for me, and it's making me feel better. He's a good friend. I think he likes me. I wish I liked him, but you can't really pick who you like. I never imagined that Gage would ever like me, but he did.

We kind of got together by accident. I've known him for a long time, but we were always in a group of people. But then I started running in the early mornings, and Gage was out on the same trails at the same time. We started talking and running together. We had this relationship that was away from everyone else. He told me things about himself I never imagined, how he felt the pressure of his parents to always be an overachiever, and that sometimes he didn't even really like football. I told him about my dream of traveling the world, being independent, feeling like the sky is the limit, like I could do anything. He said that I made him feel more optimistic, like he could do anything, too.

And then we took our run into this beautiful, shaded cove and we made love. Maybe he would say it was just sex. But it felt like so much more than that to me. We spent half the day there, talking, laughing, kissing, touching. I thought it was the first of many days, but then Gage stopped running that path, and he avoided me when we were in a group.

I think he wanted to pretend it never happened, but this baby makes that impossible.

I want to tell Willow about me and Gage. I've thought about telling her a million times, but I don't think she'll like it. She doesn't care for Gage, and she has good reasons. I just don't want to hear them. I've seen a different side of him than she has. He likes to make fun of her and that's mean, but I think it's just because he puts on an act. Everyone looks to him to be a certain way, so he's that way. He needs to grow up. He needs to be worthy of being the father of my baby. I hope that will happen.

I'm going to tell Willow later tonight when we meet at the falls. I was going to tell her earlier, but she wanted to party with Ben. I don't know who she thinks she's fooling. She's in love with Drake. And I've seen the way he looks at her when he doesn't think she's watching him. He likes her, too. But he's a big college man now. He can't like a high school girl. He's being stupid.

I think something might have happened between them. I wish Willow would tell me, but I'm not telling her about Gage, so I guess I can't blame her. She probably thinks I won't like it because Drake is my brother. I actually really like it. I just don't want Drake to hurt her. Willow has a soft heart, and Drake could break it. I also don't want her to break his heart. Maybe that's why I haven't said anything, either. I could never take one of their sides, because I love them both.

Well, they'll have to figure it out. I hope they can get out of their own way. I hope Gage and I can find a way to at least be friends again. I don't want us to hate each other.

Guess what? I just got a call from Mrs. Chadwick. She said she's with Gage, and he wants to talk to me. She cares a lot about me and wants to make sure that we have a chance to work things out. She sounded really sweet and kind. I'm so glad Gage told her I was pregnant. That's a huge step for him. Now he wants to talk to me. Maybe this will work out after all. Fingers crossed.

I blew out a breath as I turned the page. There was nothing else, no other entries. Melanie had died a short time later.

"She had no idea what she was about to face," I said to Drake.

He gave me a deeply pained look. "It feels almost worse to know that."

"She had so much hope for the future, not just with Gage, but for every other part of her life."

Silence fell between us as we processed what we'd just read.

And then I added, "I understand better now why Dillon thought that Gage was at the house. Melanie told him she was going to see Gage. If Dillon read the diary, he would have thought that both Gage and his mother were there."

"Dillon told the sheriff what he thought happened, and the sheriff covered it up," Drake said. "Tom shut down the investigation as quickly as he could. He tried to point my family toward a stranger abduction. And then he tried to blame my dad." He shook his head, his lips tightening with anger. "I'm glad Tom is dead, Willow. There's a part of me that wishes Eileen was dead, too, but you were right. She will suffer more this way."

"She will." I blew out a breath. "I don't know that I'll ever get past the pain of losing Melanie, but from here on out, I just want to remember the good times we had. She loved me, and I loved her. And she loved you, Drake, and you loved her. That's what we have to hold on to."

He gave a tight nod. "I'm going to try. Melanie made some good points in her diary," he added, a gleam in his gaze. "About us."

"Is there an us?" I asked warily.

He looked deep into my eyes. "I want there to be, Willow. I know I hurt you. Do you think you can ever forgive me?"

"Well, you saved my life. That's a good start."

He shook his head. "I don't want that to be the reason you forgive me."

"It's a good reason."

"Not good enough. You'd be forgiving me out of gratitude, and I don't want your gratitude."

"What do you want? It's a question you keep asking me. Maybe it's your turn to answer, Drake."

"I want what I was too scared to say ten years ago. I want you in my life."

My heart skipped a beat. "Really? Are you sure you're not saying that because…well, this is a really emotional moment we're having?"

"It is emotional, but that's not why I'm saying it. I care about you, Willow. I messed it up ten years ago. I messed it up this week. I'd like a chance to get it right. But that depends on you, on what you want."

I thought about his words, about all that had happened between us. But there wasn't a decision to be made. I knew what was in my heart. "I'd like to see what could happen once we get off this damn island."

A smile lifted his lips. "Where do you want to go? Seattle? San Francisco? Some place new? I'm up for anything. For the first time in ten years, I feel free."

"Me, too. Melanie wrote so much about the future, about seeing the world, living our lives. I haven't been living like that, and I don't think you have, either. So, let's change it. Let's take a risk on us."

His smile broadened. "I'm in."

"Good. And for the record, I don't hate the island anymore." I looked out at the sea. "It wasn't the island that was evil, it was just one person, well, maybe two. But Eileen and Tom can't hurt anyone ever again." I held out the diary. "You should keep this."

He made no effort to take the book. Instead, he jumped up and pulled me to my feet. "I have a better idea."

"What?"

He led me to the edge of the ocean. "Melanie loved the sea. And that's where she ended up. I think the diary belongs with her."

"What about your book?"

"I don't need her diary to write about her. Everything we read today, you and I lived through with her. We know her story. We know her heart."

"Yes, we do. For a long time, I kept her out of my head, but I can see her face clearly now, her wide-open smile, her eyes gleaming with excitement, anticipation. I can hear her lilting laugh. I can even hear her complaining, telling me to hurry up, so we could do something else."

"I can see her again, too. I feel like she's right here with us."

I wished she really was here with us, but I was happy to let her back into my head and into my heart. I no longer felt numb or dead inside. I was alive, ready to do what she'd always wanted to do—find the next great adventure. I gripped the book in my hand, then I brought it to my mouth and gave it a kiss. "I'll love you forever, Melanie. You always made me better than I was. And now I'm going to do what you said—get out of my own way." I looked at Drake. "With your brother."

He grinned. Then he kicked off his shoes, and I kicked off mine. We walked into the water. The current was tugging at my knees when I threw the diary as far as I could. At first, it seemed to come back to me, and then the current caught it and swept it out to sea.

Drake put his arm around me, and we stood there in the

freezing water for a good fifteen minutes, until we couldn't see the diary anymore. Then we turned to each other.

"No more looking back," he said.

"Only forward."

"Give me a kiss, shy girl."

"I hated when you called me that," I said with a smile.

He grinned. "I think I can find a way to make you love it."

"Fingers crossed." Melanie's laugh rang through my head as I let go of the past and grabbed onto the future.

# # #

ABOUT THE AUTHOR

Barbara Freethy is a #1 New York Times Bestselling Author of 75 novels ranging from contemporary romance to romantic suspense and women's fiction. With over 13 million copies sold, twenty-nine of Barbara's books have appeared on the New York Times and USA Today Bestseller Lists, including SUMMER SECRETS which hit #1 on the New York Times!

Known for her emotionally compelling and thrilling stories of suspense, romance, and page-turning drama, Barbara enjoys writing about ordinary people caught up in extraordinary adventures.

Visit her website at http://www.barbarafreethy.com

Made in the USA
Middletown, DE
13 March 2022